Also by Holly LeCraw

The Swimming Pool

The Half Brother

A Novel

Holly LeCraw

Doubleday Canada

Doubleday Canada and colophon are registered trademarks of
Random House of Canada Limited.

Library and Archives Canada Cataloguing in Publication

LeCraw, Holly, author
The half brother / Holly LeCraw.

Issued in print and electronic formats.
ISBN 978-0-385-66795-1 (pbk.). ISBN 978-0-385-67966-4 (epub)

I. Title.

PS3612.E38H34 2015   813'.6   C2014-907393-3
                                            C2014-907394-1

Book design by Michael Collica
Jacket design by Jaya Miceli
Jacket images: (foreground) Doug Menuez / Photodisc / Getty Images;
(background) Gregory Olsen / E+ / Getty Images
Printed and bound in the USA

Published in Canada by Doubleday Canada,
A division of Random House of Canada Limited,
A Penguin Random House Company

www.penguinrandomhouse.ca

10 9 8 7 6 5 4 3 2 1

Penguin
Random House
DOUBLEDAY CANADA

for my parents and my brother
first teachers

I learned to walk into a classroom wondering what
I would say, rather than knowing what I would say.
Then I learned by hearing myself speak; the source
of my speaking was our mysterious harmony with
truths we know, though very often our knowledge
of them is hidden from us.

—*Andre Dubus*

Love bade me welcome: yet my soul drew back,
      Guiltie of dust and sinne.

—*George Herbert*

The Half Brother

I

May

One

Mid-August. On the quad, the only sound is a far-off angry machine, a leaf blower, somewhere in the vicinity of the library. Otherwise I'd say I have the whole place to myself, except for the bees. They're delirious in the heat, in the flowering shrubs and trees, buried head-first, ecstatic. As I walk by a seven-foot-tall rose of Sharon I hear their intoxicated hum and realize the whole little tree is vibrating, throbbing with them.

Summer here in the North still surprises me. The heat, when it finally comes, is heavy and thorough, and must be appreciated while it lasts, which the bees know. I walk slowly up one of the diagonal paths. I could stop right here, lie down in the hot green grass; do a dance; get naked. Of course there's sure to be someone in the quiet buildings, behind a window closed for the AC, someone who'd look down and see Charlie Garrett pulling a nutter—but if I had to lay money, this very moment, I'd bet no. I'd bet I was all alone.

Into the cloister. Or cloister-let. Ah, the Anglophile benefactors of the Abbott School! My shoes whisper against the flagstones. The air is suddenly chilled, almost wet. There are stone benches along the walls, and ahead, the heavy wood of the chapel's side door, closed today. And, just before that door, a girl—or rather a girl's legs, long brown legs stretched out, and I know them. Most definitely, I know them. "Miss Bankhead," I say.

I call her that automatically, without irony, although there's no need for formality anymore. May Bankhead is twenty now, no longer my student; I'm twenty-nine; I can be her peer. In the letters we used to write, during her first two years of college, we'd been edging toward that equality, but I haven't heard from her in months. "Hi, there!" she says. *"Mr. Garrett."* Quicker than I. Of course.

"You look so cool," I say. "You always look so cool."

She smiles, a private smile. Otherwise she doesn't move, but she gives the impression not of complete stillness but of an almost imperceptible undulation, as though she were an underwater plant.

"I'm ruining your solitude," I say.

She shakes her head, dreamily. "I love it here in the summer," she says. "I love the silence." At that exact moment the leaf blower revs again, and we laugh, and whatever spell was on her is broken. "Aren't you going to sit down?" May says, and scoots over a little on the bench.

I sit down and now we are spectators together, looking out at the empty green. "So you come here too?" she says. "To indulge your monkish fantasies?"

"What, do you have nun fantasies?" I say. Her incongruous dimple appears. Normally, she looks rather serious. "Well then."

"I come here and pretend I'm a stranger. Trespassing. I lurk around."

"Well, that's . . . interesting."

"It's nice," May says. "I've never been anonymous here." May's a fac brat, daughter of the chaplain. She's lived here all her life.

"So you must be looking forward to Paris."

She gives me a quick, penetrating glance. "Exactly. You knew about that?"

"I hear things." And I wonder, for the dozenth time, if the letters dribbled away because she's got a boyfriend. "You're going for the whole year?"

"Yes." She sounds proud.

"Will you come home for Christmas?"

"No, Mom's coming over."

"That'll be nice."

"Possibly."

I almost say, *You'll be gone a long time*—but she's already gone. Her returns from college to Abbottsford, and her father and his moods and that otherwise empty house, are a slender thread to hang anything on; my disappointment is deep down, familiar, almost invisible. For the moment, it is even easy to believe that it's the same thing I feel whenever an alum turns up without warning, a kid I was fond of but have, without meaning to, forgotten: discomfort at the reminder that my eternal present, filled with eternal teenagers, is an illusion. (Although the cycle still has some novelty. The alums don't yet feel like ambassadors from another country, the country of my youth.)

The leaf blower whines up one last time with that ruthless insistence, corralling whatever detritus it has managed to find in August, and then stops. We are poised for its beginning again, closer to us, maybe; but a minute passes, two. The quiet gradually takes hold but we stay alert, scanning the empty quad. It's as though we're waiting for an exotic animal to pad into view, or an enormous bird, in a brilliant swirl of plumage. Some interruption, or prize.

"Where have you been?" she says abruptly. "I've been home a whole month. I thought I'd see you."

The nauseating depth of my disappointment surprises even me. A month! Wasted! A month where she was just waiting to bump into me! "I was home," I say. "In Atlanta. With my mother and brother."

"What did you do?"

"Hung out. Taught him to drive." Pretended I still live there. Assuaged my guilt.

"To drive? How old is he?"

"He just turned sixteen," I say. "He's my half brother."

"Oh." There's a slight awkwardness at this hint of how little we know of each other—how little she knows of me. "Is he a good driver?"

"He's awful," I say. "He gets distracted. By things that strike him as wonderful. My brother is frequently amazed."

"That's sort of cute."

"He's sort of cute," I say. Which is a ridiculous understatement. My half brother, Nicky, tall and auburn haired like our mother, turns heads on the street. He has a profile like a prince's on a coin.

"You're a good brother," May says. "To spend all that time."

"If I were a good brother, I'd live there. I guess."

"But you live here," May says, shrugging, as though I were as native to Abbottsford, Massachusetts, as a toadstool that has sprung up in the night. "People leave home." She shrugs again. "As a matter of fact, I'm on my farewell-Abbottsford tour right now."

That plunging stomach again. "What, you're never coming back?"

"Who knows? I don't know why I would," she says. "Anyway, I've done the town. I've done school. I've been sitting here for an hour." She's suddenly languid, older. She uncrosses, recrosses her legs, and I almost expect her to lift a cigarette to her lips. "All that's left is to go to the pond. But I'll have to do that later. Daddy has the car."

"I could take you," I say.

"You have your car here?"

"Well, I didn't walk," I say.

"I thought you lived with the Middletons."

Those are my old landlords, who used to own a two-family, just off campus. "They moved," I say. "When Booker got the promotion. They live on campus now—didn't you know? In the Averys' old house. And I bought a house of my own. Outside town."

"Daddy never tells me anything," she says. "So you're all by yourself?"

"I like it," I say, shrugging, and this is not a lie, not at all; but as I say it I also realize that I believe my solitude will be temporary. That I'm poised on the brink of something else.

SOON WE'RE WALKING DOWN the trail to Abbott Pond. From here, we could walk to my house, which I don't mention. I might later, when I can point through the trees in the exact direction. But I might not. May's cheeriness has taken on a determined edge, and its meaning is clear to me: she really did want to be alone. I've ruined a ritual. I'm mortified that she agreed for me to come out of mere politeness.

It's past noon now and hotter, even in the shade of the trees. Cicadas sing shrilly, up to that pitch of emergency, and stop, and start again. May is ahead of me on the path. Her hair was up in a messy knot earlier, but now it's come down; it's the longest I've ever seen it. It swings and shines. She seems to be tramping along to some rhythm.

She told me she's traveling around Europe before school begins. I was taken to Europe by my mother and my stepfather, Hugh, when they were newly married, and I'm remembering myself there, age twelve, sensing some beckoning clarity of experience and freedom, but pretzeled by puberty, timidity, indecision. The sheer *foreignness*. And then replacing that boy with this May, striding forward, grabbing at the world—oh, she will burst across that chasm, away from me and my kind, and go glimmering.

I hear, "The *woods* are *lovely, dark* and *deep*." I haven't seen her like this, so careless and open. She's put her arms up above her head and as she walks she taps the low-hanging whippy branches. They sway in her wake. "And *miles* to *go be*fore I *sleep*." She's trying to take in as much of the forest as she can.

And then we curve around to the right and there is the pond, the smooth center of it blinding in the sun.

May goes straight to the water and for a second I think she's just going to walk right in, but she stops at the very edge. There is probably some specific plan, an agenda. She spreads her arms wide. We have no shared memories here so I can't help, and I think once again how I'm superfluous. But I can't just disappear. I go down and stand next to her. "Do you love it here?" I say.

"Yes." She is busy absorbing. Then she reaches some kind of capacity and turns to me. "We used to come here for picnics," she says, her arms dropping to her sides. "And then I'd come with my brothers and we'd go skinny-dipping. But eventually they wouldn't let me come with them anymore. Shut out."

Jesus H. Christ. "So is that what you came here to do?" I say.

"No." She's lying.

"I won't look," I say. "I'll go up there"—and I point to the trees. "Far be it from me to thwart this important rite."

She looks at me, excited, half-convinced. "You really won't look? You don't mind?"

I raise my hand. "Scout's honor."

"Or . . . you could come too," she says. Her face is as unseductive as a child's. "It's really fun."

I smile with the most avuncular expression I can muster. "No, no. I'll be right up there."

I go up the bank to the edge of the woods and, true to my word, sit down with my back to the pond. I imagine I can feel her hesitation behind me, and then her undressing—the whisper of cloth against skin—and also her periodic looks at me, checking. Then I really do hear her, footsteps slushing along in shallow water, and then a splash. "Aaaah!" she cries. "Oh my God it's amazing! Don't you want to come in? Oh!" Another enormous splash. She must be flinging herself, full-length, into the water. Silence: she's sliding along, slick as a fish. All that water, touching all of her body.

"Charlie! It's okay! Really!"

I think she means I can turn around, so I do.

Her clothes are in a little pile at the shore. It's true, she's too far away for me to see anything. She's swimming out to the middle of the pond. Her stroke is the elegant product of years of summer camp. I think she might go all the way to the other side, but no, she gets to the center and turns around. Without thinking about it, I take a step backward, but she keeps coming in, closer and closer, until she can stand, the water up to her shoulders, and then stops and waves. I wave back. She slides under, springs up, and then begins to cavort, to *gambol,* twirling in a circle and scudding water up with her cupped palms, flipping forward and backward. Her splashes screen her and I try not to look for details but once I see her breasts and then her buttocks, flashes of roundness, nothing more, white where the rest of her is tan. She dives, surfaces, dives again, sharp ankles and pointed toes. Dark head sleek as a seal's.

Needless to say I am hard as a rock. Sitting there in the shadows.

I did not consider her invitation to join her for one millisecond, and thank God. Besides. My white, flabby self. My completely unsuitable self. She is great armfuls of girl and even if I caught her I surely couldn't hold her.

Her splashes subside. She dives again, surfaces with only her head showing. I can see ripples where she's treading water. "Okay," she calls. "Getting out now," and I turn back around.

I'm still sitting. It won't take long for her to get dressed. I am scrounging for every boner-deflating picture I've got, a trick I haven't had to pull off in years, by the way. I think of the time I threw up in the junior-high cafeteria right across from Annie Stanton. Of enormous hairy nonagenarians with bad breath. Coffins. I even try to summon Hugh, my stepfather, when he was near the end, an image I avoid because it always breaks my heart, but it's like his very ghost is against me and the memory won't come, no grief or pathos, nothing . . . and there's John Thomas stiff as a soldier. Goddamn you, David Herbert! Flowers winding in the mound of Venus—no!

"I'm ready," she sings. "All decent."

I stand up, creakily, but I don't turn around.

"The water was *glorious*! You should have come in!" Taunting me. I put my hands in my pockets and try to adjust. Desperate measures. Ineffective. "Charlie?" Her voice is coming closer. "Charlie?" I hear her swagger dissipating. "Is something wrong?"

I make my last calculations, whirl around, grab her face between my two hands, and say, "Don't you ever do that again."

For a moment her eyes are wide; but she can't look down and that's the main thing. "What?" she says. "Take off my clothes? Swim?" She tosses her head a little in my grasp. "Why do you care?"

And I kiss her, hard. I didn't even realize I was planning it. I am brilliant! Of all the diversionary tactics! I'm bending forward from the waist; she can't get anywhere near my groin. It's ridiculously awkward and so I pour everything I can into the kiss, making her mouth and mine the only real estate that counts. She's startled at first and then she begins to loosen and warm. I have to keep my hands on her face as ballast but I am beginning to lose myself too. *May-May, it's you. It's you.* I've woven my hands into her hair and under my fingertips I feel her humming and growing, feel the *fact* of her, and I know I could give up, step forward, admit myself, she'll feel it all— but, no, she's twenty years old, headed off to some Paris *quai,* some slick new life, and so I will myself to stay rough. I fight her tongue with mine. Our teeth knock together. It's all strategy. A battle. This is war.

But she doesn't seem to realize. Her hands are cradling my face now too. "Mr. Garrett," she murmurs. "Charlie Garrett," and I gentle, I'm softer than I meant to be, this could go on forever, and I pull away and stalk back down the trail.

I realize that, aside from my greeting back in the cloister, I haven't said her name at all, in any form.

I've put myself into a kind of shock but I'm also listening for her, and soon I hear her behind me, no more the jolly tramping. I consider stopping and waiting for her; I slow down, but she stays well behind me. Shame begins to seep in. Also, terror. I've declared myself, finally, but maybe she doesn't even know. Maybe she just thinks I'm a monster. The upside—or not: my erection is thoroughly gone.

We reach the trailhead. My car is the only one in the little unpaved lot. I start toward it and then I realize she's not following me anymore, and when I turn around I see her, a few yards from the end of the path, still definitively in the woods.

Her face is uncertain, but also stubborn. There's a brief standoff. I feel now that I'm only error and all I can do is compound it. Then, from these twenty paces, I see her sigh, and she puts her hands on her hips, and that's that. I walk back to her. "I'm sorry," I say.

"You are?"

I kiss her again. It's a proper, medium-length, generic kiss that doesn't say much. She knows it, and steps away before I do.

Then we get in the car and I drive her back to her house, and the whole way we don't say a word. I pull up at her front walk but leave the car running. There's a silence and I wonder if she knows I am just taking in her warmth, her smell, the way she fills the space next to me. Then she's reaching for the door handle. I want to stop her, but I don't.

She gets out and slams the door, not too hard. Then she leans down to the open window. She rests her folded arms on the frame. Settles in. Won't let my eyes go. I can see the rings of near-black around the dark blue of her irises. Her lashes are still wet, clumped into tiny points. She considers me one more moment, then gives me an enormous smile, like I've just spoken aloud, and she's gone.

Two

I had come to Abbott seven years before. Teaching English there was my first job, right out of college. I'd driven out to my interview, two hours from Cambridge, in a haze of unreality and anxiety; I was still in school then, a senior surrounded by seething ambition and limitless confidence, but for me the idea of being employed at all, at a job that entailed skill and responsibility, was unreal, ludicrous. The only time I felt even slightly proficient at life was when I was holding a book in my hand. Thus, this interview.

It was my first one and I was proud of securing it on my own, without any connections or string pulling, especially from my enormous, eager stepfamily, the Satterthwaites—although how they, back in Atlanta, could involve themselves I couldn't imagine.

That day I met with the department head, Strickler Yates. He was finishing his twenty-eighth year there, he told me (long-termers are not unusual at Abbott). He said, "Harvard. Good man. Class of fifty-six myself." We discovered a shared admiration for the metaphysical poets. Then he declared that literary criticism was "hooey," and asked if I agreed.

"Absolutely," I said, jettisoning four years of college posturing in one fell swoop.

"Those people don't love literature," he said. "If you want to find a bunch of literature haters, go to a college English department." I noticed he said "littrature."

"That makes me feel better," I said. "Because I was wondering if I should get a PhD."

"God no," he said. "No, this is the place for you. A naïve, excitable teenaged reader is a beautiful thing. Someone who's never heard of Elizabeth Bennet or Jay Gatsby, until you tell him. And they all still believe in truth. *That's* the fun of it." Then he released me to the care of an assistant dean, to show me around.

Abbott is in north-central Massachusetts, near the Vermont border, at the top of the Metacomet Ridge, soft mountains younger than the Berkshires. On that day, the air was thick with a fine, chill spring mist. Heavy silver drops hung from azaleas and cherry blossoms, and the flat glow of the overcast sky made the new greens of the grass and of the tiny-leaved trees almost fluorescent. As the dean, Adam Salter, and I walked away from the main quad and past the dorms, the land dipped and rolled, and the green opened and flattened out, as did the abundant white sky; the mist accumulated and draped itself beneficently over the tops of trees.

Salter, a thirtyish, earnest guy with a red flattop haircut, had done me the favor of assuming I was athletic, and we were headed to the lower field to watch a lacrosse game. At the field, mist shrouded the players; the spectators looked like huddling druids. Salter said he was going to introduce me to a few people, but when we stopped at the sideline he couldn't tear his eyes from the field. There were three minutes on the board. "We could wait till the end," I said, and he looked at me with outsized gratitude.

"This is our biggest rival," he said. "Essex. Very important game. Tendency to play dirty, if you ask me, gotta keep an eye on them. Do you play? Well, no matter—what a shot!—almost—oh, hey. Charlie. That's Preston Bankhead over there." He gestured vaguely to a tall, graying man on the sideline, down near the Abbott goal. "Southerner like you. Chaplain. Beloved. Beloved man. Jeez, look at the size of that guy—hey, whoa! Slashing!" There was a whistle. "Finally," Salter said, and then he turned to me for one quick, focused moment. "I'll introduce you in just a sec. He's an institution," he said. "Bankhead."

Then play started again. "No problem," I said. I looked down the sideline at this Bankhead. Middle-aged, fit, tall; patrician nose, assertive chin; graying hair receding in front, longish in back. Abbott was a nominally Episcopal school, and under his all-weather jacket the man wore a collar.

Then he turned slightly in my direction, and though I didn't yet know him, I immediately recognized him—not in any specifics, but instead in his general, privileged mien, the Scotch-Irish narrowness of his face, the lean, symmetrical features and high forehead. It was, collar aside, the fortunate face of southern lawyers and businessmen, of proficient golfers and casual hunters, of my late stepfather. I knew dozens of faces just like this one, back in Atlanta.

Hugh, though, when I had known him, had never been so vital. Bankhead was an exceptionally square-jawed, vivid version of the type, whereas Hugh had been wispier to start, and had gradually dwindled down to a red-eyed shade. But this Bankhead—and the collar, the chin, the slightly artistic hair—held a certain glamour. His eyebrows were on their way to bushiness, which always seemed to accompany a piercing gaze of wisdom. I was susceptible to such gazes.

He was standing with two teenaged boys with his height, but vivid blond hair, and a woman I assumed to be his wife, petite but formidable—she was another type I knew. Thin lips, thin eyebrows, thick straight hair (blond like her boys') incapable of being mussed. In a moment, we'd be introduced and she'd look into my eyes and be so pleased to meet me, and dismiss me. The boys—all three: as the family cheered, I realized there was another son on the field—would be, like their mother, able to recognize fellow tribesmen at fifty paces. They wouldn't recognize me.

I thought, as I so often did, of my brother, Nicky, who was only nine then, but even so would have approached with his glowing, open face, stuck out his gentlemanly little hand, won them all.

And then I realized that if by some miracle I got this job, I'd be the boys' teacher, and maybe my tribe, whatever it was, wouldn't matter. I would have a different authority. I would be different.

The final whistle blew—Abbott won 11–8—and I assumed my most promising interview expression: open, flexible, go-getter, trouper. I'd be ready for this Bankhead, maybe even for the wife! But as I watched, the family rapidly gathered itself together. Umbrellas, collapsible chairs. Amid the busyness Bankhead stood straight, aloof, until the wife said something to him, her pretty face sharp as a blade. "Hmm," Salter said, watching them, sounding both concerned and unsurprised. "Maybe now's not the time. Oh, there's Divya Lowell. You *have* to meet her. She'd be in your department."

I noticed now a small sag at the corners of Preston Bankhead's lips. The deep lines around his eyes suggested a sort of ontological disappointment. What oppressed him? The seeming perfection of his little clan? Or maybe his faith was fraught. Maybe he sighed in the mornings as he fastened the collar around his neck.

Then I realized a girl had been sitting in one of the chairs, at Bankhead's far side, all along. As soon as she stood up, one of the Visigoth brothers yanked the chair away and began folding it. She looked eleven or twelve, tall but still with a child's body, and also olive skinned, dark haired, unlike her mother and brothers. A sport. Her family seemed fearfully complete without her. Her brothers, gear stowed, sauntered off full of their careless authority, high-fiving, slapping backs, but she stayed close to Bankhead, slumping away her height. Her face was that of a child just moving into adolescence—bored, impatient, wistful.

"Charlie?" Salter said.

"Coming!"

Then the girl looked up at her father in some silent communication and he looked down at her. As they turned away from the field he put his arm around her and they were suddenly united, and I thought, *Ah. She is his.*

I GOT THE JOB, which felt both inevitable and surprising. Suddenly, I had a plan, for at least a year.

I moved into the first-floor apartment of a two-family near campus, and for several years after that, when I was back in Atlanta to visit, I rather enjoyed mentioning to the Satterthwaites where I lived and watching their faces at the word *duplex.* But wasn't I teaching at a *private* school? Hadn't I gone to *Harvard*? I jammed their radar. Living up north, I'd become exotic to them. They'd expected me to come back, and I hadn't, and now they didn't know what to think.

Neither did I, to be honest. I had no agenda; I was twenty-two; I was still thinking in semesters. My mother said, "We're fine here. Live your life," and I listened, because she rarely had an agenda either. It was the Satterthwaites who voiced distress about my absence, but this was pro forma. They were a fundamentally generous bunch, and they'd always wanted to claim me; but, as much as I'd wanted to be claimed, I'd never thought that the operation would work. Living far away just made it easier. Besides, they still had Nicky, the child who was really theirs, who'd been born correctly. He would be more than enough.

MY LANDLADY, ANGELA MIDDLETON, née Siegal, was a cheerful, big-boned blonde, like a former-jock older sister, always carrying at least one kid on her hip—they had three, the youngest an infant. She was a real-estate agent—"*very* part-time," she said. Booker, her husband, was assistant head of grounds at Abbott and six-five on a short day. He was African American, with a very dark, square, faintly Asiatic face, and not a smiler. He was in the air force reserves, and every summer he spent a month away training at the base in Chicopee.

When I first moved in, he said, "You're from Atlanta."

"Yes sir."

"My people are from South Carolina."

"Ah," I said. Booker was a broad man. Broad lips, broad cheekbones, broad shoulders. He was as solid as a concrete block, and my landlord, and the conversation was not going to end until he decided it would. We were in the small common vestibule of the house; my door was open—I'd been about to go in. "You ever get back there?" I said.

"Used to spend the summers there. Which didn't make any damn sense, when you think about it."

"No, I suppose not. But . . . but you were born up here?"

"My mother came up when she was two years old. I was born in Boston. Hear you went to school there. To Harvard."

"Yes sir."

"I grew up in Roxbury."

"Ah."

"You ever get over to Roxbury, Charlie?"

"I never did." He nodded, waiting. "I didn't have a car. I didn't leave campus much, I guess."

"Makes sense."

"Actually, I never left the library. I was hanging on by my finger-nails."

He smiled a little. "I don't believe what you're saying, now."

I thought about myself in college. "It's the truth." He was wearing a hat with the insignia from his squadron, and I was desperate to change the subject. I pointed to it. "Do you fly?"

"Tactical aircraft maintenance."

"Ah."

He finally relented. "Well. Welcome to the house, Charlie. Welcome to Abbott. It's a good place."

"Yes sir. It really is."

He turned to open his own door. I felt like a dog whose leash had been stepped on, then the foot suddenly removed. "My father was a soldier," I said. "Marines. Enlisted man."

He turned back. "Is that so."

"He died in Vietnam," I said. "Before I was born." It was the story my mother had always told me. I believed my father had been a man (a twenty-one-year-old high-school dropout, just barely a man) named Jimmie Garrett, USMC, PFC.

Booker regarded me. A long second passed. "I am sorry to hear that."

I nodded. This time he let me turn away first.

I REALIZED HOW TERRIFIED I was of teaching on the night before I was to begin. The next day, beams of adolescent attention trained on me, I was nearly flattened. At first I thought only about survival. But then a stubbornness I didn't know I had kicked in. Somehow I didn't undermine myself by thinking about all I wasn't doing, how unex-traordinary I was being; I just clung to a new persona I was making up on the spot, a tweedy, knowledgeable, unflappable self. Pretending to be someone I wasn't was, in itself, comfortable, or at least familiar.

I'd heard that I should move around while I taught, and so I walked, I paced; I strolled to the window; I lifted mine eyes unto the hills. My classroom was on the second floor, facing west, away from the quad, with a sugar maple right outside the window, and beyond all was openness—rolling green dotted with neat buildings of gray stone and white clapboard, a little farm of learning.

Sometimes I wished we were facing the quad and its honeycomb of crisscrossing paths, but I developed an appreciation for looking away instead, out beyond to the edges of campus. I wasn't thinking of escape but of mystery, discovery. And that tree became an anchor. Day after day, I would gaze at that tree, at the autumn sun filtered through leaves gradually transforming. I thought of other bygone teachers watching the same tree. When the sun sank in the late afternoons and threatened to become blinding, I lowered the shades reluctantly.

And then I'd turn back around. *Miss Myrick. Mr. Bratton. Miss Aaron. Miss Rourke. Yes. No. Absolutely. Due on Friday. Good God, do you think that plural needs an apostrophe? Please tell us why. Exactly.*

I thought that if there were any tactics I could use to age myself, then I should use them. I'd copied the formality, the *misters* and *misses,* from an old teacher of mine. It held them at arm's length, but it was an equalizer, too: I was Mr. Garrett; I held them to my own standard.

I was exhausted by the expansion of myself into these new, sturdier outlines, but I felt myself growing stronger. I allowed myself to believe I'd made this particular new person, who could withstand the force of their energy, all alone, from almost nothing, from bits of cloth and borrowed words.

Yes, please read, Mr. Bratton. John Donne was quite a sensuous writer. What's the central image here? Mr. Sprague. Is there more than one type of compass? Sometimes you have to take hold of the end of a sentence and pull. Miss Garard. Mr. Maxwell. Yes, absolutely. See me after. Good work. Today, Miss Hobson, you are on. Mr. DeAngelis, you're off. Yes. Keep going. Exactly . . . exactly.

Every day, I tried to pull it out of them. What? More than they knew they knew. More than they knew they had. I found that I could gather the force of them into reins in my hands, steer, and then let them lead. At the window of my classroom, looking out, I was in the prow of a landship, forging ahead with my new self, built on the scaffolding of these names; then I turned around and my own energy went forth, joined theirs, became something new and larger. I had not expected to feel my own self slowly emerging as I tried to draw out theirs. I had not expected to love anyone, is what I'm saying. Sometimes they looked at me in amazement at what came out of their mouths.

THE FIRST FULL CHAPEL of the year, Preston Bankhead gave the homily.

He looked even taller in his robes. His hair seemed to have grown and, while still respectable, flowed over his collar impressively. He ascended to the pulpit, looked down at us for a long moment, and began what I later called (for I was to hear it more than once) the Grey boys sermon.

As I learned that day, the chapel had been the gift of a southern cotton planter who lost both of his sons, Abbott alumni, in the Civil War. After the war was over, the heartbroken and now heirless father sent the remainder of his fortune north too, in a gesture of simultaneous penance and defiance, to build a grand Gothic quadrangle on a rolling green campus in central Massachusetts; but the benefactor, Phineas Grey, died before the quad was completed, as did the money, which was why the chapel stood alone, with its truncated wings.

There was a plaque, Preston's main subject, beside the chapel's wide, arched front doors:

GREY MEMORIAL CHAPEL
IN MEMORY OF THE SONS OF ABBOTT
WHO MADE THE GREATEST SACRIFICE
TO THE CAUSES TO WHICH THEY WERE LED
BY CUSTOM, CULTURE, AND CONSCIENCE

REQUIESCANT IN PACE

and then the Grey boys' names, ranks, and dates.

"The wording of that plaque," Preston would say, as he did that particular morning, his voice tinged with deep, if weary, tolerance for the sins and foibles of others, "was wrangled over for years. Finally it was determined by two elderly nieces, one of the abolitionist persuasion, one not. It was difficult to find common ground. So what *did* they find? They found *custom*, and *culture*, and *conscience*." He leaned forward over the pulpit. "We all find these. We don't just find them, we *swim* in them. But which is more important?" He let the pause reverberate. "What if they don't agree, those things? What if they're at war with one another?

"Custom. Is that an excuse not to think? Culture. Heaven forbid you should upset anyone! And conscience. Probably you'd say *that's* the one. That's the most important. And I concur—but how can we be sure it's our conscience that's speaking? What if it's some other voice? If you listen to the wrong voice, my friends, the consequences can be dire." He leaned over the pulpit and for a moment the congregation was still. I found myself leaning forward too.

"So you depend on culture, and custom, and conscience," Preston continued, "but then you leave home, and let's say you go to boarding school, and all the sudden you think, *This is my chance to make myself from scratch.*" He came down from the pulpit then and stood on the chancel step, as though he couldn't resist us any longer. It was, as I would learn, his signature move. "I never went to boarding school myself, but when I was a young boy my father left us, and I never saw him again. That was *my* reinvention. I had to decide right then who I was, all on my own, and who I was going to be. In a way it was a freedom—a sad freedom. I had to look at my family, my past, my future, and make myself. Who I'd been didn't matter anymore. I decided I was going to be new and different.

"And so here I stand before you today. My own creation. But is that true? Certainly not. I've been made by culture, and custom, and I hope not least of all conscience, even though I thought I was completely free of those things." He smiled broadly. "Or at least the first two." Everyone laughed, in thrall. "Your time here at Abbott will, I hope and pray, have a little less drama than my experience. But your task here is similar, to decide what to jettison, and what to keep. Who you want to be. And it's to figure out, once and for all, which voice is your conscience. It might be the quiet voice; it might be the least persuasive. But if you are truly listening, it is also unignorable." He turned away, as though he were finished, and then turned back to us once more, as though he'd had one more thought, just that second. One more flash. As though he hadn't thought of it all before, hadn't done the choreography of that little pivot in the privacy of his study. "If you ignore your conscience," he said, "that still, small voice, you will regret it the rest of your life. That is always true. Till the end of time."

And then we were singing the school hymn. "In wisdom, stature, love for man . . ."

After chapel, Preston made a point of greeting everyone at the door, like a regular parish priest. As I waited, I absorbed the medieval kitsch of the chapel: soaring vaults, carved friezes, and every face in every stained-glass window solemn, with dark-ages circles under the eyes—but I was ready to love it all. All around us, the names engraved in the stone blocks of the walls—the unfortunate young dead, captains of industry, do-gooders, past headmasters and their wives, a couple of senators, and, by the door, the Grey boys—bore silent witness to the sturdiness of the past, to virtuous productivity, and, if one lived long enough, the accolades waiting if one followed certain scripts thoroughly and well. If one listened to one's conscience, at least some of the time.

When it was my turn to be greeted, the directness of Preston's gaze, his effortless simulation of affinity, enveloped me. "I didn't know that about your father," I said, which of course was asinine because I didn't know anything about him. "That he left."

"A difficult thing." He'd taken my hand to shake it, now covered it with his other one, a gesture that felt provisional rather than warm. "It was a long time ago." He cocked his head at me, a polite nudge.

"Charlie," I said. "Charles Garrett. English department. From Atlanta."

"Of course. A fellow countryman." He smiled his saddish smile and gave my still-enclosed hand a tolerant pat. I didn't know yet that he exuded intimacy only from far away, in the pulpit. "A long time ago," he repeated. "We survive, don't we? Ah, and here's young Mr. Bratton," he said to the boy behind me, with the same consuming recognition, and the large, dry hand was withdrawn.

AND THAT DAY, that first day, when I'd seen May beside the bright green playing field, in the mist?

They took a picture that day, the Bankheads. It turned out to be one of those fortuitous snapshots that acquires a distinct identity and function over the years, or so May told me. Someone would say, "In the lacrosse picture . . ." and everyone knew which one that was, although there were a lot of lacrosse pictures. And in this particular lacrosse picture, there wasn't even much visible lacrosseness, except for Laird's uniform, which was mostly hidden by others' shoulders, and Laird's sweat, which had glued his hair in a perfect tousle.

The three boys and their parents: William, who was already in college, and who *refused* to answer to Binky anymore, *do not call me that;* Henry, the youngest boy, the sweetest; Laird, the best athlete; and then Preston and Florence flanking them, the frame fully filled with their five faces, the day's flat light perfect, making the colors bluish and poignant. You can see why that picture survived, why it ended up as an eight-by-ten on the grand piano (which no one played) in the living room, along with more official portraits of weddings and graduations and christenings: by some trick of light, some alchemy of chance, they all look relaxed, with themselves and even more unusually with one another.

They look like a family that laughs every night around the dinner table; Preston looks like a father whom the sons consult regularly, respectfully, gratefully—a father who takes long walks with each son in turn, scuffing through fallen leaves in a pretty, civilized wood. Florence looks like a mother who rules with a firm but fair hand, a taskmaster of the domestic who'll make you fold your laundry and set the table and write prompt thank-you notes, a woman whose price is far above rubies. Her head is flung back with both satisfaction and gratitude: her sons are nearly grown, look what she has wrought! And the boys look solid, full of good humor and fondness. It is exactly, perfectly the picture that should be on the piano in the rectory of a boarding school.

Their youngest member, however, cold and bored, had wandered off, trying to escape yet another of her brothers' games. But they'd taken the picture anyway, and so, for that captured moment, it had been as though May didn't exist.

"The happy family," May said to me, years later, as we stood in front of the photo, her hand in mine. "Fuck that."

Three

Henry Bankhead, the one in the center of the lacrosse picture, was the only son left at Abbott when I started teaching there. Binky was in college, and Laird had just graduated. Henry was a senior, and so to both my relief and slight disappointment wouldn't be my student, as I was teaching freshmen and juniors. As it turned out he was a popular kid in a way I could appreciate, not much of a jock, instead sort of ramshackle, with a tendency to resist the system, which I saw in his occasional columns for the school paper ("The Tyranny of Lights-Out," "Why Can't Ultimate Be a Letter Sport?"). I hoped I might get to know him a little. May was then still too young for Abbott.

After Christmas break, though, I didn't see Henry around. Finally I asked Divya Lowell about it. "Oh, Charlie, you *are* out of the loop. He's gone to St. Luke's. In Rhode Island."

"But he's a senior."

Divya looked at me with what I could only call a sympathetic glare. "Drugs. All handled quietly. It would have been different . . ." Her voice trailed off.

"Is Preston okay?"

She looked at me with surprise. "Probably not. I haven't talked to him." The bell would ring soon for the next class. "You can ask Win about it," she said. "Will you come on Friday?"

"I'm afraid you're going to get sick of me," I said, happily.

"Nonsense! We'll talk then." The way she said it, I knew she didn't think the situation so important. But to me it seemed the first chink in the finely wrought Bankhead armor.

DIVYA AND WIN LOWELL LIVED near campus, in a big, drafty, very old house on a double lot. They, and the house, were famous, as I'd recently learned, for their annual Christmas parties, and also for the boxwood labyrinth in the back forty, as Win said, which had come with the place. On the street side, the house had an enormous Greek Revival portico. "I didn't expect to come north and find Tara," I said to Divya.

"Nor me living in it," she said, winking.

Since school started, they'd been having me over for dinner nearly every week. Sometimes there were other Abbott people there, and sometimes it was just me. I was pretty sure they felt sorry for me, but I didn't care. "There's not much to do in a tiny town like this," Divya said, shrugging, and then she would put me to work with some simple task I couldn't screw up, like draining pasta. We would sit at the big table in the kitchen, with their two young sons, Anil and Ram, eating at lightning speed and then zooming off somewhere, leaving us with our wine. I'd been legally drinking for mere months at that point, but no one ever mentioned that. As it got colder, sometimes we would go to the living room after and sit in front of the fire.

Divya's living room—"It's her house," Win said, "I just live here"—had bright white walls that stretched up to eleven-foot ceilings. She had painted the ceilings pale blue. "It must be delightful up there, with all of the heat," she would say, drolly. Stretching all the way up the walls, above the abundant yard-sale furniture and odd Lowell heirloom, were paintings, vaguely representational, done by various friends, Anil and Ram, and Divya herself, in the colors of kings and queens: cobalt and canary and verdigris, ruby and sable. She had a fondness for canvases with the paint layered on until it rose in little topographical drifts, and every now and then she would let her hand hover dangerously close to the surface of one, as though she might read it like Braille. "I wish I could stroke them." She looked to either side, in high espionage mode. "Sometimes I do," she whispered.

If Win caught her, she would move her hand away. "I think it would be good for them," she said defensively. "Good for them to feel our electricity, to remind them that they are *made* things. Like us." Win rolled his eyes. "He is not allowed to touch them," she said severely.

"I don't want to," Win said.

"Exactly."

The story of the labyrinth was that it had been put in by the house's original wealthy owner, to cure his homesick Mississippi bride. It was boxwood, thigh high and forty feet square, and was a copy of one on the plantation where the wife had grown up. If I ever called it a maze, Win would correct me. "A maze, you get lost," he said. "A labyrinth, you don't."

He had turned himself into a garden historian to restore it and keep it up. He liked to complain and talk about the vegetables a plot that size could produce, how they could feed the town on it. But countless times I found him out back, planting replacement cuttings, or trimming away at a hedge that was already marvelously squared-off and smooth, humming to himself.

"Do you know if it worked?" I asked once. "For the homesick wife?"

"No idea."

Win's own first wife had died when they were both young, in a car crash, and he said he'd nearly given up hope (in what, he did not specify) before he met Divya, who was now in her mid-thirties. He was a decade and a half older than she was. She had come to America to study literature, and then, when she came to teach at Abbott, "I snapped her up."

He wore plaid flannel shirts and ancient tweed trousers, and a graying buzz cut. He seemed like the kind of man who would know how to fix your dishwasher or your car or your furnace—the old-time, Greatest Generation kind of self-sufficiency, although in point of fact he'd served in Vietnam, something he rarely mentioned. She often wore saris, although she was not above wearing a fleece vest on top, to stay warm in their leaky house. Inside, Divya was often barefoot and Win, grudgingly, in slippers, his boots at the door, at the perpetual ready for mud season. He was, of course, from Vermont. Their sons had Divya's wide dark eyes and Win's square jaw. His hands were big and calloused but he touched the tops of their dark, glossy heads gently.

That night I asked about Henry Bankhead. "Pot in his gym locker," Win said shortly.

"Seriously? How stupid can you be? Who found it?" I said.

There was a pause. "I did," Win said.

"Oh."

I supposed Win had known Henry his whole life. I imagined Win confronting him. Imagined him standing there with the baggie in one of those big hands, shaking his head. "Even though it was a first strike . . . ?"

"It wasn't. Thing was, he was dealing too."

"My theory is he wanted to be caught," Divya said.

"You realize that once this would have been nothing," Win said. "Or not much. Used to be sex was the boogeyman. Drugs all over the place when I first started here. I was a dorm master for years—believe me, we looked the other way. All the time. Not now, though."

"Why did you say he wanted to get caught?"

Another pause. I felt complicated currents of hesitation flowing between them. "Preston has had his troubles," Win said.

Divya raised an eyebrow and I knew instantly that—no surprise—she disliked Florence. She said, "It's not always a happy house."

I seized on the *not always.* Meaning sometimes it *was.* It looked happy to me. The Bankhead house, the physical house, looked ideal in fact, if a slightly less quirky ideal than the Lowells' multicolored behemoth: it was a big Victorian, a couple of shutters missing, paint on the front steps worn away, piles of sports equipment on the porch. When the garage door was open, you could see a sculptured heap of bikes and camping gear, and in the side yard were tomato cages with dried vines left over from the summer. A little sloppier than I would have expected from a woman like Florence, but I chalked up the disorder to the boys, who were still in and out on weekends, and to a cheerful ethos of industry, of numerous projects in various states of completion.

"I think perhaps Florence imagined something different," Divya said. Win radiated silence. "She's from some very old family, down south. And what's her father again? Win?"

"He's a bishop. In Virginia."

So Florence Bankhead had had thoughts of something bigger: a grand rectory somewhere, visiting dignitaries. And southern warmth. Instead she was stuck here, ninety miles from Boston, at the Abbott School—a place genteelly clinging to the second tier, New-England-boarding-schools-wise. A place I already loved, but maybe she did not.

I wanted to ask more, but I resisted, and Divya, seeming to sense my restraint, reached for my plate to give me seconds, whether to reward me or fortify me I wasn't sure. "It's not a big mystery," she said. "I just think they're not as well matched as they seem to be. Those two." She handed me back my plate. "Henry will be happy," she said, as though I'd asked. "Don't worry." The eyebrow again. "There are *far* worse things than being kicked out of one preparatory school and going to another one. My God."

"So there's just the daughter left," I said.

"May."

"Poor kid," Win said. "I wouldn't want to rattle around in that place with Preston and Florence, I'll tell you that."

"*Win*ship."

"Well, I wouldn't," he said, and Divya looked obscurely pleased.

I had just about given up on figuring out Preston's purported magic. Sometimes, during a sermon, especially if he was quoting, say, Eliot or Auden, I felt a tingling of uncanny inspiration, a nerdy mind-meld that made me giddy. *Now I have something to tell him.* But up close, he seemed surprised that anyone, including me, would feel a claim to him.

Now, in the hallway beyond the wide living room door I saw, and heard, the boys whiz by. Ram wore a crown and a cape; Anil, in a cowboy hat, was whacking at him from behind with a thing that I thought was a sword but then realized was a wand, tipped with a silver star. "I have turned you into a toad!" he howled. "Quit running! Quit running!"

"I'm *hopping*!" Tremendous thumping up the stairs.

"How was your vacation, Charlie?" Divya asked. "How was Atlanta?"

I told them a little about the enormous Christmas dinner (table for twenty, multiple forks) at Bobo and Big Hugh's, my step-grandparents', one of the usual command performances that no one seemed to mind but my mother and me.

"You're a regular southern gentleman," Divya said.

"I guess you don't know many southern gentlemen."

She tilted her head. "Do you feel like a foreign person there?"

I felt a familiar shame: I needed to appreciate what I had. "It's where I was born and raised. So that wouldn't make any sense, would it?"

"It's very hard to go home," Divya said.

"Div knows what that's like," Win said. "But you came here knowing you wouldn't go back, didn't you, Div?"

"Ha. I was forced to stay," Divya said serenely. "I was cajoled."

"You wanted to be cajoled."

"So wise, Win Lowell," Divya said. "So wise."

Her voice lilted along. I loved that voice. I wanted to ask her to read me a bedtime story.

The flames of the fire licked and rose; the childlike paintings glowed on the walls. I thought of Divya's palm hovering. Win ignored her, or seemed to, but happiness moved, nearly imperceptible, like a slow ocean swell over his face.

ONE DAY I RETURNED home to find Angela Middleton in the driveway unloading her minivan, the baby clinging precariously to her hip, the two older kids in full tantrum, and a bag of groceries scattered on the ground. "Oh jeez," I said, "let me help you," and bent down to grab a can of chicken noodle soup.

"Could you just take him?" she said, and without waiting for an answer she thrust the baby at me.

"Sure," I said, but he was already in my arms. He was heavier than

I expected, and I slid both arms under his padded butt. "Hi, there," I said. "Hi, little baby." The other two were screaming so loudly that no one would hear a thing I said, except for the baby, Zack, himself. Who wouldn't tell.

I hadn't held a lot of babies but whenever I did I thought of Nicky, still a vivid physical memory—he'd been a trusting, soft-spined lump on my hip, requiring two arms. I remembered that. And always the smile of joy, as though he'd been waiting for me. How when I took him the responsibility was suddenly fierce: he made no babyish efforts to disguise his dependence. And why would he?

But this little Zack was erect as a soldier, using me as support, not comfort. He regarded me with great seriousness. "Hey, Zackie," I said. "You're an independent soul. Where'd you come from, anyway?"

I was remembering how it was with babies. That you could look and look at them with abandon, and they wouldn't object; that they had no personal space; that they literally didn't know where they ended and the rest of the world began. Even with my face so close to his I was not another person, but a small moving piece of the vast world. A baby could not be offended.

Baby Zack's skin was light caramel, his lashes ridiculously long. His eyes were a greenish hazel, baby clear, clear as water. "You're a handsome dude," I said, and those eyes, which had been wide and blank as clean plates, suddenly crinkled into a smile. In his mouth I saw two snow-white dots of teeth. Drool glistened on the curve of his bottom lip and then dropped in a long string onto my shirt. "Buddy," I said. "That's gross."

I made a face at him, which apparently was hilarious, because he laughed, and his laugh, too, was like water.

When I had to give him back my arms felt abruptly light, as if they'd rise into the air on their own with his weight gone. "You're a lifesaver, Charlie," Angela said. "He took to you. He never does that. Watch out, maybe he imprinted."

"No problem," I said. "That would be nice."

I went into my apartment. It was dim and quiet. I felt content to be alone again. Then I heard the little thumping footfalls above my head, the rising high voices, and unaccountably I was glad of those too.

Four

May Bankhead started at Abbott my second year there. I was still teaching freshmen, but she wasn't in my section. The following year I taught sophomores, and she was. She hadn't changed much, had only grown taller, but she usually slouched, her slender body almost comically neurasthenic. Sometimes she walked with her long hair hiding her face. But at other times she would stand up and push the hair away, and in those moments she was one of the changelings, she was becoming.

In class, she was quiet, but when she spoke she was direct and didn't suffer fools gladly. Occasionally I saw Florence in her, and was sorry.

Sometime during the summer before May's senior year, Florence moved out. The whole thing happened quietly. She moved to a house in Amherst, a half hour away, but May stayed with Preston, and eventually Florence went back to Savannah, where she'd been born and all her family still was. It was said she had a boyfriend there, a childhood sweetheart who'd been carrying the torch all this time. I don't know where that story came from.

That fall, May was in my senior seminar. The first week, after class, I asked how she was doing. I wanted to let her know I knew, that we could be honest.

"I'm fine," she said. Her eyes beetled at me—cold, then abruptly warm: Preston's trick, which she had inherited, or learned. She tossed her head a little, and then looked at me again and all of a sudden seemed to decide I was all right. "It's a relief, frankly."

"How could it be a relief?" I said, without thinking. I realized I wasn't sure what color her eyes were—dark, but I couldn't tell if they were brown or gray; I wanted to know, but I would have had to say *Come close,* so of course I didn't.

"I don't like lies," she said.

I was uncomfortable. "There's a funny southern expression," I said. Blue? Were her eyes actually blue? "When they tell you not to lie they say, 'Don't tell stories.'"

She nodded. She didn't smile. "Yes," she said. "I've heard that before."

I'D SEEN PRESTON just days before at the Labor Day tea, an annual event in the headmaster's garden, the day before classes started. I hadn't known yet about Florence—I'd just returned from Atlanta, and Divya hadn't gotten me up to speed. I did notice an odd aura around Preston. People approached him warily, as if he'd recently been quarantined; if they came close, they'd lay a hand on his arm; I also saw he was alone, but I assumed Florence was somewhere at the other end of the garden, probably with Louise Hueffer, the headmaster's wife. I was surprised when Preston planted himself near me and said, without preamble, "I've had enough goddamn *vacation.* Enough of the *picayune* demands of *women* and *children.*" Then he downed half his Tom Collins in one gulp.

In spite of those cold eyes, I knew I was supposed to act like what Preston had said was a joke. I went for halfway in between. "May's a senior," I said. "I don't think she'd be happy, being called a child."

He gave me a sidelong look of measured disappointment and finished the rest of his drink in two long swallows. I thought about Preston enduring all the long summer, his family immune to him, a prophet without honor, missing his sea of captive faces in Grey Chapel. I realized he was a man without reserves. Still, May seemed to need defending. "She's in my seminar," I said. "She's so . . . bright. Looking forward to it."

Preston moved his shoulders around loosely in his coat. He looked down into the ice cubes in his highball and rattled them a little and then smiled at me again, transformed: he was suddenly warm, complete with a fatherly twinkle, confidant instead of confider. "Win Lowell tells me you're a chess player," he said.

"Not really," I said, startled into honesty. "I mean, Win's a lot better. And my brother. In Atlanta. He's kind of a genius at it." I'd just come back from Atlanta the week before, where I had, in fact, played with Nicky, who could now demolish me in a handful of moves, although he tried to string it along for my sake. I had been the one who taught him, as Hugh had taught me.

"Come by the house," Preston said. "After supper." Was his voice suddenly more southern than it had been just moments before? *Suppah.* His voice caressed the little absence of the *r*, which was entirely different from the Yankee way of chopping it off with no mercy. "What about Thursday?" *Thuhsday.* When I hesitated he said, giving every impression of indulging me for my own sake, "Or another time. Name a day."

"No," I said, "Thursday's fine."

Which was how I became, for a time, Preston's chess partner. I went over every couple of weeks. Preston would have had me more often but I begged off, saying I had grading or lesson planning, and it was often true, because I was teaching new courses, with syllabi I'd designed just that summer. I wasn't fed at the Bankheads', but I was given as much alcohol as I wanted. Preston was a silent player; afterward we sometimes sat and had one more drink.

I knew all about southern manners, but he was exceptionally good at graceful obfuscation. Sometimes I worked up the nerve to push him. "How old did you say you were when your father left?"

"Ten. Just turned ten."

"And that was in New Orleans."

"Oh, no. I was born in the Delta. Moved to New Orleans to be with my mother's people." He gave me a look. "When I was ten." He nodded slowly, and the shadows rose and fell on his sunken cheeks.

"The Delta. I thought I heard that in your voice."

"Ah. You like accents," he said, as if some suspicion had been confirmed. "The illusion of identity."

He never asked me about my own origins. I wouldn't have told him much; I didn't know what he wanted to hear. And yet, at the end of every evening, I left feeling that we had somehow been on the brink of connection.

When I was there, May was usually upstairs doing homework. Sometimes I never saw her at all. But I was aware of her, over our heads, in a bedroom behind a closed door, and I hoped the sound of our voices was comforting to her in that big, empty place.

It was still stuffed with detritus from the days when a family of six had lived there, and if you'd said they were all about to troop in the door I would've believed it. In the mudroom, there were coats on all the hooks, and a row of boots of various sizes on two boot trays, and a pile of sneakers. There were old birthday cards on the mantel, and the refrigerator was covered with magneted postcards and cartoons and outdated team schedules. On the closed top of the baby grand piano, there was the village of silver-framed photos. Percy the golden retriever, his muzzle nearly white, was still extant, along with his dishes and leashes and bones and drippy tennis balls. The house still seemed to hold life.

Once, though, I was sent to the kitchen for club soda; when I opened the fridge I found, besides the two bottles I'd been sent for, an orange, a jar of pickled cocktail onions, a half-gallon of skim milk, a can of grocery-store ground coffee, and a wedge of moldy Cheddar. Which could not have been the way it was back when there were six mouths to feed, three of them teenaged boys.

I stood there looking into that sad white expanse and then felt someone behind me. There was May, her head tipped, a wry expression on her face. Here at home she looked older, I thought. Or just more relaxed. "I eat mostly on campus," she said.

"Well, thank God for that," I said.

"May-May!" It was Preston, a sudden bellow. "Help Charlie find the goddamn fizz!"

We exchanged a look. "I've got it," I called back, and reached in for one of the bottles, which May promptly took from me. She loosened the cap to test it: no *whoosh.* She handed me the other, unopened one. "Sorry," she said, with a general shrug.

"Don't be," I said, and thought I sounded condescending, and hated it, but she'd already turned and left the room.

AT THE LOWELLS', Ram wanted to play chess with me. We set up the board and he went at it hammer and tongs—it was just a game to him, not an intellectual contest. In rapid succession he lost half his pieces. I let him put me in check four or five times before I finally ended it. "Again!" he cried.

"Fine. Set it up."

"I'm going to beat you, Charlie!"

"I have no doubt," I said. "If not now, then soon."

Win came in and stood smiling, his arms crossed over his chest. "Be careful, *bachcha,* Charlie is merciless."

"Only sometimes." Which reminded me. "You told Preston Bank-head I was a chess player."

"I did," Win said.

"Well, so are you."

"I thought you'd be better company for him."

Ram was arranging the pieces very carefully. I loved his skinny little fingers. "Why does Bankhead rub you the wrong way?" I said.

"I think the feeling is mutual. Doesn't mean I don't have sympathy for the man."

"Well, thanks."

"Don't go if you don't want, Charlie." There was a mild rebuke in Win's voice that I was not inclined to unpack. Maybe I'd spoken aloud more than I'd realized about wanting to know Preston Bank-head.

"Charlie," Ram said, bouncing up and down in his chair. The board was ready, he'd moved his pawn.

I shrugged. "No," I said, "I don't mind."

ONE EVENING I CAME HOME and found May in the vestibule of my house. "Hello, Miss Bankhead," I said. My brain in suspension: *Of course she's not here to see you!* "What's up?" What I said to kids who came to my office hours. My voice came out unnaturally deep.

She looked at me quickly and then turned back to stare at the door. She was hugging a few textbooks to her chest. "I'm babysitting," she said. There must have been something strange about the silence. "The *Middletons*."

I felt the laugh bubble up between us—*Oh we are absurd*. Felt it squelched, all silently. "First time?"

"No," she said, and finally looked at me. "I'm here a lot. Every other week or so."

"Oh," I said. "I didn't realize."

I'd babysat a couple of times myself but Angela and I both quickly realized that I was better one-on-one. So I took Zack into town sometimes for ice cream, or to Abbott Pond to fish. He was five now.

I heard Booker's heavy footsteps on the stairs behind their door. "See you," she said. The corner of her mouth lifted. "Or not."

Miss Bankhead. I'd wanted so badly to age myself, and now it was the quirk I was known for. I was trapped in it.

That night the thumping over my head was louder than usual. I wondered which feet, which sounds, were hers; I fancied they'd be a different, distinguishable timbre. But how many times had she been up there, right above me, and I hadn't even known?

The running turned to walking, the creaking I normally didn't notice anymore. Gradually all grew quiet. She must have put the kids to bed. She'd read them stories and turned out the lights. Smoothed Zack's forehead, if he let her. He liked to have a book of his own read to him; he held himself apart from his brother and sister, was conscious of being only five. Maybe she knew that, too.

Now she'd be sitting on the sofa doing her homework. Feet curled under her. Chewing on a pencil.

I liked that she was there. That we were in a small town. That these connections were everywhere.

When I was finished with my own work, I poured myself two

fingers of bourbon and sat drinking it with a satisfaction that was mysteriously giddy, that teetered on the edge of epiphany.

MY SENIOR SEMINAR then was British poetry. Old-fashionedness was not discouraged at Abbott, and a nice, thorough British survey was felt to be just the ticket to prepare seniors for the world; so that particular day I was teaching John Donne. I have always been fond of the metaphysicals. Strickler Yates, who was retiring that year, thoroughly approved of my syllabus, and I never forgot that I might have owed Donne, that old apostate, my actual job.

I was sitting at the edge of my desk, and in front of me the three conference tables were pulled into their U. It was the period after lunch and from the looks of things that day's mac and cheese was sitting heavy. "Readers? Anyone? For 'The Good-Morrow'?" May was in her usual spot at the lower left-hand corner, and slowly her hand went up, a shy sea anemone waving in the current. "Take it away, Miss Bankhead," I said, and she bent her head down to her book.

I wonder, by my troth, what thou and I / Did, till we loved? Were we not weaned till then? / But sucked on country pleasures, childishly?

There was the usual chortling at "sucked," but I held up a hand and it died away.

Or snorted we in the Seven Sleepers' den? Someone else might have hammed it up, but her voice was steady. I kept glaring, and all was quiet.

'Twas so; but this, all pleasures fancies be. / If ever any beauty I did see, / Which I desired, and got, 'twas but a dream of thee.

I'd been at the Bankheads' the night before. When I'd arrived the air had felt odd, as though I'd just missed a fight, but Preston was alone. Had he just had a phone call with Florence? Or with a lawyer? Henry?

He had the board set up and was regally, almost impatiently, waiting. The emptiness of the house was a roaring silence, but as usual I was supposed to ignore it. I went to sit down, ever obedient, but as I did I realized he was the person at Abbott around whom I felt the youngest, and that I was sick of it. "Is everything okay, Preston?"

A glare, suppressed. "My boy, I don't know what you're talking about."

"You look upset."

"I am perfectly fine."

And now good-morrow to our waking souls, / Which watch not one another out of fear.

We began to play. The silence thickened, grew purposeful. But beneath my concentration was a different current. *I think I'm giving up on him.* Preston remarked that I was distracted. He'd gone back to a solicitous tone, as if he were ready to impart wisdom. But I knew enough by now—this was a revelation too—to ignore it.

For love, all love of other sights controls, / And makes one little room an everywhere.

After half an hour I heard the back door in the kitchen open and close, and May murmuring to Percy, but she didn't appear. Preston was beating me but not badly, not yet, and I knew if I concentrated I could hold him off a while longer, but I felt an unfamiliar impatience and found myself thinking of Nicky—of how he took in the board in one gulp, of how he seemed to see the dance of the pieces far into the future, all possible attacks and counterattacks, more brilliantly than any general. Of how, winningly, he still tried so hard to let me win. And I felt one of those infrequent moments of guilt, like vertigo: *What am I doing here? In this foreign land?* I stared blindly at the board.

Let sea-discoverers to new worlds have gone, / Let maps to others, worlds on worlds have shown, / Let us possess one world, each hath one, and is one.

And then—not a noise. Mere movement in the air; and May was standing in the doorway. I smiled at her. I began to speak—she pointed to her father's bowed head and held a finger to her lips, and smiled. I smiled back, helplessly. In the fireplace behind me, a log had popped, and I'd started, and then she was melting away, silent in her stocking feet, going up the stairs.

The classroom was quiet, and I realized she'd finished. I looked up. "Thank you, Miss Bankhead," I said. "So. What screams Renaissance here? What says Sir Walter Raleigh and Christopher Columbus? The New World?" A few limp hands went up. "Miss Kellar?"

"'Sea-discoverers,'" said Catharine Kellar.

"Yes. More?"

" 'Hemispheres.' " " 'Maps.' " The voices began to get a little livelier. "And, 'worlds,' like, there's more than one." "He's saying like forget exploring, let's just fall in love."

"Well, in a manner of speaking," I said. "So, all right, what about 'sucked'? What about 'weaned'? I'm serious here."

There was a pause. "He's talking about like growing up?"

"Um, duh."

"Mr. Pedersen. A little respect. And, people, I'm going to start charging you for the *likes*. So. These metaphors, they wend their way through the whole poem. Remember what Samuel Johnson said. What Eliot quoted, in the essay we read. Which I am *sure* you recall." I turned and wrote it on the board. " 'Heterogeneous ideas yoked with violence together.' He was ahead of his time. So what is Donne doing, with these seemingly disparate ideas? Miss Bankhead?"

"He's talking about becoming yourself. Discovering a person. A person is a world."

"Yes."

" 'And now good-morrow to our waking souls.' They're"—she blushed, but forged on—"they're waking up together. So they're, um, lovers. But they're also awakening—their souls. The explorers are going far away, but he's going inward, they're going inward—and outward to each other at the same time . . . ?" Her voice trailed away.

"Yes. Excellent." Easy now. "Donne loves these paradoxes. It's the essence of his thought, in a way." I wrote *paradox* on the board, and under it *in-out, small-large*. "And if you think this stuff is sexy, you're right." I said this in my ironical voice, but I came down, perhaps, a little too hard on *sexy*. "Donne was a very sensual writer." There was widespread skepticism. May's hand waved again. "Miss Bankhead?"

She had that hyperalert look kids have when they're *getting* it, in real time, right in front of you. "And the 'hemispheres' are their eyes," she said. "Like the globe, the explorers, only they're seeing each other. In the globes of their eyes. The small is enormous. Infinite. Like you said."

And makes one little room an everywhere. I could have stood up, left the board, the fire, Preston, gone into that kitchen. Sat down with her under the white globe of the hanging light. Her long brown hands stroking the nicks and grooves in the pine table. The house quiet around us. Only her voice. I'm lost for a moment, I can see it, hear it, think it happened.

"They've transformed," she's saying. "They've"—she grins a little, showboating now—"they've landed on the shores of their new selves."

"Yes, May-May. Exactly."

The silence was like a door slamming. Everyone froze, and I realized what I'd done.

Of course I couldn't look at her but at the edge of my vision she was motionless too, sitting very tall but with the triumph gone out of her. I had betrayed her utterly. I saw glances exchanged, hidden grins. Everyone was certainly awake now. Catharine Kellar looked like she'd just been given a present. The patter welled out of me, pure autopilot: "Landed on the shores. The exploration of the self. What are some other oppositions here? What is this 'mix'd equally,' what about 'true north'? What do you think Donne means?" I turned to the board again, felt the eyes on my back.

And now good-morrow to our waking souls.

I wanted to sing it. Instead I wrote it down. "So scan this. What's the meter? Easy one." I marked the feet with the chalk, *ba-DUM ba-DUM ba-DUM ba-DUM ba-DUM.*

May-May, May-May, May-May.

"It's like music," May said. Her voice was frightened and determined. I could not turn around. *Yes, that line has sung in my brain ever since I first read it and you knew that.* She was saying *It's all right I know* and I was shouting *I am blameless, I have done nothing.* The chalk clicked. I took a dramatic step back, examining the words.

"What we need to think about," I said, without turning, because I could not turn—*because I do not hope to turn*—no, because I had to protect her from myself, "is how the Renaissance idea of individual consciousness was very different—how groundbreaking Donne was—Eliot said, 'A thought to Donne was an experience; it modified his sensibility'—do you remember that? From the reading? I knew you would . . ."

By the time the bell rang, the charge had dissipated. I made a point of looking several kids directly in the eye. Nothing seemed amiss. Still, as everyone was leaving, instead of standing next to my desk as usual, I sat down behind it. I hardly ever sat at my desk. It was good thick oak, solid as a ship, and I shuffled my knees under its bulk. "Bye. Next is George Herbert. The pages are up on the board. More God. Up on the board. 'Cause we're all guilty of dust and sin, that's why. Bye now. Papers next Monday. Bye."

Everyone was clattering past and then she was there. I couldn't look up. But I knew they were her hands in front of me, those long fingers twisting together. Stopping here was a huge risk to her. Miss Kellar would say something, for instance, or file it away; Miss Kellar let nothing slide. And then May would have to answer. To laugh at herself, or me. I hoped she would laugh at me.

But instead of her protector I felt younger than she was, a schoolboy with wet-combed hair. She was still there. I was going to look up. Her eyes would be dark blue and I looked up and they were dark blue, hemispheres of ocean and sky, and I was sailing over them using only the old knowledge of the stars.

YEARS LATER, MAY SAYS, "Do you remember that?"

"Of course I do," I say.

"I thought I was going to die."

"It was a mistake. I wasn't trying to send some signal," I say.

"I know."

"I wouldn't do that."

"I know."

"Not on purpose."

She smiles. "I know."

Five

When I was born, my mother brought me home to a small apartment
in a complex near the public city hospital, where she worked as a
nurse. She'd come up to Atlanta, already pregnant, from her hometown, deep in south Georgia. The apartment was a run-down place in
a run-down neighborhood, and I remember it only because we drove
by it once, years later, and she pointed it out to me. "I didn't know
any better," she said, half to herself, and shook her head. "I was lucky
to get any job at all."

I usually understood her non sequiturs. In this case she meant that
the luck of a job, in her condition, had made this place near the hospital both inevitable and an afterthought.

But then she found the "good" side of Atlanta—the north side, the
white side—got a job at a different hospital, and found the first home
I truly remember. Technically, it was a guesthouse, although its
parent wasn't a mansion, or at least what would have been thought
of as a mansion in Buckhead. It was, instead, a comfortable colonial,
gracefully ordinary, owned by the McClatcheys, a nice family with a
mother and a father and a son and a daughter. The guesthouse, which
my mother rented, was down at the end of the steep driveway, canti-
levered over a little ravine—suspended in the trees, a dream of green.
Two tiny bedrooms, a kitchen, a living room. It was a womb, a cradle,
out of time.

From my earliest memory I felt layers to life that I didn't understand. Atlanta seemed to me a place that had recently been a small town; a miasma of familiarity was in the air. The ghosts were thick. We lived in an established, old-Atlanta neighborhood, but the lots were large and nature barely held at bay, and in the trees around our house I could feel many eyes, benign mostly, layer upon layer of creatures who knew the land as though their own bones were the limbs of the tulip poplar trees, their fingers redbud branches, their blood made from red clay, creatures at home.

There were other houses visible through the trees but the little valley behind us was a serene and quiet bowl. The area was dotted with historical markers documenting every move of the troops during the Battle of Atlanta, on that very soil; there was one at the corner of our street. It was easy to picture blue and gray flung down behind the ridges and hillocks, easy to hear in my mind the contrast of birdsong and gunfire, and even to go farther back and imagine the Creeks and Cherokees before they'd been hounded away. But now the land felt so gentle. The tree canopy was high, and little creeks, and big ones, ran everywhere, and it wasn't hard to find a waterfall or a fallen log crossing a stream.

Up the hill the McClatchey kids were teenagers, and I could see the son playing basketball with his friends in the driveway, and the daughter having car doors opened for her by her dates. The McClatcheys had a patio in the back and we could hear their dinner parties and barbeques and laughter when it was warm out. Down the hill, my mother and I never had parties, but I think we both drew some kind of vicarious satisfaction from all the activity and jollity.

Hugh—Hugh Satterthwaite, Mrs. McClatchey's brother—went to our Episcopal church (or we went to his), and starting when I was eight or nine he often dropped by on weekends to say hello to my mother and me. He wasn't married, although he was the same age as Mr. McClatchey; they had all grown up together in this very neighborhood. He was tall and thin and balding, courtly and a bit stooped, with sadness ringing his eyes.

At some point I said the magic combination of words to Mr. Satterthwaite: "father," and "soldier," and "dead." He had always been kind, but after that was even kinder. Whenever we crossed paths he did little-kid things that I loved for their predictability. He'd pretend to steal my nose. He always had gum in his pocket. Even at my age I thought these seemed like carefully learned tricks, but that made them, and him, only more endearing.

He told me that, as a boy, he used to find minié balls and arrowheads in these same woods. I was susceptible to the romance of history, more of Mr. Satterthwaite's imagined childhood than of the war, and so several times I dutifully went looking, but I never found any.

Long before he became Hugh to me, I viewed him, and his family, as the real article. When he told me about the minié balls it was like he was giving me his own memories, his rootedness. For a long time, I thought the McClatcheys were letting us live in their extra house just because they were nice. Perhaps there's an element of truth to that. And when Hugh finally became my stepfather, I discovered that my other suspicions had been true: that there did exist people who had grandmamas and granddaddies and great-granddaddies who lived down the street, whose names were on road signs or buildings or both; who had cousins; who had a great web of people spread wide and sticky over Atlanta; and they did the things they did and had the jobs they had and went to the schools they went to and married the people they did because all that great web had figured out the best way to live and showed them how. These people were supremely, effortlessly legible to themselves, and I waited, in vain, for the effect to spread to me.

Years later, when I met Preston and Florence Bankhead, of New Orleans and Savannah, I knew immediately they were of the same ilk as the McClatcheys and the Satterthwaites. I believed I could tell them their own history. I could see Preston gripping a log bridge with his bare toes, and scuffing through the sweet funk of fallen, decaying leaves, and braiding sharp, sun-hot pine needles, and running home to a white house full of family when he heard the dinner bell ringing, and sitting at a table set with mellowed family silver, and getting treats in the kitchen from the maid, whose favorite he was. Even after I knew his father had abandoned them, I was sure he'd emerged unscathed, materially and in every other way. I thought I knew Preston right off the bat, and I hoped, and feared, he would know me too.

———

ONE DAY I SAW a small blue velvet box on my mother's dresser. It held a ring. We contemplated it together. "Why aren't you wearing it?" I said.

"Well. Mr. Satterthwaite thought maybe I should let you get used to the idea."

I could imagine him saying that, and realized how implicitly I trusted him. "That's okay," I said. "You should put it on."

A faint smile crossed her face and I thought about how she was good-looking. I suppose I had always thought her pretty the way little boys think their mommies are pretty, but now I felt a new, adult, not unfriendly distance, and I looked at her dark-red hair and the rise of her cheekbones and the arch of her brows and approved. She put the ring on and then held her hand out for us to look at, but not in a showy way. My mother hardly ever wore jewelry.

Then I realized. "Where's your other ring?" I said. "From my dad?"

Her eyes were fastened on the diamond. Then she abruptly closed her hand and looked up. "I put it away, Charlie," she said. "A while ago. I guess you just didn't notice."

After that, the changes came thick and fast. We moved into Hugh's big, underfurnished Tudor house around the corner, on Peachtree Battle Avenue. I went to a new school. My mother quit working. We had a maid, named Rosetta. And I suddenly had grandparents (Big Hugh and Bobo) and aunts and uncles and cousins, or at least I was assured they were mine. I was even now related to the McClatcheys.

The Satterthwaites had nearly despaired of Hugh getting married, of finding happiness, and so their gratitude to Anita and me was out-sized, even embarrassing. They acted as though all the benefit had been to Hugh and treated us not like interlopers but royalty, which perversely made me feel even more like a fake. And then Nicky came along. He was born in the trough between the clump of first cousins and their offspring, the only baby in sight. He was the dauphin, the tsarevitch in his sailor suit.

I think Hugh and my mother were happy for a little while; I do. I know Hugh was. Beautiful wife, baby son, and he made me feel like I was a bonus.

Hugh was an unabashedly devout Anglican. He loved the smells and bells, the Midnight Mass, and every now and then at dinner would announce it was the feast day of Saint This or That, but the thing he seemed to like best was the long stretch after Easter, Ordinary Time—no events, no drama, redemption accomplished. I remember him saying it at the beach, where we now went for regular vacations, his paler-than-pale self parked under the umbrella, his white feet, skinny as rulers, digging into the sand: "Ordinary time. Isn't it wonderful?"

That's all he wanted, St. Hugh. The ordinary. He'd never expected to have this life. Perhaps he thought he didn't have a talent for it, or didn't deserve it. And then he lost it. A chicken-and-egg proposition.

Even so, it was Hugh who kept me in the orbit of the family, at least for a while, Hugh's manly, leathery, book-lined study where I felt the most at home—maybe because there I was an acknowledged guest, it was out in the open. In the rest of the house I was supposed to feel like an average citizen, with equal rights. No one seemed to notice that I tried to be as neat and unassuming as a maiden aunt grateful for a bed. I was a pimply teenager; I was the son of a vanished man named Jimmie Garrett. The deal had been struck with Anita long before that I would not ask too many questions, and in return she, hunter-gatherer style, had procured Hugh, and this house, and my new school, the tennis court in the backyard, the new books that lined my shelves—and now a brother. Still, I felt that anytime this Buckhead caravansary could collapse.

AN AFTERNOON AT A MYSTERY HOUSE. That is, I don't remember whose. Gracious people, maybe from church, friends of Hugh's, probably—people he'd grown up with; there were a lot of those, a lot of friends who wanted to get to know my mother and me, who were full of goodwill. Bobo and Big Hugh were there too. Someone said it had been such a nice summer, but there was still August to go. So it's July.

I'm the only teenager there. The adults take an inordinate interest in every aspect of my life. They ask questions, seem fascinated. This attention never used to happen. I don't understand such an anxiety to be polite. What I absorb is that I am difficult to like. That my attractions are sparse.

Nicky, on the other hand, is the star, the only baby as I am the only teenager. There are toddlers there, the children who will become his friends, the ones he'll grow up with, but he's the only one still crawling, cherubic. And there's something else: I don't know if all babies have this light, or if it's only Nicky. His red-gold curls draw the sun. When my mother holds him in her lap, her arms curl around him. When she looks at him, her hand goes to his cheek. Everyone calls to him, everyone wants to hold him. He's oblivious, of course. He doesn't know he's Abel, Jacob, Joseph.

Meanwhile Hugh has a glass of bourbon in his hand and I know it's not his first, and that I'm supposed to watch him; my mother has already given me a look, enlisting me. But he seems so relaxed, in his element, here on this green lawn beneath old trees, that I don't want the job.

Instead I excuse myself and go inside and after a perfunctory use of the facilities I linger, drifting from room to room, watching the afternoon light playing on the smooth worn banister, on the creamy heavy paint on door frames, on the antique rugs thin at the edges. But then I hear the voice of the hostess and another woman as they enter the kitchen. If I could stand here long enough, maybe a layer of the mystery on the surfaces of these lives would be peeled away, but if they find me I certainly won't be able to say that, and so I slip out through a French door to the side yard.

As I walk back around I hear cheering, and when I round the corner to the wide circle of chairs in the green grass I see Nicky, in the middle of the circle—walking. They're his first steps. He's stiff kneed, a miniature lumbering giant. His face is full of surprise and he stops, swaying, and laughs. Laughs! And everyone around him laughs too. And he looks all around him and takes in all the adoration, swallows it whole, as is his due.

And then sees me. And makes a beeline for me. His face is clean with joy and I crouch down and he lurches into me, his fat hands splayed on my knees with unthinking ownership. Everyone else loves him but he's chosen me, and I feel myself giving in, as helpless as the rest.

THE DECLINE WAS GRADUAL. Nicky was at least three before I noticed how I'd quit relying on Hugh—that he was often literally unavailable, in his study with the door closed. Sometimes he even slept there. He was such a gentle drunk, never ugly or belligerent; he would just gradually disappear, over the course of an evening, the smile on his face delicate as paper, and half an hour, an hour after he slid away you'd finally notice he was gone.

But it turned out he was still paying a little bit of attention, and there was still something he wanted to do for me.

He asked me to meet him at his town club for lunch, which I'd never done before. It was hushed and male and famous for, of all things, hot buttered homemade saltines, which were absurdly good. The waiter knew him and seemed uncommonly fond of him. "We haven't seen you for a while, Mr. Hugh," he said. He brought Hugh a double old-fashioned without asking. Every black person there called him Mr. Hugh. The white men at the front desk called him Mr. Satterthwaite.

As Hugh gestured with his glass, he explained that the men in his family had always gone to Harvard, "and I want to do that for you, Charlie." I didn't ask how. The Satterthwaites were humble, affable, down-to-earth, but things often got done with undue ease, bypassing the usual channels; it was a different time. Calls could be placed. Cousins turned up in useful positions. Someone had been someone else's best man and I remember your sister so fondly, and don't say another word.

I wasn't principled enough to resist his offer, but, more important, I couldn't resist Hugh. As we spoke and I tried not to eat all the saltines, and the waiter quietly brought him fresh drinks, I realized in my dumb seventeen-year-old way that he was following a script in his head with immense, heartbreaking care. Old courtesy, old order.

"Maybe you should slow down?" I said, when the fourth drink was set in front of him. With just the two of us, and the clairvoyant waiter, I couldn't help counting as the glasses appeared and disappeared.

He smiled sadly, as though I had just stumbled on a great, inevitable, adult truth that he had wanted to keep from me for as long as possible. Before him his water glass brimmed full, untouched. He didn't seem any more or less inebriated than usual. "Son," he said (he'd asked long before if he could call me that, and of course I'd said yes), "don't worry about me. Fruitless endeavor. You worry about yourself, now. Eat up. Have another cracker." He handed me the linen-lined silver tray. "There's a couple you missed there." And then he said, "Charlie, I love your mother, and so I love you. Simple as that. You didn't do a thing to deserve it, but that doesn't negate it. It just is."

So I got into Harvard, which I had assumed I wouldn't, even with Hugh's help. When it was too late, I was ambivalent. Suddenly I had grand ideas of independence. And of course I was also scared. I took Hugh at his word and worried about myself, decided I'd been well behaved for long enough, kicked and screamed a little, slammed a few doors, was briefly, theatrically moody—and have regretted it ever since. I never told him thank you. Then, several weeks before my high-school graduation, on a day he'd actually made it into his office, he got a stomachache so painful that he took himself to the emergency room, thinking he might have appendicitis. It turned out his organs were shutting down, one by one. He was gone in three days. I hadn't known people really could literally drink themselves to death, but they can.

Near the end of our lunch that day, he'd said to me, "Charlie, you need to know something." His face had suddenly sagged, as though he'd been holding his breath through the entire meal and was finally letting it go. "I have known exactly who I was, who I am, my entire life." He waved vaguely around at the dining room, the black waiters in their white coats, the city outside that was his. The wave nearly threw him off balance. "And it hasn't done me a damn bit of good." His right hand made a fist, and then, driven more by gravity than passion, came down heavily, muffled on the thick tablecloth. His silverware rattled faintly. "Remember that, Charles Garrett. Son of no one. Count your blessings."

I WENT TO HARVARD, on my dead stepfather's recommendation, and on his dime. I could not have felt more like a fraud.

In his honor, I did as well as I could, which was not well enough, and drank very little.

And then, all of a sudden, graduation was approaching. And, surrounded as I was by seething ambition, I began looking for jobs, although I had no idea about that larger thing, a career. Nevertheless, I'd do it on my own. I didn't involve my mother or, God forbid, the Satterthwaites, although once again what I said or didn't say turned out not to matter.

IN EARLY MAY, that year that I was twenty-two and graduating from college and deciding where in the world to go, my mother, Anita, was at Hugh's parents' for Sunday dinner. After Hugh died, the family was more often there, on a Sunday, than at the club—even by then, when he'd been gone for four years.

In the town where my mother grew up, there had not been a single house like the Satterthwaites', or like the one she now lived in. She'd been raised by her grandparents, who believed in hell; if they were still living, they surely believed she was going there. She didn't know her father's name. As it was every Sunday, at the Satterthwaites', she believed her job was to not let on to these facts, and not to forget them herself.

She'd escaped to the empty formal living room. At times, she needed a moment. Everyone forgave her these moments. The Satterthwaites loved her, as they liked to love most people, but were a little intimidated. This was not, by the way, an uncommon reaction to my mother.

The living room had antique china in niches by the mantel, maps of Civil War–era Atlanta on the wall. In front of her, on the coffee table, magazines were carefully fanned, no doubt by Bobo's maid,

Willie Mae, who was Rosetta's sister. My mother's fingers twitched because she wanted a cigarette, but her smoking was the only thing the Satterthwaites frowned upon, and since she agreed with them, her hand didn't go to her pocket, and she didn't get up and go outside to some isolated grassy corner. Instead, she picked up the magazine at the top of the fan, which was an alumni magazine from a place called Abbott. Hugh hadn't gone there; he had gone to a day school in Atlanta, the place I was also sent. Anita didn't know a thing about this other school.

When she opened the magazine, she saw green rolling fields and white buildings, a chapel of gray stone—foreign but familiar, like scenes from a picture book or travel guide, peopled with teenagers as white toothed and smooth browed as the Satterthwaites. She was always encountering things like this magazine in the Satterthwaites' houses. They were documents in a language in which she would never be fluent. She didn't know how ordinary, in its own way, Abbott was.

It was around then that Bobo came in and sat with a companionable sigh in the wing chair across from my mother. "That Nicky had three pieces of pie," she said. "Two apple and one pecan. It's Willie Mae's pecan pie and you know how it's so rich. I told him he would get a stomachache, but then I just let him."

Anita said she didn't mind. She long ago accepted that here, Nicky would be spoiled. He reminded them too much of Hugh.

"That's where Big Hugh went to boarding school," Bobo said. "Way up north. Don't ask him about it or he'll start talking and he won't stop. He wanted Little Hugh to go there but I said no, there was no need, because by then we had good schools right here in Atlanta. I just didn't want him to go so far away. There was no need."

Anita knew it was small of her, but she didn't look up right away. The expression on Bobo's face would be the bleak, brave, moist-eyed look she got when she mentioned Hugh. Whom Anita also mourned, but didn't miss. She steeled herself, turned another magazine page to stall.

And there was Preston Bankhead.

He was in robes and a collar. That was not a surprise to her. Neither was this: he stood with a lovely blond wife and three blond sons, the only word for whom was *strapping*. They were all radiantly healthy and solid. With the green hills in the background, the well-cared-for northern trees, the pure air.

"I know it's a wonderful school," Bobo was saying. "It's just so far away. But not far from Charlie, I suppose. How is Charlie? How is he doing, Anita? He's a senior, isn't he? Is he looking for a job yet? How is that wonderful boy doing?"

The blond boys in the picture have a great deal that I do not. But once again the way is clear for my mother, and she can make sure I get what I deserve.

Six

May graduating: I see it over and over. Boys in navy blazers, girls in white dresses, processing. In my memory the line is endless. The girls and their wreaths of white flowers.

I was standing right along the path where they walked after the ceremony, everyone grinning, the boys high-fiving me, and some of the girls too, but I was waiting for May. When she walked by me and her eyes landed on mine it was as though she'd spoken my name aloud.

In the milling about afterward we found each other—but is that true? I was looking for her, and then there she was. She had a lot on her mind; she was eighteen years old. I doubt she was looking for me.

The flowers were a cloud around her face. Snow in her hair. "You look beautiful." I said it. There was a division, before and after, and now it was after. Now she had graduated. She knew it, that was the look, we were in perfect agreement.

Except now she wouldn't meet my eye. "Have you smelled this stuff?" she demanded, pointing to the flowers. "It's baby's breath. But who knew that baby's breath smells like old cheese? Smell it!" And she leaned forward so the wreath was touching my nose.

Possibly she was right. But I couldn't smell a thing. Or see, or hear. I was frozen.

She sensed it; she froze too. The air around us twined and thickened and I didn't want to move and didn't but then I did. "You're right," I said, stepping back. "Camembert. Roquefort."

"Crazy, right?"

"Miss Bankhead?"

And finally she looked. "Yes?"

"Write me a letter every now and then."

"I plan to," she said.

A YEAR OR SO EARLIER, B.J.—Booker Junior—had taken up the drums, directly over my head. I kept my mouth shut, though, because Booker ran a tight ship, and I didn't want any complaint of mine to spell the end of B.J.'s musical career. Who knew where music might take him? Then he started a band. They moved up to the attic, but still, every Saturday afternoon, sometimes into the night, the entire house shook, not always in a discernible time signature.

But then the solution appeared. Booker was promoted to head of facilities, and a faculty house opened up for them on campus. They'd sell their house and Angela would help me find a new, quiet one of my own. "Early spring," she said. "You hit it exactly right, Charlie."

At first she showed me houses in Abbottsford proper, the historic district, but buying there seemed so audacious. Yes, I loved the Lowells', the Bankheads', but could I claim such a spot? No, I thought, so we kept going. We headed northwest, where Abbottsford dwindled to a dinky strip mall, a garden center, a hardware store that serviced snowblowers, a last service station, and then the county highway turned straight and fast.

We spent a couple of Saturdays this way. I found out she and Booker had met at U Mass. They were each the first in their families to go to college. "Booker's family wasn't too happy when we said we were raising the kids Jewish," she said. "And my family wasn't happy about him being the wrong color." She glanced at me and I realized it would be okay to laugh, and so I did, with her. "And that's why we like it out here in the country, away from the in-laws," she said, in her city Bahston voice.

I told her the money for the house came from Hugh. "I don't really feel like it's mine."

"But he must have wanted you to have it."

"I suppose."

"So we just have to find the perfect house, then, don't we." *Puhfect.*

One Saturday afternoon I went outside to wait for her and found Zack in the driveway, shooting baskets. I lowered the goal for him all the way so he could dunk, and then I put it back up at B.J. and Cassie's height so they wouldn't get mad, and picked him up so he could dunk that way. This was our routine. But he wasn't smiling and cheering like he normally did, and when Angela came out he took the basketball and went and sat on the front steps and didn't look at me.

I went and sat down next to him. "I'm looking for a house with your mom," I said. "She's really good at finding houses."

He didn't say anything.

"Your new house is really cool. Have you seen it?" No answer. "Hey, Zackie Bear. Want to come with us today? Will you help me pick out a house?"

A very slow nod. Angela rolled her eyes but looked pleased. "He's *not* happy," she said. "He does not like change."

"I know how he feels," I said.

We were still looking outside town, going farther and farther down that highway, and I was beginning to worry there was nothing to find. That day, as we drove around looking at ranch houses, exposed in the country way on large windy lots, worry gave way to bleakness. I had no idea what I was looking for. Plus, early spring depressed me. The trees were still leafless and the bare ground brown but the light was higher, intrusive, dragging us awake, out of hibernation. I liked hibernation. *Midwinter spring is its own season.* But it was also the first weekend that the local dairy bar was open. "Let's get ice cream," I said. "My treat."

I got rum raisin and Zack got vanilla with jimmies, and I sat down next to him on the bench attached to the picnic table. "I think I should just get another apartment," I said. "What do you think, Zackie? Little place in town. Little bachelor pad. It'll be hip. It'll be a happening place."

"I thought you wanted a house," he said.

"Well, we can't find one."

"I liked the one with the pool."

It had been a sagging above-ground pool. "That was pretty spiffy," I said. "I think I'll keep looking, though."

What I didn't say was that I wasn't sure I should stay in Abbottsford at all, even though my mother was in favor of the house plan. "You'll have room for us to visit," she said. "You seem happy, Charlie. You seem to have nice friends. Don't come back here on our account. I'll take care of Big Hugh and Bobo. Nicky's fine. He's fine."

But I was looking for signs and portents. If there was no house, my way would be clear: I wasn't meant to stay; Abbott had been a way station.

Angela was going through papers in the car. Then she got out and came and sat on the bench with us. The dairy bar was close to the road, and cars whooshed by. "There's one last place," she said. "It's way too big for you. And it needs a ton of work. But who knows," and her face settled into the vatic calm that I have since learned is the special province of talented real estate agents.

"It'll be dark soon," I said. Behind us, they'd put out the Closed sign.

"Well, it's not much farther. And it's empty. The owner died."

"He *died*?" Zack said.

"A while ago. Don't worry, sweetie. He was very old. He was ninety-two," she said to me. "It's been in the same family for a zillion years." *Yeahs.*

We left the dairy bar and drove another couple of miles. The sun was lowering fast. The landscape grew hillier, hovering in anticipation. Finally we made a left turn, west off the highway. At first it was just another road, with more ranch houses, but then the suburban feel died away along with the pavement, the road narrowed, and then there on the right was the last big aluminum mailbox, with the smaller plastic newspaper box beneath. No house was visible from the road. "Hmm. Mysterious. What do you think, Zack?" I said.

No answer.

The gravel driveway bumped slightly downhill through thick trees, where it was already dusk. We rattled along the ruts for a minute or so and then the driveway flattened and we shot into open pasture; an eighth-mile ahead of us, on a little hill, silhouetted against the sunset, was the house, long and white. On its hill, although there were low, gnarled apple trees to the side and in back, the house was completely exposed. The tree branches, still bare, were black against the sky, rose fading to deep blue, stars already appearing.

It was a clapboard farmhouse, Federalish, with tall windows and a porch with columns, a thoroughly New England mishmash that, even so, struck me as a little southern. The house looked like a true destination. A place you'd be relieved, over and over, to reach. We pulled into the half circle of pea gravel by the front steps and got out. Zack stood close to me. I said, once again, "What do you think?" and this time he nodded. He climbed the steps with me, and we looked around at the porch and then turned to face the woods, the meadow beyond. "I think maybe you're right," I said. "I think maybe this is the one."

Eventually I realized what my earlier misgivings about owning a house had been: that somehow I did not deserve certainty. For years afterward, as I drove down the driveway, I'd sometimes let myself imagine that the house wasn't really there, that I'd made it up. Then I'd turn the last corner out of the overarching trees, and there it was. In its sudden space of air and light.

THE LETTERS WEREN'T FREQUENT but they were regular. She sometimes wrote in purple pen. They were often fat letters. When one arrived in my box I would let it sit for a while. An hour or so. I'd look at it and hold it. Then finally open it.

They were always chatty, sometimes a little coy. Perky as the minutes of a student-council meeting, and I would think, *Just stop.* She would mention parties and dances but not boys. She signed them *Yours.* Maybe she meant to be old-fashioned, or formal; maybe not.

THE SECOND YEAR, when the letters dropped off, I felt deep contempt for myself and my surprise. I heard she was going abroad for her junior year, to Paris, which would make no difference in my life whatsoever, other than her letters, if she ever wrote again, having foreign stamps.

She came home for the summer, but I didn't see her until the week before she left, when I drove her to Abbott Pond, and she went skinny-dipping in front of me.

A FEW WEEKS AFTER MAY went to France, Preston, who had a chronic cough that had gotten worse and who'd begun losing weight, learned he had melanoma. There were two different moles he'd been ignoring— he'd always tanned, never burned, that's what he said, absolving himself. But the cancer had spread. There was little to be done.

Divya told me the details. She'd heard them, in turn, from Win— Win, of all people. Preston had gone alone to his appointment, gotten his test results, gone home, sat with it for an hour, and then called Win Lowell. It was the oddest thing I'd ever heard. And yet not. Preston was in a situation; Win was a fixer. It was possible that Preston thought of him as the only worthy comrade left at Abbott, since most of the old guard—Strickler Yates, Larry Saltonstall, the legendary hockey coach, and Fred Hueffer, the previous head—had left by then. Win became the liaison, at least temporarily, the mediator between this abrupt hand of fate and the rest of Preston's ordered world; he was the one who, like some kind of glorified servant, had called May in France, and then handed the phone to Preston.

Family descended, briefly. I went over once, before May arrived. I was given lemonade and a cookie. Preston informed me, regal in a recliner and a red plaid bathrobe, that he couldn't play chess that day, as though we'd had a plan, which we hadn't. I wanted to say that he'd gotten a tough break, or something like that—something manly, but no southern manners bullshit. But in spite of myself I felt stupid and years younger, there in front of Laird and his pretty pregnant wife and Florence, who had greeted me with that enthusiasm that makes you think you've broken some rule; the air of emergency in the house seemed mild, almost jovial, slightly embarrassing, a brief thing that was just an obstacle to normalcy, and so I said very little.

"Chemo once a week," Preston said. "They're fixing me up. We never know how long we have, anyway." He didn't even sound brave. He sounded amused.

I hadn't seen many people die.

Seven

And then she was back.

She hadn't written or called. I just heard about it. I didn't know what to do. But I knew people brought food. Whatever else people do, they bring food, so I went to the trendy little bakery in town and picked something up and drove over there.

When she opened the door she didn't look surprised to see me. Or she pretended she wasn't. Instead she presented herself like she was the guest: "Well, here I am. Charlie." She smiled a little. My name still had the whiff of a joke. Or—it had lost that scent, but now it was back?

I followed her into the kitchen and handed her the white box. "Éclairs," I said.

"Éclairs? Oh," she said. "Do you want one?"

"Sure." Then I looked around, foolishly, as if I expected Preston to pop out of a cabinet and join us for an éclair.

"He's sleeping," she said. "I took him for chemo today." I nodded, *Oh yeah, chemo, I know all about that,* but it didn't fool her. "It's not to cure him," she said, in a clipped voice. "It's just for pain." Then she sat down, gave down, really, into a chair, there in the kitchen.

The box sat in front of her. She looked at it but didn't touch it. "Actually I haven't had dinner," she said.

I was so stupid. I was a useless man. I said, "I should have brought that instead."

"I'm not really hungry anyway." The emptiness of the house rang around us. "Mom's in Savannah," she said. "She said she would come back if it got complicated."

"But your brothers will be around."

"They've got jobs," she said. "Henry, for instance, is extremely busy building boats in Newport, and maintaining his supply of weed."

I should have been used to this family by now but I wasn't, and I felt a strange internal roar of protectiveness. Even though I was probably the last person she needed.

But then she looked at me quietly for a long moment. It was an expression she used to have when she was younger and trying to convince herself of her own bravery, a look I'd seen in my own classroom. I didn't know if she wanted to present this character to herself or to me. Then she looked away again and said, "Mom did arrange for nurses, at least. If we need them. But it's not *complicated* yet." She reached out and fiddled with the string knotted around the bakery box. Her nails were short, but not bitten; the effect was well cared for, sensible; they were startlingly familiar; I found I loved her hands. This presented itself as a discrete and private fact. "I mean, the boys come on weekends. He's not in a lot of pain right now. I don't really have to do anything. Just keep him company." She started to cry.

"May-May," I said, in that kitchen that was thick with history that wasn't mine. Paralyzed with noticing my own awkwardness—but not caring about Preston at all; no, at that moment, not at all. He was an old man who was dying, they'd left her alone. Suddenly I was wild with not caring.

"He's so selfish," she burst out. "He always has been. Selfish and horrible and full of *shit*," and she stood up and then I knew what was going to happen.

She stepped into my arms and, after all, she had been there before. By the lake, with her hair wet, the memory fresh of the nakedness I hadn't seen. I'd kissed her and tried not to feel foolish, in a conversation with myself and not with her, and I'd been sure that for her that day would be only one experience in a long list, that she was already gone.

But now she hit her forehead on my chest. She was sobbing, she was full of feeling that had nothing to do with me. Still, I seemed to be giving her comfort. This was astonishing.

Then she looked up at me and said, "I was *glad*." She said it like she had murdered someone.

"About what? About what, sweetheart?"

There was the smallest *tick* while she registered my word. And then went on. "When I heard how sick he was and that I had to come home. I was glad because of you, and then on the plane I just thought of you. Not even of Daddy. Just of you."

And so. Now we were both astonished.

Then there was a change: we knew. A shift that was suddenly fact, that we both accepted. Pieces slid, could not be moved back. And then I was kissing her. And there was nothing wrong. And I was speaking only to her, not to myself or Preston or anyone else.

I don't know how long we stood there. We started off gentle and rapidly became near-frantic—it became clear how we wanted, we wanted. If I had dared to imagine that far, I would have said I'd be another version of that sad sack standing motionless with his hard-on on the banks of Abbott Pond. But that man had disappeared like smoke. Every moment was further confirmation. I was a believer.

Then she took my hand and led me out of the warm yellow kitchen. Into the front hall, through the formal living room, to the little den. "We'll hear him here if he comes down the stairs," she said, matter-of-factly, and I nodded, utterly serious, and then we began to smile, smug smiles at the universe, because weren't we somehow beating the odds? Having the last laugh?

But sitting on the sofa was different and at first uncomfortable. Rearrangement of height, of limbs was necessary, sitting up less efficient than mashing against the wall in the kitchen; there, all had been wild and effortless but now shyness reentered, a small stutter, but was it really time to lie down just yet? And did we feel suddenly teenaged on the sofa, in front of the dark TV, the urgency, the moral clarity and imperative of the crisis-suffused kitchen now gone—were we slightly absurd? I was beginning to wilt. It wasn't overly concerning, it was for the best. I would not take advantage. We'd truly kissed, we could keep kissing, the situation was plain now and there was no going back, and maybe next time—

May reached behind her and turned off a lamp. Now just one light remained; the corners of the room were suddenly velvety dark, the blank TV screen no longer shone. It was better, she was right. Her expression was inward, oddly determined. "I don't *care,*" she said. "I don't *care.*" Then she stood up and said, "I want you to see me."

She pulled her sweater over her head. "May."

"What."

I stood up. "Sweetheart." I wanted to say it over and over. I reached to stroke her hair; she stepped away; she would not be dissuaded. "We don't have to. To do anything. Not now."

"It's *time* now." She unzipped her jeans, pushed them down her legs. She straightened and reached behind her with that lovely sudden wing-motion that women do, and her bra was loose and then she leaned forward with a little practiced shake and slid it off.

Up till now she could have been alone, getting ready for a quick shower or bed, her movements had been so rote and everyday. But now I saw her fingers trembling. Then she hooked them at her sides into her underwear and slid it off and stepped out, one leg, the other, and then she stood up and looked at me and her bareness electrified the air, stilled every noise.

"I want you to *see* me," she said again, and her voice was firm.

I was aware I was staring and that the scientific gaze was a refuge, and I blinked, try again—and God yes, her breasts and the roundness of them, sloping into her ribs, enough to break your heart.

I'd always thought the rest of her body was a little boyish—not that I cared, not that that wouldn't be just fine with me—but now I saw I was wrong, with her naked I was completely wrong. There was a swell of buttock and a curve at her hip, the secrets I never knew. I stood up, and put my hand gently on the hanging sweetness of breast and stroked down, down her side, the curve of her, the line of her, oh how she is here, right here, right here. "I see you," I said.

There were certain planes and angles that had to be mapped and verified. There were her arms, there were the sockets of her hips. The tautness of her waist was an announcement and I touched it and its downward flare again and again.

She was reaching then for the buttons of my shirt and it was only fair. "You are beautiful," I said, as explanation, apology.

"Shhh."

I felt the air like hands on my chest and I didn't want her to know my paltry self, but it was far too late for that, wasn't it? So late that I could not possibly care. I would just have to be acceptable as a created thing. As the body that held my heart. She leaned forward and kissed my chest, she brushed her cheek against the hair there and sighed, and her hands were at my buckle and I had to let them work, not push into her, with my fingers sunk into her soft backside pulling her to me, erasing all the space between us, *See me, see me too,* I said, *shh* and *yes* and we were on the floor.

I was careful, I shoved the coffee table away with my foot, I put a pillow under her head and she let me, watching me the whole time. I am not going to say we did not choose it all. *It's time.*

And we are both asking and answering: *Do you know how long Oh yes I know Do you know So long Oh yes. Oh please.* Our words flow under and around and together, we say what must be said. If Preston comes down the stairs we won't hear him but he won't and it wouldn't matter anyway. We try to be quiet then we laugh and then we are past laughter.

I've been formless and void but now I have shape, meaning, I am myself. I did not know how it would be, to be myself. *Oh do you know.*

Do you know how long.

Yes I know oh I know you yes.

I am conscious for just a moment of Preston somewhere above us in his drugged sleep inching toward death, as indeed we all are. I am sure though that, being closer to it, he has attained new wisdom, I am sure he would approve, I am sure that all he wants for us is love.

"SOMEONE'S IN LOVE."

"Divya." A match has been set to my face. "Be quiet." Panic.

But she says, "I think it's all right."

"Do you?" It's all I can do not to say *Please please tell me this is all right.* I need, I trust her calm, her twinkle.

"Are you serious about it?"

"*Yes.*"

"Don't flaunt it."

"No, of course not."

"It just started." She doesn't say it as a question.

"Yes."

"Honestly, she seems older than you do. If you don't mind me saying."

Of course she's right. I do not mind a single thing.

She considers me. "You've been boring a long time, Charles, so there's that in your favor."

"I'm counting on it."

"Everyone will know anyway, of course—"

"Not if you don't tell them."

She smiles. "Tell them what?"

HER HAIR WAS IN TWO BRAIDS. She was standing in the front hallway of my house. She was seeing my house.

It was my first fall there, and soon it would be the first winter, the first spring. I'd cycle through again and then again, digging myself in deeper and deeper. As I stood there looking at her, I realized that's what I wanted. And that right now was the beginning of everything.

She had been back two weeks.

"This is a big house," she said. "It's so much."

"People do buy houses," I said.

But even at twenty-nine I was a little young for this place. We both knew it. Especially because I had no need of all those bedrooms upstairs, not yet.

She walked slowly farther in. Her footsteps were gentle and the old wooden floors received them. She walked to the wide door of the living room as if she were approaching a sleeping baby. She said, "I think this house is a life."

I didn't dare imagine what she meant. I wanted, I wanted.

She was looking all around, up into every corner, down to the rough boards, taking the house's measure. "What's that?"

"A floor sander."

"You're doing it yourself?"

"Win's helping me."

"He can he fix anything."

"Yes."

Her face was alight. "I like him so much," she said.

So much more than a squealish *Oh I love him!* May could do that. Say things very deliberately, things you actually believed.

"Yes, any fuckups you see are definitely mine." She was still looking all around at the empty room, the empty shelves. "I've moved everything because of the dust," I said. "Look though. C'mere."

I took her hand and we walked down the hall, where all the books were piled against the walls under tarps, and into the kitchen. Her hand was in my hand. Even though we'd done everything—as we might have said in high school—it was still so new, and just that touch, now, exhilarated me. I led her to the sink, and the window above it, and said, "Look."

Her face between those braids (I'd never seen her wear her hair like that before) was as entranced as I had hoped (which was not at all a sure thing, since for her these little Massachusetts mountains had long been ordinary). So I took her outside through the kitchen door.

My property backed up to conservation land, and through the luck of topography you couldn't see another house. The mountains rolled bluely westward, away and away, giving the illusion of progress to an unseen land, a shining sea, that might be perfect, paradise even; the mountains were pure, untainted possibility. I was sure she saw this.

She looked out for another moment, and then down, at the flagstones. She could tell that every detail was important. I said, "That was the first thing I did when I moved here. The patio."

"Without Win?"

"Without Win. I was overconfident."

"Well, you managed this."

"It was really just putting together a puzzle. Although I have to redo that mortar over there. But, see. We're facing southwest. It's warmer than anywhere else. Sun all day long."

She turned in a half circle, orienting herself. "And it sets—there," she murmured. "Over that mountain. So here is the sunset." She swept a hand across the view, confirming it.

Then she began to walk very carefully, one foot directly in front of the other, as though she were balancing on a narrow beam of a path. She walked the perimeter of the patio and looked out to either side, through the apple trees, down the slope. I thought that in her mind she was walking even farther, through the tall frozen grass beyond us—down into the woods, taking the measure of the land now. The measure of me.

I didn't know that in the years to come, I would often return from work, go in my front door, through the house, and straight out the back. As though the house existed only as a foyer for this view. That I would stand and look out like a parched man gulping from a spring, that the mountains' chief beauty would be that their seeming infinity stopped thought.

But then she shivered and so we went back inside, which was good because I needed to show her the rest of the house. *Needed* to. I took her hand again, we went quiet, urgent. Already we were rarely shy with each other. Upstairs there were, sure enough, five bedrooms, echoing empty except for mine. But at the bottom of the stairs, my conscience smiting me, I had to ask. "Is Preston really okay by himself?"

"Mom's with him. She's here for a little while."

"Oh."

"I know."

"Does she know where you are?"

She smiled. "I needed some time to myself."

I wasn't going to ask if she was ashamed of me, because I knew she wasn't. She was just prudent. Just smart. This was only ours, for now, we were keeping it.

Instead I came closer and reached out and took her braids, one in each hand. "What are these?" I said. "Who are you? Gretel? Heidi?"

"Hmm." She thought. "Your milkmaid." She tipped her head and simpered.

I let go. In this moment I wanted no role-play, no hints of anything sordid: it was all too new. "Are you feeling young?" I said. I was ready with my guilt.

"*No.*"

I wanted to touch her again. My hands burned with it.

She said, "I don't feel young. My father used to like my hair like this. I suppose I did it for him, or something. I don't even know."

I saw tears in her eyes. She tossed her head, drove them away. She reached up and pulled the white bands off the braids, raked them apart with clawed fingers until her hair rippled loose around her.

"I don't feel young at all," she said. "Come here. Come here right now."

"THE HAPPY FAMILY," May said. "Fuck that."

We were at her house, standing in front of the piano, looking at the lacrosse picture.

"I think I'd gone to the bathroom. Anything to get away from the *field*. I was always having to watch someone's *game*. Or I was just wandering in the administration building, to get warm. I loved it there, when I was little. I pretended it was a palace. Because of that crazy marble floor in the main hall, and the columns. Being alone there, gliding around—I loved that."

For a child who grew up at a boarding school, May seemed to have spent a lot of time alone, at least some of it by choice. Which I completely understood.

"That picture even went into the alumni magazine," she said. "Lickety-split. Without me. Did you know that? I think that picture is Mom's ideal." She cut her eyes at me. "I know. I'm being self-pitying."

I pointed at another picture, in another silver frame, of May solo, at about age five. "So what's that?"

"Compensation." But her voice was light.

Now we had each other. Self-pity on any count was absurd. "I want it," I said, pointing.

In the picture, May was sitting in a miniature Windsor chair, wearing a green velvet dress with a white collar. Her hair was a short pageboy, ending just at the childish fullness of her cheeks, her bangs martially straight (I imagined Florence wielding the scissors), her child's hands folded in her lap. It all would have been sort of fatally *American Gothic* if she hadn't looked so utterly self-contained, with a hint of exasperation in her dark eyes. Over them the brows were like delicate wings of birds. "Did they try to get you to smile?"

"Of course."

"And you wouldn't."

"Would *you* have?" Now she was smiling. "Take it," and she reached forward over the squadron of other frames.

"Oh, no, that's—" Her hand hit the lacrosse picture and it toppled, taking others with it, in a falling line. I heard her quick intake of breath, although it could have been my own, and then we dissolved into laughter. "See, May-May," I said, "you can't upset the gods that way."

"I don't see why not," May said, and turned to me. We left the rest of the pictures fallen, as they were.

"WHAT WOULD YOU BE DOING if I weren't around?" I said. "How would you be amusing yourself?"

She turned to me. We were naked, in bed. We had been there for hours. We were pretending Preston had no idea. We could do whatever we wanted. "Charlie." She advanced on me. "Poor sad Charlie." She climbed on top, straddling me. She leaned close, her breasts swaying, but her knees were pinning my hands. "Poor *pitiful* Charlie. He is *fishing* for *compliments*."

I stared straight back. "Yes." I was shameless in my need.

Outside, it was snowing. It was only midafternoon but because of the snow the low light cocooned us. The house was practically silent. Preston was asleep—we knew this because there was a baby monitor on May's bedside table. Every now and then it lit up and we heard him moan or sigh, one floor below, in the study that was now his makeshift bedroom, since he had quit climbing the stairs. Sometimes we heard the thump and snuffle of Percy rearranging himself on the floor next to Preston's bed.

May's room, where we were, had the semi-stripped mien of a place that was in the process of being left. The posters and construction-paper locker decorations were artifacts from high school, still on the wall only because of inertia. Sometimes I scanned them for signs of what May was like before, *before,* but there still wasn't enough distance for me not to feel prurient.

But right then I wasn't looking at anything. The kiss, however, ended before I was ready, May pulling away, and I felt it before I opened my eyes: she'd switched modes, she must be light for a little while, we had been so serious, sometimes it was frightening. Sometimes, she required facts. She wanted to build us a foundation; she was absolutely right; she was erasing a deficit, acquiring knowledge of me, my family, and it had to be a bit of a joke because she knew so little—there was an imbalance. "So tell me," she said, as she'd said before and would again.

She knew the outlines, even Jimmie Garrett, although I had done my best not to Horatio Alger myself—not to Preston Bankhead myself. But right now she was interested more in my generation. "I thought all brothers hated each other," she said.

"Of course not."

"You talk about him like he's perfect."

"Well, he's not. And how is that hating?"

"Not hating exactly."

"He's just the opposite of me. He looks like a model. He's a math genius. He can't spell."

"You *do* hate him."

"I adore him," I say. "He's a slob. There're always holes in his clothes. Always needs a haircut. Girls call him all hours of the day and night."

"Lovely."

"You'll have to meet him to understand." There had to be some way to explain. "His charm is untainted. He will always be loved."

She looked at me and in the half-light her face was sober, almost stern.

I said, "Why did you quit writing me? Last year?"

"Because it seemed hopeless," she said, without hesitation. "Because I did not want to be a silly girl."

I reached up to her hair. Her face. She settled down into me.

The light was almost gone. We drank that cup of time, pretending it would never run dry.

Then her voice came. It was nearly dark. "How could you ask that?"

"Ask what?"

"Earlier. How I'd be amusing myself. *Amusing* myself? Don't you *know*?"

"Yes. I know." She sank down, under, I held her, covered her. "I know." I could barely see her face, the sea-deep eyes, as I curled around her in her childhood bed.

PRESTON INSISTED WE GO to the Lowells' Christmas party.

Usually he didn't like to be left, and at some point I realized this particular instance wasn't magnanimity but an effort to pretend all was normal. "Why *wouldn't* you go?" he demanded. We called the visiting nurse service, and didn't tell him until the woman showed up at the house and it was a done deal. Meanwhile, he sat motionless in his chair, his hands precise on each armrest like a statue. It was almost funny, how the lightning bolt seemed to be materializing in one fist, but then he nodded at her stiffly. "There is a television in the back bedroom," he said, meaning *Stay away from me,* and the LPN, who knew the drill already, smiled at us to let us know it was all right.

The party was crowded. At the front door, we looked at each other and then stepped apart. We weren't willing to broadcast ourselves. But as the party went on the distance became more and more titillating and finally I said, "Do you know the best view of the labyrinth?"

"Show me."

We wove our way, separately, through the people we knew so well, people who must have been wondering, but I didn't think about that. Divya glanced at us, smiled. I went up the stairs; May followed a minute later. Behind us the noise of the party died away. On the third floor were several pinched, icy maid's rooms (I heard Divya's voice: *My God, this house is a British novel*) and then the attic. Straight ahead was a round window that swiveled on a horizontal axis, and when I reached it I pressed open the solid old brass window locks, letting in the cold air, and tilted it up for her. Carefully, she put her head through; directly beneath us, laid out like a map, was the laby-rinth.

People down below were laughing. The sound floated up. May laughed too. "Don't you feel like they're little puppets?" she said. "Like you could reach down and flick them along with your fingers?"

"Shh," I said, and put my hands on her lovely ass in the smooth black dress.

Outside in the cold people bumble and laugh. How Win trims the boxwood. Oh the hours! And Divya with her private smile. The home-sick southern wife, so very long ago. I can see past May's head: snow lay on the dark green, the circle right-angling, giving way to another circle.

Everything is beginning. I believe everything is still beginning. And when May draws her head back in, white flakes melting into her hair, she is smiling.

I'D LIKE TO SAY that dying brought out the best in Preston. I'd also like to say it brought out the best in me. Both would be lies.

One night after dinner Preston said, "Goddammit, when's lunch?"

May and I exchanged a look. She said, "Daddy, we just ate. Do you want a snack?"

"Do not patronize me!"

He'd also said, in recent days, "Fred Hueffer wants me on the fucking steering committee," and, one afternoon, sitting in front of a history documentary on TV (the only kind of show he'll consent to watch), "I am just not going to get the sermon written, and that's final."

Once, May left the room and he leaned in to me. "I've been faith-ful to Florence throughout our whole marriage. Completely faithful."

"I admire that, Preston," I said.

"It was mostly out of my own pride," he said, and then May came back and he shut up.

I pondered that one awhile, but never told her.

Quietly, it was agreed that someone should be with him at all times. He only ever wanted May, but sometimes, during the week, I stayed at the house while she ran errands. By then I was regularly staying overnight. She was vague about all this with her family. "They've never really thought I'd do anything interesting," she said. "I don't think they'd even notice us. If they were here."

One afternoon, when I was with him, he was fidgety and petulant, refusing music, TV, me reading to him, a nap—and then all at once he smiled and said he would set up the chessboard.

I half expected him to ask for a drink; he'd become increasingly belligerent about habits and routines, and if he remembered that he usually started his game with a scotch on the rocks by his side, we'd be in trouble; but instead he moved his pawn, tipped his head coquettishly at me, and broke his cardinal rule, which was no chatting during play. "Charlie," he said, "I like to know about people, and I realize I don't know your middle name."

He didn't seem like Preston at all, but like an actor, a character. A genial nursing-home resident I could josh around with. "You're asking after all this time? Well, I don't know yours either," I said.

The old, the real, Preston would have bristled. This one smiled indulgently. "I am Preston Broussard Bankhead," he said. "Preston from my father's mother, and Broussard from my mother's mother. A family tradition."

He was formal as a paper doll, and it was at that moment that I realized, once and for all, that Preston was dying. That sooner rather than later, he would not be there. He would be merely an absence. A space, nothing.

And I further realized that he wasn't in his right mind, and I could say whatever I wanted. I could—not to put too fine a point on it—just make shit up. It was cruel and, in the moment, made complete sense to me. "I'm Charles Satterthwaite Garrett," I said.

Which was untrue. My middle name was Spooner, my mother's maiden name. How could Preston have known so little about me? How had my name never come up in conversation? He seemed to know everyone's middle name. It was the sort of detail Preston Broussard Bankhead used to suss out on his own, climbing up people's family trees to inspect the view.

I waited for him to call me on it, to furrow his brow and wonder aloud if he was confused. But he didn't.

I was aware that *Spooner* would not impress him, might be a detail he actively disliked. Maybe I was protecting my mother from him. And protecting myself. Maybe I was seeing that hot little town she came from, where she took me only once, and even then I had no desire for Preston to sense any of it in me, to smell it on my breath.

I was protecting something that I hadn't entirely figured out. It was, in the purest sense, none of his business.

He was waiting, I realized. "Satterthwaite's from my father's side," I said, "an old name," and I'd told another lie that felt like play and protection at once.

"I've been thinking about these things. I have a great deal of time to think now," he said, waving a hand magisterially. He sat back in his chair, the game forgotten. "It's important to know who you are. To know who's around you. Because I'll tell you." And then, all of a sudden, he's launching into the Grey boys sermon.

Always the same phrases, the same arc. "So, do we have relativism?" he intoned. "Isn't *one* the most important? But what if it's tainted? *Cus*tom, or *cul*ture, or *con*science? Or all three? Because I'll tell you, friends. Someday you'll wake up and you'll be on a different ride at the fair. You'll be alone at the top of that Ferris wheel. You'll be looking down at the landscape below. Little tiny people like ants. You'll be alone but not lonely. You'll realize how *powerful* you are, and that you *never knew it*."

This was different. This was new. I leaned forward, in spite of myself.

"The notion of reinvention will seize you. You will excavate some larval form of yourself, some sixty-year cicada. Some ugly, horny bug! Do you hear me?"

Why couldn't I give him one last chance, in this addled, unguarded state? To impress me, enlighten me? I'd been waiting for that, expecting it, since I met him.

"You'll venture forth with wet wings and no baggage. These ideas will destroy your sleep, but you won't care! The world finally knows who you are, you're destroyed—rebirth is all you will have left! Be GRATEFUL!" He shook his head, and I knew, beyond the shadow of a doubt, that in his mind he was stepping down from the pulpit, coming down to the chancel step. "Be grateful," he whispered. "That's what they say. Be *grateful*."

I heard the back door open into the kitchen, but I didn't turn around. I sent a silent prayer that May wouldn't call out. I wanted the spell unbroken.

"The days will speed up. You're in an ecstasy of possibility. You will have unspeakable choices before you—you've been expecting enlightenment—you've been *bursting* with *hubris*! But no—"

May was behind me now. She touched my shoulder and I covered her hand, pressing her quiet.

"—the brightness begins to fade. The grimy details are reappearing. The Ferris wheel . . . lowers." I wanted to laugh but he was so utterly serious, holding us with a fierce whisper. "Everything is rotten. Autumn that year is rainy and the leaves are knocked off the trees before their time and the light is never properly golden and *then one day you wake up and you shit blood*."

"Oh, Daddy," May said, her voice catching.

It was done, over. That final, minor performance, capped by that last, grotesque, and ultimately false detail—because, while the cancer had spread to his bones and, clearly, to his brain, I knew it wasn't in his bowel. Although I was glad beyond measure he had no idea I knew such things.

He was shaking his head, slow and mournful, ignoring us. Lately he'd refused both haircuts and shaves. His eyebrows were gray thickets. I thought of bearded Moses out on some crag, looking down on the Promised Land, forbidden to enter. Perhaps I'd say this to May. Perhaps not. We were both still, waiting for a coda, which made no sense because it seemed like he'd said his piece.

But as we sat in the stretching silence I felt my senses open. Someone had dropped dinner by earlier; I smelled roast chicken. Beside us, the fire crackled. The lamplight in the corners of the room reflected off the thick old woodwork, the creamy walls; Percy was asleep on the sofa; the Christmas tree in the corner glowed. May and I had decorated it a few days before—she insisted. She'd come around now to sit on the floor next to my chair, leaning, just barely, on my leg, and I felt a rising giddiness, a happiness so distilled it was almost painful, which surely could not be right, could it, with this old man disintegrating in front of me?

"Charlie," he said, "do you believe life is infinite?"

"Yes," I said. "Absolutely. Yes." Oh the abundance.

And he pounced. "Charles, you of all people. Do you think I'm waiting with bated breath for the many mansions? For the streets of gold?"

"No," I said, willing to believe for another moment that I would like what was coming next. "Not literally."

"Not *literally*," he minced. "Oh, but we *do* believe life goes on. And on and on. That we never stop learning, or some other highfalutin' version of immortality. Like the gods of Olympus! Or perhaps we come *back*! As a king the next time! A movie star! Sheer egotism! That is what I've realized. Terror at the thought of the world without one. Without one's *miraculous uniqueness*! That is the infinity." He looked down at the board, suddenly aware of it, and moved his bishop out to the middle, foolhardy, a move Ram would make. "Oh, why ask *you*, Charles, my metaphysical friend," he said. "I think *all* is glorious to you, *right now*." May moved closer. Preston saw, and smiled—and I felt a rush of relief. Yes, finally. Name it! Tell the world! Truth and love!

I looked at him ready for the warmth I never stopped expecting, and maybe his blessing (oh we're fools), and met instead a strange, off-kilter glint. "I think you are waist deep in the present right now," he said. "Or should I say cock deep?"

"*Daddy*." May stood up. Preston gave me a triumphant smirk.

"Am I wrong?" he said, turning to her. "Are not you and young Mr. Garrett here buried deep in the glorious mud of the mundane? Wallowing in the *peccata mundi*? The exquisite flight of young love, etcetera, et cetera? And you think that it will always last? That you will live forever? Making the beast with two backs?" He wheeled back to me and raised his arm, pointing a long finger. "Charles Satterthwaite Garrett. You shoeless piece of trash. *Do you think I do not know what goes on in my house?*"

It was like a fairy tale, a myth, where the name is the locus of power, the true name, and the good guy literally disarms the bad guy by calling it out—or vice versa. But I, of course, had gamed the system.

I started to speak, but May was ahead of me. "That's not even his name," she snarled. "You don't even have his name right."

He looked at me, caught off guard. "It's true," I said mildly. "I'm Charles Spooner Garrett." I shrugged: *It's all right, old man.* "Not Satterthwaite. That's my stepfather."

"You said . . . stepfather?" He looked from May to me. "Spooner?"

"After my mother. Anita Spooner. It's a family tradition." I glanced at May, saw the tears standing in her eyes, and stood up. How was I actually happy, just moments ago? "Come here, sweetheart," and she came inside my arm, close to my side.

"May-May." He looked back and forth, between us. His face was oddly askew. Out of the corner of his mouth, a thin string of drool. Back to me. "You said. You said you said."

"Maybe we should get you to bed, Preston," I said.

And then his arm comes down on the board; the pieces fly. "Do not patronize me!" he roars, or at least I think that's what he wants to say, to bellow; but it's gibberish, and all the words that come next are gibberish too except for *May-May, May-May.* She goes to him but his arms are still stretched past her. For a moment, I even think he is reaching for me. One hand is a claw, his mouth drooping, and as May sinks to her knees, her arms around him, I go for the phone. "Daddy, it's okay. It's okay," she croons, but over her shoulder, his still-wild eyes on me, he is shaking his head.

THE IDYLL WAS OVER; the family descended in earnest. Preston, who could no longer speak, became agitated whenever he saw me, and so I began to keep my distance. May came more often to my place, but even though she said she was glad for a break, she was distracted, and I was distracted in turn, for my job was to hide the euphoria that persisted, even though I knew a man was truly dying. Isn't a man always, somewhere, dying?

I was lurking around at the Bankheads', trying to see May, trying to stay out of the way, and one afternoon I walked into the study, which I'd thought was empty. But on the loveseat Florence was sitting sideways, knee to knee, with Laird, who I now knew was her favorite. She was crying, moaning really, "I'm not a *bitch,*" in a way that I knew was not a response to anything Laird had said. Her eyes were squeezed shut, but as I began to back away, she opened them and saw me.

Florence and I didn't meet each other's gaze for some time after that; but then, I'm not sure we ever did.

BY NOW I KNEW the Bankhead house better than my own. Odd to think May and I had had only six weeks, beginning to end, but in that time I'd absorbed her as mine, and also the house; I knew every knickknack, knew it all as a museum of May. But now the house belonged to the brothers again, and any gesture of familiarity on my part—opening the correct kitchen cabinet for a plate, finessing the tricky deadbolt on the door to the cellar—rattled them, readied them for a battle they were primed to fight. Their incipient grief had to go somewhere. So the house they hardly visited was *theirs,* along with Preston and May, and these lowest members (as May would have it) nevertheless could be claimed by no one else, least of all me.

One day I went by after classes and found the tension in a new phase: Preston had been unconscious since the night before. May took me in to see him. His mouth was open, his brow clenched with insentient effort. I touched his waxy hand. He was May's father, and I was sorry, and sorry too he hadn't ever been what I'd wanted—but that was an old thought, one I was used to, and without any real grief. Why had I ever wanted anything from him anyway?

I wished that I felt more; but I had so much. I reached for May, for her hand, beside mine. I ached only for her.

We said good-bye in the mudroom. It was crowded with coats and snowy boots, fully alive again, but it also felt, in that moment, anonymous and private, a way station. "I want you to stay," May said.

"You should be with your family."

"I am."

"I'll come back whenever you want. But right now you all need to be together. They want you to themselves."

Indecision in her eyes. She said, "You shouldn't mind them."

"I don't." I stroked her hair, pressed her gently back against the coats—felt her body known against mine, her mouth, her tongue—oh, it was laughable that anyone else claimed any importance, even Preston himself. And now here was the euphoria, which grew every day—our bodies together were a single artifact, iron, no, gold, durable and shining; I wanted to pour myself into her, make a new self, together we were entirely new—

"Jesus Christ." It was Laird. May held me tighter, but I looked up and saw him standing in the doorway. Unlike me in the study, he let his gaze fall fully on us, with undisguised hostility, before he turned away. And all at once May and I were separate.

"It doesn't matter," she said.

I kissed her cheek, her temple. Touches. Her skin living and moving. "I'm going to go."

"They said it could be in the next twenty-four hours. At least in the next two days."

"Call me. Call me in an hour. Whatever's happening."

"They don't know, though."

"No, they don't." Her hair. So smooth. She leaned in to my hand. "It's time, though, sweetheart."

Her eyes began to fill. "I don't think he's ready."

All I could do was murmur platitudes, clichés: *Yes he's ready, no more pain, is anyone ever really ready?* I wouldn't say he was going to a better place; but how useful the streets of gold would be right now! "He's going to find what he wants," I said. "He won't want anymore." The tears fell. "Oh, baby. Do you want me to stay?" Through the tears, she shook her head.

Is that what she did? Why don't I remember each second, each portion of a second? Or was there more, more yes-ing and no-ing, more *go* and *stay,* the dance of touch and withdrawing touch, hating the nakedness of being alone—was there? Were we there five minutes or an hour? We were there among the coats and Laird came in, and in spite of him I should have stayed, God knows, should never have left.

But the door opened and the air was cold and then I was in my car on the way home, exiled.

It was early twilight—it was, I realized, the solstice. Christmas lights were on the houses, Christmas music on the radio. Outside the liquor store a mile from my house, a life-size Santa turned slowly back and forth, waving, and at the turn to my road the neighbors had a sleigh with reindeer on the roof. Rudolph's nose lit up, on-off, on-off, and I laughed aloud. Sometimes the holidays were sadness itself but here, just here, I could be happy, I could isolate it, hold it quickly to me. May was miserable, and so I shouldn't have been happy; yet I knew she'd understand. *On the plane I was glad,* she'd said, *because of you.*

I turned into my long driveway, drove down through the trees, emerged around the bend and there was my house, silhouetted in the last of the light, the bare branches of the trees, my trees, black against the last blue edge of sky. I regretted my lack of decorations and thought that maybe I would wind some lights around the columns of the porch. Inside I had a tree, though, in my bare-ish living room, a tree May insisted I get, *ours.* That was a precious afternoon stolen: we bought the lights and cheap ornaments, we made paper chains and a ridiculous star with glitter. It was all May's idea, a joyous regression and progression of playing house, and I pretended to indulge her, but now whenever I saw that tree with its kindergarten trimmings it filled me with that same euphoria. *This is what you have now, and what is coming.* I saw a life.

But the tree, the lights, reminded me. Christmas was also coming, and I too had a family, and I needed to call my mother. If Preston really went soon I might not make it home, even though my ticket was already bought; I believed, though, that she would understand. It was Nicky who would be disappointed.

I talked to my mother fairly often, if briefly. Neither of us were phone people much, but I liked it when she first picked up and I heard her voice. I suspected she felt the same. That was all we needed. We didn't really share news. I hadn't told her, for instance, about Preston's illness. Possibly I'd never even mentioned him. Nor had I mentioned May. I hadn't told anyone about May. I'd been holding my news of her, of us, like a prize, waiting to bestow it on the right person at the right time. It seemed like now was the right time.

First, though, I told my mother about Preston Bankhead. I tried to leave out my disappointments, his pettinesses; I thought instead of May and her grief, and realized that the man might become legendary anyway, and that that would be fine, that was as it should be. To my surprise I was crying. Then I told her about May. The order of things seemed clear and profound. If my mother asked about these strange laughing tears I would say no, they weren't confusing at all, because an old man was dying, but I was a young man full of joy.

On the other end of the line my mother was quiet and then she said, "Preston is dying?"

Yes, melanoma, spread to the brain. Terrible, too young. I was still flying. Away from that house, my happiness was unfettered. But there was something—at the edge—"Why did you say 'Preston' like that?"

"You're in love with Preston's daughter?"

"Why do you know his name?"

"Preston has a *daughter*?"

"Yes! Yes!" The happiness again. I would sing it. Shout it. When this small trouble was settled.

"But you are Preston's son," my mother said. "You are his first son."

I SAT AT THE FUNERAL. With Win and Divya, not the Bankheads, which was understandable, I wasn't wanted (oh no, not at all), that was now a relief, a blessing. I watched, in the front pew, that row of blond heads. At the end, one dark. May turned and looked at me, her eyes pits of need.

A hymn, tunefully British, saints going to tea. Laird reading scripture. Too many eulogies.

"I thought there was time," my mother had said. And, "He didn't deserve you."

Avoiding her had been difficult. May. She had called and called. She drove to my house and I stayed hidden inside. Because I wanted her too much. Because I was afraid I wouldn't tell her.

"I fell in love," my mother said. "In a little town. Called St. Annes. He was in seminary."

I didn't care. I didn't want a story.

"He loved me. He wanted to be better than he was. But he left, he couldn't do it. He didn't know you were born. He didn't know he was your father. I was going to let you decide. I thought there was time."

My mother had never apologized to me before, for anything. Her doing it now turned my stomach along with everything else. Her begging on the phone. Her becoming a different person. We are all now entirely different people. Preston has a *daughter*?

"Charlie, you look awful," Divya whispered.

Yes I'm sure I do and I pushed out of the pew and headed blindly up the side aisle and out the door, through the snow to the woods beyond the chapel, slipping in my good shoes, and once I was in the thick of the trees I began to vomit, over and over and over, down to the bile.

And in the middle of this pure sickness, I understood. There had been a decision to be made, and now it was done.

I saw that if I told May I would become a victim, like her, of this stomach-churning fate. But what if I were the villain instead? Then the villainy would be the consolation. May hating me would be part of the sacrifice. Throwing myself on the grenade: that was the route I wanted. *I* would be the sickness. I would choose it.

I would end it, and tell her nothing.

Once the past had happened, once it was past, it seemed in stone to me. I was like my mother in that way. It was done.

I straightened up and slid, on my tractionless soles, out of the woods, away from the chapel, to my car.

I loved May. We *were* love. It was a thing that existed in its own time and could not be changed. And now I would be leaving that house. I would abandon it but I didn't want to tear it down, to change the landscape of the past. I didn't want May to know it was a place that never should have been built.

Neither did I care for her to know that Preston was a coward and a cad—old-fashioned, true word. I didn't want to destroy that house either, that shrine, where she would still go for comfort. I would save her. Leave me that little bit of control. Leave me that.

So I made my decision and didn't think about whether it was my right. I left the past. I started the car and drove away. I let the wood of that house we built petrify, transform, become hard and lasting. Whether we wanted to be or not, we were our parents' children, and I was my mother's son as well as my father's. So forward, forward, forward.

II

Nick

Eight

The house—my own house—saved me.

It was lifeboat and anchor. I needed the tangible. I could believe only the corporeal. The walls around me, the house's rising sturdiness on the hill. It seemed a loyal, patient entity, the immovable thing I could care about. It wasn't a house of the past or even, oddly, of the future (as maybe it once had been) but of only the absolute present, of one moment and then the next, which was all I could face.

And so I let it become an all-consuming distraction. I needed an obsession, and the house was ready. It turned itself inside out for me, its own labyrinthine puzzle, becoming larger and larger the more closely I looked. It might have even overcome me, become another antagonist, if Win hadn't been there. He too was loyal and patient, and gradually in some way my own house and Win Lowell became almost interchangeable: one was the other, each and together they were safety.

The house seemed steeped in the histories of other people, and that too was a help. Additions had been made along the way—a wing, a lean-to, an ell—making it thoroughly asymmetrical. It was filled with nooks and oddities that were decisions embodied. (Why was there an old knob-and-tube outlet in the crawl space under the stairs? Why were the windows in the kitchen different sizes? What had happened in the living room, where the wide-plank pine was patched?) My fascination was sudden and strange and deep: the house was a country I was ready to claim.

I was astonished at all the forms wood could take: clapboards, shingles, floorboards, banisters, crown moldings. Pine, spruce, hard-rock maple, oak. Win taught me the patterns of the different woods, and I began to notice both the grains exposed in the house—the old gumwood cabinets in the kitchen, the attic stairs—and the chalky texture of the paint where the wood was painted. I would run a finger along the groove of a chair rail and think of the rough board before it was cut. I thought about how the shingles had been nailed on one by one. Sometimes I imagined all the pieces of my house flying apart and then coming back together as if drawn by a giant magnet. It moved me that the house had existed for so long before I'd ever known of it.

I began to buy tools. For the first time in my life, I read nonfiction with complete absorption—how-to books, handyman books, carpentry manuals. I learned how to hang doors. I bought a secondhand lathe at an auction, and, after dozens of tries, was able to replace a broken spindle in the staircase. I learned how to mud in sheetrock and how to plaster. After some hesitation, I bought a book on masonry and eventually, several summers in, repointed the chimney.

The house was in danger, of course, not of spectacularly disassembling in a magic reverse cyclone, but of disintegrating piece by piece. Parts of it seemed to be held together with only varnish and brown age, so I felt a certain legitimate urgency. And Win never told me I was crazy to spend so much time. He knew what I was doing—knew, that is, that I was erasing May, or filling her absence. I never told him, or anyone, the rest.

"Where'd you go after the funeral?" he said once.

"West."

He nodded, unsurprised.

I'd been gone three days. I'd been thinking of the Pacific, had made it as far as Iowa, a flat, white, unending world, close enough—and finally I'd been calm enough, or numb enough, to turn around.

I didn't tell him that either, but if I had, he would have understood.

———

WIN WAS OF THE GENERATION that understood what ownership was, that had been raised to fix things, and the more intractable the problem the more patient, or stubborn, Win became. He decoded plumbing, wiring, collapsing cabinets, crumbling concrete. All was a series of rational steps, for everything had an explanation, and mysteries were solvable.

The only thing that really made Win irate was plastic. Luckily, there was very little of it in my house. Win would say, "You're lucky, Charlie. I'd rather fix honest wear and tear than mistakes." Or, "No one's gone and ruined this place, Charlie."

The largest job we undertook was shoring up the staircase. His directions were sure and instinctive. "Had to do this before," he said. "Cellar stairs. Did it for my mother, summer after my dad died. Bad heart. He'd started it, and I finished it. I was seventeen. Didn't end up pretty. But it was solid as a rock."

These bits of information came out over the space of long minutes. His monologues were slow, but I'd learned that if I was patient, the words would accumulate.

"Later on I did it at my first wife's parents' place. That had to be a prettier job, you know. Boy was I sweating it. Had to pretend I knew what the hell I was doing. Think I fooled 'em. Hand me that level.

"And then had to do it over on Summer Street." That was his and Divya's house. "Thought that would be the last time." He smiled at me, which I took to mean he was glad to have been wrong.

After a minute, I said, "What was your first wife's name?" I knew she had existed, but this was the first time he'd ever mentioned her outright to me.

"Girl named Jennifer King. Jennie. Beautiful girl. Love of my life." He noted my face. "You can have more than one. I found that out."

"Oh."

"She was just a good, good-looking girl and we were in love, and you know, Charlie, I was cocky, I thought I'd dodged a bullet. No mediocrity for me. Found the perfect girl, was going to have the perfect life. I'd gone to Vietnam, I was back. I deserved it."

The story, such as it was, could have ended there. Win spoke very completely: that is, every pause seemed like the end of a story. But he must have sensed I needed detail, and took pity on me. "She looked like a magazine ad. Blond hair, blue eyes. What they used to call an Ivory girl. We were married two and a half years, and she was pregnant. Six months along. January. Hold that right there. That end. No, just a finishing nail. Good.

"Driving on the icy roads, you know. Hairpin turn, that one up by the pond. Textbook. Hit a tree."

"God, Win." Did you say you were sorry? Years later? When a person was in another life? "I'm sorry."

He nodded. He didn't seem affected, but he didn't meet my eye. "So your life ends one day, but you're still living it. So you have to get used to that. I tell you, Charlie, thinking the universe is angry at you—that is its own kind of hubris, Charlie. No puppet master upstairs pulling any strings. You just have to get on with it." Long pause for hammering. "I did some stupid things. Because I was angry. Then I stopped." His tone had hardened with something both stern and long dead, and I knew I wouldn't press, although it was hard to imagine Win and any sort of dissipation together. If I couldn't respect secrets, then who could? "And then I met Div and straightened up."

"I imagine she wouldn't have it any other way."

He grinned, which involved mostly his eyes. "You imagine correctly, sir."

There was another long, companionable, productive stretch. I loved how I was beginning to anticipate his movements, like a surgical nurse.

Then he said, "You ever talk to May anymore?"

"No."

He nodded slightly. "But you were kind to her."

"I was as kind as I know how to be," I said.

"Well. It'll be all right, then." He stood up, creakily. Contemplated the new treads we had put in. "You know, Charlie," he said, in the tone that meant he was finished for the day, "you made a real find with this place." He looked at me. "I mean it."

"Thank you."

It was an honest compliment—Win made no other sort—and I always remembered it. Sometimes I even said the words to myself like they were lyrics to an old song: *You made a find. Although you didn't know that you were looking.* Win never asked what a young fellow like me needed with fourteen acres. Never said or even seemed to think, *What are your intentions, Charles Garrett?* (As if I were defrauding life.) The empty bedrooms upstairs. Decisions not yet made, life not yet lived. Win believed in doing; he assumed I did too.

NORMALLY I WENT HOME to Atlanta for a good part of the summer. But this year I decided Nicky could come to visit me. "You need to see my place," I said to him, on the phone.

"What about Mom?"

"She has to work."

"That's what she *said*," but then Nicky's voice trailed off. He hated conflict. He wasn't going to ask, because he didn't want to know.

"Just you and me," I said. "It'll be great. We could look at colleges too."

"Yeah. I want to come up there for school anyway," he said quickly, as though he'd been waiting for me to mention it first and now was afraid I'd disapprove. "I've been thinking about it."

"See?" I said. "It'll be perfect."

The first night he was at my house, at sunset, he strode to the edge of the patio and threw his arms wide, a yawp to the world. "My God, Charlie!" he cried, as the red boiled up in the sky, and the green of the mountains turned dark. "I love it here! I'm never leaving!" He turned to me, his arms still outstretched. "I understand why you're here," he said, and he was taking me in, along with the mountains. "I get it."

His reddish-blond hair was shaggy, his T-shirt full of holes, his bare feet dirty as a pilgrim's. He was still just a twice-a-week shaver, but he'd grown again and was a full six inches taller than I was. He had Hugh's slender, ropy look; but he was far more golden, vital, thoroughly seventeen. Muscles popped under his skin whenever he moved as if they couldn't contain their exuberance.

And despite his dubious personal hygiene anyone could see why girls flocked to him: in his gorgeous openness there was also something unattainable, unreachable. Something fine, that couldn't be owned; but a challenge was always attractive. His energy flowed out, artless, unchecked.

People would always reach to touch his hem.

LIVING WITH SOMEONE AGAIN was odd but not unpleasant. I was aware of Nicky's presence in the house from the moment I woke in the morning. I would creep downstairs and go out to my front porch, facing east, and feel some mute longing for the possibility of solitude I sensed in the light coming through the trees. And then, of course, a little guilt. He could not have been easier, once he was awake—he was content to be led nearly anywhere.

The Middletons were down in South Carolina while he was there, but he met Win and Divya and Ram and Anil and fell in love with them all. He walked the labyrinth with a delighted smile on his face, like he was on a ride at an amusement park and genuinely didn't know where he'd end up: "This is so cool!" He and I drove around to dozens of schools, easy to do in New England, and went, of course, to Harvard, where he wanted to know every landmark of my dingy years there.

As we walked through the Yard, I told him about my lunch with Hugh at his club, not mentioning the old-fashioneds, and Nick looked wistful. With epic unfairness I, the stepson, remembered him much better.

"I mainly remember his study," Nicky said. "I mean, him in it. On that leather sofa, with his feet up. Or behind his desk. Like the president. I thought he was the president."

I was glad that Hugh was, in some way, still a hero to him. "I remember his study too—that's where I always see him first, too," I said. "Handing me a book." We spoke of the library as though it were mythical, vanished, but of course it was part of the house Anita still lived in. "He let me read anything I wanted. And of course the first thing I took was *Lady Chatterley's Lover.*"

Nick looked blank. I had to explain. "But he didn't mind," I said. "He said it was a great book. Actually, he said nearly great. Which is accurate. And he said to reread it, when I was older." I remembered sweating in his study, trying not to mention the part where the game-keeper makes her breasts swing like bells. And also the flowers in the pubic hair, which I had thought was both the grossest and most erotic thing I had ever heard of. His quietly amused and sympathetic face. "He also said he wouldn't tell Anita," I said. "That it would be between us."

"I wish you'd call her Mom," Nicky said. And then walked up the steps of Widener Library, past the plaque to yet another fallen young man.

A MONTH LATER Nicky was back home and I walked up the hill to the headmaster's house, to the Labor Day tea, and I walked under the arbor, petals of the late roses falling like confetti, and got a gin and tonic and mingled in the seersucker and the summer dresses and the civilized glow, all of us held there in the garden within the old, low piled-stone walls. There were people missing, but at a school there are always people missing, people always cycle away, and it's easy to forget how or why. Shocking how quickly the September light was already fading. I knew this slant of light, this ending and beginning. It was familiar, something that would repeat and repeat; there always would be a Labor Day tea; and Win was there, and Divya, and I thought, *There are people here I love, and maybe I am lucky.*

Four days later, while teaching his junior trig class, Win had a heart attack, like his father before him. He died on the way to the hospital.

Divya was the only one I wanted to be with. When I was there, at their house, she was wordless and severe and I played with the boys. She endured a good deal of my presence, and I hope I was a help to her somehow. I hope I was a help because she could be wordless and severe and I expected nothing else. Neither of us would jolly the other.

She began to pay an absurd amount of money to a landscape company to take care of the labyrinth. "The roof can wait," she said. "The gutters. I sleep better knowing it is trimmed just so."

"I'm glad. Whatever it takes. I'm glad you're sleeping."

She ignored me. "Such lovely absurd order," she said. "Someday I will do it on my knees like a pilgrim. I truly will."

"I'd like to see that."

"I will let you know."

Once I was at her house for dinner. Not right away—several months after Win died. It was winter. I remember that she had said something and I had laughed and then she had laughed, and through a look or a tilt of the head we had silently acknowledged that it was the first laughter in a long time. Then Ram and Anil hurtled through the kitchen; the back door slammed and we listened to their footsteps thundering across the wooden deck and down the steps to the yard below.

She was standing at the stove, stirring a big pot. I wondered if she was still smiling, looking out the window into the snowy yard, her sons flying across it, the white outlines of the labyrinth beyond, but then she turned to me, without warning. "Oh, God, Charlie. Oh, God." She looked flattened, overtaken. The long wooden spoon dangled from her hand, dripping stew onto the floor.

"The sea is finally calm and empty," she said, "and then a ship sails into view, an enormous black rusted-out thing. That's what I dream of, these enormous things coming at me. They fill everything up. And I can't breathe."

I opened my arms. I wasn't like Nicky. I was not inviting an embrace, or wanting to drink the world. Instead, for a moment, just a moment, I felt a brute endurance, some new version of myself; and I let the ghost ship sail over me instead and it was weightless and it did me no harm.

I realized that withstanding its onslaught would be my only accomplishment for a very, very long time, and perhaps it didn't hurt me because I was already drowning.

"Thank you, Charlie," Divya said, and she turned back to the stove.

DURING HIS VISIT Nicky had asked, "Did you know you wanted to be a teacher when you came here?"

"Not at all. I didn't even know it when I graduated. I just wanted a job."

"But you're happy now?"

I didn't miss a beat—because, of course, he was asking about my professional life, not any other sort. "Yes. Sheer luck."

"But maybe you were intuitive," Nick said. "Maybe you knew what you were doing all along." He always wanted to give me credit.

After Win died, I decided he might have been right. Teaching began to be quite literally the only thing making me get up in the morning. I'm not sure there exists any other job that could have functioned in the same way: my mind needed to be outside myself, to be centered on others' thoughts and work, and I needed objective evidence that I was being useful. To that end I could see students progressing, mostly under their own steam, but still I could feel a small measure of utility. Finally, I needed to be dealing with people who were far more interested in themselves than in me and yet couldn't be faulted for it—in other words, high-school students.

I endured the loveliness of all of them. All of them, even those nature hadn't favored, even the ones without silky eyebrows and flat stomachs and effortless muscles—they were changelings, they were becoming. Sometimes there were kids who were simply born to be thirty, or fifty, or seventy; I could see their unfinished teenaged faces overlaid with the transparencies of their aged selves and had to resist telling them so—that the maturity they wanted was going to happen, that someday they would look as completed as they felt, in their fleeting, truest moments. That someday they would be magnificent.

Others, seemingly fortunate, were at their peak at seventeen. All their physical edges were already smooth, they rarely had acne, their hair seemed to keep itself cut. Their fate was to go no further.

And sometimes there was a girl, or boy, whose beauty was both dewy and odd. He might stick out; she might be invisible. But there was some clarity there that was so finely drawn it was easily missed, until one day it all melded and became striking. Of course I am not speaking of only physical beauty. And I tried not to think of May.

Every morning I was met with their energy. They were full of their dramas and their innocence and there were some who might be president or queen or martyr and some who might ruin themselves—

but there was still time for them to turn back, still time for us to save them. And did they care if I had a personal life? If I did anything besides teach them? No, bless them, they did not.

Every day I gave them what I had. Poured it out onto them, my pitiful measure of oil. Gave them all my treasure, anointed them: go forth. Then went home, read, graded papers, slept, woke, did it again.

On Saturdays I was alone and liked it and thought I was resting and recovering, well deserved, and I would fix something around the house or mow the meadow or putter around the tired old apple trees or maybe even plant a new one, but by Sunday I would be panicky with lack of schedule. So I went to church. I didn't go because of Preston, surely, who had failed me, in ways I still couldn't absorb; or because of my mother, who'd been raised in a little country church with hellfire and prophesies, and who had failed me too; but instead because of Hugh, who had knelt with such gravity, who'd held his mouth open for the wafer in the old style, a waver of palms, a receiver of ashes, ready every Sunday morning with his eyes red and watery, bourbon on his breath—but off we would go and he didn't miss a word.

So years later I too went to church without fail and stood and knelt and sang and said the same words over and over (indeed resented when some eager-beaver young theologian got modern and mixed them around) and never thought about whether I believed them or not, because I understood, like Hugh, that there were things you had to cling to, that belief was a luxury, belief was beside the point.

LATER—YEARS LATER, when Divya was no longer wordless and severe, at least not usually—she said, "Charlie, are you going to stay at Abbott forever? Because you can leave, you know. There are other schools. Other jobs. Other *much* larger towns." I don't know what my face looked like, but I could guess because she said, at once, "I'm not try-ing to get rid of you."

"Oh, I know," I said, and it was true, I wasn't hurt; it was more that I couldn't comprehend what it would be to leave. I was like some primitive islander who had no idea there were other lands past the horizon. But I didn't much care.

"The thing is," I said, after a longish pause, "I still haven't finished the house," and Divya rolled her eyes and smiled. Because I would never finish the house. Because its surfaces and innards were vast, and even though they weren't infinite they might as well have been, because whenever something *was* done, something else that had been done broke. It was a joke between us, and we felt Win's ghost and his ghostly capable hands and his silent laughter, and though I knew a house was, in a way, like a life—that it was constantly changing and decaying, that despite all efforts to shore it up for good it eventually would have to be left in an unfinished state—I knew now was not the time.

Nine

Without any help from Hugh, except from beyond the grave, Nicky got into Harvard. Maybe he couldn't spell, but he was either president or captain of everything, and besides, he was born fluent in numbers; he saw patterns laid out as clear as maps, although couldn't explain any of it to me.

Whenever I went to visit him at school and we walked through the Yard, or went out for a meal, the parade of people greeting him would be endless. Once he was having a particularly hard time during finals, and I drove in to make sure he was eating. But despite his dishevelment—he was unshowered, hair matted, his teenaged three-day beard patchy and soft—or maybe because of it, one girl and then another just happened to stop by our table to say hello. A preppy girl, and then one with piercings and black eyeliner. A guy with black eyeliner. A rower. The blessèd, the cool, the meek. He and the guys exchanged complex handshakes. The girls all touched him—his shoulder, his arm, his filthy hair. As for the rest of us, we managed half a conversation, and then he said he had to go study. "Where do you hide?" I said.

He grinned. He was much more cheerful, I had to admit, than he had sounded on the phone. He'd turned punchy. "If I told you, I'd have to kill you," he said.

"Get some sleep," I said.

"Overrated."

He graduated summa in math. He was awarded a prestigious post-grad scholarship to England, but at the last minute he turned it down (and dumped a girlfriend of two months, who'd already bought her ticket to follow him). He said, "Math at this level is really just like conceptual art or something. It's beautiful. It just doesn't have any point."

"Beauty is its own point," I said. "Very few people can do what you do. See what you see."

"Okay," he said, and he went to Haiti.

He was supposed to be handling an NGO's computers but organization was loose, and he ended up teaching math to elementary-school kids, in a cinder-block school with no plumbing. He sent pictures of himself, very occasionally, tall and golden brown, his hair and seemingly his teeth bleached by the sun, surrounded by children, pressed around him as close as they could get.

He lived in a cold-water apartment with three roommates and many more roaches. (Rather gleefully, he also sent me pictures of those.) He seemed to feel elementally comfortable in privation. Maybe it seemed to him to offer the possibility of purity, of a straight and radiant path. Anita called and asked what we should do. "Nothing," I said.

You would not believe this place god the shittiness but it is gorgeous it is paradice and people live with both those thinges, he wrote. *there is way more bullshit sometimes litteraly (cows ha ha) but also less I don't know if they need me here althogh I am working my ass off I probably need it more.*

He continued to fall in love constantly. His letters were riddled with girls' names. *I see someone on a bus. I see the back of someones neck. Or their crossed legs sitting down when a bus is crowded and you cant see what belongs to who, just peices of a person and I see some girls calfs something clicks. Thats it.* There were Marie-Jacques and Toinette and Claudine, and Catherine, an American, and older women, other Americans cycling in and out of the country, whom he mentioned frequently without quite admitting anything.

There were guys too. *Its something to experience love is good right?* I wrote back immediately that yes that was fine but he damn well better be taking precautions, all around. *Im not stupidd jeez Charlie also on balance as they say I like women more so Calm down Charlie.*

He'd told me before that he promised nothing to a girl, or boy,

ever. *No point. Things here change to fast.* I restrained myself from telling him he'd grow out of it. I imagined him facing one person, then
another, with his clear, utterly honest eyes. *Thats it.* If he broke hearts,
it was through no fault of his own. He never mentioned drama.

I saw him once a year or so, when he came home to Atlanta, and I
made myself go there to see him. I watched him with his high-school
buddies, and when they talked about old times—drinking at Collier
Park, stealing the Big Boy and putting it on the roof of the gym, *Oh
holy shit remember? remember?*—he laughed as loudly as all the rest but I
could see that he *didn't* really remember, that he had no access to that
self anymore, and that their wistfulness baffled him. They were all in
real estate or banking or law, and that baffled him too.

When he was home, he couldn't talk about Haiti the way he could
in his letters. His vitality seemed to pale. When I'd take him to the
airport for his trip back, he'd be nearly quivering with excitement and
relief, holding it in for my benefit I supposed, not understanding that
I knew quite well he wasn't escaping, but returning.

He was resolute in not acknowledging the tension between Anita
and me. But an entirely tense country? A hand-to-mouth existence,
disease, poverty, death? *O Charlie,* he wrote, safely back in squalor. *I
am living I am living I am living.*

THEN 9/11 HAPPENED. Then the war in Afghanistan. It took him nearly
a year, but he got there. He started working for a relief organization in
Kabul and took trips outside the city, to visit schools, to give vaccines.
He didn't want to be in the capital but no other westerner was crazy
enough to live outside it if they weren't military, and he relented. I
thought he missed Haiti but when I asked him, during a rare phone
call, he said, "No, I was done there." But then he launched into a
tirade about Kabul's too-convenient plumbing, electricity, restaurants.
"People think it's so bad here. This is *civilization.*"

I was getting sick of his weird purity. "Well, for God's sake, are
you actually making any difference?"

"No," he said, and his voice was full of despair. "It's angry here.
Everyone's angry."

"It's a fucking war, Nicky."

"That's not it," he said. "I'm not close enough to it. Not close enough. I can't get to it."

"Close enough to *what*?"

But he couldn't, wouldn't, answer.

HE GOT SOME INTESTINAL PARASITE that made him drop thirty pounds that he didn't have to lose. I was surprised he even told Anita. He'd gotten so confused, so out of touch with the way normal people, *we,* reacted, that he thought her being a nurse would make telling her okay.

Instead, she called me. "I need information. I don't even know what he's taking. He says he's better, but he won't tell me what he weighs."

"He probably doesn't know."

"If he's going to a doctor he would know."

"He's not going to ask. If the doctor told him he wouldn't remember."

"All he has to do is—"

"Jesus, Mother," and I felt her cringe, because she was still a country girl and you still didn't take the Lord's name in vain, but I didn't care. "I can't make him do anything. I don't know why you're asking me. What are you asking me to do here? What power do you imagine I have?"

I ignored my own worry—no, fear—and the kinship she and I had because of it. Instead I thought how I could push her like this, now. I could be cruel and she would say nothing. I didn't do it much and I didn't like myself afterward, but it was almost a discipline, to make myself so blunt, unmerciful: it was my role now, it was my due.

AND THEN, ALL AT ONCE, it was over. He was traveling outside the city, in a small convoy, when the van ahead of them drove over an IED. His car went off the road and he lost consciousness, but just for a few minutes; that was all, that was it. But afterward he couldn't sleep. Woke up every night screaming, and finally they, whoever *they* were, convinced him he had to leave.

I went to Atlanta. He looked desiccated. He slept a lot, and in between Anita took him to doctors. He was drinking special milkshakes. She'd never been much of a cook, and she loathed waste, but now she was making food all the time, mounds of unseasoned chicken and white rice, throwing most of it away untouched. I felt superfluous—or worse; Anita said, "He doesn't want to collapse around you."

I didn't know what to say to that. "Do you think he *would* collapse? I mean—maybe he needs to."

"Of course he doesn't," she said.

We were in the living room. I don't know how we'd ended up in there. Maybe because it was the farthest from Nick's bedroom. Maybe also because that part of the house smelled the least of smoke. I could tell my mother had started smoking inside again. But the living room didn't even have an ashtray.

When Anita and I had moved into that house, Hugh's house, the baronial living room had been nearly empty, and twenty-five years later it was still underfurnished, a beige, corporate-looking sofa and two chairs lonely on the enormous Oriental rug. She had told me years before that she'd only stayed in the house so when Bobo and Big Hugh drove by they could know that she was still there, part of Hugh was still there, although she had no feeling for the house one way or the other. I found myself inspecting the carved limestone mantelpiece, the moldings and coffered ceilings with a new eye. I wished Win were there to compare notes with.

"They all had training," my mother said firmly. "He's going to be fine. He knew the risks, they knew all about it—IEDs, snipers, mines. They all knew what could happen. And he was already weak, because of the GI situation."

"Mother."

She didn't answer. She wanted to start talking in medical lingo. She knew I knew it. She went over and sat down on the window seat, limping a little. "You need to see someone about that leg," I said, but she ignored me.

She was still young, only sixty-one, and in certain lights looked younger, her features still fine, her auburn hair thick, her figure still voluptuous, impractical—her body had never fit her. But the direct sun coming through the bay window revealed that smoking had done its work, etching rough lines and graying her skin, which had once been milk white.

She was sometimes short of breath, and one leg tended to swell; her legs had always been elegant, but now she wore pants almost all the time. She'd shifted to a desk job at the hospital and would not admit it was because she couldn't be on her feet. Her aging enraged me. But we stayed out of each other's business. That was the pact. So only Nicky was left.

"He's not good," she said finally.

"No. He's not."

"There were children. In the van. That hit the mine. That blew up."

"There were?"

"I don't know why we let him go," she said. Behind her, through the leaded bay window, I saw the yard sloping up, behind the cracked and weedy tennis court, and daffodils dotting the ivy. It was mid-March. "I don't know how we did it. Nicky of all people. How could we—Charlie. Charlie." She was looking to the side, through the little diamond panes, not at me. "He picked them up. Bodies. Limbs. Pieces. He saw all of that. Nicky saw all of that."

He'd made a bet and lost. He'd been looking for a present so intense it would envelop him, and now he had a moment he could never leave.

A FEW DAYS LATER she said, "I want him there with you."

"With me?" There was a pause. "At Abbott?"

"Yes. Please."

Her voice was matter-of-fact. Anita did not do guilt or guile. It was a request, not a command.

"He can teach," she said. "He'll be good at it. He'll be happy there with you. You know he will." She didn't beg, or clasp her hands, but that was the closest I think my mother ever got to getting on her knees in front of me. I heard it, in her voice, some dire knowing.

For a moment, just for Nick, my mother and I were co-conspirators, as of old. We were planets, and he was the sun.

I thought for a moment of Divya, when I had held open my arms for her ghost ship of grief to engulf me instead, and how I had done it, and was stronger now.

I was thirty-eight. It was remarkable to contemplate. And my house had been empty and waiting for a long time.

Ten

The row of blond heads in the front pew, and at the end, one dark. She turns and looks at me pleading, and I stand and push past the knees and out of the pew and out the door and into the blinding white world. And vomit to the bile. And get in my car. And disappear.

In my mind sometimes I'm still there, moving, road gray and frozen ahead of me, I have never come back.

MAY AND I HAD SPOKEN only once more.

She'd gone back to Paris after that and written letters, and called and called, and one day finally I'd picked up and she'd said, "Is there someone else?" and since that was as good a reason as any I'd said yes, because I wouldn't sicken her the way I had been sickened; it wasn't truth that sickened, but knowledge—truth was there regardless, but did the tree's fruit exist if you did not eat of it?

She'd said, "You loved my father more than me. That's the real truth. You wanted to get close to *him*. And that is fucked up, Charlie." I'd said she was right. I hadn't sounded like anyone I knew, least of all myself, certainly not any self I had ever been with May. Maybe that was why she'd been crying, because I'd transformed, I had tricked her, legless belly in the dust.

She'd said she hated me and I'd said, good. Although the safest thing was not hate but the end of hate, passion replaced by cold neutrality. I wanted this mostly for her sake but for mine too, because I wanted so much to make a sacrifice in the name of atonement. To have her look at me, hear my voice, and feel nothing. And I would feel the punishment of that pain.

And I'd believed I'd heard it, then: the space, the moment where she'd decided, or realized; when she killed something, or gave it up, or watched it disintegrate. It was a before and after, with finality, and I'd almost said *Now you're grown up* but I didn't. But I had been glad that the thing was done.

And then she'd said that she was the one who was never coming back. Abbottsford was mine if I wanted it, she didn't care. I'd heard that ice in her voice, the absolutely genuine disinterest even beneath the tears. I hadn't thought I would get my wish so soon. And so that had been the last time we spoke.

I heard news of her, sometimes, inadvertently: she'd gone back to Paris, she was teaching in Dallas. Still, when I saw her, day after day— whenever I saw a tall girl, a dark-haired girl, a girl dipping her face shyly away, or hugging her books to her chest and hunching as she walked, regretting her height—my first thought was always *No.* Even before the excitement and then the disappointment and then the relief when the girl turned and was not May. Because she was supposed to be living a shining life, elsewhere. Because, elsewhere, she was glorious: I hadn't hurt her at all.

AUGUST. THE LONG ABEYANCE. Zenith of ordinary time.

Heat, and perfect stillness.

Nicky was ensconced in Abbottsford. He'd gained a few pounds. He'd thought Abbott was a good idea—a great idea. "I get it," he said. "Time to grow up. But I love it here anyway." He'd refused to live with me, though. "I'll crash with you all the time," he said. "But I need my own place. Besides, I don't think you want a roommate. You wouldn't like that much, Charlie," and after one open-mouthed moment I'd shouted with laughter and relief. "It's going to be all right," he said, laughing too.

Still he could drop by the house anytime, with his light and need; but today, he'd gone to Boston, to see friends. So I was off duty. Off, on—both new to me.

When Divya called I almost didn't answer, but then I did. (Either way, of course, would have changed nothing.) "Did you see the e-mail?" she said.

"What e-mail?"

There was a pause. Then, "Oh, Charlie. My dear." Her voice was a long sigh. "Your ramparts have been well and truly breached."

Eleven

There was a Labor Day tea. Because there would be a Labor Day tea for ever and ever amen. And Divya wore an orange salwar kameez, and her hair was complicated (as Ram would have said), and Anil was home from law school, tending bar, which was a long folding table in the corner of the garden. I asked for bourbon. "It's kind of swill, Charlie," he said, holding up the bottle.

"Do you think I really mind?"

He didn't answer, just gave me a look and poured, generously. He didn't know. Divya hadn't said anything. What would she have said?

Then Adam Salter—the very one, the young assistant dean, who was now the middle-aged headmaster—began his usual remarks. *So wonderful this special place true excellence the whole person the Abbott family.* He'd start his introductions in a minute, and I pivoted discreetly, scanning the crowd. Salter caught my eye: *Where is he?* And all I could do was shrug. Because my brother was not the issue, no, not at all. Then Salter's darting eyes stopped somewhere beyond me and he broke into a huge smile. "There he is! Excellent timing, Nick!"

"Thank you, sir."

I turned and there he was, looking sheepish, probably having just realized how fine he'd cut it. His khakis were a little rumpled. He had on an old seersucker blazer that I guessed, by its sacklike tailoring and slightly wide lapels, to have been scavenged from the remnants of

Hugh's closet. He'd remembered a tie. But he'd forgotten to change his tennis shoes, and I knew that if you looked, not all that closely, you'd be able to see his left big toe through the holes. He was as gaunt as a saint, and his red cheeks were clear and ardent as a boy's—as if he'd just come off some twilit playing field in the snapping air of autumn. As the weight of everyone's gazes sank onto him, one hand crept up and snaked through his flopping hair.

Then he smiled and all around me I felt the silent sigh, and I knew he was forgiven henceforth and forevermore.

"The newest member of our math department!" Adam said. "Via Haiti and Afghanistan! Boy, has he got some stories to tell. He's just gonna knock the kids' socks off. Oh, and by the way, it's all in the family, Nick here is the brother of our own Charlie Garrett—"

"Half brother," I said. I moved closer, reached up to clap Nick on the shoulder, allowing the inevitable inspection. "Obviously."

For a moment, gazing at Nick as though he were the last wild dodo, Adam looked supremely satisfied, as only Adam could, and only Adam could be forgiven for.

But that wasn't all. As I'd known he would, he'd saved the best for last. "Folks, folks!" he cried. "And finally! One of our beloved Abbott families. It just hasn't been the same without a Bankhead!" He ticked through all of them, even Florence, not mentioning the pot or the academic probation or the divorce, lauding instead the southern refinement and warmth, the lacrosse and wrestling and crew, the *esprit,* oh so dearly missed. Preston an institution. "A cultured and cultivated citizen. A patrician in the true sense of the word . . ."

And meanwhile there she was. There she stood.

Through the whole hagiography I waited for that slouch, the look that meant she wanted to disappear, but it never came. Salter wound down and then looked at her expectantly, waiting for an answering paean to school spirit, but May just raised her hand in a gracious little wave.

She was back, she was twenty-nine, and it was breaking my heart.

And then she was walking over to us, she was kissing Divya on the cheek and then me, and I didn't even feel it, and I must have introduced Nick because then she was saying to him, "I think I saw you already. So *that's* who you are."

She was wearing a suit. Pale yellow linen. Three-quarter sleeves, pearls, Jesus all she needed was the pillbox hat. "You look so cool, May," I said. "You always look so cool."

Behind me, Divya sighed.

I saw recognition in May's eyes, but she only smiled. "Thank you, Charlie."

That suit: it was buttery. I had to bite my tongue not to say it. *You look like butter.* Not just the yellow linen but it made her buttery, she herself, oh, I was a blithering idiot, she looked so *rich.* Her skin was creamy brown from summer, summer, the bare heels flicking down in Abbott Pond, the head sleek as a seal's, and I could not think these things, I had to find a way to not think them.

Her smile was china white; she was perfectly in control; her hair was shorter, cut to her shoulders, straight and shining, oh, the woods are lovely, dark and deep. As soon as was polite, sooner, really, if the truth be told, I extracted myself, set my empty glass on the nearest table, wove my way through all the seersucker and white, all the last rites of summer, and out under that arbor, beneath the last roses, beneath their falling petals.

THE TABLES WERE IN A U. The maple outside the window was still green. It was my seventeenth first day, but in a complete reversal from that young teacher standing terrified, years ago, this classroom was now my safety. This was the safest I would be all day. With May somewhere in the building, as she would be, from now on.

And so I began. "Well, look—at—all—of—you. Huh. *Who* is responsible for this?"

I walked slowly around the tables, feeling the wattage of my seniors' attention on my face. I had no doubt I looked engaged, mock stern, in control, because I could see myself, in fact I was nowhere near my body but floating elsewhere, pulling all my old moves out of the files, my old speeches; no need to reinvent the wheel. "Mr. Pentecost. Miss

van Slake. Mr. *Bolling*?" They started to grin. "Mm-hm. Mm-hm . . .
Miss Hirschfeld. And Mr. *Middle*ton."

I hardly ever called people by their last names anymore. Today it
was just for effect, and they knew me well enough—I was known,
here at Abbott, well enough—for them to realize. The habit had died
away gradually, as I began to use it more and more ironically, until it
lost its significance, its protection. Until the protection was no longer
needed. No more the great division. No more the professor on high.

Syllabus. Handed it out. Expectations For The Course. They listened with open, serious faces: there were colleges to be gotten into,
high, slick walls to be scaled against all odds. We all knew this. We all
knew too that actually I was on their side. Poor seniors. Poor fetuses,
still floating warm and safe. Teetering on the edge.

I turned and wrote on the board (oh the comfort), turned back. A
senior seminar (this one was the Observer and the Hero) was really
a bunch of my favorite books with a theme attached because, by
God, that's the point of a senior seminar. Well-known fact. I even
told them that, and they liked it, liked that I was honest with them,
giving them the skinny, letting them in on the code.

I tried to take them in. Because they deserved that, my dramas
aside. There were Abeje Chukwu, earnest all-rounder, and Darius
Flake, ramshackle charmer, and Candace van Slake, of the streak of
fuchsia hair, inveterate arguer, either side, didn't matter; there were
Daisy Coomeraswamy, determined nihilist, and Minnie Zheng, who
favored animal prints (today she wore zebra-patterned shoes of a
dizzying height), and Dexter Angus Pentecost, ginger-haired class
president, who wrote his full name on every paper, test, and quiz,
without fail, as well he should, as we all should, if our name were
Dexter Angus Pentecost.

(Over the course of seventeen years my classroom had become
diverse, even international. Challenging but better. More real—
maybe. Just last year I'd had the son of a Nigerian oil baron and the
daughter of a sheikh.)

Marina Hirschfeld, making sidelong glances at Dex. Will Bolling
and Victor Onyango, whom I'd had to separate in my class sophomore
year—let's see if they could control themselves now. Celia Paxton,

slight, Asian (adopted? Chinese girl baby, abandoned, now cherished?), long braid down her back, oval face like a young novice's; a sweetness to her, a breakability. Celia of the graceful duck walk: she was a dancer.

And Zack Middleton. I'd been looking forward to finally having him in my class. He towered over me now, fully Booker's height, his shoulders even broader. He was a running back on the football team. His essential reserve hadn't changed. Cassie and B.J. had both been easily confident, rarely awkward, dependably popular, but Zack seemed to fall into the interstices of the social system. He was most frequently seen alone—or with Celia Paxton. They'd been an item since the previous year, glued to each other, adoring, one of those couples occasionally scolded for PDA. Yes, Zack would be the loyal type; he'd find a girl, wouldn't let go. At this very moment Zack was draping his arm over the back of her chair, and I glanced at him, pointedly. He could damn well canoodle on his own time. He dropped the arm.

Celia's expression didn't change. She was private too—but she sometimes reminded me of May. There was a look I sometimes caught. Aimed at no one. A sudden, homeless glance.

But I could not think of May.

There was a little chitchat, who's read any of the books already, *what?* you didn't read them all for me over the summer?—ah, well. Zack was watching me with a seriousness that was almost hostile. Maybe he didn't want to exploit the connection. Good man. I'd missed him. I felt oddly shy around him, too. How had adolescence descended on him so heavily? His face was pitted from breakouts, his nose too big, his features not settled. Becoming. His springy light-brown hair was close-cropped now. His eyes were the same, though—pale green, heavy lashed.

"Mr. Garrett?"

I'd have to get used to the name. I wondered if he felt the same way. "Yes, Zack?"

He lolled back in his chair. "I did start reading *All the King's Men*. And there's *nigger*. On the first page."

I sighed. "I know it," I said. "I wish it weren't." I noticed that Darius Flake, who was president of the Diversity Forum, was rolling his eyes. "How much should we excuse? Because of the historical context? It's an active question. And the book is no *Huck Finn* either." Zack watched me with that flat gaze. "In *All the King's Men* there's no Jim, for better or worse. Very few black characters to speak of. None, really, except for one in an extended flashback, and I'm not sure she even speaks. Although she drives the plot, in a way . . . so what we can talk about, *when* we get to that book, is whether it's about race. Because somebody could say, hey, there are no black characters, so how could it be about race? But on the other hand, how could a book set in 1930s Louisiana *not* be about race?"

I was overanswering, shutting him down. I was watching myself do it.

"Some of you have had me before, and you know that I think it's all there. In the text. It's where you look. It's where you dig. Sometimes we want to put things there that aren't there. Sometimes we don't want to see what *is* there. Right? But here's the thing. Sometimes what isn't there, isn't there deliberately. It's an elision that has great meaning. Maybe the book is based on information we aren't given outright, but we have to find it, we have to deduce it by its absence. Sometimes it's what we *don't* know that is the *point*. That drives *everything*."

I had to stop.

"So when we get to the Penn Warren, we'll talk about that. Let's get out our first book though. Here we go. *The Good Soldier*." Shuffling and mumbling. Books appeared. "A great deal we're not told. At least not in the order we expect it. One of the most famous unreliable narrators in the English language. Along with Humbert Humbert. Heh. Some other year."

I had them read the first five pages, and then I gave them a micro-quiz, a gimme, on what they just read, to show what I was looking for. Or was it to fill the time? On the first day? I had to do right by them. I felt myself ache with it. Celia's foot was pressed alongside Zack's. I could see it perfectly well under the table. All the heads bowed over their papers.

There was no first-day freshness in my soul. It wasn't fair to them, not fair at all. Instead there was some sordid thing in me giddy with panic. Maybe all I could do was laugh. I felt it bubbling up. "Okay. Time's up. If anyone didn't get one hundred we've got a problem," I said. "Any questions? Zack."

"Is Mr. Satterthwaite really your brother? The new math teacher?"

I assumed a wry tolerance, copied from Divya. "Is this a question about the quiz? Or this *class*?"

"No sir. Just general knowledge, sir."

He was being very thorough with the *sir*s. As though determined to remind me of how long ago our closeness was. "Yes, he's my brother. Half brother."

"He's got a southern accent."

"Yes, I know. He's managed to retain the signs of his origins."

Minnie Zheng said, "I *like* his accent."

Daisy Coomeraswamy said, in either horror or agreement or both, I couldn't tell, "Oh my *God,* Minnie."

Zack said, "Where's *your* accent?"

"I used to have one. You were too little then to remember, Mr. Middleton." There. He looked away. "I guess I've lived up here with you heathens for too long. And besides. My brother was born with a great deal more charm." I had to tell them, somehow, that I knew the differences were glaring. Although I was disturbed to think I had any pride about that anymore. Here at my school. In my place.

Zack's expression, anyway, said that he gave not one flying fuck about charm. "Be nice to him, everyone," I said. "He's new." Just then, the door opened. A sudden, zinging snap of attention. "Speak of the devil," I said.

"Hi, everyone," Nick said.

"Bye, people. First three chapters tonight. Dig."

At the door, every girl giggled, then went silent as she brushed by Nicky. Even Celia glanced up, then quickly down. Zack was one of the last to leave. "Hey," I said, as he went by my desk. "A moment?" He stopped, huge, even forbidding, backpack slung over one shoulder. Celia hovered just outside the door. "Are we good?"

He shrugged. "Sure." But he didn't move. "You don't know what it's like to read that word," he said.

"No. You're right. I don't."

"It's like I'm *not there*."

"Let's talk about it," I said. "Okay?"

"We don't need to talk about it, Charlie. You just need to know."

He waited a moment, the hint of insolence still in his posture. Zackie long gone. Was he just tired of his status of being known, of long histories with adults who remembered him when he could crawl? "We'll have a good discussion," I said. "I'll do everything I can. And I'm always here. If you change your mind." He gave me a curt nod and turned, free to sling his arm around Celia again. The hardness in his face melted when he looked at her. He had it bad.

Out in the hall it was like joining a school of fish headed to a spawning ground. We were carried along down the stairs and into the first-floor hallway, where there was an obstruction, dividing the flow: and as quick as that, there she was, there was May, I had seen her, here at school, and it was done.

She was the one blocking the current, talking to Zack, with Celia still at his side, although they'd detached themselves for the moment. Zack was taller than May by a head; she looked up at him, delighted. There was an embarrassed half smile on his face, but he didn't look displeased. Celia was impassive. Then May reached out and gave him a half hug, one arm—all we were allowed, if that—and then let them go.

"Hi, May," Nick said. "Are you going to lunch?"

This was what would happen. Every day. There was no way around it. It must cease to amaze, it must become normal.

When we emerged from the building, Zack and Celia were a little ahead of us, relinked. Nick said, "They're in one of my calculus sections. That kid is huge."

"Football and hockey," I said.

"Nice kid?"

"I've known him since he was an infant. So has May." Nick waited. "He's a very good kid."

"Not nice?"

"Something's up with him. Gotten tough, lately. I guess."

"Oh, Charlie," May said. "He has a tender heart."

Oh Charlie.

"I used to babysit him," May said. "Remember?"

"Yes," I said.

"Well, charm is overrated," Nick said cheerfully.

We crossed the quad and headed down the hill to the cafeteria. Yesterday, at the tea, it had been properly golden and elegiac, roses fluttering in the slight breeze, but it had rained overnight and the tender, clear autumn air was gone. Now it was overcast and muggy, with that weird, shadowless, heavy light. Still, it felt like the first day. Energy and freshness spilling over. I wanted to ask May if she remembered this feeling—couldn't I ask her that? Well, another time.

I felt how stiffly she was holding herself, how steely her determination. She was damn well going to say *Remember, Charlie?* and make me behave too. She wasn't going to give an inch, she was becoming formidable. Maybe it was the Florence in her; but I didn't have to like it, although it would make things easier for both of us.

As we walked, Nick in the middle, I reflected that no one really remembered about May and me. It had been hush-hush, muted further by the speed of Preston's dying. And the students—bless these kids, as usual. They had no idea. I tried to forget May's proximity. Instead I tried to bask in Nick's reflected glow. Beside me, his face was open and happy; he was incapable of self-consciousness, maybe because he didn't notice attention anymore, maybe because it never ceased.

Candace van Slake glided by. "Hi, Mr. Satterthwaite," she breathed.

"Hi, Candace." Nick was good with names. He'd have everyone memorized already.

She blinked, dazzled. I glanced up at Nick, wondering if he would smile, and at the same moment May looked at him too, and May's and my gazes crossed and tangled; but Nick walked on oblivious, to us, to himself; and May and I saw it all.

Twelve

Mid-September. When the heat gentles and the light is thick gold.
The green of the leaves is darkening, still vital, and time hovers, folding up and back, memories thick on the sides of the road, not even
mine, not even Abbottsford's: the wistfulness is general over the world.

And I'll get confused, because the light is so pure and equalizing,
and think it is June instead of September; or that I am driving down a
road in the South, not the North; because the light holds all memory;
and maybe I am headed to that guesthouse in the trees, or even to
some town where I've never been—one of the unknown towns of my
faceless ancestors; and a little farther down the road, in that light, over
the hill, almost visible, almost here, is the home I have always looked
for, the white wooden house filled with voices.

I WAS WALKING down the hall during one of my free periods when
I heard a woman's musical voice, full of confidence and wit, even
though I didn't know what she was saying. It was like seeing someone
familiar in disguise.

The voice rose and fell, May's and yet not. It ascended in a tart
question, clearly rhetorical, because the class burst into laughter.

I edged to the open door, peered in at an acute angle. There were

Celia, Zack, Dex, looking up at her, engaged, alight. Zack was smiling, a hint of the old sweetness. Then Celia Paxton saw me, her attention flicking to me and back. I couldn't look in on May's straight slim
self, her grown-up clothes, her hair swinging as she moved, and I was
grateful. Instead I had no choice but to assume my usual preoccupied
gait, the one that was expected, and so I clasped my hands behind my
back and cast my eyes down, knowing I was unwatched as I continued
down the hall and disappeared.

I KNEW VERY LITTLE FRENCH. In high school, I studied German, in
order (I would say later) to read Rilke and Goethe, but really it had
only been a decision of useless nonconformity. Eventually I'd realized
my foolishness and in college switched to Latin, with an idea of add-
ing a major in classics, but it was far too late for that (I was already a
sophomore), I never even got to Greek, and I ended up, as I thought
to myself, with plain old English.

What I'd really wanted was an old-fashioned British public-school
education, minus the paddling. That breezy assumption of knowledge,
that unquestionable canon, already outdated by the time I desired it. It
was the sort of learning I'd assumed of, for instance, Preston, and once,
when he was still reliably lucid, I had said as much. "An American version, I mean," I said.

"I went to a very fine Episcopal school. I was a scholarship boy.
Then Sewanee. Scholarship. But I did major in classics. I had Greek
and Latin, and then, in seminary, Hebrew and German. I wonder how
you knew that."

"Just a guess."

"We're not so different, Charles," he'd said, and there it had been,
a chance to confide in him; but some different instinct, which had
surprised and puzzled me, had whispered, *Oh yes we are.*

I thought of this exchange after Preston died, when May had
gone back to France and was still writing to me, baffled, disbelieving,
and holding out a different canon, temptations that were not herself.
Would I come visit? "I promise to speak nothing but French the whole

time. I know you want to read Baudelaire and Mallarmé in the original. And Flaubert, and Proust, and Balzac, and simply *everyone* who matters!"

It was nothing close to her own voice, to what either of us knew. I'd wanted to tell her that I, too, could hardly believe I had the capacity to break someone's heart.

And now, every morning, there she was! Mended! I should have been used to her. I had been seeing her for years, all the tall girls, the dark-haired girls. With all the false Mays I conjured over the years I'd feel reflexive joy, then hope, then disgust, and finally the numb acceptance to which I'd trained myself—all those things quick, quick, a millisecond, a sequence hardened over time to a diamond I could toss over my shoulder, faster even than the realization that once again it wasn't May at all. But now, when I saw her, she was real and true, existing completely independently of my imaginings. Now I was supposed to let her become ordinary. Had to: that was my job.

THE DOOR WAS OPEN. I knocked on the frame. It was late afternoon, the stolen half hour when sports hadn't ended, conferences were over, dinner was still cooking, over in the big kitchen—still the day, but at a lull. But May was around, and we hadn't been alone in a room together, and this must be gotten over.

She was sitting at the desk. Her arms lay relaxed on the arms of the chair; her hands dangled down, graceful and still, a pen held loosely, papers spread before her.

She was wearing a different suit today. This one cornflower blue. Not the blue of her eyes. I wondered if Florence had taken her shopping. I wanted to make a joke about a Suit Store. Then I thought that maybe these were uniforms and she didn't believe in herself, that maybe she was playing a role—but she wasn't a new teacher, a young teacher, anymore. Another thing I couldn't get used to. It was just me who thought she was a little girl playing dress up. If I said that to her! What she would do! I almost laughed aloud.

No, this was who she was, she was in a young-Dallas-matron suit.

She'd been engaged there, to a banker she'd gone to school with. Divya, bless her, had been doing reconnaissance, until I told her to stop, that I didn't need a dossier.

So not married. Still a maid. *Oh Charlie how lovely to see you.* The jacket was draped over the back of the chair. Her blouse was white and pressed. Collar notched and flat. The pearls glowed on her neck and she was neat and clean as a blank envelope and it could have been 1942, or '52, or '62, and *who was she?*

She looked up and for a moment, before she wrapped the professionalism around her like a lab coat, her face was warm. "What's up?"

"I don't want to interrupt."

"You're not," she said. She didn't put down the pen.

I edged into the room. "I overheard one of your classes. You were speaking French."

"Yes." She smiled, and looked like she meant it. "The rumors are true."

Uninvited, I went all the way over to the window and looked out. Kids were dribbling onto the green; sports must have just ended. "This was Win's room, for a while."

"I remember." Her voice gentled. "You must miss him."

"I do," I said. And suddenly time was enormous.

"This all must be strange for you," she said.

She'd gotten up from the desk and come around to half sit against the front of it. Maybe to signal her openness, her willingness to listen, and also her mastery. She'd taken some seminar. I didn't want to look at her legs, which were crossed, and long and brown—yes, I could see that from my peripheral vision. Her sensible heels. *Jesus, May-May.* "Yes," I said. "A little strange."

She nodded like a doctor who was pretending to be solicitous but really was just thinking of her next patient; or lunch; or how your case was hopeless and uninteresting. But had she noticed that her Camelot jacket was hanging not on one of the ancient slat-backed oak chairs (I still sat in one in my room) but instead one of the snazzy new mesh-seated models? Had she noticed the whiteboard? (I fought to keep my blackboard, they'd sighed and let me.) Was she, in short, seeing all the tiny things that had changed since she was last here? Because I could see them as though they were outlined in fluorescent paint, but she seemed to feel not a whiff of strangeness.

I turned again to the window. Nicky was crossing the quad. Heads turned; quickly, he was besieged. "There's my brother."

"You must be so happy he's here."

"Absolutely."

"Aren't you?"

"Of course. I just said I was."

"You know, I saw him before school started," May said. "In the post office. Standing in line. I thought he was a PG. Isn't that funny?"

A postgraduate. "Nicky will always be young," I said. "He will never not be young."

"He looked familiar to me. It was so strange."

"You must have remembered pictures."

"You never showed me a picture." A veiled rebuke. Our time together had been short; I'd failed. "No, it was something—here." She swept a hand across her eyes. "That reminded me of you." I gave her a look of darkest skepticism, but she just smiled. "I was so relieved when I ended up meeting him. That I wasn't crazy."

Her smile was full of friendliness. We seemed to have jumped to some different category. "He asked about you," I said.

"Oh?"

"Right after you met. After the thing. The tea. He figured out that we . . . already knew each other. I said I was the bad guy," I said. "I made that clear."

"I was clear on that," she said.

I was supposed to look wryly amused. I gave it a go.

"I was surprised, though," May said. "When you introduced us."

"Why?"

"I could tell he'd never heard my name before."

I didn't answer.

Her eyes were steady on me. "If I had had a sister, I would have told her everything. Over and over."

"May-May—"

"No."

There was a long silence. I should leave now. "May. Why did you come back?"

"To your school?"

"It's not my school."

"No, Charlie, it's not." She sighed. "They offered me a job. And I didn't like Dallas."

A dangerous moment. Because there was a hint of humor in her voice, a hand reached out, because she knew I'd hate Dallas too. "All right," I said. Moment over.

"Do you believe me?"

She'd said she was never coming back and I had believed *that*. What I felt now was duped. I couldn't say this, of course. "Yes."

"Good." Of course I couldn't mention the ex-fiancé. "I came to the point where I needed to see the place that formed me," she said primly. My God. Her twenty-year-old self would be howling!

Finally I said, "You could have visited."

"I need to be here." Her expression was pleasant, and completely closed.

I glanced again out the window. On the quad, someone was trying to get Nick to play hacky sack. He probably would. "In a few weeks it'll be dark by now." I looked at my watch. "By five o'clock."

"Oh, Charlie." In her voice was a vast sisterly relief. "Don't be gloomy."

"I'm not. Right now is the golden time."

I seemed to be stuck at that window, watching that petri dish of character down below. All those kids believing they could make themselves from scratch. Didn't we all once believe that? "Charlie," she said, and I turn back to her. "You can consider the box checked."

It was a dismissal, and I was relieved she'd done it.

But when I left and crossed the quad myself—unaccosted—I did think I'd fulfilled a small duty. And that I'd been bested; and I was glad about that too. And glad also, I couldn't stop myself, that she remembered my essence, she still knew it, enough to detect whatever infinitesimal resemblance existed between Nicky and me.

Later I thought that's when I should have told her, straight off: that my half brother was bare as a green peeled stick. But I didn't think I had to tell her. Why would it matter? Why would she need to know Nicky? And besides, she'd known him when she saw him; she'd seen some essence. I thought she knew all she needed to know.

I KNEW THE DAY she was thinking of, the day she'd first seen him. When she'd known and not known him.

He and I had been unpacking boxes in the August heat in his new apartment. He didn't have an air conditioner; he said he didn't need one. He'd been bare chested, I could count his ribs—and then he puts on some T-shirt full of holes and saunters off, to buy stamps, because our mother liked letters, still letters, never mind that e-mail, but really he's falling in love with Abbottsford and wants to go be part of the citizenry, he wants to scatter his light as he walks, it is new and strange and quaint and what he loves best is a new place, a blank slate.

He walks the six blocks, stands in the longish lunchtime line. In the way of little towns, the Abbottsford PO is still much used. There is no air-conditioning there either. It's broken, and instead there is a tall old-fashioned fan roaring in the corner, and the big old leaded-glass awning windows propped ajar. He'd described it when he got back. Every detail was charming.

And I can imagine him there, and also May, standing a few people behind. She can't believe she's here. She's been in this room a thousand times. It is so real to her it has reversed itself, feels like a movie set. She both anticipates and dreads being recognized.

She is holding her hair off her neck in the heat—and then she sees a boy, ahead of her in line, thin as a stalk of wheat, dressed like a vagrant, but with a profile that cannot be true. Glamour is thick around him. She knows that when he turns the illusion will be shattered (isn't that always the way?) and his face will be too round or too long, ordinary after all; and then he gets to the front of the line and he speaks to the woman behind the counter, and the woman laughs, clearly dazzled, and Nick laughs, and then he turns his head slightly, reaching for his wallet, and she sees that it's not a trick of angle or light, that there's no imperfection, and she cannot believe that the boy can be, that he can exist, and that everyone else in the line is not staring too.

And then he reminds her of someone. But that fact is secondary. Is lost, until she remembers it, later, when she sees, as she's known she will, the man she thought she used to love; and then May-May, though she is just twenty-nine, just before she makes the connection between my brother, Nick, and me, is thinking, *How young I was, back then.*

AND IF I HAPPENED to spy on one of my brother's classes?

Worship.

I WAS HEADED to the parking lot one evening when the headmaster stopped me in my tracks. "Charlie!"

"Hi, Adam."

"I know I've said it before, but I am so glad you brought your brother to us. He is just terrific."

"Yes, he is."

"He's a Pied Piper! Kids trailing around behind him! Have you seen that?"

"Indeed I have."

Adam was actually rubbing his hands together in delight. "Brilliant guy. These kids are just hungry for the *real world*. You know, you and I are so contented here, right, Charlie, in our little mountain home, and we get the kids here in Happyville and teach them a few things and send them on their way and we forget that maybe once we thought we'd do the things Nick has done. And that maybe these kids want to do those things too. He makes them think of *possibilities*. They are just *riveted*."

I wanted to get home before sunset. Adam's feet were firmly planted, though, in preparation for conversation: I knew the signs. "Are you plotting escape, Adam?"

"Ha. Bethie would kill me. But maybe we should rotate in and out, huh, Charlie? Get out there, get some dirt under our fingernails?

Come back and share the story? What do you think?" He relaxed back into his pelvis, got comfy.

"We do that," I said. "They're called sabbaticals. But it sounds like getting blown up is going to become part of the requirement."

"No, no, of course not! Ha!" He stood up straight again. I could see Adam's headmaster brain clicking through actuarial tables, annual giving reports. "Blown up?"

"It's rough over there," I said.

"But Nick's fine."

"Of course. Obviously."

"Do you think Nick's glamorizing that side of things?"

"No."

"Well, of course he wouldn't."

I took pity on him. "He loves it here," I said. "Tells me all the time. I mean it. That's a fact."

Adam took a step back, suddenly deferential. "Well, Charlie. It's a good fit. Just like May! About time she came back home! Born teacher like her dad! Another good fit. Love it when we get a good fit."

"Yes," I said. "I wouldn't want him anywhere else."

NICK HAD INDEED ASKED ME about May on the evening of the tea. We'd been walking back to his apartment, where I'd left my car. "So?" he said.

"So what?"

"You never told me something had happened with a student, bro," he said.

"Nothing ever has."

"What about May Bankhead?"

"That was after she graduated," I said, automatically. "My God, Nicky, I wouldn't do that."

"Not ever?"

"*No.*"

"Seems kind of hard to avoid. Lotta options."

"You're joking, right?"

"Of course I'm joking," he said. "But, whenever it was. You never told me about her."

"So you could tell." He nodded, hyperalert. Usually when we talked about girls, they were his. "It didn't last long. A fling. Under sort of extreme circumstances. I ended it." I told him a little about Preston. The strange season of love and death. "A mistake, frankly. *In extremis.*"

"Have you kept in touch?"

"Not really."

"I think she's still mad at you."

"Doubt it."

"And you're sure—"

"Positive," I said. "Nothing there."

"Well, bro, I don't think I'd want her mad at me."

"I guess she's gotten a little frightening," I said.

"Is it weird?" Nicky said.

Our shoes scraped along the twee brick sidewalk. "No," I said. "It's not weird at all."

AS EVERYONE SETTLED into the year, Zack Middleton got surlier. I heard he nearly got into a fight in the locker room and was pulled off of Darius Flake just in time; he would have had to be benched, and he was the team's top scorer. I wondered if there was something going on—maybe steroids? He was so *huge.* I talked about it with Divya and then finally, after a good deal of hesitation, I went to Booker, because, after all, hadn't we known each other a long time by now, weren't we colleagues, peers, finally?

And no. There was no way, no possibility whatsoever. "He knows what I'd do if he was taking that crap," Booker said. "You think I'd let him do that?"

"No, of course not."

"My pop is the same as him. Huge man. It's in the genes."

But Booker did say Zack had gotten a pretty hard knock on the head that summer at football camp. They'd said it could affect his mood for a while. "But of course he's fine to play. You think I'd let him play otherwise?"

"No, of course not."

"He giving you any lip?"

"No—"

"Don't take any crap. I'll talk to him."

"He's not giving me crap."

"I'll talk to him anyway."

"I wish you wouldn't."

"Then what's the problem, Charlie?"

"He's not himself."

Booker's nostrils flared a little at me and I waited for the next challenge. Jesus, poor Zack. But then Booker stuck his hands in the pockets of the maintenance-green chinos he wore, rocked back on the heels of his work boots. "He's all worked up. That girl. College. You know how I know he's not taking anything? Because he's applied to the Air Force Academy, and he's not going to fuck it up."

"Oh," I said. "Wow. That's news. You must be very proud of him."

"Didn't get in yet," Booker said.

"Right. But to make the decision."

"Keep it under your hat." It was a command. "Let Zack bring it up. He'll be asking you for a recommendation any day. Should have already. Decided over the summer. He's got his letter from the congressman and everything."

"I'd love to write him a recommendation," I said. "I really would."

"He wants it bad and he's nervous."

"I understand."

"So maybe that's what you're seeing." He rocked back on his heels once more. It was a reminder to himself. He had trained himself not to loom over people. Zack did it too—the looming, not the rocking. "I appreciate you keeping an eye out, Charlie."

"That's what we're here for," I said.

"Yep. Boy wants it bad," Booker said, and his face relaxed, all at once, into a rare grin, a different person. "Boy wants to fly."

Thirteen

Late October, and we are hurtling down the brilliant slope: clear Friday morning today, and the light has sweetened and deepened and now, five o'clock, it is rich as honey, we are all rich, drunk on it. The grass glows bluely, I am standing at the edge of the quad, I should move, I should call out, I should answer—*Hi, Mr. G., whatcha doing, are you coming to the game tomorrow?*—but I am fixed in the cement shoes of being, I stand here, I cannot move, it is too beautiful.

The voice will come—*Mr. G.! Come sit with us!*—and I'll follow it and lower myself to the cool dampish grass and huff and arrange myself and they'll be amused with me; they'll want to impress and yet also feel an unthinking superiority; there is no way they'd choose my mysterious, dull adult life over their own, not now, not this afternoon. They are starring in their own epics, they are miserable or ecstatic or enthralled, and they sense I love them for it. That I will indulge them, that I have their backs, that I will protect their idyll while I can—

But today the voice didn't come. Instead I saw Nick, coming from the direction of the gym, Nick in an old green sweater I recognized, that made his eyes shine. His hair flopping and wet from the shower. Minnie bounced up from Dex's side where she had been and skipped, literally, over to him, and then Dex followed, and there was Celia, and more and more, and Nicky was the tallest, and he shook his hair from his eyes.

There he stood, happy, and alive, pulling them all in, their center. They thought he was their leader and guide, but I knew he was burying himself in their energy. And instead of seeing my brother they saw what they wanted to see, they saw their own dreams.

And there was May. A silk scarf draped around her blazer in her new style and I thought of her in Paris. Where I was not. She tucked her hair behind one ear and I missed again its length; it now stopped above her shoulders. Thick and straight, shining. She laughed. She was happy, there was no reason for her not to be. The circle opened for her.

And football must have just ended because here came that little army, burdened with their muscle, curving arms and thick necks. All a game, their bodies responding at a whisper, *grow!* Tomorrow they were playing Essex, here at home. They were puffed with prebattle importance.

And last was Zack. Who went to Celia and encircled her with his arm and they stood apart, just barely, and I saw how she held him up, that tiny girl. How much he believed he needed her. Zack who wanted to fly.

I must move, I must move.

And then, too late: *Mr. Garrett! Are you coming to dinner? Sorry, chickadees, headed home. It's taco night! Ah. Tempting. Are you coming to the game tomorrow? Wouldn't miss it.*

Wouldn't miss it.

Oh, the light slants away. *Son, we are in Ordinary Time,* Hugh would say. *Isn't it marvelous?* Nicky brushes his hair back and I raise a hand to him, only him. May watches me, unmoving.

At the bend in the walk I look back and they are all still there, my lovelies, my beauties, standing together.

BY THE NEXT DAY the weather had turned, one of those abrupt New England rotations with the power to erase all sensory memory of the day before. Now it was an entirely new world, gray, barely fifty degrees and felt like thirty, and we huddled in our anoraks in a raw drizzle. But Essex had driven fifty miles for this, and they wouldn't call the game unless it turned into a monsoon. Or if there was lightning. Because lightning was dangerous.

Next to me, barely visible under her down hood, Divya announced, "Everyone is invited to my house after. For toddies."

"How imperial of you," I said.

"There aren't that many forms of hot alcohol."

On my other side, Nicky watched the game with unusual attention. He was dressed semi-effectively, in an old bomber jacket, cracked and soft, with a balding sheepskin collar. But he was the only one of us who was hatless, and a sheen of droplets clung to his hair, like mist on a spiderweb. "You're getting soaked," May said to him, on his other side. "You'll catch cold."

He ran his hand through his hair, slicking it back, and then looked at his dripping hand with mild surprise. "Huh. It's not so bad."

"Charlie," May said.

Nick's wet head had been bothering me, but May noticing was worse. "Hey, Nicky."

"Yes, Charlie."

"Put on a hat."

"Will do," he said, his gaze back on the field. May humphed, but this exchange seemed to please her. She herself was nicely bundled: neat belted jacket, scarf and hood, fuzzy green gloves. Years away in the lazy Texas heat had not made her less practical.

May knew I'd first seen her by a misty field. The one next to us now. I could have turned my head and seen the spot. That *mist* would now have a fucking *connotation*. Mist, by God! I hoped she'd forgotten. When we were first together, there had been that exhilarating period of confession, *The first time I knew, I felt it when, I knew I knew you.* All that talk that says *Fate, fate, synchronicity!* And it seems one is the very instrument of God. Ha!

But I was better today. Better than yesterday, that is. The clouds helped.

"Did you see there are recruiters here? Looking at Zack?" May said.

"Isn't it a little late for that?" I said.

"I guess not if you're not getting money. Maybe *recruiter* is the wrong word. But look, down there. With Booker."

I was beginning to think the Air Force Academy application was a myth, but I held my tongue.

People went for coffee; others joined us; we rearranged ourselves, huddling for warmth. Around us the students were rowdy, oblivious to the cold. I saw Celia near the front, in a clutch of girls. We scored—Zack scored—and then in short order Scooter Lewis, the quarterback, was at the thirty again and was nearly sacked, but his arm with the ball flashed up just in time; and Zack was there, suddenly arcing away separate, the ball too an arcing missile, then caught two-handed somewhere in the air and for a moment cradled to his chest like his heart had flown away and returned, and then it was crooked in one arm, small and safe, and a path created itself in front of him and we scored again.

I remembered Nicky doing exactly the same thing—what seemed like the same thing—when he was very small, three or four. Hugh had thrown a ball, a tennis ball I think, and I was about to say *I usually throw the big red rubber one to him* but then Nicky's arm went out and the ball flew straight into his hand, like it was flying home.

In the end zone, Zack never celebrated. He'd shoot across the line and then stop, his body suddenly loose and unconcerned, his head down. He looked like a sprinter who'd been practicing starts, the same absorbed nonchalance, like the race hadn't even begun. *That one didn't count.* And as everyone cheered around us I thought of little Zack in the driveway of our old house, practicing baskets, and how I'd lower the goal for him, and he'd enjoy the sudden ease but for only a little while. I remembered his face, his soft furrowed brow as he'd aimed, again and again.

Huddle, then it broke; a businesslike crouch, zigzag pushoff, and he was lost in the scrum. The whistle bleated for some offense I didn't understand and even that sounded sodden.

I heard Nick say, "So why *did* you come back?"

I stood up. "I'm getting coffee," I said. "Anyone?"

"I'll wait for the toddies," Cletus Maxwell, the chaplain, said. I squeezed past knees and out of the row and was halfway to the stairs when I heard, "Charlie." I pretended at first not to hear. Was there a name for mingled annoyance and pleasure? Probably some useful Yiddish word. But when May called again, I turned around and waited for her.

The little green concession stand was at the far end of the field, near the long-jump pit. We walked for a minute or two in silence. The low gray sky made the world small. I didn't feel the need to make her comfortable, or I shouldn't. Finally she said, "You should have seen them all over him yesterday."

I said, patiently, "I'm not sure what you mean."

"Nick. At dinner. With all the kids. Girls, but the boys too."

"I've seen it."

"But he's very graceful about it. It's not like he's holding court. He is just purely *engaged*."

They were out of coffee so I got hot chocolate. It was like drinking chocolate-flavored soapsuds. May bought a bottle of water. We had to smile at Amy Maxwell, Cletus's wife, running the concession, and say how lucky she was to have a roof over her head. May's dimple flashed. I stepped away the first moment it was decent, and waited.

"What's the deal?" I said, when May rejoined me. "Is something about Nick worrying you?"

"Not at all. He's just really good with them. I wanted you to know."

"I've heard."

She was having trouble unscrewing the cap with her gloved hands. I took the bottle, opened it, and handed it back. She accepted it silently and then said, "Why's he here?"

"He needed a place a little calmer than Afghanistan."

"When did he—"

I stopped. "May, look, you can ask him. I'm not his manager."

"Of course not." Her face closed.

I started toward the stands again. "Ask him anything. I don't mind."

"Oh. Well, *thank* you."

"I didn't mean it that way," I said. "What I meant was, he can tell you his own story."

We passed a trash barrel and I threw in the half-drunk hot chocolate. The wind was picking up. Jesus Christ it was cold. I couldn't even remember why I'd felt the need to come to this game, Zack wouldn't have cared, no one would have, woe was me. I wanted to be at home, in my house, in front of my fireplace, maybe barricade myself for the winter, not emerge till the world was washed clean in the melting snow. And I thought maybe I could tell May; maybe she'd come with me; we'd be two little souls lost in the wood, brother and sister who couldn't find the breadcrumb trail out. I thought about this and for a moment it was like I was dreaming on my feet it seemed so utterly possible.

"Charlie, stop it," May said sharply. "You can't look at me that way."

"Like what?"

"Like I'm dead. Or a figment of your imagination."

"Well, you most certainly aren't," I said.

Cheers rose up again and May said, "I'm glad for Zack. He's really good. I didn't expect that. How good he is. I wonder why he wasn't already recruited."

"May, you don't have to make conversation."

I could almost pretend my annoyance was genuine. Because it was exhausting, holding myself away.

She put her head down against the wind, walked ahead of me, did not look back.

I nearly turned around and walked to my car but *I had to not care* so I went back to the cold metal bleachers and sat down on Nick's other side again and cheered and joshed and told Divya that the thought of toddies was the only thing keeping me upright. And there was May, ignoring me, good, with her straight shoulders and her surprising, carrying yell (*Brothers*, I heard her say to Nicky, *had to hold my own*) and if I glanced to my left and caught them both in profile—my God look at them, look at them. He was light, she dark, and oh their matched fineness. Divya saw me looking and I shrugged: Didn't she see it too? Fact? The two of them, the tall beauty of them together, a fact?

It had begun to rain for real but they wouldn't call the game, not now. We hunched into our hoods. Nicky was getting soaked, wouldn't listen to protests. People began to file down off the bleachers to the sidelines, not because they were leaving but because they were putting up umbrellas and didn't want to block the view. We were a polite bunch. A considerate bunch. The sidelines filled, and this reflexive kindness and the colors of the open umbrellas lifted my spirits sud-

denly and strangely. Something was going to happen. Maybe all would
be well, and all manner of thing—

It was a rout. We were twenty-one points ahead. There was a rush on
the field—it was a third down—and grunts and the thudding of bodies,
and the band oompahed away, and in the middle of it the whistle. For
a few seconds the air was still loose and happy and then it changed and
thickened, the players hanging back. "Someone's down," Cletus said.
He was an alum, one of my first students, Cletus was. Dogged. Oddly
calm, even as a teenager. I wasn't at all surprised he became a priest.

The pause tipped. Some muffled mystery came over the loud-
speaker. Then I saw Booker moving onto the field, through air slanted
with rain, Booker and his eternal blue cap, and he was walking purposefully but fast and then he gave up and broke into a jog. May stood
up. "I'm sure he's fine," I said. She seemed not to hear me. Celia hung
over the barrier at the front of the stands, her friends already petting
her, solicitous.

Then Nick was moving. "Nicky, wait," I said.

"Charlie," May said behind me.

"Nicky. Wait."

He didn't turn around. He pushed his way through, down the
stands, and I followed him. Once I felt May's hand on my coat behind
me. *Is he moving? Is he moving?* The stillness of the crowd eerie in the
rain. Then something else on the field, beyond the knot of people
around Zack, where the two teams had been slowly edging in, slowly
mixing—and there was a swaying contraction, a darting dispersal,
and then all at once they were on each other.

There was a collective gasp and seemingly on its strength we
lurched forward. "He moved. Zack's moving," I said. But no one was
listening. Everyone was watching the scrambling knots of bodies now.
Players were throwing off their helmets and rushing in.

Then right in front of me Nick found a space in the crowd at the
rail—seemed to conjure it—and then he was leaping sideways over
the bar, up and over with that ridiculous grace, and he was running
across the eight lanes of track to the field. "Charlie!" May cried. She
grabbed my arm.

And I turned to her, right into her face, her eyes, and shouted, *"I cannot do anything about him!"* Then I yanked my arm away, squeezed under the railing, and dropped to the ground.

Nick had shouldered his way in and was peeling Abbott guys away, pulling them close, whispering as if passing a signal, or a spell, his arm briefly around each neck, and then he'd push them down the line, and it was up to someone else to herd them and that was me, and Cletus, who was suddenly beside me, because everyone else was still with Zack.

All those years of hyped-up bad blood with Essex, the rain and mud and merciless scoring, kids needed some drama, fucking testosterone, and then I saw an enormous Essex kid land a blow on Nick's face—and Nick was exploding, and I was running, swearing, the kid under him, Nick's arm a piston up down up down.

"Goddammit, Nicky, Nicky, it's me, Nicky stop, it's me, it's Charlie, Charlie." I had his arms. He was so thin. I looked around, wild, and met Cletus's eyes, and then I sensed them, Abbott boys circling us like a fence, and together Cletus and I held Nick and tried to pretend that wasn't what we were doing and those boys stood around us, sentries looking out, streaked with mud and rain and their heads small and lost coming up out of the shoulder pads, their eyes solemn, and I said, "Shh, Nicky, Nicky Niccolo, shh, it's me, you're with me, you're at home, shh," until he finally stilled and whispered, "Sorry. Sorry. I'm sorry."

In the middle of it all, they were lifting Zack onto the backboard. I saw him move arms, legs, in fact I saw other hands pressing him down, gentling him too. I was unaccountably furious with him, lying there in a neck brace, covered with mud and soaked with sweat and rain. There was blood too on the shearling collar of Nicky's jacket but nevertheless I wanted to knock both their heads together, once more, a blinding, ringing blow; I wanted to save them both.

Fourteen

By Monday Nicky's eye was still magnificently black and only partly open.

He'd insisted on coming to school. Sunday night, at his apartment, I'd said, "You're going to make everyone cringe."

"Is it really that bad?"

"*Yes* it's that bad. Jesus. And it'll be worse tomorrow." I winced, only partly for effect. And yet I kept wanting to touch it, whether to confirm its existence or to magically smooth it away, I didn't know. I felt my fingers tingling toward his face, like the old hypnosis trick where your arm rises of its own accord. "It just—it's like a car wreck," I said. "You want to look away, but you can't."

"Well, great." This was the first argument that seemed to give him pause, but after a moment he said, "I just don't want them to have to get a sub. I'm fine."

"We know you're a hero, Nicky. We get it."

"I am not a fucking hero. That is not the fucking *point!*"

"I'm kidding," I said. "I know."

"*I* am not the point!"

"I know, Nick, I know. Look." And I waited until he looked. "Does that happen often?"

His green eyes were bleak. "Every now and then," he said. "If someone comes from behind. I thought it was better."

"You should have told me," I said. "You don't know how lucky you are."

But at school, sure enough, the waters parted before him; whispers and murmurs billowed behind. Fist bumps, high fives. He was abashed. "I'm fine," he said, "I didn't do anything," over and over, batting at the air in front of him as though he were beset by flies. Several players from the fight had been benched for the next game, and the general feeling seemed to be that they were the unlucky ones Mr. Satterthwaite hadn't stopped in time.

He often sat with students at lunch, but that day he beat a retreat to the teachers' table and sat with Divya and me. "Oh, Nicky, Nicky, Nicky," Divya purred, and I watched her hand rising.

"It's nothing. It's fine," he said, and waved away at the flies.

The dining hall, the most modern building on campus, held its usual brightness, from the clerestory windows high in the roof ridge. It was a boon on a day like this, gray and wet with the last of the storm that had finally moved in for real on Sunday, blowing branches bare, plastering the leaves to the brick paths on the quad. The light was flat, full spectrum, honest. It shone without mercy or comment on Nick's eye. I could see the shadings of color, from blue black to the healing greenish yellow at the edges.

Behind Nick, Adam Salter was approaching. He raised his hand to clap Nick on the shoulder and I barked, "Don't!"

Nicky's eyes widened, fastened on me for dear life, and Salter's hand stopped in midair. "Not from behind," I said, and sat down again. "He's a little jumpy. You can imagine."

Salter's eyebrows knitted slightly and then the look was gone. "All hail the conquering hero," he said, pulling a chair catty-corner from the table to face Nick and sitting on it backward. "You saved their asses, Nick. We'd have had to suspend the whole team."

"S'what I figured," Nick said.

"What I want to know," May said, "is what you *said* to them."

"I don't really remember."

"Well, it worked!" Salter said. He reached across to Nick and completed the proprietary gesture he couldn't be dissuaded from making, patting him hard on the shoulder, *attaboy attaboy,* but in Nick's full view this time. "Natural leader," he said. "Leader among men. Hey, so Zack Middleton is out for a couple of weeks. You heard that."

"Yes." I'd been aware all morning of Zack's absence. There was a strange lightness to the student body—all, of course, in my mind. We were starting *All the King's Men* this week, and he was going to miss it.

"Just waiting for the dizziness to go away. He's champing at the bit. Angela's making him stay home."

"I should hope," May said.

"He's got to think about hockey season now. Probably done with football for the year. Wants to save up. But he's fine. Had all the tests." He looked at his watch. "Got a conference call," he said. And he was off, navy blazer flapping in the breeze.

"Zack's only playing football in the first place because of his dad," Nick said.

Another pause, more complex. We all wanted to like Booker. "Who told you that?" I said.

"He did."

"He did?" May said.

"I wrote him a recommendation for the air force."

"The academy," I said.

"Right, whatever. I made him talk to me a little, so I had something to go on. He said football's like a job to him, but skating's like flying."

"He always loved to skate," May said. "I remember him on Abbott Pond, pushing around a milk crate. When he was, like, two. Trying to keep up with B.J."

"He asked you to write him a recommendation?" I said.

"Senior math teacher, it's required or something. But I also tried to talk him out of it," Nick said. "I told him there was a war going on. I told him the military is only gonna think of him as a body. Meat. Fodder."

"Oh, God, Nicky." I wasn't even surprised. I was glad that Salter had gone. "What did he say?"

"Not much. He wasn't going to listen."

"You're not going to sabotage him, are you? To save his soul?" May demanded.

Nick looked surprised. "No, of course not. I told him I'd write the rec. I wasn't lying." He grinned at her. "But that's an idea."

"I mean it," May said. "Don't do it."

"I mean it too," Nick said. "I won't. It matters to him," he said patiently, "so I won't." He looked at her, a little wide-eyed, for another moment and then his gaze shifted to me. "Besides, by the time he's done there the war'll be over, right?"

I shrugged. "They'll think up another one." Nearby I saw Celia Paxton get up from a table, with a phalanx of friends—Minnie, India, Marina. She was laughing, laughing so hard that her mouth was stretched wide. I'd never seen her so raucous. The four of them were collapsing on one another, bent double with their hilarity, and the whole cafeteria could hear them, but for the moment they seemed not to care, these girls who were pretty and smart but not at the top of the social order, not used to attention, to doing exactly as they pleased. Somehow in this moment, though, they felt an unusual freedom. They picked up their trays and sauntered off, tossing their hair.

I thought about how just a few days before I'd seen Zack steer Celia down the hall by the elbow, like they were long married and old, old.

"Well," May said, laying her fork and knife neatly across her cleared plate, standing to leave. Divya rose too. "I suppose he can have visitors. I'll go by and see him later. Maybe speak to Booker."

"He's like your little brother," Nick said. "You really care about him."

May smiled. "I guess you're right. He was always my favorite. I used to rock him to sleep. But don't tell him I said that."

The limpid gray noon streamed down, the clearest light, casting no shadows; it shone on Nick's cheeks, raggedy-edged rose, on the red-gold hair flopping in his eyes. He had no idea he was being watched; he was watching the girl.

When May and Divya were gone, I stretched my legs under the table. Nick and I both had frees now. It had become our new habit, on Mondays, to linger here. As he drank the rest of the coffee I said, "So. May."

He put the cup down. It looked small in his long hand. "She's a tough one," he said.

"She likes the straight and narrow," I said. "That's new."

The cafeteria was emptying. But inside was warm and bright.

"You know that whatever was between May and me could not be more over," I said. "That is God's truth." He played with the food in front of him that he hadn't eaten. Which was most of it. He hollowed out a roll and balled the soft part up between his palms, examining it with an empirical seriousness, then dropped it on his plate. "What is it?" I said, patiently. "Tell me. Fingers? Earlobes?"

He smiled at me like I was crazy, like he was merely tolerating me, but didn't meet my gaze. "Whole package. Not that it matters."

"But I thought it didn't work that way."

There was a long silence while he grinned to himself, and finally he said, "Eyes."

"Ah."

"They're blue. I just realized that today. Just now. The way the light shone in." I nodded helpfully. Father confessor. "They're so dark— I've never seen that color. I didn't realize." He was filled with wonder, at May's eyes, at the shift that had happened, in him, again.

AFTER LUNCH. After that free. Last class of the day. "Okay, people. Time for an indulgence. I'm going to indulge myself. I've been waiting for this one." They didn't know it, but I said this every year. Every year, when we had finished *Gatsby,* I read the last page aloud.

Also, every year, I wept. I hadn't realized the words moved me so much until one year I just teared up, right at *And one fine morning—* After that, I was Pavlov's dog. I almost looked forward to it. Crying once a year is probably necessary. Not that it was full-on sobbing, not at all. More a welling up. But it was involuntary, almost external, like being rained on, a nourishment, and it made me glad that I could feel that deeply, or had once.

So I read the closing passage.

He had come a long way to this blue lawn. I read along, anticipating the *tick,* the turn, the switch flipping as it always did—it was outside feeling now: my eyes would suddenly heat, and there we'd be. *His capacity for wonder.* The collective embarrassment would be thick; they'd be thinking, *Is he really crying over a* book? But I figured my annual display was good for them. If not your English teacher weeping over literature, then who?

And I always wondered: why did no one ever point out that Fitzgerald wanted it both ways? Which eventually I would do. Show them the time circling. The dream behind him, the future receding in front—which was it? Both? *The orgastic future*—ah, Nick Carraway, ah, Scott, he felt and felt. And the tears would come.

But then, that day, I came to the end. The boats were beating against the current: I held the class in my hand, one more moment; *borne back ceaselessly into the past.* And my eyes were dry.

I paused, and of course they thought I was being dramatic. Their eyes on me—Candace's, Dex's, Celia's. But really I was waiting. Just waiting. Nothing happened. The streak was broken. And that was that.

AFTER PRESTON DIED, and after May left, I began to have a dream. I'd dream of an ordinary day, and how I was waiting for her, my student. The reality of the present crept in and wound into the past, and time lost all its markers, and I dreamed that I had loved her when she had been a child, that I had seen her in mist and she had looked up and known me, that we had been infants in the same crib. In the dream she was so familiar she was faceless. I knew exactly when she would walk into my classroom and sit down, exactly when she would walk into lunch, and she would float over to me in this dreamworld Abbott and we would take each other into ourselves.

The dream was day after day after day all twined into one. I waited, and then she was there. Over and over, disappearing, appearing, dream, forgetting, remembering. *Is it true? Is it true?* and it always was. As I woke, though, transgression would begin to pollute the softness; I would start to scream my innocence, but either I was voiceless or no one listened, and when I woke the warmth and the dream and May were always gone.

I WENT TO HER CLASSROOM. Again I leaned against the doorway, just inside. No, I wouldn't go farther. Probably ever. "Hi, Charlie," she said.

"I only have a minute," I said.

She cocked an eyebrow. For some reason she sensed a joke. And she wasn't wrong, really. "What's up?" She smiled. The joke was going to be good. She'd chosen to forget our tension at the game. She took a sip of coffee, as if to fortify herself.

But I had frozen. She didn't seem surprised. She suffered me the way you'd suffer a child. Tolerantly, she began to chat: She'd been to visit Zack. Out for another week. It was driving him crazy—said he felt fine. Funny how he'd opened up to Nick, wasn't it? Before Nick ruined it with his hippie talk—and she smiled.

I cleared my throat. "Well, that's why I'm here. In a way."

"What is?" she said.

She had leaned out over the labyrinth and laughed. Her face and body had been so clean, unmarked—better than innocent. Instead waiting and confident. Like Nick, like Nicky should be.

"Charlie?"

I said, "You need to understand."

"Understand what?"

"My brother is twenty-six."

"Yes," she said politely.

"And he's a better man than I will ever, ever be."

"Oh, now. Charlie." She smiled a faux-wise smile. Her back was stiffening.

"I'm not just talking about his recent heroics," I said. "He always has been."

"Oh, please—"

"Since he was a child. Since the moment of his birth."

She put down her coffee. I saw her shoulders tense, her fingers stiffen on the lip of the mug. But oh, I wanted her to be laughing! Howling! I wanted to pick her up and rattle some joy loose! "Why are you saying this?" she said.

"Because it's something I want you to think about."

"About how Nick is better."

I thought of Nick glowing. "Yes. I'm irrelevant."

"That's one word for it." Then her control cracked. "Oh my *God,* Charlie. Spare me the narcissism of your self-loathing."

"That's pretty good," I said. "Have you been saving it?"

"It's completely accurate."

I shook my head. "No. You've got it wrong."

"I know what you're doing. This is absurd."

"It's not."

"Charlie, *I didn't come back here because of you.*"

"I believe you."

"I know you wanted my father, and not me. That was pretty clear. Weird, but clear. To me. Eventually."

And I didn't protest because it fit, fit perfectly, so I'd deny it at my peril, or hers. Instead I said, "I told Nick it was all right."

"I don't need your fucking blessing!"

She realized what she'd said.

"I just don't want you to think he's underhanded," I said. "That's all. He's the finest man I know."

The anger in her eyes was white-hot. "I don't need some kind of consolation prize, either."

"I know you don't!" I snapped. Nicky as consolation? I could be angry too.

There was a long pause. On her face, feelings fought to surface, were quelled, mitigated, transformed. It was like looking out the window of a speeding car: the scenery was almost homogeneous in the blur, details were impossible to discern, and yet the progression, the fact of it if not the substance, was unmistakable. You began on the mountain, ended in the cool green valley. She fought the journey, fought this destination I'd suggested. I knew though that if the idea had not also been her own, she never would have moved an inch. Would not have arrived where she did, which was considering it. Considering Nick. In spite of herself.

I was seeing Preston in her now, too. A haughty, highly defended frailty. Maybe I'd exacerbated that quality in her—although I didn't want to claim that kind of influence. Maybe it had always been there. Maybe I sometimes looked the same, had that same set of shoulder. Who can see essences? Who can see himself?

"You should see him when he talks about you," I said.

She was silent for a long time. Her face had finally gone completely still, the current of thought now deep, deep. Oh, I wanted inside her mind. All the doors opening and shutting. The maze she was in. I was sorry, I was sorry. But Nicky—beautiful Nicky! Here he is!

Finally she said, "Is that all?"

"That's all." When I left, I closed the door behind me.

AT THE OLD, unlovely Atlanta stadium, years ago. Nicky is five. It's the summer before I go to college, the summer after Hugh has died. I'm leading him down to our seats, ten rows above home plate. In those days, you had your pick.

There are many stories I could tell to explain myself. This is only one.

I say that Hugh brought me here, and then feel an irrational fear that Nicky will envy me this knowledge of his father—irrational because for one thing, Nick's too young to make that kind of connection, and for another I already believe that the capacity for envy is not part of his nature.

I tell him everything I know about baseball, which is not much. But Nick looks at me like I'm a genius. I say, "Your daddy knew a lot more than I do."

He gives me a serious nod, because what greater truth could be spoken, and then turns to the game. His stare is straight ahead. His feet don't touch the ground. "Hey, you want a Co-Cola?" I say, like Hugh, old Atlantan with his few, gentle affectations. "I'll get us a couple of Co-Colas."

I also buy peanuts, hot and dusty. I show Nick how to shell them. He barely believes me when I say we can drop the shells right at our feet. A few minutes later I buy hot dogs. He holds the food stiffly in each hand. "Are you hungry, Nicky?"

"Okay, Charlie," he says, answering a different question altogether.

Every time a hawker goes by, I raise my hand. Nicky watches me without surprise: grown-ups (and to him I am a grown-up) do this around him. I buy Cracker Jack, and a hat, and a souvenir pennant. A deluxe commemorative program. Cotton candy. I scan the crowd for anyone selling anything and pay attention to the game only if I hear the crack of a hit. I will leave no junk unbought.

Anita watched us leave earlier this evening. She'd stood in the doorway as we went down the front walk to my car, me holding Nicky's hand, and I'd felt that with every step I was shouting *Don't worry, don't worry:* not about this particular night, or my driving, or muggers, or that Nicky might get beaned with a fly ball or anything as mundane as that, because my mother was not a worrier—no, it was that Anita, and we, were on a ship, an ocean liner, enormous but empty, devoid of crew, a situation we'd grown accustomed to, and now Nicky and I were rowing away in a leaky dinghy. Maybe we were seeking provisions; maybe this was a practice run; or maybe this was what we would have to do, now or someday, to rescue ourselves. And my mother didn't care about being left, or being alone or even wasting away, once the hardtack and water were gone; she just wanted to know that I would never abandon that tiny vessel, tonight, ever.

She watches us drive away and it is July in Atlanta and the humidity is thick and sweet and the green grass damp and the trees not yet tired and dusty looking, and the light long.

I love my mother and she loves me, but the feeling between us is quiet, and more and more Nicky has become the conduit between us—Nicky the young and open, the mascot of us all.

At the stadium, there is a home run. The men, miniature even from these seats, run their geometry on the floodlit green. I can scarcely believe this is my life, Nicky beside me my brother: How did we get here? How were we given each other?

When I buy a mini bat, glossy and light, and perch it on the top of the pile in Nick's lap, it slides off, but I catch it before it reaches the ground. "Sorry, buddy," I say, and place it again, more securely, a tiny weapon against the world, Nick watching me all the while, the look on his softly rounded face one of infinite patience.

SEVERAL DAYS LATER, late in the afternoon when classes were over, I saw Nick walking toward May's classroom. His face was pale and filled with concentration and a faint exaltation, as though he were processing to the gallows. Dear God, he was doing it. He didn't see me at first and, suddenly panicked, I looked around for an empty room to duck into, but I wasn't quick enough and he saw me and his face filled with light, it *glowed* at me. For one dicey moment, I thought he was going to give a thumbs-up.

But I gathered myself and looked back with an expression that was patient, encouraging, and the faintest bit stern, since that was what he always seemed to want. He gave a nod and then stepped to the closed door. His chest rose with a cleansing breath, and that was when I turned away, but as I walked in the other direction I could hear his gentle knock, and May's muffled voice.

I went straight back up to my own room, my errand to the copier abandoned, and closed the door. I couldn't decide if I felt like a wounded animal in its den or an expectant father in the waiting room, wreathed in cigarette smoke. Nicky would be standing there, unaware, as usual, of his assets. Was that true? Raking the hair out of his eyes. And maybe May had not yet decided. Maybe she too felt cornered, maybe she'd be as cool with him as she was with me—oh, I could see her, on the road to becoming forbidding, to being the sort of teacher students both feared and secretly pitied—oh, May-May.

Nicky would be looking reflexively at the clock above the door. Had she already politely shut him down? It would be quick. And inevitable—oh, I saw it now. Madness.

But then May, not yet lost, would blurt, "Don't go."

The corner of Nicky's mouth would begin to lift and he'd look just like Hugh. (Hugh who, before he was so thoroughly broken down, could manage to look both serious *and* amused, or wry *and* impatient, or regretful *and* unyielding. Hugh both complicated and gentle, Hugh who was always on one's side.) Nicky would say to May, not knowing where the cojones came from, "Calm down."

And of course she can't believe it. She can't believe any of it. How can he say that to her? How can Nick stand there, the blush flaming on his cheeks, and look both tentative and confident at the same time? How does he emanate this *delight*?

Was her face hungry? Incredulous? Outraged? Did her eyes never leave his?

The thing is, she knew what I said was right: that I was irrelevant. She didn't want to admit I was right, but she certainly didn't want to admit I was wrong. She didn't want me, Charlie Garrett, to influence anything she did, and so what would she do if I didn't exist, and this man were standing in front of her, grinning like an angel?

Sound. The doorknob turning. And there he was. "God," he said, walking into the room. "This is crazy." He ran one hand through his hair, for the tenth time in as many minutes, by the looks of it. "I thought she was going to put me in detention or something. I hope it isn't always this hard."

"So you didn't—?"

"Oh no," he said, meaning *Yes I did.* "This Saturday. Seven o'clock."

He couldn't stop smiling.

I knew that what was supposed to happen next was a debriefing, a discussion of local restaurants, and a pep talk. I did my best. I recommended a new place in Northfield, half an hour away. "If you go to the Abbottsford Inn, you might as well put up a billboard. Write a news item for the paper." I don't remember what else I said; I do remember that he looked a bit disappointed in me. Maybe I wasn't enthusiastic, or wise, or jocular enough. Perhaps I seemed cold. I think though, honestly, that by that time we were each too distracted to care.

After he left I spent several minutes gathering papers and putting them in a pile—the neatest, most squared-off pile that had ever been or would be. I realized I was waiting for May to walk through the door. I thought of calling Anita. She'd be surprised I was calling her. Still, though, she'd ask what she usually did, both of us understanding that Nicky was our main, our only link now, and I would say, *He's good. He's really good.* The satisfaction of it! Of telling the truth! Of the yawning wound, the wholehearted sacrifice! What more could I do now? I'd done everything.

Books in the briefcase. Papers in a pile. I was going. Here I went. Going, going, gone.

Fifteen

Zack Middleton was back, Celia at his side again. But the ease he'd had when she was near him had evaporated. I had always assumed the intensity around and between them came from infatuation and sexual frustration (or not: surely they'd found hiding places; there had to be some), but now the agitation seemed different, more urgent. Sometimes, also, Celia was bolder. I'd see her alone, or with her friends—but then she'd be folded into his side again.

One day, Zack waited till everyone else had gone after class and then sauntered up to my desk. Celia wasn't waiting for him. "Mr. Garrett," he said. "I need an extension on the paper. I'm still . . . catching up. I guess."

"We had some great discussions while you were gone," I said. "I missed you. We talked about erasure. Presence and absence. Origins. Exactly what you brought up." He looked blank. "On the first day of class."

"Oh."

"Hey, why don't you and I get a cup of coffee, and I'll get you up to speed?" Students usually loved it when you asked them to meet for coffee. It sounded so adult and urban.

"I'm pretty busy. Practice and all that. I'm sorry." There was a quick, hooded shame in his eyes. "I'll get the paper done, I promise. Just a couple more days."

"No rush," I said. "I think you're supposed to be taking it easy. Right? Maybe we could just skip this paper."

"I can't have incompletes."

"Well, then you won't."

"Our first game is next weekend."

"I'll be there."

"I have to be able to play. In good academic standing and all that bullshit."

"You need to stay healthy."

"I am healthy. That's the point." He blinked.

I sighed. "One more thing," I said. "It's probably too late—but your dad mentioned the Air Force Academy, and I had the impression I needed to write a recommendation."

"I got Ms. Hawkins to do it," he said. "It could be your junior or senior English teacher. I had an A in her class," he said, and he shrugged, and I couldn't tell if he was embarrassed or accusatory. In my class, he kept dipping to a B minus. "So. You know. Sorry. And," he said, his voice getting louder, "she hasn't always *known* me. I'm not the fucking janitor's kid. The fucking diversity dream."

"Jesus, Zack—"

"Just a little black. Not black enough for some people but black enough for them."

"Come on. Really? You think that's how I think of you?" He glared at me. His face was white, and fine beads of sweat stood at his hairline. "Zack, is your head hurting right now?"

"No. It isn't."

"Zack—"

"It's not. Thanks, Charlie." And he was gone.

THOSE LAST DAYS OF NOVEMBER. Leaves gone. Sky cold indigo. Chill sliver of moon, chill spark of Venus. If I timed it right, I could get home when there was still a line of burnished light along the horizon, behind the house. On the grandest nights, great columns of purple cloud made operatic strokes over the mountains. Five minutes too late, though, and the sky would be gray black. As if nothing had ever happened.

———

NICK AND MAY'S FIRST DATE was successful. I discovered this, however, only when I found out they had gone out again, and then again. Nick was cagey. "Nicky," I said. "I don't want details. I don't care. It's really fine."

"No details. Okay." And I knew he was trying not to grin. That there were details.

The Saturday morning came when I called him about our plans for a hike that day, and he wasn't home. I hung up the phone and looked at the clock: 8:00 a.m. I had done it to myself. Done it to myself.

I had never seen the inside of May's place, a narrow blue town house a few blocks from Nicky's.

The kids sniffed it all out, inevitably, although I never saw the two of them closer than several feet together at school, although Nick still ate with students, and at chapel he and May were never in the same pew. I was a little surprised at the total restraint, attributed it to May. But then one evening I was walking past the gym to my car and there they were, pressed against a wall, sheer Hollywood. It was the route they would have taken to walk to either of their houses, and so what had happened was that they *just couldn't wait.*

Her hands on the back of his head, pressing; he was wearing the bomber jacket and between his legs I saw hers, moving; I saw his hips, saw them wanting.

Anyone could have seen them and I realized how she needed him, how she wanted someone to help her break the rules.

I needed to not think of any time ever when I had pressed against her like that and it had been a long time ago and never should have happened and no, I could not remember, I could not remember a thing, no scents or sounds or whispers, and it was the next day at lunch that we were all sitting together and May across and down the table from Nick and her wall up and so cool *Ah May you look so cool* and then I looked down at her hands on the table and saw them lying there, so still, still, I realized, with effort. Was she thinking she would never be twenty again? That she might as well? That this was her last chance to be carried away in this fast-moving current? Or was she not thinking at all?

Her hands trembled to reach across, to cradle his face. To once again confirm his reality. To keep him.

NICK AND I SPENT THANKSGIVING at Divya's, with her boys, home from college and law school, and a few of their friends, assorted vagabonds and castaways who lived across the country, too far to go for a holiday weekend, plus a guy who Divya whispered was Anil's new crush. Divya often had other teachers or foreign students from Abbott, but this year it was just us. I wondered, had things been different, if May would have come; she was the classic example of the Abbott teacher who might want to avoid family, might claim hardship traveling when, really, the truth was that her colleagues felt more like family, in the end. But her family was too close for excuses. I assumed she was at Binky's, in Providence.

The usual script, in matters large and small, was followed. "Ram," Divya said, "I don't mind if the football is on the TV, but turn it down. You aren't even *watching* it."

"It's part of America, Ma. It's aural wallpaper."

"Those poor boys who don't get to have their Thanksgiving dinner," Divya said, of the college players.

"Those poor boys who can't *read*," Anil said.

"I like having the game on," I said. "Ram is right. And if you were southerners, you'd know those boys are gods. They'll get their turkey."

"Oh, God, *turkey*," Divya said, as she also did at some point every year, "this huge ridiculous bird that no one really likes—"

"Ma!"

"—someone come help me carve."

She had first cooked a turkey when she and Win had been a young couple. He brought it up, every year. He always said it had been wooden on the outside and bloody on the inside.

"It was an act of love," Divya would retort. "I cooked it so you could have your Norman Rockwell fantasy." *Fahnt-a-zee.* Looking at

Win purse-lipped. And there he'd sit in his bow tie, and he'd look at me and wink.

She was still cooking that turkey for Win, every year. When it came out, golden brown and, indeed, Rockwellian, it was a sanctified bird.

Ram sat at the head of the table—the tide had been pushing me that way, but I felt it wasn't right and I'd sidestepped at the last minute. However, I ended up carving. Ram claimed he'd wreck it. Anil said he was better at scooping, as in mashed potatoes. "Oh, Charlie, just go ahead," Divya said. "Everyone is hungry." I wore my bow tie in honor of Win. I touched it when I made a toast to him. Ram and Anil looked indulgent but secretly pleased and Nick looked entranced and said, "Hear, hear," when I was done.

Nick seemed to be taking the place of a long-lost relative, familiar and yet with a veneer of the strange, who had this year dropped back in on a family and on rituals he had forgotten but found irresistible. At the table he was a bit bashful and listened intently to everyone else talking, with a slightly distracted, almost anthropological air.

"Nick," Divya said, "where is May today? I forget what she told me."

His mouth was full. "New Hampshire," he said, muffled. He swallowed. "I forget which brother it is. A lake house. It's about an hour and a half away."

"Binky lives in Providence," I said, before I could stop myself. "He must be doing well. Buying a lake house."

"No, I think it's Laird," Nick said. He didn't even hesitate on the name.

"It's on Lake Winnipesaukee," Divya said. "Now I remember."

"That means 'place of drunken waterskiing' in Wampanoag," Ram said.

"Not in November it doesn't," Anil said.

"Well, I asked her to stop by," Divya said. "If she was back in time."

She was warning me. This consideration, if that was what it was, made me livid.

"Doubt it," Nick said, his mouth full again. "Think it's an all-day, all-night deal." She was the secret he was holding within himself. In the moments when he seemed to be disappearing in front of me, he was thinking of May.

Anil and Ram watched us, eagle-eyed. Something was up, but they didn't know what. "Hey, Charlie," Anil said, "could you pass those beans?"

"Sure thing."

"You made these, right? As usual?"

"It's my highest culinary accomplishment," I said.

"Doesn't it involve, like, cream of mushroom soup? And a can opener?" Ram said.

"Maybe."

"Well, they taste just like Mom's," Nick said.

"I got the recipe from her. Such as it is."

"She doesn't cook much either," Nick said to the boys.

"There's mixing involved," I said. "Stirring. Must be done to precise standards."

"How is your mother, Charlie?" Divya said.

"Doing fine."

"Do you know her, Divya?" Nick said.

"We've never met. Oddly enough. After all these years."

"She's coming for Christmas," Nick said.

"Really! That's wonderful!"

"She's going to stay with Charlie."

Divya looked at me quickly and I gave what I imagine was a rather wan smile. "Time for her to finally see the place," I said. "Don't know why it's never worked out before."

"Well, now she has two of you here. Now there is no excuse."

"That's right," I said. "None at all."

"THIS RIDICULOUS CHINA." This was also an annual complaint. It was Win's mother's expensive heirloom wedding china that couldn't go in the dishwasher. She always said the boys expected it. I can't imagine they would have noticed, but the ritual was in stone and Divya would not admit she'd done the chiseling.

I heard cheering, and looked out the window above the sink. Between shreds of cloud the sky was a watery blue, and the sun was casting long shadows. Nicky, Anil, and Anil's friends were high-fiving one another while Ram and his friends looked on in mock glumness; then they all huddled and re-formed. White teeth and handsomeness abounded. "The Kennedys appear to be playing football on your lawn," I said.

Divya came over next to me and looked out the window. "Some of them are remarkably tan," she said. She watched for a minute, a hard-won contentment emanating from her. The light shone through the bare branches of the maples at the edge of the yard, and for a moment I was blinded. "Look at the sun," she said. "So low. Ah, it'll be dark soon."

"We're in the last days of Ordinary Time."

"That sounds so ominous."

"Just the inexorable march of the liturgical calendar."

"That doesn't help, Charlie."

"Actually we're all waiting for the solstice. Deep instinct. Primordial."

"Maybe you are nothing but a pagan after all," Divya said.

"Maybe you're right."

They re-formed and ran another play, and as we watched Nick went diagonal and then reached up a long arm, casually, almost as though it were not a part of his body and instead controlled itself, and caught the ball. He loped easily to the goal line and there was more rejoicing, and then I saw a new figure walking into the yard, a long-legged girl in jeans and tall brown boots, and as I watched May walked straight up to Nick and kissed him, in front of God and the college kids and everybody. For a second they were together, so tall, complete, and then she stepped back, she was laughing.

"Oh good," Divya said. "She was able to get away."

I knew that there were many possible comments to make: That she had escaped in record time. That the traffic must still be light. That it was good she'd gotten home before dark. That I, myself, would rather sleep in thumbscrews than have a long dinner with Laird and Binky. That I had believed it when Nick said she was staying there overnight, if I had thought of it at all, which I must have been because here I was thinking *I thought she was going to stay overnight.* But not saying it. Because nothing bothered me.

"I'm sorry I didn't warn you before today," Divya said. "But I doubted she would really come."

"I didn't need a warning."

"I thought Nick would mention it to you."

"Nothing needed mentioning."

We washed and dried in a heavy silence. Divya was shaking her head. "I was wrong. Wrong, wrong. I am sorry." She put a plate down with a *clink* on the stack on the kitchen table. "Charlie, what have you done?"

"What have *I* done? What are you talking about?"

Divya dried another plate, came back to the drainer. She didn't look at me. "Charlie. It's not good."

I gave up pretending ignorance. "You talk like I have control of the world, Div. Would that it were so."

"The only conclusion I can come to is that you have lied to him." I didn't answer. After a moment she said, stubbornly, "To Nicky."

I sighed. "About what?"

"Tell me I'm wrong."

"I told him that May and I were an item, briefly, a long time ago, and that it's good and over, dead as a doornail, and that is the truth."

"I never knew why it ended, Charlie."

"Doesn't matter. We were too young or too old or too stupid or whatever. Preston was dying. It isn't even interesting—it seemed terribly profound at the time, but we were just a mismatch."

"I know you would do anything for him," she said. "But that doesn't mean you have to."

"You seem to think I'm very noble, Div."

"Maybe you are."

"Ah, no."

"Charlie—"

"Leave it," I barked at her, and then was ashamed. "Please."

"And I am surprised at May too."

"She has my blessing. I told her so. Not that she needs it."

She put another plate on the dry stack. "Charlie. You won't let anyone help you."

There was a wet plate in my hands, and the only reason I didn't raise it up and dash it into soapy pieces on the floor was that I could remember Win in this kitchen, holding what might have been the same plate, a towel tucked into his waistband, humming. "What kind of help, precisely, are you offering?" I said. "To fix what problem? I have a brother who is in love. I have a brother who is happy. I have a brother who is in Abbottsford, Massachusetts, also known as the Yankee fucking Shangri-la, who is not going to get blown up by an IED or some crazy-ass fundamentalist suicide bomber while he's here, and because he is in love and he is happy, then maybe he'll stay. If there are other issues you'd like me to take up, let me tell you I am fully occupied at the moment, and I am completely content." I rinsed the plate under the tap. I put it in the drainer with great care. I kept my back to Divya and my eyes on the sink. From outside I could hear clapping and laughter, ringing in the dying afternoon, the unmistakable sounds of our paradise on earth.

IT WAS TRUE that Anita was coming for Christmas, and true of course that it had been Nicky's idea. Not long after his first couple of dates with May, he had said, "What are we doing for the holidays? We have to decide." Oh, *we*. "I just realized I'll *be* here for them. I mean in the States."

"Traveling is a bitch over Thanksgiving."

"Okay."

Too easy. He had that sad, hopeful look, and I knew that once again he wouldn't ask why Anita and I rarely spoke, no matter how hard we pretended for his sake. Instead he would just stand there (okay, right now he was sitting, we were sitting on the patio) with his buoyant longing.

I was braced and thinking that Atlanta wouldn't be so bad if Nick was actually there. I'd done it plenty of times since Anita and I had fallen out, I'd pretended for a long time. But Nicky said, "I was thinking Mom could come here."

"Here?"

"And stay with you. You always say you rattle around here. In this house."

"That's true."

"So, I think she would like it."

"Have you already asked her?"

"No," he said.

I believed him. He could not dissemble. "I was just wondering. If she'd said anything to you."

"No. She didn't. But has she ever been here?"

"No."

"Why not, Charlie?"

"Because I always went to see you."

"Oh." He wanted to trust me. He *did* trust me. He soldiered on. "I think she would like it," he said again. "We can show her everything. Introduce her to everyone."

So he wanted her to meet May.

"And she needs to see this," he said, and gestured out to the mountains, and then for good measure bounced out of the chair, roamed off the flagstones and into the grass. "This is you. She should see this place."

Oh, his particular genius. Exactly what I did not want her to see. Myself, everything I couldn't change. But as always the easiest thing to do was to roll over, hum a mindless little tune, admit no complication. "Okay," I said. "Sure. Christmas here."

"The beginning of a new tradition."

"Sure."

"Maybe there will be snow," Nick said. "Someone was telling me. There are all these signs. This farmer's almanac stuff. Like, there were a lot of acorns this year. And the caterpillars were fuzzier than usual. That's a thing. Meaning snow. Meaning a heavy snowfall."

"Signs and portents."

"*Yes,* Charlie."

Oh, how he was stymied by his dour older brother. Oh, I saw it all, what he wanted: sleigh bells, perfection. Perfection and harmony weren't usually his gig, though—it was like he wanted it for me, for Anita, as though he knew our chances were dwindling, that maybe this was as close as the stars would ever align. "Sure," I said. "A white Christmas. Chances are good. Chances are always good."

Sixteen

Going back down the stairs I passed Celia and Zack on the landing, oblivious to anyone else going by, in tense conversation as usual; but even though they might have been on the verge of breakup, I envied them. Then was quickly ashamed. That pain: of course I remembered it. But oh, how it *mattered*.

CHRISTMAS PARTY AT DIVYA'S. One of the things that could be counted on, and wasn't I fortunate to have so many of them? These rituals that stood alone, that couldn't be altered or ruined?

Faculty, spouses, little girls in hair bows, little boys in knitted vests. Sprinkling of garish Christmas sweaters. This year Divya wore a green sari shot through with gold threads. Her bun was complicated. Her jewelry was so abundant that I thought she might clink when she moved—but it was too loud in the house to tell.

Seniors in good standing were invited, by long tradition: Win's idea, years before. He thought they should be treated like responsible adults. The joke was that they would stand by the bar and try to mix themselves drinks, waiting to get caught by Bethie Salter, who long ago had appointed herself overseer. By now the exchanges were as stylized as kabuki. The only student who had ever succeeded in spiking the punch was Henry Bankhead.

The tree stood in the foyer and was twelve feet tall, blanketed with the ornaments that people brought every year. (Tonight Dex Pentecost had triumphantly produced a tiny toilet with "Plumbers' Local 1" painted on it in red and green, provided by his brother, Amos, '00, who knew the drill and had been on the lookout.) All was illuminated with big, blinking colored bulbs. Otherwise the only light, throughout the house, was dozens of candles. Around every door were paper chains and evergreens and mistletoe, and in the dining room enough food for a multitude of parties. The fires in all the fireplaces—dining room, living room, library, front hall—were lit. In the kitchen it was nearly impossible to move, and seated around the table were a dozen people of varying ages, playing penny poker.

I made a polite circuit and ended up in the front hall next to the tree. Through the wide doorway into the dining room, I watched as May and Nick stood next to the table, examining the food. They made no move to pick up plates. May was in a navy velvet dress that was nearly off the shoulder. Her collarbones begged for a finger to run along them and admire their fearful symmetry; with luck Nick would think of this.

I edged a little closer to the doors, staying half hidden. Sip of eggnog: high-octane. You've got raw eggs here, Win said. You need the bourbon, you see, to kill the bacteria. Health precaution, he said, and *glug-glug-glug* went the amber into the punch bowl. The merest of twinkle in his eye.

That doorway: nestled in it were the pocket doors. Since Win had restored them, they'd glide on their tracks with a touch of a finger. He'd showed me, proud as a child with a tower of blocks.

Now May and Nick were holding hands. A bold move! I noticed students noticing. Minnie Zheng, on the other side of the table, loading up on Divya's samosas, swept her gaze over the two of them like she was reading a flowchart, and then whispered something to Marina Hirschfeld. Darius Flake and Will Bolling cut their eyes over and then nodded in admiration. These kids assumed they were looking at their own bright futures. No matter their current state, someday they too would be good-looking and in love. Singlehandedly, Nick and May made adulthood appealing.

With an air of great purpose, I turned and went up the stairs. On the second floor the electric lights in the hallway made the house ordinary again and the party noise from below, muted and equalized, became the essence of nostalgia, the sound of every good party that had ever been, every wonderful life: every night where you flirted with someone and were flirted with in return; where you felt her eyes on you and knew finally that you weren't imagining things, that the person you'd come to the party hoping to see had thought the same of you, and you were about to enter into that mutual understanding that, being tacit, still had enough edge of uncertainty to make it excruciating and delicious. *Hi, Mr. Garrett. Miss Bankhead. You're home. Yes. Are you drinking the* adult *eggnog, Miss Bankhead? Certainly not.*

Going up to the third floor, the stairs were uncarpeted, and narrower. Meant for the servants, after all. Even the moldings became plainer, made with a simpler knife. I found the light switch and flicked it. Plain fixtures along the passageway, which was empty, and I heard no scuttering of either mice or people: no intrepid students had made their way up here to make out. Too well behaved, our kids today. Too meek and unadventurous. Henry Bankhead probably scored up here at least once.

Ahead, at the end of the short corridor, the door to the attic. Another switch, now bare lightbulbs. Here it was so cold I could see my breath. Ahead the round window. I flipped the good strong brass locks, nudged the frame, and it opened with a woodeny *pop,* tilted out on the horizontal axis—and there, below, was the labyrinth, edged in white. It had snowed perfectly earlier that day, obscuring the outlines just enough to make them look devilishly confounding to those who didn't know the pattern. And now the moon was out and the shadows were sharp and blue, and the voices floated brightly up.

The labyrinth was overtaken by kids, the only ones game enough to leave the warm indoors. They bumbled along, caroming off the shrubs, and I almost yelled out right then: *Take care, you little bastards!* But there was Booker Middleton, his arms folded, watching. Ah, a true groundsman. He would appreciate the labyrinth, the work that went into it, the care.

And also, I now saw, Dex Pentecost, blue blazer, no coat, red hair shining an unearthly brown in the moonlight—he was also scolding. "Guys, easy," he was saying. "No cheating, heh, heh," when Will Bolling made to crash through the boxwood rather than follow the path. And next to Dex, Marina Hirschfeld too. God love them! Yes, indeed, love them. Why couldn't I? And what a couple. I'd been blind! Dex and Marina! Solid, solid citizens. In the next ten years, I'd get a wedding invitation, baby announcements. Twenty, and we'd be interviewing their kids. They'd visit at homecoming, seek me out—I'd be gray at the temples but otherwise the same, they'd say it, *You look great, you look just the same,* delighted that their memories were safeguarded in our preppy Brigadoon, and relieved, too, that they could leave and go back to their own world which moved (they would no doubt believe) in a line, not an endless loop.

The work of two minutes to marry them off and exile them to a center-entrance colonial in Lexington or Rye! To a menorah and a Christmas tree both—they'd manage! To the PTA, to wealth management! Was that love? I had said I wanted to love them.

A door opened directly beneath me, two floors down, and babbling and music spilled out into the snow; several people emerged, I couldn't tell who, not yet, from the tops of their heads; then the door closed, and the bright voices took over again. "I'm stuck!" someone cried.

"No you're not!"

"You guys!" someone hollered. "This is supposed to be *spiritual*!"

Then I saw, midway between the center and the far right edge of the labyrinth, Celia and Zack, deep in conversation. Or rather Zack was talking. Pleading? He was hatless and in an odd, illogical reflex I worried for that head, exposed, as though cold would hurt the bruised brain inside. He was bending over her, too close—was that possible for those two? Yes, it was, it had become possible: she was rigid, shrinking away. Other kids edged past them, giving them as wide a berth as possible in the narrow path; arguing couples were kryptonite. Besides, no one would tell Zack Middleton to move.

Then suddenly Zack turned and began to push his way straight through the maze—through the boxwood. He made it through one wall but the next one was sturdier and he kicked once, twice, at the branches with his enormous foot. "HEY!" I shouted. "ZACK MIDDLETON! Cut it out!"

I knew Booker was right there. Did I think I was tipping him off, that he'd take over? But instead every face swiveled up to me. The spy unmasked.

Zack was cutting straight across to the back border of the maze and the dark yard beyond. The double lot sloped downward and away; in the moonlight the other houses receded. At the next barrier, more vicious kicking. "*ZACK!*" Another ragged hole. "Goddammit, what are you *doing*! Stop it! You little *shit!*"

I whirled around, leaving the window open, the ghostly maids shivering in their pinched little rooms. Down the stairs. Second floor, the party near again. Down one more flight, a tunnel of sound opening up, and sudden heat and multicolored light; no one here knew anything was amiss. Smiling faces turning to me in inexplicable expectation: what was I bringing them? The dining room and then the library, the French doors to the outside. By now Divya was following me, disapproval trumping concern. "Charlie, what is the matter?"

I opened the doors and stepped out into the cold. "Booker, what the hell?" I waved at the broken hedges. "Win planted those!"

"Charlie!" Divya said. "*Charlie.* Stop now."

"He kicked right through them! Zack did!" Booker's face was stony. "Do you know how old these are?" I hollered. "Do you know how much Divya spends on this?"

Divya looked, eagle-eyed, between Booker and me. "Charlie, it doesn't matter," she said.

"It does matter! Look at that. Look!" Now I could see: the branches were broken all the way at the base and they flopped to the ground, seeming for all the world like the pitiful stiff legs of some dead songbird. I wanted to prop them up. See if they would mend themselves. And then I saw him, far at the edge of the yard, in the shadows, watching, it seemed, waiting. "Zack." I looked around at the staring faces. "Let me go," I said, but no one was stopping me.

I broke into a jog past the boxwood. He waited. Then I had my hand on his arm. "Zack. What the *fuck* was that?"

He looked betrayed. "I'll pay for it."

"You certainly will," I said, but the fire was going out of me. "What happened?"

His chest was heaving. He looked back at the house, the lighted windows, the floodlit labyrinth. "Tell her I'm sorry," he said. "Ms. Lowell. I'll fix it. Okay? Please?" His face was suddenly younger. "Please, Charlie?" And then he saw something, someone, behind me, and his face hardened again. "Get the fuck out of here."

I turned. Nick was standing there, his hands up like he was surrendering. "Zack." He looked at me. "I saw. I just wanted to help."

"You're a fucking *fraud*," Zack snarled. "Get away from me!"

Nick took a step closer. "I know I'm a fraud." His hands floated down to his sides. His face was slack, empty. "I know it. You're right."

Zack stared at him. And then slowly shook his head. "No," he said. "No. You don't get to do that."

"Zack, I don't know what I've done—"

"Get away from me."

"Nicky," I said, and shrugged: *I don't understand either. But just go.* His hands rose again, he backed up a step, two, and his face, turned full to Zack, filled with concern and regret before he turned and walked back to the lights and the labyrinth.

We watched him go. And then Zack said, "Celia's always talking about him. He has *ideals*. He's *brave*. He *cares* about *others*. All that hearts-and-minds bullshit. He's *perfect*." His voice trailed off. "*You* don't believe that, right?"

I absorbed this, and then I said, "Do you love her?"

"Yeah." He nodded and swiped at his eyes, full of shame. "So much," he whispered.

"Oh, Zackie Bear," I said. "I'm sorry."

He looked at me with dread. Then he turned and slowly walked away, into the dark at the edge of the yard, and then broke into a run, back toward school.

Seventeen

Two days before Christmas, Nick and I drove to the airport, in Boston. We parked the car and headed to the baggage claim but Anita was already there, standing straight, at the curb.

She hugged us both and I admit there was a moment of pure disbelief, something close to excitement, that we were all standing here in foreign Boston together, in the gray, winter airport atmosphere; it was as though the three of us had met to begin a journey, rather than to fetch Anita at the end of one. Nicky started chattering away: How was the flight? Wasn't it cold? She made good time! She just had the one suitcase? Well then hey, where were his presents?

And I felt myself receding, as I always did when it was the three of us. I let them love each other, let them carry all the energy. I trundled along, Charlie the driver, but as they talked, although I felt separate as ever, I found myself aware of my mother as I never was in Atlanta. I realized, in this foreign and neutral place, this way station, how the flow of Nicky's talk wrapped itself around her, both slightly annoyed and relaxed her. I was acutely aware that she'd never been here before—*felt* it, was inside her senses: I tasted the metallic air, here so close to the water; noticed the white slashes of seagulls wheeling and crying and realized how strange their presence would be to her, these summer beach birds roosting on concrete, in this bleakness of terminals and parking decks. I saw unsmiling people hurrying in dark coats, saw the ridges of black salt-pocked snow along the road. Snow to southerners was fluffy fairy-tale stuff. How had she let me come so far away, and stay?

But Boston was always foreign to me. We needed to get out of the city. That was all.

"Mom," Nick said, "are you limping?"

"I'm stiff from the plane."

"You're awfully stiff."

"It'll walk out."

"Did you get that graft? Or whatever it was?"

"What graft?" I said.

"No," Anita said. "I didn't do it."

"In her leg," Nick said. "Hardening of the arteries or something."

"Doctors like to overreact," Anita said. "Never talk to a surgeon if you don't want an operation."

"Why were you talking to a surgeon?" I said.

"Son," Anita said, "I am fine, and I am here to have a good Christmas."

I couldn't remember the last time she called me *Son*. She was hobbling along beside me through the parking lot, dragging her suitcase herself, her mouth set. "Well, Mother," I said, "I like it when people have clear goals."

And she looked at me like I'd caught her at something. I remembered how she used to say *You are so smart. So smart, Charlie,* and it had bothered me because it meant she knew what I was saying was clever but didn't understand why, or did not approve of my sarcasm, or was refusing, once again, to laugh at herself; but this time she smiled. I reminded myself that I was not going to be lulled by our old complicity.

She wasn't exactly short of breath—that is, she didn't stop walking, I didn't hear wheezing. But she was surrounded by a cloud of effort, transforming her, blurring some essential outline of intentionality she had always had.

NICKY STAYED OVER both Christmas Eve and Christmas night, which I enjoyed more than I ever would have admitted. Anita seemed to view herself as a charity guest on an Elderhostel tour, which suited me just fine; she was polite and appreciative and private. I knew I could not keep up my own good behavior forever—sharing the kitchen at breakfast, making bland, polite conversations—but as inoculation I thought often of Anita marching herself painfully over that asphalt, in a straight line, all decisions made, my only job to follow in her wake. She did seem to improve, physically, too. We walked around my property, we walked around the campus. It was true that when Nicky wasn't paying attention she would slow down. I pretended not to notice and she pretended not to notice me not noticing. All was smooth. The line was straight.

In my living room I had a tree (I didn't always) and on Christmas morning Anita said, with satisfaction, that it was nice. Meaning the morning, the scene. She was supremely unsentimental—I had forgotten, really. A holiday for her was just a day, and the fact that I had bought the lights for the tree two weeks before, and the ornaments on sale at the drugstore, and that memories and meaning did not drip from them—well, that was fine with her, it was what she expected. It was Nick who might want more, Nick who expected magic to pop out of a box or a song, but Anita and I could lovingly stare him down— together we could have no expectation, no buildup or letdown.

I hadn't expected this truce, and I didn't trust it.

On Boxing Day we woke and had coffee and eggs and then Nick said he had to go home and get some clean clothes. Nick never cared about clean clothes. I asked when May was coming back. She had gone to Providence.

"Today," he said.

"Aha."

He looked from me, to Anita, back to me. I was acting as well as ever, so well that he broke into a grin.

"Go, you," I said.

By now we had thoroughly discussed the labyrinth incident. Nick said he had no idea what Zack was talking about. Yes, they were both in his class. Yes, Nicky talked to Celia outside of class, in groups, like he did with everyone else.

"Why'd he say you were a fraud?"

"I don't know—"

"Why'd you agree?"

"I'd had too much of that fucking eggnog," he'd said. "That's the truth. I just wanted him not to be upset. It seemed like a good idea at the time. I should try to talk to him again—"

"Absolutely not. He wants someone to blame. He's getting his heart broken. Teen drama," I'd said. "Don't attach much weight to it." And so after that when I saw him with May, even when I caught them snuggling in his classroom, I was relieved.

After breakfast, once he'd left, Anita said, "Do you know what you're doing?"

"Nope."

"Charlie."

"I don't see how I could know. I'm no fortune-teller. And if I did know, it wouldn't matter," I said. "My knowledge and vision are irrelevant here. I would say this is a fairly unique set of circumstances. A baroquely odd pickle."

"Charlie," she said again. Her voice was soft.

"Look, Mother, I think they're in love. Okay?" And as soon as I said it out loud, I knew it was true. It was what I'd been seeing. It was past infatuation. Maybe Celia even sensed it! The strength of it. And was jealous, in an illogical teenaged way. "Did you see his face?"

"I did. And does she love him?"

"Yes." Out loud, it was solid. "Yes, she does." I shrugged. "Nicky is Nicky. Nicky gets the girl."

"Charlie." She sighed. She couldn't say *honey* or *sweetie*.

We needed Nick to come back. Anyone. What I wanted to say was, *This is why I can't be alone with you.* The last thing we needed was to start telling the truth.

"He's easy to love," Anita said.

I got up and poured more coffee into my mug. Sat down again. I said, "I don't know what the hell that's supposed to mean."

She shrugged. "Nicky always has people following him around."

"She's not like that. She's not frivolous."

"All right, son."

Don't call me son. I kept it in, just in time.

She finished her eggs, rather delicately. Mashed the crumbs with the tines of her fork, ate them with her last shard of bacon. She always cleaned her plate. I realized I'd never thought of it until now. She didn't eat to excess, hardly ever had seconds; just ate what was put in front of her, all of it, without comment. It was the habit of another generation. Such details seemed clearer to me, seeing her in my own kitchen, on this unfamiliar stage.

She said, "I am just not sure. That she shouldn't know."

I hated her tentative voice. She was never tentative. "I think you're missing the point," I said. "The point is, everything is hunky-dory. Don't you think, Mother? Haven't we had a nice couple of days?" She would hear the threat and understand it. Things might be mended, but the joint was unsteady, the glue not set. Rattle the pieces and they'd come apart. "Nicky is really happy right now," I said. "Everything is going beautifully. Exactly the way it is."

Her lips pressed in a familiar line: she understood. "So. I am meeting her tonight," she said. "I've always wanted to meet her."

"I'll bet you have," I said, and she half hid a smile, and I took pity and laughed a little, and then we both laughed just a little more, just enough to twitch closed the curtain that camouflaged the absurdity of the whole thing. And I knew our laughter made her happy but that she would also be looking for Preston in May's face, and she'd see him, and wonder; and she knew I knew, and between us we knew far too much.

She took another sip of her coffee and then her hand slipped down to the pocket of her bathrobe, in a gesture like a madeleine. That searching pat, the almost-invisible look of impatience and agitation, which would always be followed by the click, the flare, the efficient inhale, the hidden relief and satisfaction—

She saw me noticing her patting hand, and stopped. "I thought you quit," I said.

"I have one in the morning, and one at night."

I knew she was telling the truth. She possessed that sort of self-control, and also the inability to lie, just like Nicky. So: a decision to make, here. Nick would get upset, would be incredulous. Or, more likely, she would not have even made the gesture in his presence. But with me she let her guard down. Let it all hang out with Charlie.

I cradled that to me for a moment.

"You could go out on the patio," I said. "It's warmer than you would think, out there." She nodded reluctantly. "You don't want Nicky to smell it," I said. And she smiled.

DINNER THAT NIGHT was at Divya's. Ram and Anil were home, and Anil's friend from Thanksgiving, now boyfriend, was visiting again. The two of them were trying not to act besotted, and failing. I was hoping my mother had gotten modernized and wouldn't mind. The enormous tree was still up and I looked at it and tried not to think about the party, and no one mentioned that night or my exit although I imagined they were thinking of it. But no, everyone behaved. Everyone was just lovely. It was a casual dinner, at the big table in the kitchen. May was wearing a turtleneck sweater that was just too god-damn tight. She and Nick sat next to each other, and it bugged the hell out of me trying not to think about whether or not they were playing footsie. (There was no doubt about Anil and Jackson.) Goddammit. Nick glowed. The table was lit with a dozen candles, half gone from the party. There was a lot of glowing.

Talk turned to my mother's retirement. "I worked for thirty-five years," she said. "Altogether. I took some time off when Nicky was little." Because Hugh wanted her to, I did not say. Because Hugh and she both wanted to believe that the two of them had been trans-formed, and were embarking on a picture-book life.

"But you went back because you missed it so much," Nick said, proudly.

"It's a bit of an addiction, isn't it," Divya said. "Feeling useful."

"I don't know about that," Anita said.

"That doesn't sound right," Divya said, laughing. She was immune to Anita's Puritanism, and my heart warmed. "I suppose I'm trying to resign myself to the idea of retirement."

"But you're not retiring," I said.

"Oh, but Charlie. I will. Rather soon, too. I have directed my sons to get well-paying jobs in a nice warm climate, and then I will come join them, whether they like it or not." Ram and Anil looked at her indulgently, but I could tell it wasn't a fabrication.

"But you love it here," I said. "You've become a New Englander. We're dug in, Div."

"Charlie, my bones are frozen. Soon they'll forget how to thaw. Did you really think I could stand it forever?" She laughed the laugh I loved—the laugh I thought of, in thorough political incorrectness, as wisely Indian: a laugh formed by the ideas of reincarnation, of multiple capricious gods, of our smallness. Of the fecklessness of life.

"But Charlie will never leave," May said, with a superior sort of fondness.

I shrugged. I felt the shrug in my eyeballs; I needed to calibrate my drinks more carefully. "Who knows," I said.

"You said you're dug in."

"I'm an in-the-moment kind of guy." I waited for someone to laugh out loud but no one did. "Right, Nicky?"

"Oh yeah," he said, his warmth automatic. He wouldn't decide until later that he disagreed, if indeed he thought of it at all.

I could feel Anita's eyes on me.

I decided I had contributed quite enough to the conversation for the evening.

So from then on I tried not to concentrate too hard on anything much, and whenever anyone gave me a look that might have been significant I ignored it. Instead I watched Anil and Jackson. My mother, I noted, watched them with a benign curiosity, which was a fairly new level of tolerance. But I decided Jackson was blond and Waspy and pretty, and therefore exquisitely boring, and Anil deserved better, and it was all I could do to not lure Divya into a corner so we could talk about him; I wanted to be cruel to a blameless stranger. Meanwhile, Anita watched May, and May in turn was aware of Anita. She held her smile at the ready and whenever Anita spoke to her it brightened. I had never seen either of them try to charm someone.

At the end of the night Anita and Nick and May and I said goodbye together, leaving Divya in her yellow-lit doorway and Anil and

Jackson beginning to entwine on the sofa, and Ram the wry single brother who would head upstairs to sleep alone, and we walked out into the snow to my and Nicky's cars and our voices suddenly rang in the frosty air and the snow was a rounded cushion on the rooftops and it was all very Currier and Ives.

May was wearing a long red wool coat with black velvet epaulets, a Christmas gift to herself, she said, now that she was back north. "You're very dashing," I said.

"Well, thank you, Charlie." She turned to my mother. "I hope I see you again before you leave," she said, almost shyly.

"Well, I hope so too."

"It was *so* wonderful meeting you," May said, as if she hadn't already said the first thing.

Anita was skeptical of extroversion and enthusiasm, except in Nick, but now she took May's gloved hand in both of her own. "I'll see you soon, May-May," she said, and I caught my breath. "That's your family nickname, isn't it. May-May."

"Yes."

"I hope you don't mind if I call you that."

"No," May said, "I don't mind at all." Nicky looked on, beaming. "Two more days you're here?"

"That's right. And then *I* will go home to thaw." She tipped her head, proud of her little joke.

"Charlie," Nick said, "I'm just running May home."

"Take your time," I said. "We'll see you tomorrow." He began to protest and May looked down at the snowy ground, half smiling. "Tomorrow, bro." And Anita and I turned to the car. I opened the door for her, helped her in. Walked around, the snow crunching beneath my shoes. What a splendid time. Oh, so well behaved. So many things unsaid! Good night, good night, good night.

AT SIX THE NEXT MORNING, Anita was at my bedside. Sleep was warm water, pulling me back, but I swam upward—time for school, the morning cold, the windows gray, in my old narrow bed, she'd hold out my clothes, slide on my socks, *Oh Charlie wake up it's time.* "Mom?"

"Charlie. *Charlie.*" Her voice catching, containing something I'd never heard there before. It was fear.

I sat up, in my bed in Massachusetts; she was gripping the door frame with both hands; one leg was drawn up, all the weight was on the other, and I knew she'd waited as long as she could to wake me.

III

Anita

Eighteen

When I was four years old, my mother drove me south to meet her grandparents, who'd raised her. There was a long car ride, hours and hours, the hot wind roaring in the windows, my cheek stuck with sweat to the vinyl seat where I lay down; and outside endless fields, corn, cotton, peanuts, and drunken shacks on the side of the road, corrugated roofs listing, wood silver gray, entire houses sliding down from civilization into something almost wild.

At the end, there was a town, and a big house, all white, porch, shutters, siding—or it once had been; now it was flaking, disinte- grating, the most leprous house I had ever seen. We went inside, and a woman who was my great-grandmother gave me ginger ale and showed me a bobbing glass bird that drank water from a cup. At first the bird fascinated me, but then it bored and then frightened me, because it would not stop, because its will and its thirst were endless. Its pointed red beak dove down to the water, again and again.

These were the days of *yes ma'am* and *no ma'am* and spankings and *don't sass me* and *I'll wash your mouth out with soap*—codes and pun- ishments that shifted and softened, later, when Anita married Hugh, and which by then didn't affect me that much anymore; but when I was small and Anita was closer to her old life, they were simply part of the world, part of what I knew, just as I had known these people existed, these two old people, people who had nothing to do with us and yet were at our heart, my mother's and mine, and now here we were. I had known that this hot little town existed too, had divined it somehow from my mother whom I watched so closely, whose breath I listened to without realizing it, all the time; and, finally, I knew that my father had been a soldier and had died in Vietnam. There was Vietnam on the TV and grown-ups seemed to accept it as another given, and my mother had told me about this father, not at any time I particularly remembered, but had simply given me the knowledge, before memory, to absorb with my child's osmosis. All these truths were somehow a structure, they were of a piece.

The old man's eyes, my great-grandfather's eyes, were pale and hot at the same time. He had not yet come close to me. I told him this absolute truth, that yes I did too have a father, and about Vietnam.

He looked at my mother and said some boy wanted some before he shipped out and the apple don't fall far. My mother stood up and the old lady said, *Oh Nita, please don't leave.* I was sent out to play.

Outside was a wall of heat, and insects singing with a weird primordial urgency, and the gray beards of old men hanging from the trees. I had told the truth, a fact at my core, but somehow it had been talking back, acting ugly, telling a story: I had miscalculated. Now I'd been exiled, and was waiting for whatever was coming.

But then we left the big white house—I don't remember the good-byes, I was done, what child remembers good-byes?—and there was no punishment. Now my mother was in charge again and we would go back to ourselves. The sun had lowered, the heat had lessened, a small edge of mercy.

We drove, just a little ways, and then we were outside a church. It was a child's drawing of a church, a white box with a steeple. Long shallow steps along the front. I don't know if my mother said then, "That's Granddaddy's church," or if she told me later and the knowledge seeped backward, or if she'd told me before and I already knew.

Even inside the car I felt like we were being watched, and we probably were.

Up until then, the pictures from that day are muddled to me, malleable. I know I've arranged and enhanced them: the sloughing white paint; the bird and the ginger ale; my great-grandfather's pale eyes;

the Spanish moss; the flat yard with gray sandy soil I was banished to, that I still see as enormous, stretching away and away, when really it could not have been, because it was in the middle of that town, in the middle of streets. And me wandering in it, sifting the small, crackling, fallen brown leaves of what must have been live oaks through my fingers. I had begun to feel I had to get closer and *closer* to things, all the time, see their astonishing *thingness* as thoroughly as I could. There was a reason and order in deep hiding—although now I felt a new confusion: *all I did was tell the truth*. And I was still limp with relief, because a large punishment had been coming, but it had passed me by.

Then as my mother and I sat in our car in front of that squat whitewashed cinder-block building she told me a story, about being right there, on those steps, when she was about my age. Though I don't remember the sound of her voice and the story has grown in my mind and is probably as tainted as everything else now, still I know that as she spoke, I saw her there, snapped into focus—a little girl, long skinny legs, red hair, utterly alone on those steps, in singing heat, the white of the church in the noon sun nearly blinding, and I knew that little girl was also a truth, and she joined us.

I hadn't thought of that little girl in years, until my mother came to my house in Abbottsford, that last winter.

"WHAT ARE WE GOING TO DO?" Nick said.

No one else was there, but still we muted ourselves. We were in the lounge area on the surgical floor. It was dinnertime. I was lightheaded from adrenaline, the wine from the previous night at Divya's, the sudden reversal of fortunes.

"They said she'll be in the hospital for a week. Then rehab. For I don't know how long."

"And then?"

"Then she can come back to my house."

"She'll want to go home."

"Well, I don't know how that's going to work," I said.

"What about all her stuff? She needs her stuff. What about the house?"

"We'll figure it out."

"Maybe she should live up here. We can find her a place. For when she's ready."

"Yes," I said. "We absolutely can." I had already accepted this obvious reality.

"But in the meantime she can stay with you."

"Yes." And that one too.

"We'll get her one of those things that goes up and down the stairs. Those seat things. That attach to the banister. That they advertise on the crappy TV stations." I didn't answer. "I'll pay for it."

"Nikko, don't worry about that."

"But I guess it would wreck your stairs." He said this without reproach.

"No it won't," I said. "A house is to live in." Someone seemed to be handing me these lines; it was merely my job to read them. To not lose patience. To let him talk on, and on, frantically weaving his fragile little rope bridge of control.

If Anita were here, awake, listening, we'd exchange a look. We would be stronger than Nicky. Our bridge would be wood or stone.

Then I noted I was actually wishing for her presence; felt my surprise for a moment; moved on.

My mother, as it turned out, had had several operations already on her leg. When she came up to Massachusetts, dry gangrene was beginning to set in, because the arteries had closed almost completely and there was no blood flow. She had been taking painkillers the whole time. She had known she would lose the leg, eventually. All she said to me was, "This was not supposed to happen here, Charlie." In stiff, silent fury at herself. She had wanted to have Christmas. She was more sentimental than I'd thought.

The operation could have waited, but not long. She couldn't fly. It was better to have it done here. Better to have her here. A surgeon was available. She didn't want to go to Boston. "Just go ahead," she said.

The doctor said to me, outside her room, "She's done her research. She's ready. You need to know she is in extreme pain right now."

I said that I knew.

We had gotten in the car, in the soft early morning, we had driven to the hospital, and the whole time her mouth had been a grim matter-of-fact line and she'd resembled nothing so much as a nurse with a dull, textbook patient, somewhat slow, the patient being herself. I'd waited until after eight to call Nick. Because I'd known I would have to call him at May's. Although I told myself that I was just letting him get a good night's sleep before it all began, *it* being as yet amorphous and mysterious, and open-ended.

And now he was here. With me. Under the fluorescent lights, sitting on teal pleather chairs. "Charlie. What's she going to *do*?"

"She's going to recover and get a prosthesis and be fine."

"She quit smoking!"

"Well. I think the damage is done," I said.

I would let Nick talk on and on, I would let him install this thing on my stairs, let him remodel, even dismantle and rebuild my whole house, so he would not have to talk about her now-missing leg, or wonder why she hadn't told us, or about what the doctors had said, what I hoped he hadn't heard crouching in the jargon, enfolded in the boilerplate of their speeches—which was that this was just the beginning of a long string of bad luck, if you could call it luck, something random, which you could not. *What we see in this population,* the doctors said, which meant smokers, in other words a population that turned onto the wrong road and then just kept going, hell for leather, like there was still a chance they might end up somewhere pleasant.

Well, she had ended up in Massachusetts. In my house. So, maybe I missed her, here in the teal waiting room, with its out-of-date magazines and sturdy potted plants and soothing water feature (bad things happened in this room) plashing in the corner. But I wouldn't have to miss her for long.

"Charlie, what the hell are you smiling about?"

"It's just strange."

"I don't know what the fuck you're talking about."

"Nicky. It's okay."

"No it's not!"

"I mean that we are all here together. I am just glad. Even though it's like this. That's all."

He looked searchingly at me, not that he ever would have disbelieved me. Rather he was looking for the quality of my reassurance. I shifted in the chair and tried to look solid, imperturbable. I am a rock. I am an island. An island broken off, because the solid ground itself of my solitude had turned out to be unmoored, and I was now marooned on a renegade sliver of it, floating away.

Then Nick stood up, because May was there, in the door. "How is she?" she said, her eyes going from me, to Nick, to me. She was wearing the long red coat. *Ah, here to take charge.* Then Nicky was beside her, had her in his arms but really he was in hers, his head was on her shoulder, she was murmuring to him. He folded himself around her. I saw what he did, open, porous Nicky: he infused himself with the other person, made himself whole and strong that way, or at least a little closer to whole, a little stronger. I saw how thoroughly he had absorbed her. So she would be with us too. All of us together.

I HAD THOUGHT life was full, but I had been woefully, laughably wrong. *Now* it was full: after only four days in the hospital and another four in rehab—surely losing an entire limb was more involved than *that?*—Anita was back home with me. There were physical therapy appointments to drive to and decent food must be available and a small cadre of nice women must cycle in and out of the house, at least for now, helping my mother with the things she temporarily (that was the attitude we were taking) couldn't do, many of which I need not inquire about, and odd equipment appeared, and I had to account for my whereabouts, and plan. We had set up a bed in the dining room so she wouldn't have to contend with stairs, but after the first week she nixed it. The stair chair, as Nick called it, was installed, and she said she could manage just fine with that thank you very much. Her arms were surprisingly strong. She scooted the wheelchair around and handled the crutches without complaint. Nicky and I rolled up all the smaller rugs and put them away so she wouldn't trip. I tried not to look at the pinned-up pants leg, or the remaining, still-shapely leg emerging from a skirt. The stump was an obscenity. She shooed me away from it herself. She had taken it on; it was her job.

One evening, when Nick wasn't sleeping over, I seized the opportunity and said, "Just how did you think this was all going to work? Were you going to do this all by yourself?" She didn't answer. "You've been planning. It's why you were going to retire."

"Of course it was," she said. "And there's money. That's what we have, Charlie, money, and I would have worked it all out."

"And you weren't going to tell either of us."

I was baiting her. We both knew it. Telling me anything would have been breaking our rules of engagement.

"There was no sense in worrying you," Anita said.

How many hundreds of times in my life had I heard Anita begin a sentence with *There's no sense in . . .* ? I nodded. "And then you started working out," I said. "For the crutches. Since when do you have arms like a weightlifter? You can't fool me."

Her face had its usual stubborn, inward look. Then all at once she lifted her arm, shook her sleeve down toward her shoulder, and flexed her biceps for me. "That's pretty good. Isn't it."

"Yes, it is," I said, both smug and, finally, surprised.

She pulled the sleeve back down. "Well, it was something to do."

"It was smart, all right."

We were in the living room, with a fire going. I was grading papers and Anita was doing Sudoku. In deference to me, the TV—a new addition—was off, but she didn't seem to mind. I told myself we were not in limbo. I told myself this was the new normal. We were waiting for nothing.

As if determined to contradict my fragile peace she said, "Charlie, I am not going to stay forever."

"You can't fly, Mother."

"Well, I will be able to soon."

"I was talking with Nicky. We'll drive you down at spring break." She didn't answer. "I know it's a long time to wait. Maybe we could take a week sooner."

"You don't have to do that."

"Well, one of us is going to fly down and check on the house for you though."

"Dodie's taking care of it. Lord knows she needed a project. It's fine."

A silence. "You need to sell it."

"I know." I started to speak again; she waved a hand. "Nicky's been talking to me, Charlie, I know all about it. You two have it all worked out." I saw that the *you two* gave her pleasure. "Now. It's about time for me to turn in."

"It's only eight thirty."

"I'm tired."

But I had seen her face hardening as we talked, a barrier to a different feeling. "Mother. You need to take one."

"No, I don't."

"It's only been two weeks. Good God. Take the pain meds. They prescribed them for a reason."

"I've seen what that stuff does to people."

"Those are people who don't have legitimate pain."

"I'm fine." She reached for her crutches. I helped her up off the sofa and then let go at the first possible moment, the first instant of her balance, so she wouldn't bark at me. She inched over to the stairs, not looking back at me, pretending she didn't know how closely I was following her.

Just before she got in bed, she relented, and took a pill. Just one.

THINGS ARRIVED FROM ATLANTA. Aunt Dodie, Hugh's sister, had overpacked. "I don't know what Dodie thought I was going to do with all of this," Anita said. "She sent everything. Summer clothes too."

"We do have summer up here," I said.

"Summer's a long way off," she said, exasperated. "Does she think I'm never coming back?"

"Aunt Dodie likes to be thorough," I said.

"She likes to over*do*."

Anita was sitting on her bed, taking things out of the boxes.

Smoothing the folds, stacking clothes in piles. It was something to get used to, her staying in one place for minutes at a time; I hadn't realized until now how she had always been moving—not restless, just purposeful. Now she purposefully planted herself somewhere, gathered her energy in, resisted asking for help as long as she could. "Well, the dresser over there is empty," I said. "You can fill it up, and the one in the other bedroom too, if you want." Although Anita had never had that many clothes in her life.

"I'll get May to help me," Anita said.

"May?"

"She wanted to come visit. She called."

"Oh."

She looked up at me. "I wanted to tell her not to come but I wasn't sure how to put it."

"You don't have to do that."

"This is your house, Charlie."

"I'm aware of that."

"So she doesn't have to come here."

"There's no harm," I said. "She's been here before." I let that marinate.

But Anita would refuse to acknowledge a sexual innuendo even if it came and sat in her lap. Instead she regarded the stacks of clothes in front of her with a casual disapproval. Then she opened another box, leaning awkwardly over her stump. If her leg had been there, the box would have been sitting on top of it. This one was full of odds and ends—toiletries in a quilted bag, books, and several pairs of shoes. She took out a pair of sneakers and looked at them sternly. In the olden days, this was when she would have taken a long and contemptuous drag on her cigarette. I thought I saw her fingers twitch.

She set the left one on the bed next to the clothes and tossed the right one into an empty box on the floor. "I don't need the visiting nurses as much now. I'm going to redo the schedule."

"You're the boss."

"And I'm going to have the PT come here. It will cost an arm and a leg but what is the point of having all this money?" Money again. She sounded fretful, aware of yet unwilling to acknowledge her joke.

"Anita, you can do whatever you want."

She ignored me. "Lord above," she said. "She sent bathing suits."

"You'll use them eventually," I said. "What? You're never going to swim again?"

She kept looking into the box, her face filling with something like surprise, lips pressed together, toughness gone. It was a sudden self-pity, the first I'd seen, and who could blame her? That handsome body, the shapely leg. Still it made me wild. I didn't know if I could stand it. I clutched my hands at my sides, wanting to shake her, to throw something—then I realized she wasn't on the verge of tears, not at all; instead she was trying not to smile. *"What?"* I said. "Goddammit, what?"

She started a little at my tone, but still looked amused. "The problem," she said, "is that I might go in circles."

"What the hell—oh." I felt myself deflate. "Swimming?"

"That's right." Her shoulders shook. She covered her mouth with her hand.

I was trying to think when I'd seen this Anita before. "No more straight lines for you," I said.

"That's right," she said. "My rudder is broken. Around and around in circles. Oh, my."

I pictured her in Abbott Pond, in the shining blue center, making endless rings. "You'll never get anywhere," I said.

"Nowhere."

"You're stuck."

"Stuck. Oh, my." She held up a bathing suit, bright red, by the straps, and made it do a dance. In amazement I watched the mother of my youth.

BEFORE THE BREAK ENDED, Divya asked if I wanted to offload a course or two. "No, thanks, I've just got three this semester, and Nicky already dropped one of his," I said. "We'll be fine, and frankly, I need to get out of the house, Div."

"Is someone going to be there all the time?"

"Most of the time. She is refusing to be babysat. Nick and I have figured out a schedule. And, um, May is going to help out too." Divya raised an eyebrow. "And there are visiting nurses coming, and physical therapists and all that."

"I think you are crazy."

"This is all temporary."

She rolled her eyes. "I've got good subs available. A very nice woman who used to teach at Northfield Mount Hermon. You don't know what might come up. Maybe just drop the seniors. There are other electives open. That would be best—"

"Absolutely not. That's my baby, Div, come on. It's a great class. I didn't think I'd get anyone for Rilke and Eliot, but there you are."

"Charlie," she said. "You silly man. They're there for you, and you know it."

"No, I don't."

"False modesty doesn't become you. What about Nicky?"

"Good luck if you try to take *him* away from anyone else."

"But, I mean, how is he?"

"Fine."

She tipped her head, a telltale sign of exasperation. "Charlie, listen to me. May told me he's having nightmares. She said he's not sleeping at all."

"He's okay at my house. Sleeps through the night." Like a good child.

"Are you sure he's sleeping? Or is he wandering around?"

"Of course he's not wandering around."

"Because that's what he's doing at May's," she said. "And of course, Charlie, she couldn't talk to you about this."

"Of course she could."

"Charlie."

A few days after that, or nights, when Nick was next sleeping over, I woke up and heard the creak of floorboards. Footsteps only, no crutches, no chair. We had walkie-talkies set up for when Anita needed us; mine was silent.

I heard him going down the stairs. No lights went on. I heard the back door open and close.

I refused to look at the clock. I didn't want to know. It was dark, deep dark, one or two o'clock with any luck, with a cushion of real night left; there was time to get back to sleep, to recover, to have these sentient moments seem like a dream, if I remembered them at all.

Was he wearing a coat? Was he even wearing shoes? Was he hungry? How long had he been awake?

The creaking steps, silent, was that a sound, no, I listened for the door, I felt my body grow less heavy. Awareness beckoned. If I tipped over into it. And the gray light would begin to edge the windows. And the night would be over and day would begin and I could not. Could not.

Could not.

Nicky sitting motionless on the patio. He had taken himself there. I turned over and fell back to sleep. It was much easier than I had thought it would be.

ONE DAY I WALKED PAST Nick's classroom and saw Celia Paxton huddled at the seminar table, her shoulders heaving, Nick beside her, a decent distance away. And the door was widely, properly open—why wouldn't it be? I lingered at the door for a moment, and finally he saw me and shrugged. He looked concerned but preoccupied; he didn't have that rapt, tragic look I watched for, the one he got right before he was sucked down his vortex of empathy.

He told me later that she wanted to feel bad about breaking up with Zack, but didn't.

"Is that all?"

"They were together a long time," he said. "He's pretty wrecked about it. She feels like a bad person. She asks me these questions. What is selfishness? What is love? So, yeah, Charlie, that's all."

"And what do you say?"

"What do I *say*?" We went outside and he turned right, without comment, in the opposite direction from the parking lot, and so I knew he wanted me to walk to his apartment with him, or just walk—we did that sometimes, walked in circles, and I didn't ask where he wanted to end up. "I don't know," he said. I heard the edges of his voice fraying. "I don't even know what I say. I tell her I have no idea. Charlie, why do people come to me? Why does anybody *ever* come to *me*?"

I stopped and turned to him. I wanted to shake him senseless, to smooth him down, to fold him up, put him to bed and watch serenity overtake his face, tuck him away, sleeping prince. There were circles under his eyes. "Tell them not to," I said. "Especially Celia. Tell them to go away. Tell them to come to me. Anything." I held the knobs of his shoulders in my hands, held them too hard, but he just stood there. Why did they think he was bottomless? That he of all people could carry extra weight?

Next time I would get up, I would sit with him outside in the snow all night long if I had to.

"Nicky," I said. "I know you're not sleeping. You know Mom is going to be okay, right? She's here with us. She is going to be fine. She's safe at home in my house and she's going to be fine." He glanced up at me and gently stepped out of my grasp, and I thought that the look on his face was the closest he'd ever come to disappointment with me—but if he had fully admitted it, he would have also had to say the unsayable to himself.

And after that? I could have gone to May. Or Divya, or Celia's advisor, Louise Henri. I could have called in reinforcements. This was Abbott, we knew our kids, this was the kind of thing we didn't let go under the radar, that we didn't let fester, or blossom. I could have gone to them; I could have.

ANITA SAT ON THE STEPS of the church in noonday heat. Her granddaddy was inside, in his office, and she was waiting for him. She had new sandals, with two straps over the foot, and absolutely flat soles. They meant summer. She stood up and walked across one of the long steps and back and listened to their *slap slap*. She sat down again and looked around her, closer and closer. The light so bright. Along the step, a line of ants, walking like crumbs. She was not alone. Creatures of the earth.

She was four or maybe five or maybe six. Old enough to remember. Then there was larger movement and she looked up. A man was approaching, familiar, as most adults in the town were familiar to her, but she didn't know his name. He was wearing overalls and work boots and no hat. The white lines in his red face were wrinkles from squinting into the sun. He walked along the road from outside town, came up the sidewalk to the church, stopped in front of her, and considered her awhile. "I hope you're grateful to your granddaddy," he finally said. "Taking you in like he done."

She wasn't afraid because she knew that adults said anything they wanted to to children. But she didn't answer.

He seemed to expect shame. He was telling her the answer to a question that was a constant in her life, a condition. This *taken in*. How her mother did not live in their house, or town—how she would reappear with no warning, blond, beautiful, wholly unlike Anita, and then leave again. Her own presence, her mother's absence, her father's seeming lack of existence were facts; they snapped into a whole and made her. She did not understand it, but now, all at once, she believed it.

The man exuded a baleful patience. And then, abruptly, he turned and walked away. The bulwark of Granddaddy's church was behind her and she waited for the inrush of safety, but she hadn't felt what she was supposed to, she'd refused the shame that was her due, and so the safety didn't come.

Nineteen

I was waiting at the house for Nick to show up so I could run some errands. Anita scoffed at our caution, but I didn't feel good about leaving her alone with the stairs and her crutches for too long, and Nicky enthusiastically agreed. He'd said he'd be there as soon as his last class was over.

But instead the doorbell rang, and it was May.

"Nicky had to stay for some conferences," she said. "I guess there's a test tomorrow and people are freaking out."

"He didn't mention that."

"Well, he wouldn't. He thinks everyone's brilliant. He thinks his tests are easy."

She was carrying several bags. She was going to make us dinner. Nicky hadn't mentioned this either. She was going to make a double batch of this chicken dish, no, *coq au vin,* that was the official name, she said that, and then we could freeze some. She also had soup, muffins, spaghetti sauce. "I didn't know you cooked," I said.

"Any fool can watch cooking shows," she said. I followed her into the kitchen, where she found space in the freezer for the soup. "I was very bored in Dallas. I got very domestic." Once again I didn't mention the fiancé. I wondered if she had gotten domestic because of or in spite of him.

She put the muffins in the bread box on the counter. "They'll keep a couple of days and then you should freeze the rest of them too. You can just defrost them one at a time in the microwave."

"Okay," I said.

"Will you remember?"

"Tell Anita."

"Right." This seemed to amuse her. "You're welcome."

"Thank you," I said. "You're very kind."

Had she ever stood here, in my kitchen, before? Of course she had.

"May-May? Is that you?"

She turned to the voice. "Hi, Anita!" she called, and disappeared into the living room.

I heard Anita say, "You've still got your coat on! Charlie didn't take your coat?"

"Oh, I can hang up my own coat!"

"I'm going," I said. "Ladies?" I heard laughter. "May-May?" I wasn't speaking loud enough to be heard. I knew it. "Bye," I said, to the empty kitchen.

I BEGAN TO NOT feel surprised when May walked in the door. Or when I walked in and found her already there.

But I could feel the effort my mother was expending not to talk about her. When her name did leak in, I knew it was only one of maybe a dozen times that Anita had almost said it.

One day, after May had left, Anita began, "Charlie—"

"No."

"You don't know what I was going to say."

"You cannot tell her."

"But, son—"

"It would wreck her," I said. "You don't want that. And don't you see how happy Nicky is? Don't you see that? Aren't you glad? Do you want to wreck that too?" She looked down at her hands, folded in her lap. "It is the *only thing I am asking you,*" I said, and I felt like stone, forbidding and eternal, and Anita didn't say anything more.

———

HOW HAD MAY BEGUN IT? "Nicky has told me so much about you"? "My mother is from south Georgia too"? And Anita feigned ignorance, but May sensed there was something she was supposed to hunt for, something easily missed, a golden egg hidden in deepest underbrush?

For Anita was telling her stories.

One evening my mother said, "You know, I used to like sitting under my grandmother's table. In the kitchen."

"Like a fort?" Nick said.

"No, I'd do it when she was sitting there. With her lady friends. In the middle of their legs." She chuckled self-consciously. "I can't imagine why she let me. Except that it kept me quiet."

"How old were you?" May said.

"Little. Little-little. But old enough to remember. And one of the women one time—it was our neighbor. Memaw didn't like her much. This neighbor would come over and Memaw would be in her housecoat and slippers and she wouldn't even change. So that's how I knew. And one day this woman said something about a redheaded stepchild. I'd never heard that before, and I thought she was talking about me."

"But she wasn't?" Nick said.

"Oh, no. It was just an old expression. For someone you don't treat so well. You say, *They treat her like a redheaded stepchild*." Her fingers were twitching beside her plate. No one would notice but me. But I knew that right about now there should be a long drag; then a tap in the ashtray, without looking. (*Charlie, empty this ashtray, please. Charlie, find me an ashtray.* They were the only requests she used to make of me that had been anywhere close to favors. I'd done the dishes, taken out the trash, cleaned my room, but she would never have dreamed of asking me to bring her a glass of water, or the book she was reading, or a deck of cards to play her solitaire;, but I'd see her patting her pocket, and if she came up empty I'd go to her purse or her coat or the pocket of her other sweater. It was what I did for her. She'd favored pockets, then.)

"She said something later though," Anita was saying. "That time, or a different time. I don't know. They would just forget I was there, I expect. I would sit there quiet as a mouse."

"What did she say?"

"She said something about my complexion. Memaw wouldn't let me out in the sun, but I went anyway of course, and I got the worst burns. She said she'd never seen a child so pale. So the neighbor lady said, well, at least you know there's no nigger in *that* woodpile. And Memaw said, yes, there's that at least."

"Mom," Nicky said.

"I didn't say it, son," Anita said. "It was just another expression. But it used to be so important." Her fingers twitched. "To know. People used to think it was very important."

"Because they didn't know who your father was," May prompted.

"Yes. Because of that."

There was a fiction afoot, which was that I knew all these stories. Anita and I let it stand. The truth was our business. As a child, I had felt the past sitting there, undeniable, but I had known with great certainty that my mother only looked forward. Together we pretended that history, by definition, was dead and could not hurt us anymore, or rather she pretended and I, not knowing any better, believed it. Now the past was filling in. Hints and guesses and ghosts gaining color and weight. Beginning to breathe.

I thought about what she'd just said. How she'd heard in that woman's voice that she'd done something good, *was* something good, unintentionally, which also meant the reverse: that she could sin anytime and not know it. That she was keeping some secret she didn't know she had.

"YOU KNEW MY GRANDFATHER was a preacher," Anita said.

"I don't think I did know that," May said.

"Oh yes. In a little country church. No denomination to speak of. He was self-trained. He felt the spirit. He could interpret tongues."

I was coming downstairs when I heard this conversation happening in the living room, and I stopped, unseen, on the stairs.

"They spoke in tongues there?"

"Yes indeed. As a child, it was so confusing. There would be this whole stream of gibberish—oh, I shouldn't say that, I reckon—but it would sound just, well, strange. But still, every time I would think, Oh, here it comes! And then Granddaddy would interpret and it was never the end of the world or any good, interesting prophecy. Or a flood or tornado even. It was just God is mighty, and He's watching, and repent, repent of your sins." She paused and I knew without a doubt that she was shaking her head, her mouth comically tight. "It would be *boring.*"

And May burst into laughter, and after a moment Anita joined her, and I realized how seldom I heard that sound. The laughter carried them out to a glorious sunny blue sea; for a second or two I felt utterly abandoned, but that was an old thought and instead I let myself be glad, and I stood listening to the laughter baptizing my house.

WE TOOK ANITA WITH US to the winter concert at Abbott. Celia had a solo. It was a piece by Mozart. Her voice was rather thin, lacking confidence, but on key; "Laudate Dominum": that's what it was. She swayed a little with concentration during the legato notes. Her Latin was careful, foreign in her mouth. She wore her long hair down, in a long twist hanging over one shoulder. I wished someone would push it back and make her symmetrical.

As she sang I began to feel a pull, not from the stage but directly to my left; I looked over and across the aisle I saw Zack, his face rapt with dread, as though he were watching an execution, or Celia's wedding to another boy. I elbowed Nick, beside me. He turned to Zack for a long moment, almost too long, and then back to me, his expression sad, resigned: *Told you.*

The solo ended and the choir came in, repeating what Celia had already sung, confirming it now in four parts, following its path, bringing it to full life. Celia stood quiescent, her arms at her sides. Then all at once she lifted her chin, looking straight at us; she wasn't finished; and her voice came out twice as strong—strengthened by the choir behind her? *Laudate dominum.* She sounded almost free, her voice more pure, in a long slipping string of an *amen,* and I knew that during her song she had, somehow, answered a question for herself— and was singing it to *us?* No. To Nicky.

But from this distance surely I was wrong. I glanced over at Zack. No, she wasn't singing to him. "Who is that?" Anita whispered. She'd noticed me looking. I whispered back. "Oh. Poor boy," she said.

After the concert, as we were getting Anita arranged and taking the brakes off her chair, Zack came over to us and stood there expectantly. I wondered if he'd noticed Nicky's and my glances, but I knew his eyes had been fixed on the stage the whole time. I introduced him to Anita. He shook her hand, leaning down to her chair, and then when he straightened I thought he looked almost military, more erect—maybe he was practicing. Also healthier than I'd seen him, better color. "This is the hockey star I was telling you about," I said. "This guy had a hat trick a couple nights ago."

"You saw that?"

"Of course I saw it. Haven't missed a home game yet." He smiled to himself, the Zack I remembered. "And now you better tell my mother what a hat trick is."

But instead he looked back down at her and gestured at her empty pants leg. "I'm sorry about that," he said.

I sucked in my breath. I was glad Nick and May had gone to get the car. But Anita just said, "Thank you, son."

"We heard about it. Here at school."

"Not from me," I said. I'd mentioned that my mother was visiting, and was ill, that was all.

"I don't mind," Anita said, a little sharply.

"We hear things, Mr. G.," Zack said. "We young people." And he actually smiled. Then he looked at Anita, grew serious again, and said, like a five-year-old, without guile, "What happened?"

"Bad habits," she said. "Don't ever smoke, son."

"Yes, ma'am. I mean, no, ma'am."

"Mother, Nick's probably outside now with the car," I said.

"That's so weird," Zack said, and shook his head.

"I don't follow you," my mother said.

"You're Mr. Satterthwaite's mother too."

"That's right."

"Yeah," Zack said, speaking to himself, smiling, shaking his head.

"Yeah, all right. You take care now, ma'am. Mr. G." I saw him in uniform. Saluting. Some roughness had dropped away from him but I didn't believe it: when had Zack ever told me to take care?

THE NEXT AFTERNOON. A terrific clanging and I went out in the hall and saw Zack, banging into the lockers, throwing an occasional punch into the doors as he went. People were standing clear of him, looking around, their eyes lighting on me—*Fix it, fix it!* I hurried down to him. "Zack?" My hand on his shoulder. Good God, the wad of muscle. As soon as I touched him, he stopped and crumpled against the wall of metal doors. "Cool it, buddy, what's up?"

"Don't fucking buddy me."

I removed my hand. "I said *cool it,* Mr. Middleton."

He turned his face into the lockers, twisting a little, eyes closed, as though he were a little boy pushing into a closet, hide-and-seek in the coats, the warm woolly dark. The posture, the healthy color of the night before were gone, and now he looked sallow, awful—skin violently broken out, eyes puffy, cheeks hollow. "Why do you *do* that?" he said. "Get all formal and shit."

I crouched down beside him. "Zack, what's wrong?"

"Nothing nothing nothing," he said. "Nothing, fucking nothing." He turned to me and opened his eyes. They were exhausted. "I hate your brother," he said. "You're the better man. What a fucking phony. What a pussy."

"Zack, shh. You can't talk that way. You know you can't. I can't let you."

"It's all his fault. She would still be with me."

"Zack. Let's go talk. We need to talk about this."

"Don't tell me there will be other girls," he said. He was crying again.

"I won't." He looked at me and I saw the trust he'd been hiding. *Charlie, hold me up. I want to go with you. No, Charlie's taking just me.* And also despair. "Come on a walk with me," I said. "Something."

He closed his eyes for a long minute, and then he finally spoke. "No," he said. "No, I can't, Charlie." And he pushed himself to standing, and turned and walked away.

I FOUND OUT ZACK had failed his last calculus test. He was, in fact, failing the course. There were others failing too, but this was BC Calculus; was that so unusual? Nick was adjusting the curve. No, he was *not* sabotaging Zack's academy hopes. Bump in the road. Colleges would never see these grades, it would be fine. Zack would retake the test. The college counselor assured Zack she'd take care of it, don't worry, the main thing was not to worry, and I thought about all the machinations that must be going on to preserve the future of Zack Middleton, diversity prize. And I remembered what he'd said to me about the academy: *You have to earn it, that's the thing, you know you've earned it. Just you.*

In my class, he shut down completely. It didn't surprise me. I was sure he'd only signed up to be with Celia. Now, they sat at opposite ends of the table, and the rest of the class maneuvered around him as though he were a boulder in the sea at high tide.

"You people are seniors," I said. "You've all done well and you're all about to fly the coop. You've filled in little bubbles with number two pencils and sent in the applications. You've checked all the boxes, you've gotten it, you've learned how to get it, but the deal with this class is that these poems can't be *gotten* in the way you're used to.

"You need to do two things with these poems. One, you need to get down on the floor and wrestle with them. Look at every word. Every word is there for a reason, probably ten reasons. Get closer and closer. Be patient.

"And the other thing, the less academic thing, the *soul* thing, is to pull back. Intuit. Trust yourself. Like I said, these poems aren't something to get. They are something to *apprehend*. Apprehend: to take hold of. To *pay attention to*. Pay attention, and meaning will open up."

They regarded me with boredom and disbelief and bafflement and trust. Curiosity and also a little hope. "Darius? What do you say? How about the first elegy. *Every angel's terrifying*. Here we go." And the heads bent to the page—all except for Zack's. He hadn't opened his book, sat with his hands folded on top of it. He glanced at me, his face washed clean of any expectation—Was that the same thing as hope-lessness? Or better? Or worse?—and closed his eyes as Darius began to read. *Maybe birds will feel the air thinning as they fly deeper into themselves.*

But at the end of class he stopped by my desk. "Charlie," he said. "There's a game tonight."

"Do you want me to come?"

"Yes."

"Then I will be there," I said. "You can count on me."

"HOW IS THAT BOY?" Anita said.

"Which one?"

"The one I met at the concert. The poor lovelorn one."

"Lovelorn," I said.

"I worry about him," Anita said.

"I do too."

She sighed. "Charlie, I'll take a pill."

I went upstairs to get them for her. They weren't in her cosmetic bag; I found them in the medicine cabinet. So she'd taken some when I hadn't known about it. *Good.*

When I handed her the bottle she shook it, and confusion passed over her face, a quick shadow, gone. I brought her some water. "The prescription is for two," I said, resigned. She ignored me, shook out a single capsule, and then closed the bottle again with a sudden, violent twist.

Twenty

Little Anita in white dress, feet dangling, sitting in the front pew of the white cinder-block church. Friday night. Hot. The windows are open and thousands of moths flutter outside the screens. The church is a giant lantern.

Her grandfather up in the pulpit, her grandmother beside her. All around them the fans waving, a hundred sticks held in a hundred hands, back and forth, like so many unsynchronized wings of a vast, fantastic insect. On one side of the fan, a tinted picture of the town funeral home; on the other, a melting-eyed Jesus, knocking at the door of your heart. As she watches, all the fans' rhythms come together, an astonishing, undulating creature—it is about to take flight—

The heat is thick, coastal, a leaded blanket over every movement, but a child doesn't realize. A child can breathe in that heat, a child can think fresh thoughts.

The fans go without ceasing; the only thing that makes them stutter is when men (never women), in short-sleeved shirts and Sansabelt slacks, their foreheads glistening and their necks clay red, stand up one by one, a babble flooding from each mouth, a mysterious pidgin syntax. *Once we were perfect* (say the men, in the language only her grandfather understands), *but then the devil tricked Eve and sin was layered over all of us; we are made of dirt, wicked forever; and yet we can recover, in a paradox that we can never understand.*

Somehow the sin is woven in, and yet extra. It is an appendage that can be cut off, but it always grows back. We're always, forever, in need of forgiveness; we do not have one clean moment.

"Amen, brother," says her grandfather. "Brother John has been the vessel." "Brother Lester has been the vessel."

She thinks that that's her own granddaddy in the pulpit, and so she herself is chosen, there in the front pew. But later on, over and over, she realizes how wrong she was. Bit by bit she learns, and then tells herself the rest of her life, that sitting in a white dress in the front pew is an accident of birth, something unearned. As are all births, all accidents.

IN THE CHAPEL, on Sunday, the beginning of February—a short month, days already longer, we would make it through; and Anita doing well, the stump nearly healed; and I didn't wake up every day surprised.

During Cletus's sermon Anita nodded every now and then, at the most emphatic points. I thought of her in that little white church in that hot little town, and now she was in a little stone church in New England, with me, in the snow, and I thought, *This is my life,* and I was content in an unfamiliar way.

Then we were passing the peace and Anita turned to me and said something in a language I did not understand, both garbled and other-worldly, and I looked at her politely and in a split second that was days long I thought, *This is something new to learn, she is showing me something new.* May took Nick's hand but was looking at me: *Do something.* The corner of Anita's mouth was drooping, and for a moment her face was full of fear and wonder and then I saw her thinking and deciding, and she turned back to me speaking tongues from another land and her eyes were flat as a general's.

By the time we got to the hospital, it was over. A pudgy young doctor with a surprising, painful handshake said that they could do surgery but unfortunately the procedure itself could cause a larger stroke, and Nicky said why the hell would they do it then? What was this piece-of-shit hospital and what do your doctors in Atlanta say and what the fuck is this doing nothing!

"Nicky, Nikko," I said.

"Don't fucking Nikko me."

"Nicky," Anita said, in her own voice, which had come back. "That's enough. Come here. Come sit here with me. Right here," and she patted the bed next to her.

The doctor had said she'd flicked a clot. What a ridiculous word. What a transparent effort to cut the body down to size, to a comical, manageable adversary, and to absolve the doctor of this lack of control, of knowledge, over this crazy, unpredictable, corporeal self. Flick a clot here, flick there. There'd almost certainly be more.

May came and got Nick and he clung to her, embarrassingly, nuzzling her in the hall like she was in heat. "Nicky," she murmured. "Baby." She wouldn't meet my gaze, but I felt us speaking through the empty air.

After they had gone, I found Anita signing papers in her room, with a doctor as witness. "I should have done this so long ago," she said, and she handed them to me.

I looked at them. "Okay," I said. I sat down. I shuffled through them again. The doctor looked from one of us to the other, and then said he'd leave us alone. When he was gone I said, "Mother, do you *want* to die?"

"No, Charlie, I do not. I want to be clear as day about that. No I do not. But what I want does not matter one whit."

"What about what I want? What about Nicky? You don't know what they'd be able to do. If something else happened. Aren't there all kinds of things—"

"Charlie, I know exactly what they'd be able to do."

We stopped. I waited for the silence to smooth. We had been in one time, Anita and I and Nicky. And now we needed to move to another. I sat and absorbed this truth.

Finally I said, "Do you want me to talk to Nicky?"

"No," my mother said. "I'll do it."

"Be careful."

She didn't answer. I put my head in my hands and she didn't say anything. But I felt her there. A presence. Not an absence.

———

MAY'S COAT HUNG ON THE HOOK. Anita's crutches leaned against the kitchen wall. The stair chair hulked on the banister. Books tilted on my bookcase at leafed-through angles; Nicky's boots stood by the back door; his bed in one of the spare rooms sat perpetually unmade, somehow larger that way. New implements appeared in the kitchen, supplanting my lone dull knife, my cracked cutting board. Food I hadn't bought sat in the fridge. The washing machine was going, the dishwasher was going. My house was full to bursting. The ashes in the fireplace were always warm.

I WONDERED ABOUT THE SPRING, and summer. I'd plant a garden. I'd look out the window and there would be May, in a big floppy hat, tending the rows. Anita in a chair, directing. Nick sweaty and beaming. A long golden afternoon.

ANITA RODE IN THE CHAIR. She rode it when Nick came over. Wheelchair to stair chair to wheelchair to patio: she said she wanted air, she didn't mind the cold, it was refreshing. The pressure of his hope was painful for her. She hated sitting and looking; he didn't hate it, but mostly his body just didn't understand it, at least not for long. They sat on my snow-shoveled patio, bundled up, and vibrated with their effort not to move.

At night she might read, or more often play games of complicated solitaire, the cards snapping down. I learned to ignore the sound and learned also to be contented with reading passively, since that was all I could do in a room with another person. My attention changed. I took to reading detective novels, and Anita, who recognized a title now and then, seemed to approve. By silent agreement, we played cards together only when Nick came over: usually hearts, sometimes gin, and then Nicky taught us a complicated game he'd learned in Haiti called Onze, which involved eleven rounds of bidding. I set up a table in the living room where her chair would fit, and we huddled around the flame of the cards.

But what was surprising was that my old anger had become a blankness. I realized what an effort it had always been.

She said one afternoon, looking out the window at the gray-and-white February day, "I don't know how you stand this snow."

"Of course you do," I said, not sharply.

She looked out the window a long time. Outside, nothing moved. The quiet was implacable, untouchable. She said, "I guess you're right."

"I ALWAYS DID LIKE TO WORK," Anita said.

She'd started with babysitting. She preferred odd jobs, though, even physical, dirty things, like pumping gas or mucking out barns. But babysitting was the easiest job to find, for a girl. She preferred the younger kids, who were still wide-eyed and never judged, and loved simple things without knowing they were simple. She didn't like the ones who were overly mature. "Too big for their britches," she said. "Girls usually. I didn't really like other girls. Oh, that hand on the hip and that know-it-all voice. Cutting their eyes at you. They were just imitating their mamas. Those mamas pretended to like me, because of my grandparents. They pretended to be sweet, oh, if you were a girl you had to be sweet—Lord have mercy. They pretended all day long. I always said if I ever had children I wanted them to be boys."

"So you got lucky," Nicky said proudly.

"Yes, I did."

She got older and got better jobs and saved all her money. "And then I made my first big mistake. I was seventeen and I bought a car. Charlie probably remembers that car. A blue Ford Fairlane. Two-door."

"Yes, I do," I said.

"I loved that car. It wasn't much, but you always love your first car. But, you see, I showed my hand, and when Granddaddy saw I could pay for a car he said I could pay for everything else. I turned eighteen and he made me pay room and board. He made me pay for nursing school."

"What did you do?" May said.

"I got a night job and a weekend job, and I paid for it."

"Well good for you."

"Once I heard Granddaddy bragging on me. Saying how I was paying for everything myself. He said I was smart too, and I don't know what folks thought of that. Course he would never say any of that to my face.

"But, you know, that car—I had to make it worth it for myself, I reckon. So what I did was, I drove. I figured if I was going to pay for everything, they didn't need to know where I was night and day. It wasn't any of their business. And so whenever I had time I just drove around. As far as I could get, in my spare time. I liked to go to towns where I'd be a stranger. I liked to eat alone in a restaurant where no one knew who I was. I'd have the special. Or a piece of pie. Or just coffee, for a nickel. I loved that. People looked at me like they felt sorry for me, being alone, but I loved it. Or they looked suspicious— but I didn't care. Because I didn't know them and they didn't know me. And I hadn't done anything wrong.

"Then one day I went over to St. Annes, this little town on the coast."

I sat up. She saw it. I shifted on the sofa and rattled papers. She kept her eyes fixed on May, and they began to shine with an artificial brightness that came from the effort not to look in my direction.

"It was a swanky place, where the tourists went. Historic and all. Our town was twenty miles inland and hotter than Hades, you under- stand. But St. Annes was on the water. There was a breeze off the har- bor and some fancy stores. And some of the stores had air-conditioning.

"So I was walking around and going in and out of the air- conditioning when I saw some girls I knew. I'd grown up with these girls, you understand. And in the middle was a girl I'd known since I was born, and she was pregnant—that belly just high and proud. This was a girl who'd married the most popular boy in the class. Right after graduation. Awful boy. Mean as a snake." She lowered her voice as though we were back standing on that street corner with her. "I saw her with a black eye. More than once." May sucked in her breath. "Everyone knew, but everyone still thought she was lucky. They did. People could do that, think two things at once that made no sense together.

"And on either side of her were two girls who had just disappeared during high school, and then come back—who, you know, who'd gone to visit an aunt and uncle in another state for a while, there." She gave May a look: *Do you know what I'm saying?* and May nodded. It had become a story only for May. Both May and Nicky would believe that was because it was, essentially, a woman's story. They wouldn't question my mother's intensity.

"So I saw them coming toward me and I knew they'd ask what I was doing in St. Annes, all shocked, like I was committing a crime. They had all these shopping bags, but I was just walking around and they knew I didn't have the money to shop there. And before the sun went down everyone in my town would know that I'd been in St. Annes, and I wasn't doing a thing in the world wrong, but I just wanted to be left alone. And that belly was coming toward me— oh, I don't know! And so I turned the first corner, and there was a church there, a pretty little church with the pointed windows, and a big arched red door, and the door was open and I heard singing. And so I just went in. And that was the first time I'd been in an Episcopal church and oh my, it was the strangest thing I had ever experienced."

"Does anyone want anything?" I said, standing up. "I'm getting a nightcap. Anyone?"

"We're good," Nick said, not looking up.

The liquor cabinet was a shelf in the pantry that held my lone bottle of bourbon. I poured myself a double, or maybe it was a triple, and sat down at the kitchen table, but I could still hear everything.

"Late afternoon and there was a service going on," she was saying. "Up and down and up and down on your knees. And the prayer book. Flipping around in that—oh, mercy. Everyone knew where to look, of course, and I just hoped no one would notice me. Granddaddy would have said it was idolatry—all those things getting in between you and Jesus. That was the way I was raised.

"And then this young priest says it's the confession, and he said the page number so I knew where to look. I think he saw me." I held the glass with both hands. A secret heart to save me. "I think he knew I was confused. So I could follow along finally and I heard it. 'From time to time.'"

Nicky asked what she meant, and Anita pretended to be distressed that he didn't remember the liturgy he'd grown up with, but really she wasn't surprised and didn't care; I guess she knew that all those years in church he'd knelt and stood and sung he'd just been a good boy, a sweet boy, and he was now untethered and the old words had flown from his head, if indeed they had at any point taken up residence.

I left the kitchen, drink in hand, and went to the doorway. "'We acknowledge and bewail our manifold sins and wickedness, which we, from time to time, most grievously have committed,'" I said.

And she finally looked at me. "Yes," she said. "Do you see?"

"'Provoking most justly thy wrath and indignation against us,'" I said.

She turned away. "But I had thought the sinning never stopped. It was important. Important to me—he said it, that priest, so calm. So polite—'from time to time'! Oh, every now and then! Oh, we've just made a few mistakes!"

Nicky laughed. "That's way better."

But Anita was talking to May. "Do you see?"

"My father was always complaining about the new prayer book," May said. "He used the 1928. He didn't care. He wouldn't change."

"It doesn't matter," Anita said, shaking her head, as if May hadn't spoken. "But it mattered to me. 'From time to time'! To think that you were only wicked sometimes! You weren't made of sin! I didn't tell my grandfather. No sir. I don't think I told anyone. I never talked about it, I think. Until now. But it was a new life. It was a whole new kind of life."

"It's getting late," I said.

Now we'd have the regular comedy of Nick deciding whether he would stay at my house or go with May. Sometimes I liked to watch him squirm, sometimes I stayed to smooth things over so no one would be embarrassed. Tonight I just turned and went back to the kitchen. A good place for the help. Got a refill. Nick was going with May. I called good night, didn't get up, and soon I heard Anita's crutches, the arrhythmic tapping turning to squeaks as the rubber tips met the linoleum of the kitchen floor.

"I'm not going to tell her," she said. "I said I wouldn't and I meant it."

"Don't get angry at *me*."

"Don't think I'll break my word."

"Maybe she knows Preston was in St. Annes. Maybe he mentioned it once. I have no idea. Why are you skating so close to the edge?" I took a perverse delight in the metaphor. Noted my perversity. "Why? Don't you understand, Anita, that I am going to be the only villain here? Not her father. Only me."

"You're protecting him."

"Oh, God." I put my head in my hands. "I'm protecting *her.*"

"And yourself."

"No, Mother. That's absurd. I'm done. I'm cooked." I looked in her face, full in her beautiful face, the face of my dying mother. God damn it all to hell. "You don't get it. There is nothing to protect. But May—I loved her, and she loved me, and then as far as she knows I ruined it by being an asshole, but what I am not going to do is make it *sickening* for her, is make it an *abomination.* That is *my* choice, not yours. *Mine.*"

Now it was her face that was like stone. I remembered that face: it was the face that dealt with drunken Hugh. It meant she loved me but she had given up. But I didn't care. I didn't care.

She turned and tapped her way toward the stairs. I heard the grind of the stair chair. After a moment I went to the bottom of the stairs and asked if she wanted help. There were still practicalities. Her body was going to assure us of that. No peace.

But she didn't answer. And so I sat down again alone. No peace.

A COUPLE DAYS LATER I walked into the kitchen and found May making a cup of tea. Anita was taking a nap, and Nick was still at school. It was fiveish, already dark, the time when the world needs to think about a drink and some supper, the time when a man might like a little quiet. But no. "May-May," I said, "why are you here?"

Her back was to me; she didn't turn around. She poured water into her mug, replaced the kettle with a new precision that said, *I know I'm a guest.* "Don't you feel strange calling me that?"

"No. Because you're here in my house. Nearly every day." She stirred the tea slowly. That little *clink* of the spoon. It reminded me of Anita, except that she didn't drink tea, took her coffee black—so how was that? "Anita wants you here. You need to be here for Nicky. I realize that." I cleared my throat. "I *am* grateful."

"But dubious." She finally turned, gave me a quick smile, and then went and sat down. It was an invitation, but I didn't move. She wrapped her hands lightly around the mug, blew on the surface to cool it. Still I stood in the doorway. As always. Even in my own house. "She just tells stories," she said.

"Oh, and I bet they're good ones."

"You're so angry at her."

"Not as angry as I used to be."

"I don't know what happened between you two, Charlie, but—"

"May. No."

She was quiet a long time. "I think I will never understand you."

"No, probably not."

She drank her tea. Looked at her watch. "I don't know where Nicky is," she said. "He told me four."

"I don't know what she's going to say to you," I said.

"You've heard it all before," she said. "Haven't you?"

"You never know what mothers are going to say."

She was picking up her mug again but her hand slipped, and the hot tea sloshed over. Just a few drops but she gave a little cry, and then she said, "No, you never do."

HERE IS ONE THING May told me, later.

How the first time she had visited and Anita had held May's hand and said, Come back sometime, Anita's voice had been strong, wry, unadorned, but May had felt it was a shell, that the animal inside that had once been strong was beginning to shrink. Something wavered in Anita's eyes—a fleeting transparency, an absence. And her hand was encased in loose skin and seemed made of pieces of itself, no longer bonded into a strong whole. It chilled May when she felt it, and she knew what it meant.

Nick and I had been standing there and May had felt our eyes and knew we watched her hungry for information, but what? What did we think she knew?

The oddest thing though was that as May had held Anita's hand and the chatter floated in and among us, everything rudderless, all of us anxious for different reasons, May heard a bird outside, making an insistent call. It cut through the white January cold and was a *bird,* alive in winter, was life, was notice that time was moving, joyously; that, hidden, things were preparing to grow; and May had known that early out-of-place harbinger bird was counterpart to the smoky absence that passed behind Anita's gaze. Hints and guesses.

So she went back. Over and over. Sometimes she told Nick or me that she was coming by and sometimes she didn't, although she didn't hide it either. She saw that Nick was confused at first by her visits, that she did not chat about them to him, as she might have about buying her groceries or picking up her dry cleaning. She kept herself from saying *Why do you think your mother is an errand* and then realized that of course he didn't think that, that he was trying hard to believe that his mother living in my house was a routine that would last. He wanted May to visit that reality and bring back sanitized reports.

One day she told Anita she would bring her lunch. Nick and I were both at school; she might have told us she was going; if she did, then Nicky surely would have beamed with a determined pride, and I would have said a clipped thank-you. Most likely. Anyway, she went, and as she opened the front door (she told me this particularly, the materiality of that day, how the midweek, midday world made her notice the *thingness* of things) she felt the heft of it in its swing, felt the smooth clicking of the doorknob and thought of me. Imagined me with my head bent, oiling and mending, taking care of my house as though it were my child. Then she replaced my bent head, in her mind, with Nick's, Nick excited and earnest and a bit self-consciously clumsy, my calm competence (how much credit she gave me!) replaced by the pellucid concentration of a little boy, and Nicky's hands filled not with the mechanism of locks and machinery but with something living and beautiful, a bird's nest maybe with tiny speckled eggs.

She closed the heavy door as softly as she could behind her and

heard the *click*. And then listened to the silence; let the house's familiarity and foreignness surround her, fill her, and come to equilibrium.
Not hers, this house, it had never been. But somehow Anita's presence
mitigated that.

Anita wasn't in the living room or kitchen. May went upstairs,
humming a little to announce herself, then called, softly; she didn't
know why. But when she knocked and then pushed Anita's door open,
she saw that my mother was asleep. The TV was on but muted; the
remote control was by her relaxed hand and her chest rose gently up
and down. The warm arrested present of the sickroom. And in the
peace the thought descended on May seemingly from the outside, a
truth of her world, now come to light: *Oh Anita, I love your sons.*

May stood there in the column of her love. She thought the force
of her mind might wake her. But Anita slept on even though May felt
her self, her person, was shouting. She stood there and felt that Nicky
was on her skin, but that I (oh yes she said this) was running through
her veins. She could have stood there looking, picking each feature
out of Anita's face and matching it with her sons', but she also knew
she would see too many mysteries, too many people who were not
hers, whom she would never know, that it would break her heart that
they were both so alone.

Oh I love your sons.

She willed the love to dissipate, or at least become ordinary. What
was she doing? She was standing on the solid wooden floor of my
house. My house filled with things, objects that were not hers, that
had nothing to do with her but that nevertheless had a straightforward
permanence she understood and could take refuge in, unlike this
confusing transporting emotion—thank God Anita had not been
awake to see it on her face, see it surrounding her like so many flapping wings.

"ARE YOU VISITING?" says the young priest, on the steps of the stone
church, in the town of St. Annes. If he's even a priest. His sash is
diagonal across his chest like a boy scout's. She's confused, says yes, she
is. "How long are you in town?"

She explains then that she's both visiting and not. That she lives in a town nearby. He says she should come back sometime. He's a visitor himself. A deacon—he points to the sash, as if she will understand—in seminary, here on summer assignment.

She thinks the collar means he can't get married. She doesn't even know. So it doesn't matter that he's handsome. That there's something bare and hungry and essentially alone in his face, something she recognizes.

She will go back to the main street, and the girls from her hometown will be long gone. But even if they're not, she could face them. Nod hello and keep going. That's what they expect of Anita Spooner.

She says she will be there on Sunday.

Twenty-one

I'm in our kitchen, aged eleven or so, at the table with its plasticky fake-wood grain, with the salt and pepper shakers and the precise stack of paper napkins. The windows are dark but if I could see out I'd see only trees, in our little valley outside the guesthouse.

My mother's at the counter, her back to me, and I watch the shifting of the double-knit uniform as she moves, her slender ankles rising in rebuking contrast to the thick white soles of her work shoes. Her elbow pumps up and down as she opens cans. Occasionally we have TV dinners but those are expensive, and tonight we will have green beans and spaghetti heated up in pots on the stove, and an iceberg-lettuce salad, which she will dutifully provide on its own plate and will make me finish, as always, because it is fresh.

I know that she's an indifferent cook only from occasional dinners at friends' houses, and I'm aggressively disciplined about not imagining, when I'm in our own kitchen, warm cakes on glass stands or roasts emerging from ovens, or fried chicken, or pans of brownies already cut into squares.

She sets down two heaped plates and the little, inevitable salads, and we say a blessing and I feel a satisfaction—hers, mine, it doesn't matter, it's the same—at how well the two of us are doing things.

Yes, I've finished my homework, and I got a hundred on the spelling test and an eighty-four on the math test, and maybe that wasn't my best but next time will be better.

Before long—tonight, or some night soon—she'll ask if I still need a babysitter, or am I too old, what do you think, Charlie, and the long procession of Jennifers and Amys and Janets will end. Soon, also, she'll tell me that Mr. Satterthwaite from church has invited her to dinner, and I can stay home by myself if I lock the door and don't answer it if anyone comes and go to bed by nine, and of course the McClatcheys will keep an eye out like always.

But at this point there still is a girl from the neighborhood there in the afternoons, and as we're eating she remarks that this Linda or Lauren has said that I spend all my time inside reading, and Charlie you need to go outside and get some fresh air, find some boys to play with, it's not healthy.

And I say yes ma'am because that is what I always say and I am used to *Charlie get your nose out of the book,* but who would listen to such absurd advice? When a book is a time machine, taking me back and sideways to other minds and times and cities and planets but mostly forward, forward, to dinnertime, to when my mother would walk in the door and the unsympathetic girl would leave and I could re-emerge into my life, and it would be only the two of us again, my mother and me, and although I felt like I barely had her at least she was mine alone—who would give such magic away?

EVERYONE WAS SICK. Every wastebasket was filled with used tissues. I noted this to Divya and she told me not to be disgusting, and then she said, "My God, you're right." Colds turned into flu and bronchitis. The infirmary was full. The buildings were germ incubators. I waited my turn, but stayed obnoxiously healthy.

Nick, however, missed a couple of days, then came back, then was out again. He looked gray. I asked if he was sleeping and he said he was fine. He didn't come to my house for several days running, and then he went to Boston for the weekend, without May, to visit friends; then he was sick once more. Finally I said to May, "Look, I know you're lovebirds and all, but I think Anita needs Nick to come over and say hello."

She gave me an odd look. "I thought he was sleeping at your house," she said.

"No. Did he say he was?"

She looked miserable, and nodded.

HIS APARTMENT WAS DISGUSTING. Fetid, dirty dishes, unflushed toilet, papers everywhere. "Do me a favor and call before you come," he said, and picked up a few smeary glasses and carried them to his overflowing sink. He looked bad, but he sounded normal—no congestion. I insisted on touching his forehead. Clammy, not warm. "I'm getting better."

"Why'd you tell May you were at my house?"

"I didn't say that," he said. "I wouldn't have said that. I'm here because I didn't want to make Mom sick. Or anyone else."

"What's going on?"

"Nothing. Is May worried?" His eyes softened, color came into his face. "I'll talk to her."

He'd be in the next day. He was contrite. Yes, he knew, he was in trouble with the secretaries, he hadn't been calling in and they'd had trouble getting subs, but he always thought he'd feel up to it until the last minute. "Nancy Beamer came after me today," I said. Nancy was the ferociously efficient head school secretary. "And I told her it's not my responsibility. Which it's not."

"Go away, Charlie, you're breathing my germs," he said.

He didn't want anything. No groceries, he was fine. In the past I would have insisted, but one patient was enough for me.

I SAW MY MOTHER'S FACE when Nicky came back: saw her delight. Together we heard the heavy front door opening, the rattle of the door knocker, Nicky stomping his boots on the mat inside. "He's here," she said to me, just as Nicky's joyful voice came floating up the stairs: "Mama?"

———

I'D GOTTEN RELIGIOUS about attending hockey games. I made all the home games and even a few away ones. It was for Zack, and then I finally had to admit it was for me: it was a relief to have a new imperative, a new ritual; amid the dry cold of the rink, the artificial smell of the ice, I didn't have to think.

I grew used to its particular spectacle, the slamming against the thick Plexiglas, the girls sitting behind shrieking with fear and delight, like they were on a roller coaster. The players masked and padded, cartoonish, as they smashed expressionlessly into one another and the boards; I wondered if this was an aspect Zack appreciated—the disguise, the protection, how emotion became invisible because it was purely private. You couldn't even see them sweat, unless they took off their helmets. Their bodies had no expression except for that urgency, that speed.

Maybe, for Zack, it really was the speed, only that. The closest thing to flying: imagine yourself across the rink and then, suddenly, you're there, with the push of a foot. That's what he'd told Nick, anyway.

The band oompahed. They'd play the school song, some Springsteen, and some Beatles, with glockenspiel, including "Norwegian Wood," with the tuba taking the sitar part; our band director prided himself on his original arrangements. Then, maybe, something that might be AC/DC. With glockenspiel.

Once I was sitting in the front row and as Zack skated by after a whistle he waved at me. A very small wave, like a four-year-old, or a teenager.

Then, at the break, the shouts of "Book-er! Book-er!" as Booker Middleton drove out on the Zamboni. It was odd and endearing that he'd appointed himself Zamboni man, remarkable that someone, once upon a time, had thought of chanting his first name, even more so that he let them, and it had become tradition. Around and around and I'd watch with the usual mildly obsessive suspense, hoping he didn't miss any slivers. He never did. He was predictably precise. The gleam of the new ice, the careful overlapping, beginning to be hypnotic until he reached the center and then he lifted his blue squadron cap into the air; and then the wild cheers and whistles, the stomping feet.

Zack was on fire, relentless on goal, even behind the mask I could tell his focus was absolute. The other hapless goalies down again and again on rubber knees, and again and again he got past them. I brought a hat to every game, to throw on the ice, just in case.

I MISSED ONLY ONE GAME, on a Friday night when I sent May and Nick instead. I stayed home with Anita and pretended I wasn't babysitting. We watched *Casablanca* on TV, and she fell asleep while Bogey and Bacall were in Paris, and I spent the rest of the movie mostly watching her face, afraid it would twist or sag. It never did, but she didn't look peaceful either. Her brow furrowed and behind her closed lips her mouth dropped open in a look of grim, disquieting astonishment. Finally I turned off the TV and woke her up and helped her to bed.

As it turned out we lost, 2–1, but a rout had been expected, so it felt almost like a victory. Zack didn't score—that had been Darius—but he was credited with the assist. He'd also gone down once in the second period, but Nick hadn't even noticed; no one much did. It was a collision like dozens of other collisions.

Zack didn't admit to the double vision until the next day, when he tried to get out of bed and vomited just from sitting up. That's what I heard. On Monday, he was once again missing from my classroom, from everyone's. There were scans and consultations, and second and third opinions, and finally unanimous agreement: he could never set foot on another rink or field. He could not be in the military, any branch; he certainly would never fly a plane. He was lucky to be alive, and another hit could kill him.

"I THINK I SHOULD TELL YOU," Anita said. "I had another one today. It's like a curtain coming down over my eyes. It passes down and then up. And I couldn't say my name. So I sat down in a chair and I stayed there. And ten minutes later I was fine. Charlie, I just thought you would want to know." She paused. "There's nothing I can do, though."

"Then I don't know why you're telling me," I said. It was just us. Just my mother and me. She told only me because I could handle it. Charlie can handle these things. I thought of her sitting, alone, waiting for whatever was going to come next. "But tell me anyway," I said. "Always tell me."

It was afternoon—I'd just gotten home. The days were getting longer already, the sun higher; it was blinding on the snowy mountains. The kitchen was flooded with light.

Overnight it had snowed, a light powder, and now it was blowing, glittering in the sun. A southerner would be amazed. Floating snow like silver dust. Here in this foreign land. "Look at that," I said, and stepped away from the window, so she could see.

SHE SAID THAT I should go visit Zack, flat on his back in a dark room, and I said I would. She said that she'd like to go herself, and I said I'd take her. We should give it a week or so, though, she said, because that boy has to sleep, he has to heal. It would be too soon for visitors. I saw that she was looking for a patient besides herself.

"I wonder if that girl will go to see him," she said. "I don't know if that would be bad or good."

"You think about them that much?" I said.

"I had a boy like that in the ICU," she said. "In a coma. His girlfriend visited all the time. Cried and cried. I got impatient with her, I remember that. I think I kept it to myself all right though."

I made a sympathetic noise.

"They kept hanging on and hanging on, they wouldn't unplug him."

"Mom," I said. "We won't do that to you. And Zack is not in a coma."

"I know that," my mother said, inscrutable, unrepentant.

No, he was not in a coma, but neither did he want to stay flat on his back for a week, and one night he got up when everyone else was asleep and walked to the gym; he could think better in the cold, maybe; maybe the cold kept him together—that was how I felt, sometimes, winter as a bracing, binding agent, winter as discipline, and maybe Zack Middleton was the same. The cold in his nostrils and he thinks, *I'm all right, they're all full of shit, I'm fine.*

And so he goes around and around and around: flying. If there hadn't been a recent warm spell, if Abbott Pond had been thickly frozen, maybe Zack would've gone there—because, it seemed, he needed to skate. To fly. But that elemental motion was forbidden to him now, so he had to sneak out to do it. It was a little after midnight, they found out later, from the security camera footage at the rink, where Zack went instead—but if he had been at the pond he might have looked up at the geometry of Orion stretched against the sky, that gargantuan wheeling warrior, the ice of his sword at the ready, and felt a protection and wonder.

The brightest of Orion's stars is dying; I wonder if Zack knew that.

But instead he used his father's keys to the rink and the alarm and he laced up his skates and flew bareheaded and alone. The only sound the scraping of the blades against the ice. Around and around.

He knew that rink so well—he carried *that* geometry in his body; at least that's what I imagine. If he'd closed his eyes, he might've been fine. If he hadn't relied on his vision, doubling the boards like fun-house mirrors; if he had instead closed his eyes and *felt* the limits of the rink—then maybe he could have kept going, around and around, flying.

There is no Icarus constellation, I later discovered. A gross oversight. But there's a crater named for him on the moon. I looked it up. Apparently astronomers are known for their dark humor.

Someone found him in the morning. Not Booker—thank God not Booker. Instead a part-time janitor, filling in, whose name I don't know, who saw the dark heap on the ice, the crumple of Zack, who had miscalculated, who had hit his head for the last time in the night, who had fallen to earth for good.

I KNEW THAT, at the cemetery, there might be a pile of dirt and a shovel, and a polite line of somber people waiting their turn. I warned Nick, who had never been to a Jewish funeral. A shovelful of dirt and it would be final and real, I said, but also palpable, deeply right, a mitzvah.

But what I did not expect was how cold it would be that day, how Zack's grave would be on a hill, and how there would be so many people it would be hard to see; that the pile of dirt would be enormous; that there would be no explanation or announcement of this custom, this rite, just the sounds beginning. The cut of the shovels, the ringing of the rocky soil on metal. The clods thudding on the casket. I couldn't see who was digging. There was no polite line.

But then the crowd shifted without seeming to move, amoeba-like, and through gaps in the wall of motionless people I could see two men: Angela's father, and Booker. Booker was wearing a yarmulke but he was so tall I could see it only when he bent to dig. Together, they lifted the dirt and poured it in. Lifting, pouring, from the towering pile. Divya reached up and held on to my arm. My other arm around Nick. May close by his other side.

Then Booker's father, a man even taller and darker than Booker, took the shovel from Angela's father, but Booker kept going; another black man, another, then another white one, uncles, cousins, took the other shovel, but Booker would not stop, until finally his father put his arms around him and then gently slid the shovel from his hands the way a parent slides a toy away from a sleeping child.

And Booker bowed his head and wept. The hole was so deep. Bottomless. The dirt kept going in. I couldn't see Angela but I could hear her, the most defeated, wretched sound I had ever heard. And beside me Nick pulled away and I realized I'd been leaning on him and I nearly fell. "Charlie, Charlie, shhh," May said, tears pouring down, and the tears were like light on her face, light in my own eyes, and I could see her, I could see. She looked after Nick, stumbling away down the hill, and I shook my head, and May came under my arm where Nicky had been and Divya still there on my other side and we all stood unwilling to let go.

A MEMORIAL BEGAN at Zack's locker but became so large it was moved to a bank of overflow, unused lockers at the end of the first-floor hall. The notes and stuffed animals and photos multiplied day by day; Zack's name was spelled a foot high. All the girls in their dorm rooms, crying, drawing bubble letters, making collages, turning this enormity into ritual and then finally into kitsch—who could judge them? The Diversity Forum had made a huge poster. "We are all one Abbott—We love you, Zack." There were multiple pictures of Zack and Celia. There were baby pictures, some with our old house recognizable in the background. There was an enormous picture of him from freshman year, in his football uniform, helmetless, smiling, Zackie Bear oh Zackie Bear, and I saw Nicky stop and stare at it, incomprehension on his face, whenever he passed.

A WEEK AFTER THE FUNERAL. The pall beginning to lift by the merest fraction. Then: Dex Pentecost at the windowed door of my classroom. "'Scuse me, people," I said, and went over and opened it a crack. "Hi, Dex, can it wait?"

"It's Mr. S.," he whispered. "In our class. He's—I think you need to come." Our eyes met. "He's crying," Dex said.

I glanced back into my room. "I'll take them," he said. It was my sophomores. "We'll just hang out. Go."

"Invisible Man," I said.

"Got it."

I went past May's classroom. They'd come to me. Me. Downstairs. Other end of the building. His room next to last, the door closed; I don't know what I expected but when I went in it was nearly silent, the class frozen except for Marina, who was crouched at the front of the room next to Nick, slumped down under his whiteboard. "Mr. S.," she said. "Mr. Garrett's here." She looked up at me, uncertain in her new role. "Your brother's here." She patted him gingerly on the shoulder. "It's okay."

His head was between his knees, his head covered with his hands. Sackcloth and ashes. He looked horrible: unshaven, uncombed, unshowered by the smell of it. I got him up. I told the class I would be back. We went out in the hall and closed the door. "Nicky," I said.

"I'm sorry—it just—God, Charlie, I looked at his seat, and I couldn't—"

The exhaustion was suddenly crushing. I put my hand on the wall to hold myself up. "They're all crying in there, Nick. There's a time and a place. You have to give them order. You have to make them feel safe."

"It would be dishonest," he said. "They need to know—"

"Jesus," I said. "They do know. Go home. I'll come over later."

He looked stricken. "We can't just leave them in there," Nick said.

I turned my back on him. "Go home."

I went back in, alone. I apologized for my brother. To a one they looked amazed, said it was all right, and then Celia stood up and asked if she could leave, and before I could answer she ran out of the room.

I thought of her at the funeral, flanked by her parents, who had flown in from Hong Kong. They had been two of the most beautiful and expensive-looking people I had ever seen. Celia was not adopted, as it turned out: her father was a blond, blue-eyed American, her mother a Hong Kong native, porcelain skinned, exquisite; between those two visions Celia had faded to plain; the parents had looked distressed and, very faintly, impatient.

Minnie looked after her with anguish and just a shade of self-importance. "Why don't you go check on her," I said, and waved her out. Celia probably shouldn't be left alone anyway.

The rest of them looked at me with absolute credulity, with faces wiped clean of attitude, of bluff. I told them that they weren't imagining it, this was all horrible. I told them there was no way around but through. I said we had one another and to be kind. I knew what I was saying was true, but it felt like there was no truth to be had except the finality of Zack's absence.

Then I dismissed them, went and dumped the whole sorry mess in Nancy Beamer's lap—she'd round up everyone, subs, advisors, dorm parents, and I even told her to tell May; I wasn't going to do it—and then I went back to relieve Dex, who was reading aloud to the class and actually had them laughing. Oh ye Dexes, oh ye salt of the earth. Ye competent and uncomplicated. We shall rise up and call ye blessed.

———

WHEN I WENT TO NICKY'S after classes were over, it was clear May had recently been there: papers were stacked, dishes washed, pillows fluffed. That precise V dent in each one. Maybe I'd just missed her. I sensed the remnants of freshness, of purpose, in the air. How quickly she'd moved through, establishing order.

Nicky didn't answer when I called out to him.

He was in bed, on his side, facing away from the door, a position I knew, remembered, and beside him on the floor a liter of vodka, nearly empty. May's ministrations had stopped at that bottle. She had left it there for me to see. I went and stood over him, so I could see his face. "Nicky." He grunted at me, opened unfocused eyes, closed them. I could smell it now, in the room, in his evaporating sweat.

I reached down and shook him, hard, my hand, my arm seeming separate from me—they had their own ideas. I held on too tight to his ropy young self, oh my poor poor emaciated brother. I took pleasure in squeezing too hard. I felt for a moment what I could do if I let my control lapse altogether.

"Ow," he said, turning over to his back. He groaned and dragged his eyes open again. "Charlie, what the hell."

"What the fuck have you been doing?"

"Leave me alone."

"Do you do this a lot? How long has this been going on?" He curled up again, small, small. "It's just this once, right? You don't *do* this. Do you hear me? No. You don't. You don't hear me and you *don't do this!*"

He was muttering something into the filthy bedclothes. I shook him again. "I can't hear you."

I was waiting for him to start talking about Zack. Something that would make me furious. *That empty chair. Celia's so upset.* But instead he said, "I'm sorry I said I would stay here forever. I'm sorry."

I let go of his arm. I sat on the edge of the bed. I'd had a rudimentary plan when I came over: I was going to talk him down, or up, whichever way he needed to go. Then I was going to take him back to campus, in time for dinner; I was going to sit there in the dining hall with him, with his wet hair freshly combed, maybe a fresh cut on his now-smooth chin, the circles still there under his eyes, gray velvet, the circles that I'd seen May smooth with one gentle finger, and I was going to watch the parade. All the girls, and the boys too, marching, no, drifting by, lingering: all deferential, all acolytes. All hoping. A long slow line of those kids, fresh and fortunate, wanting him, as we always want the rare, the delicate, the souls with the air of elsewhere.

But instead I thought about all the times he'd been sick this winter. How he kept disappearing. I thought about his trips to Boston. I looked around the room and it suddenly seemed filled with malice, and I knew that I could look in closets and cabinets and drawers and trash cans and find evidence of an entirely different man. And yet the same. The Nick we all wanted, but there wasn't enough of him, and he knew it. My brother, my talisman.

I touched him again, gently, on the shoulder before I left, but he was asleep, and didn't move.

I WENT HOME and as soon as I walked in I knew she was there. They were in the living room, playing two-handed bridge. "Your mother taught me," May said. "This afternoon." Her eyes were red.

"I hope she's letting you win," I said.

"Not a chance." She smiled faintly, without looking up.

"She's doing very well," Anita said.

"I went by Nicky's," I said. No one answered. I took off my coat, went to the kitchen to see about dinner. I knew I was hiding. Oh solitude. Oh the lost silence. Now bits of me kept being peeled away. All the safety. And today was Friday. Now it was the weekend, two long days.

Then I heard the tapping and they were both there, in the kitchen. I turned to them and said, "Did you know he did this?"

May said, "He told me he didn't drink because of his father."

I said, "Do we believe him?"

Silence. Then May said she was leaving. "Don't go over there," I said.

"I'll be back tomorrow," she said. I wondered where she would sleep tonight. I hated myself for wondering.

The front door opened and closed. I said, "I didn't know."

"I didn't either," Anita said.

"I don't know how long he's been doing it," I said. "I don't even know what he's doing." Oh the cowardice. I didn't want to know. I was asking her, *Do I have to know?*

She tapped over to the table and sat down. "I did what I thought was best," she said. "Getting him to come here."

"I know you did."

"It was a lot to ask of you."

"He's my brother."

"And you let me ask. You let him come. Thank you, Charlie."

"Don't be so valedictory, Mother." Cold, cold. Pushing her away. "We're still in it."

She said, quietly, "I had another one today. It's fine though. I'm fine."

I pulled out the chair across the table from her and sat down. My legs were trembling, like I'd been standing for hours.

"I try not to worry," she said. "But I do. I'm not afraid of pain but I don't think there will be pain." She rubbed her forehead, as though trying to smooth it. "Aphasia is a concern."

"In English, please."

"If I can't talk." I remembered Preston's eyes, wild as he spoke his gibberish. *My mother is Anita Spooner.* "I try not to be afraid, Charlie," she said. "But that's the only thing I'm afraid of. If I can't talk to you and Nicky—"

And I couldn't stand it anymore, and I reached out and took her hand, and she clung to it, hard, and was there, all of her—fighting, dug in, I felt it. And I felt how the battle was already lost, because that was the nature of battle itself.

"Tell me," I said. "Tell me everything you want to say."

Twenty-two

She was in the town of St. Annes. In the stone church with the red door.

FROM TIME TO TIME. *In newness of life.*

When they knelt to pray it seemed a kind of idolatry. But she was ready to worship a different God.

HIS CAR HAD A RADIO and he let her find the stations she liked. It was an older car, but he'd taken good care of it. She loved his long, smooth hands on the big polished steering wheel. The chrome on the dashboard gleamed.

When not in his robes, he wore a seersucker sport coat, or short-sleeved collared shirts like a golfer would wear—like the college boy he was. He wore his hair short, no sideburns. He wore white suede oxford shoes.

HE'D HAD TO THINK of some way to stay in school, to avoid the draft; he'd never thought he'd end up a priest. "I don't know if I heard a call or not," he said. "Sometimes I'm worried I made it up. Other times

I'm sure I didn't." He nodded, more to himself than to her. "Please don't think I'm a liar."

"I don't," she said.

SHE WANTED TO KEEP seeing him only in the neutral fairyland of St. Annes. But he must come to her house in his car, he must pick her up. She wouldn't let him in to meet her grandparents. "I don't know what you're about," he said.

"I don't either."

"It's not the way I was raised."

"Nor me." She said it like a lady, looking out the window, her back straight.

She felt the pull of him beside her. She was sure he knew it. She terrified herself.

They went down Main Street and she watched everything familiar go by, looking flattened and dusty, beaten, unlike St. Annes, which was where she would see him, in her mind, for the rest of her life. "I'm from a town just like this," he said. She didn't answer. "Only worse."

"I thought you were from New Orleans."

"I was born in a town like this."

She turned to face front, glancing at him only quickly. "I don't think I would say worse," she said.

"Anita, we're the same," he said.

HE LEANED DOWN TO HER and there was a familiarity in the tilt of his head and then in the pressure of his mouth. *How many times has he already touched me?* and she felt the sudden whirling loss: she should have been counting.

"CHARLIE, IT'S LIKE HE WAS ME," my mother said. "Nothing he said surprised me. Everything was familiar. I know that doesn't make any sense." She was quiet awhile. "It was just falling in love. But I didn't know that."

————

HIS FIANCÉE WAS THE DAUGHTER of a bishop. "But I can't marry her. I can't do it."

Anita understood, fully, how she had been wronged. She understood exactly who and what the other girl was.

"Anita, I have to tell you who I am," he said.

"Tell *her.*"

But he told Anita instead. He told her how one day his father had laid his hand, warm and heavy, on the top of Preston's head, and looked with him with a kind of disbelief, and then disappeared.

Preston and his mother went back to New Orleans then to live with her family, the Broussards. It was such a large family that there were members he rarely saw. Some of these were cousins with dark skin and kinky hair. Yet they were his cousins. He had other cousins too, with light, straight hair and blue eyes, who were merely tan. Not much was said. Nothing was explained. But he understood he had a responsibility not to take his luck for granted. He also understood, now, the disbelief in his father's eyes. "You're no different, son," his mother said. "You're the same person you ever were." And he tried to believe her.

ANITA SAID SHE DIDN'T CARE. Of course she didn't. How could she? "I don't even know who my father is," she said.

But once they were bare to each other, known, the same, she fell to his own level, the level of the bastard, the mistake, the level he could not accept.

At the end of the summer, he went back to Virginia, and the blond, blue-eyed daughter of the bishop.

SHE HAD SUSPECTED before he left but had prayed she was wrong. Had prayed not to be punished. Finally though her situation was clear, and she wrote and told him.

He wrote back. He enclosed a check. He'd asked around, and

thought this would be enough to take care of it. Since she was a nurse, he wrote, she might know someone.

She knew gathering the money and asking around hadn't been easy. She felt an enormous pity for him. Which was almost harder.

SHE SAW JIMMIE GARRETT every now and then in town and their glances still held the truths of high school: she'd been smart and had graduated; he'd been handsome and wild and had not. They rarely spoke. But one day, in the dime store, he swaggered over as she stood in line. He had a way of stopping not directly in front of a person, so you were forced to turn to orient yourself toward him. "Anita Spooner. I thought you got the hell out of here by now," he said. He slid his eyes sideways at her, and back. "Beg pardon."

She paid and headed for the door, not inviting him to follow but not dismissing him. They stopped together on the sidewalk. The November light was white and thin. It was colder than it looked. She said, "I'm leaving in a month. When I'm done with school," and she knew it was true as soon as she said it aloud. She'd be four months along. Not showing, if she was lucky. Preston's check in the bank.

He regarded her with hooded appraisal. "Me too," he said. "Gittin' out of here. Vietnam."

She looked around at the storefronts she'd been walking past all her life and she thought how people would see them standing there together. People might be impressed that Jimmie Garrett was even giving her the time of day or they might wonder why she was talking to white trash, but she didn't want them to think anything. She began to walk. Again he followed her. They went half a block and she said, "Are you scared?"

"Naw. Shitty little war in a jungle." His eyes slid lazily to her, and away. "Beg pardon."

"Have you always wanted to go to war?"

"Sure," he said. He smiled an inward smile. "Glad they thought one up in time for me."

HIS FINGERS WERE ROUGH and smelled of lye soap, like Memaw used for laundry, and for just a moment she saw him washing before he picked her up, leaning over a tin sink, with an earnestness that she hadn't thought of. She tried to feel passion, reminded herself she knew now what it was like; she let him do more than he expected he'd get, she was sure. But it felt unreal to her, and she knew that, for the first and last time, it didn't matter.

"Anita Spooner," he said slowly. "Little Anita."

When he had driven back to town and was idling in front of the big peeling white house and she was reaching for the door handle, he said, "I'm leavin' soon too. In two weeks."

She nodded politely.

He said, "But you know, I can't be with a girl who acts that way." Her hand froze at the door. She nodded again, amazed at herself and at this new sin but also at a new, detached compassion: *Poor boy, he thinks this has anything to do with him.*

"I'll get me a wife when I come back." He seemed to be waiting for a challenge, but when she said nothing he went on, "But that is not what a man wants. A woman who done what you did, tonight."

"I don't blame you," she said, and got out of the car.

SHE TOLD HER GRANDPARENTS she was going to Brunswick, twenty miles south, to see about a job. Her clothes were getting tight. She had no more time. Early the next morning she got in the car she had paid for herself and drove, not south but north, six hours, to Atlanta.

She had had no idea what a city was like. She drove around and around, and the city kept going. When she finally stopped she was in front of a post office, with an impressive granite facade.

It was lunchtime and the line was long. As she stood in line, she understood that she was not known. She let her back sway, her belly protrude. Was it visible? She'd had to buy a bigger skirt. She was not known.

A man waiting behind her glanced in her direction, and she pretended not to notice. She put her bare left hand in her pocket. That was something to take care of.

At the counter, she asked for stamps. When the man handed her the sheet, she carefully tore one off, licked it, and stuck it in the top right corner of her envelope. Then, with her right hand, she handed it to the man, who had gray hair and laugh lines. "It's to my grandparents," she said. He smiled with approval and told her to take care now.

As she walked out of the post office, she smiled straight into all the faces she did not know.

Twenty-three

Saturday was quiet. My mother slept more than usual. I tried not to hover.

At one point she said, "'He never met a stranger.' Do you remember?"

"I remember," I said. That was what Hugh used to say about Nicky. Who would toddle up to anyone and beguile them. Whenever Hugh said that my mother and I would look at each other and silently agree: *We've met lots of them. We are strangers.*

"He's a person who is going to be alone in the world," she said.

"No. He has us."

She smiled, and said she was just tired.

I UNDERSTOOD I COULD ASK her no more about Preston, not now. She was spent. Everything she'd rolled up and put away years and years before, laundered and put in a brown paper sack, stuffed in the deepest of drawers—she'd gotten it all out and given it to me. And now she was lighter, but unsteady. She had to get used to me knowing.

"IS THERE ANYTHING you want me to tell Nicky?" I said. "He said he's coming. Soon. With May."

"No." A few minutes later she said, "He needs to hear things in a particular way."

Oh favored son.

She was dozing on the couch. Her head sank back. Then she straightened and said, "I burned that letter up."

"What, Mother?"

But she was asleep.

WE DIDN'T GO to church Sunday. Nicky finally came over, with May, in the late morning.

It was gray and raining, just above freezing, dreary. When he came in he shook off his wet, hatless head like a dog and wouldn't answer questions. He looked thin and strangely radiant. "I just want to see Mom," he said.

"I need to know how long you've been drinking."

"That was bad, what you saw, Charlie," he said. "But I don't drink. It just—I was desperate. Don't you get it? I'm sorry. I'm sorry you had to see that. I don't do that."

May went into the living room and sat down, her back to us.

"Where's Mom?" Nicky said. "Why isn't she downstairs?"

"She's resting."

"It's the middle of the morning."

"It's a good day for a nap," I said. "She knows, by the way. She's worried about you. So you can go explain it to her."

He gave me a look that was equal parts woundedness and incomprehension, and went upstairs.

I went into the living room. "It won't help to get mad at him," May said, tonelessly.

"I don't see why not," I said. "No one ever does. It's not going to make things worse."

She didn't answer, and went to make tea. I settled back into the work I'd been doing. The world couldn't just stop. We all had jobs and we had to do them. Anita understood that, I thought.

I concentrated on the fire, on the quiet. I read a solid B essay by Dex on nature imagery in "East Coker." I allowed myself to be annoyed that he was mailing it in, then further allowed myself to be resigned, since he was a senior. Convinced myself to not take it personally. Considered what his best work might be: Could Dex Pentecost write an A paper on Eliot? Maybe not. Although I realized I wasn't concentrating very well, and maybe this wasn't a B paper after all; actually I had no idea what I had just read—

"He has nightmares. Almost every night."

My pen stopped, hovering.

"Or I wake up and he is out of bed, just sitting at the window, staring. And I can't comfort him, Charlie. Nothing works."

I heard how many times she had comforted him. How she loved him.

"Are you afraid for him all the time?" she said. I didn't answer. "You should have told me," she said, and then shook her head, speaking to herself. "It doesn't matter. It wouldn't have mattered."

Jesus God this clamping matrix of time and feeling.

"I wanted him to see someone," she said. "He won't do it."

"He would just charm them. Fool them."

"You didn't tell me he was good at that."

I said, "I didn't know."

She was very far away, there in that chair, next to the sofa, next to me. A person I could not touch.

I went on to the next paper. I put Dex's at the bottom of the stack, without a grade, since I didn't trust myself. More and more I had to do this, duplicate my work, start over. I'd forget what I'd done. I'd lose my place.

"Charlie."

"Mm." She didn't say anything else and finally I looked up. Her eyes were wide, her head cocked. "What?"

"I don't know," she said, but then she stood and headed upstairs, and I followed her.

Anita's door was open just a crack. May stood, listening, and then opened it softly. She went just over the threshold, just far enough so I could see too.

Nicky was curled on the bed, his feet hanging off the end. His head was nestled in the space where Anita's leg should have been. He was asleep, his hands held the blankets in fists, but his slack face looked spent and weirdly plain, for the first time I could remember, ever.

Anita was stroking his hair, very gently. She looked up as we stood in the door but her own expression didn't change—her ancient, soft, sad adoration.

May stopped. She stood, frozen. I was behind her and suddenly wanted to spin her around, to see for myself what expression was on her face, what realization. We stood there for several long moments. I put my hand on her shoulder, and she turned, and we left, and she closed the door gently behind her.

We went back down the stairs, and by the time we'd reached the bottom I had no choice. I took her gingerly into my arms. Her head dropped onto my shoulder and she started to sob, burying all her sounds into my neck, hanging on to me for dear life, the nearest piece of flotsam. She was saying something. I wasn't even sure she was saying it to me. "What? What, May?"

"He's gone. He's gone."

"May, he's right here."

"You shouldn't have given him to me, Charlie."

"May-May," I murmured. "Shhh. May-May." I held more tightly. "I didn't mean to." She said something into my sweater. "Shhh."

"Yes you did. You did."

"I'm sorry. I'm sorry, sweetheart, I'm sorry." I stroked her back. My cheek rested on her hair. I said, "He is the best I have."

Twenty-four

A storm was coming, and, this being the twenty-first century, we knew it, down to the hour of its arrival. The school was battening down the hatches. I was teaching one more class but then I'd leave, ahead of the snow. It was almost March, and the snow would be heavy and wet, weighing down trees and power lines. We were supposed to get at least a foot.

But then Nancy Beamer appeared at my door, head down, tapping the glass with one knuckle, and I knew. I went down the hall to the phone at Nancy's desk, where May was waiting on the line. "I didn't want to hang up," she said. "I don't know why."

"It's all right," I said.

"I'm at the house. I came by . . . she's unconscious. I thought she was asleep but then I realized—"

"She's breathing?"

"Of course she's breathing!"

My hand relaxed on the phone. I hadn't realized how tightly I'd been holding it. And then I knew how much harder this was going to be than I'd wanted to believe. "Don't call nine one one," I said. "We have hospice set up."

"I know." There was a long pause. "I'll get the number for you—"

"I have it."

We had been waiting for exactly this moment. This stage. We'd been clear-eyed, planning for nothing else, Anita and I, and now she wasn't here. For all intents and purposes absent. I hadn't realized. I hadn't known this was part of the plan.

"I'm here," May said. "I'm with her. I just happened to come by. She would have been alone."

"Okay. Yes. Thank you." Hospice would send someone. Someone to be in charge.

"But there's that rattle, Charlie. All of a sudden. You need to come home."

I let myself shake for one more second. Then swallowed, steadied. "May, it's all right."

"I remember when Daddy sounded like that—oh *God,* Charlie."

"May-May." I heard myself, went on. "Is Nicky there?"

A small hesitation. "No. I haven't called him yet."

"All right. You try to reach him, and I'll find him." All of a sudden I wanted to see her. To imagine her, that is, as realistically as possible. "Where are you?" I said.

And she understood. "I'm in the hall. Downstairs."

"I was just wondering," I said.

"I'm standing by the bottom step. Looking at the front door. I don't know why. I'm going back upstairs as soon as I hang up. I didn't want to disturb her, talking on the phone. I know that's ridiculous."

"It's not."

"You'll find Nicky."

"Yes."

"Hurry."

"Yes."

UPSTAIRS SHE KEPT BREATHING. And she was still a presence: I'd been wrong; and, weirdly, I relaxed. I felt the completeness of the house, how she was still absolutely here, however feeble. Her body was still so active. She looked a little surprised, lying there, her mouth slightly open, air rushing in and out thickly, like the tide.

We waited for Nick as the snow began. Just a few flakes at first, gentle but inexorable. The sky was gray and heavy with what was coming.

We called hospice and while I was on the phone I heard myself saying not to send anyone. Whoever came would be stuck for the duration of the storm, and I realized I didn't want that. As I was explaining to the concerned woman at the other end of the line I looked at May, and she nodded.

Then I hung up, and we were alone.

I'D TOLD NANCY we were looking for Nick, and she said she'd find him, and I'd believed her as I always did and put it out of my mind. But he didn't come, and we called, his apartment and his cell, and left messages.

At the school they'd be hunkering down. They had generators for the gym and the cafeteria, so if the power went out it would be a giant sleepover on the basketball court. "Sorry I'm making you miss that," I said.

"I would most certainly rather be here," she said.

WE SAT AT ANITA'S BEDSIDE. We'd brought two comfortable chairs up. May left periodically; she'd return with a mug of tea, or a glass of water for me, but I knew she was calling Nick, from my land line, because cell reception at my house was almost nil. When she came back, I'd look at her and she'd shake her head. Outside the snow was now falling in earnest.

She chased me out when Anita needed cleaning up. "I'll do that," I said, the first time.

"You will not. She would hate that."

It was far, far easier not to argue, and I had to admit it was not a memory I wanted to have.

As soon as I left the room and the rattling breaths, and went downstairs where I couldn't hear them at all, I was filled with almost overwhelming relief. The non-rhythm of them had nearly made me crazy. In the living room, however, there was no sound but the wind outside and the sense, not a sound at all, of the falling snow.

I put on my coat and boots and brought in load after load of wood from the porch. I wanted to do it only once. I hadn't stopped for any food on the way home and now I checked the fridge, the cupboards: we would make do. If the power went out, we could still light the gas stove, and besides—"God damn it all to hell," I said.

"What?" It was May, at the door of the kitchen.

"I don't have gas for the generator. I used it up in the snowblower. I was going to get more and I completely forgot."

"You've had some things on your mind."

"I could go out now, quick," I said, but I knew it was too dangerous— I could get stuck on our road and then May would be alone.

"We'll be all right," May said softly.

"Is she—"

"All cleaned up," she said.

I shook my head. "I'm so—"

"It's all right. I am glad to do it."

"You aren't going to let me finish a sentence, are you."

"Probably not." We both smiled and then she said, gently, "Charlie, you know this can take a while. It might not even be tonight."

"I know. But that breathing is so bad."

"It can get better. Go back and forth. I remember, from my dad."

"I know."

"I checked her feet. Her foot, I mean."

"Jesus," I said. For a moment we both tried not to laugh. I leaned over the counter and gave in, felt tears coming to my eyes, but they were strange, removed tears, more of exhaustion, already, than anything else. And it was too early to be so tired.

"I'm sorry," May said, but there was a little laugh still in her voice.

"It's all right."

"Do you remember? The nurse who kept checking Daddy's feet and hands? Who wouldn't shut up about it? When his *extremities* were *cyanotic*. God, that awful nurse."

I knew who she meant, the officious one who liked her presence to be felt, who liked to offer advice on grieving, who told stories of the grisly deaths she'd attended and how it was her calling to ease the pain of families during this life transition. Florence had welcomed anyone who would take control and, even better, let her be an extra patient in the bargain. But May had had to leave the room whenever that particular nurse had appeared. I remembered her crying on me, out in the hall, and beating my chest with her hands, and laughing too—and how at one point we went up to her room and locked the door and she attacked me, resulting in the fastest, most explosive intercourse I'd ever had. Afterward May had said, over and over, "Fuck her. Fuck her. I hope she heard every bit of that."

"All one hundred and eighty seconds of it."

"*Fuck* her! *That* is how I am going to fucking *grieve*! God I fucking hate her! I hate her, Charlie! I hate her!" I hadn't asked if she meant the nurse, or Florence.

And the wonderful thing, now, would be to look at May and acknowledge what we were both thinking, but I just couldn't do it, I was afraid this time the dam wouldn't hold. She seemed to know this, and sighed, shakily. "Where is he, Charlie? I don't want to leave any more messages. He'll see all these missed calls and know—"

"Isn't that the point?" I said, more sharply than I'd meant to.

"Yes," she said miserably.

"He's let his phone die," I said. "Or he's turned it off, or it's under some pile of laundry. In his fucking undergraduate-lifestyle pigsty of an apartment."

"Charlie."

I clenched my teeth; but I was so, so tired of not saying things. "This is unconscionable, and you know it."

"Stop it."

"And you're right," I went on, unable to shut up. "He's finally going to turn on the fucking phone and he'll see those messages and he will *fall apart,* it will be *ugly*—poor, poor little Nicky—"

"Stop it! Please stop! *Please stop,*" she begged, and she bent over, her face in her hands, but she wasn't sobbing, just breathing deeply, shaking her head, and I knew she was trying to hold it together for me. Or, more likely, for Anita. She was decent enough to want to treat me well, for Anita's sake. For Nicky's.

"Sorry," I said. "I mean it. I'm sorry." It didn't matter anyway. Nothing mattered.

And she knew that too. "It doesn't matter." Her eyes still closed, her hands still on her temples.

"The roads will be passable awhile longer," I said. "He'll show up here any minute. You'll see. Or the phone will ring. He knows. He'll be here. He'll come."

MAY MADE US SANDWICHES. We picked at them in Anita's room in the air of a fragile truce. Her uneven breathing continued but did not grow worse, and gradually we became used to it. But the front door did not burst open with Nick's arrival, the phone didn't ring; finally I went to check once more to make absolutely sure we hadn't missed a message, and found the line was dead.

The sun had gone down but I turned on the floodlights on the patio, and we saw that the world was pure white. "He wouldn't try to come now," I said.

"He knows I'd kill him," May said. "He's a horrible driver."

"He won't," I said. "Don't worry about that."

"He'll figure something out," May said. "That's what I'm afraid of."

"He's in the gym with the kids," I said. "He'd have to be. He's walked over there, but"—I traced the sequence in my mind—"Nancy would have gone home by now to feed her dogs." She had three Norwegian elkhounds; she kept pictures of them on her desk. "So she didn't tell him I left. He doesn't even know, May. He doesn't even know what's happened. Remember that. He's worried, of course, sure, and he doesn't know where you are, he's worried about that too. But you know him. He only worries when he remembers to worry. And right now he's with the kids. Basking in the adulation. You know he is."

May laughed a shaky laugh. "Fending off Celia Paxton," she said.

"It's her dream! And Minnie's! Every girl's! After this they're all going to say 'We slept with Mr. Satterthwaite.' It will be the high point of the year. Right, Mom?" I drew my chair closer to Anita's bed and reached out and stroked her forehead. "Right?" It was strange to get no response. Her presence was still so strong; I felt it; so how could she also be turning into an object? "Nicky's at school, Mom. He's snowed in. Up here. Up north. He's got teenaged girls all over him, Mom. It's a panic. He'll tell us all about it."

"Charlie," May said.

I kept stroking. With one hand. Wiped my eyes with another. "I know," I said. But of course I didn't.

I HAD SENT MAY to go rest, on the sofa in front of the fire. I dozed off in the chair next to Anita's bed, listening even in my sleep for the continuing, irregular breaths. When, in the middle of the night, I jerked awake, I thought it was because of Anita: she was silent; I felt my heart begin to seize in my chest—and then a long rattling breath came. Then another. They had changed, become more guttural. Gradually I realized I was also freezing. The lamp I had left on wasn't on, and the red numbers on the digital clock had gone dark.

The stairs creaked and then May was at the door, or a shape something like her, wrapped in a blanket. "I'm sorry," she said. "I fell asleep."

"You were supposed to. I did too."

"Has the power been out long?"

"I don't know." There was another rattle from Anita's bed. "I think this just started."

We listened to two more breaths. They were impossibly far apart.

"It's so cold," May said. "She needs more blankets." She unwrapped the blanket from herself and spread it on the diminished shape of my mother.

In the dark I gathered up all the bedding I had from the other bedrooms and brought it to May, and then felt my way downstairs. In the kitchen I found the flashlight and checked my watch: only midnight. Wasn't there some theory, some statistic, about when people were most likely to die? Wasn't it the middle of the night? I gathered up candles and flashlights, took them upstairs, and then came back down to stoke the fire. It had nearly gone out while May had been sleeping.

May on the couch behind me.

I crumpled newspaper, shoved it under the grate. Stacked wood over kindling and fatwood. The fatwood caught and the dry wood blazed up, and I sat on my heels, watching the flames, just a moment, just a moment, conscious I was playing hooky, May was upstairs, May—I didn't know if it was the dark or the deep unfamiliar cold, or being interrupted in fitful sleep, or the hours of crisis that had settled down into a waking dream, but absolutes were dissolving in my head and when I heard the stairs behind me creak my heart leapt. *Ah she is walking into the room.* No.

"Charlie," she said softly, as though over a great distance. "It's too cold. I think we need to move her."

"Yes. That's a good idea." I prayed she couldn't feel the air around me trembling.

"I'll make up the sofa."

"Help me move it first."

I dragged the coffee table out of the way and then, wordlessly, we each took an end and pivoted it ninety degrees, until it was parallel to the fire.

Then I went to carry my mother downstairs.

May had just changed her. The room smelled of baby wipes and air freshener and the sick undercurrent of waste, and the scent seemed stronger in the dark. The candles on the bedside table made tall shadows. I folded back the thick layer of blankets, then realized I was on the wrong side and went around to the other side of the bed—because I had to have the shorter leg closer to me, the longer leg bent over my arm, for balance. I remembered how easily Nick had lifted her, when he had to. How she had looked at him with that fleeting wonder before stoicism had overtaken her face.

May said, "Are you all right?"

She meant logistically. Engineering-ly. We had become only practical: move from point A to point B. "You should spot me," I said. "On the stairs." The stair chair wouldn't work without power.

I heaved Anita up into my arms. In these situations you're supposed to say someone is no heavier than a child; but I wasn't in the habit of carrying people of any size around. Calmly, however, I readjusted her. Her head lolled back; May reached forward and propped it against my shoulder. On the stairs, she backed down in front of me. Such caution. I was carrying remnants, pure need. Comfort—warmth—was all we could give to my mother and we approached the arrangements now with the urgency of a military operation. I crept down one step at a time. "May. Hold on."

She was holding the flashlight above us, looking only at Anita's blank face. She reached out and grasped the banister. "I am."

May had made up the sofa with sheets and blankets and a waterproof pad. Anita the nurse would have approved. We laid her down and May tucked her in, tucked all around, slid another pillow under her head. We had candles on the mantel and we each had a flashlight, but in the wavering shadows I couldn't tell if my mother's hands were blue or not. They were cold, but everything was cold. She drew another rattling breath.

The fire was going well but still I added more wood, and it roared up, a column of flame into the chimney.

May sat on the floor at Anita's feet and I sat at her head. One side of my face tightened from the heat of the fire, but all around us, I could feel the wall of cold from the rest of the house. Snow had drifted up the windows. The floor was hard and after another minute I went upstairs and wrestled a twin-size mattress off the guest room bed and brought it down, and we wedged it between the fireplace and the sofa. We each huddled at an end. May leaned her head against the side of the sofa. "You should sleep," I said.

"I'm all right."

"Stretch out. There's another pillow."

She hesitated, then unfolded herself onto the mattress, wrapped the blankets around her again.

"I'm sorry you have to go through this," I said.

"Please don't say that again," May said. "I am so glad I'm here."

I had no answer for that, nothing that could be said aloud.

For a long time the only sound was the fire crackling. Then May said, "Charlie, do you think your parents were actually married?"

I waited a long time to answer. "I only know what Anita told me," I finally said.

Her voice was dreamy. "I'm sorry."

"I don't mind. What did she say?"

"She was just telling me about when she came to Atlanta, after he'd died, and when she was interviewing for a job, and I just got a feeling. How she said the supervisor was looking at her hand, and how she was glad she had a ring. How she was asking about her family."

"She had a ring," I said. "I remember it."

"Oh." She was on the edge of sleep.

THE NURSE SUPERVISOR who hired her was named Ann Fusco. Anita never forgot her name.

Ann Fusco asked who was going to watch the baby when it came. Anita said she'd put an ad in the paper to find someone. She said it as confidently as she could. "Don't you have family?" Ann Fusco said.

"No ma'am."

Miss Fusco did not look skeptical; she just looked, and did not stop. "They're back home," Anita said. "They didn't want me to marry my husband."

"I see. I'll ask around for you."

"Thank you, ma'am."

"You know you will not be paid while you're gone."

"Yes, ma'am."

"You have savings."

Preston's check. "Yes."

"What is your family, Mrs. Garrett?"

It took Anita a moment to understand the question. "Just my grandparents," she said.

"They raised you? I see." Ann Fusco's eyes flicked to Anita's ring finger and back. Although the look was quick, it wasn't hidden. Anita looked down at her hand; the gold band gleamed dully. It was surprising how many wedding bands you could find at a pawnshop. If you attached each ring to a person, to a family, it was heartbreaking. If you let yourself think that way.

"You know you don't have to keep the child," Miss Fusco said.

"Yes, ma'am. I know."

The supervisor considered her for a moment. "I don't mean to sound cold."

Anita shook her head, mutely.

"You also know, Mrs. Garrett, better than many, that things can happen to a woman giving birth."

"Yes, ma'am."

"I want you to write a letter to your grandparents and give it to me. Sealed, of course. I will only mail it if absolutely necessary."

Anita had known Ann Fusco for a week. She had met with her once before, and when she'd seen Miss Fusco taking note of her thick waist, she'd thought that would be the end of it, but here she was. She knew no one to ask about Miss Fusco. She had only her own instincts.

Ann Fusco's rather plain, middle-aged face was neither smiling nor judgmental nor superior nor kind. It was simply, utterly fair.

"Yes, ma'am," Anita said.

"All right then."

Anita wrote the letter and on her first day of work she put it in Miss Fusco's box at the nurses' station. They did not speak of it again.

I GOT UP to stoke the fire. I fell asleep and woke to May murmuring to me, or my mother. May fell asleep and I talked to Anita, feeling shy, finding nothing much to say beyond *Mama, Mama, it's me. It's Charlie. It's okay.* Sometimes I said, *Nicky is coming. Nicky is on his way.* I said, *I'm sorry it's cold. You're here with me. We're together,* I said. *Mama. It's Charlie.*

Sometimes I sensed impatience, and who could blame her? She was all unconscious forbearance. I thought each of her breaths was her last and then, an agonizing five, ten, fifteen seconds later, another would come. How laborious it was to shut oneself down.

I would fade into strange dreams and then start to full consciousness, and everything would be the same: glowing fire, agonal breaths, cold, May in miraculous, dangerous proximity.

And then finally I woke and it was light, almost blinding through the windows: the sun was shining on the snow outside. The storm was over.

May was asleep and I looked over at my mother and she was breathing, regularly, her chest going up and down, a gentle tidal sound again, waves plashing at sunrise. I watched her hard, finally reached over and touched her. Still warm. I was so confused. I felt the night hadn't happened. Maybe I'd missed a miracle—but no, her leg was still gone, she was still unconscious, still dying, and so I stood up and reanchored myself to the world. Mother, house, death, May; sun, snow, cold. Morning. No Nick. I put more wood on the fire and went to boil water on the gas stove for coffee. I felt an unaccountable, shameful sense of letdown.

Then I began to dig us out. I shoveled the front stairs and the walk and dug out my car—more useful than May's, since it had four-wheel drive. I stared hopelessly down the driveway and then began digging again. There was no way of getting out, no way to clear the entire thing. We were marooned, we were good and fucked, no question about it, but I was in such a fog of sleeplessness and upset that I kept digging, because there was nothing else to do.

Soon I'd go in to check on Anita—to check on the ladies, I thought. Dear Lord. I was getting used to having a dying mother in my house. Was that possible? Could this keep going on and on? How long? But it seemed nothing would ever change; I was lodged quite firmly and with a weird equanimity in the present and nowhere else. I was worried only about the cold. Nick only every few minutes. I would forget about him and then look up at the slightest sound, realizing I'd never forgotten about him at all—expecting to see his car miraculously slipping down the driveway, or maybe Nick on foot, on snowshoes acquired who knows where, and he would fling an arm in the air in greeting, *Heigh-ho!* And we would all be together, and somehow Anita would know. Will the circle be unbroken, by and by, Lord. The silent agitation, the waiting, would float away, the room would be filled with peace. He would have had his whole crazy journey to reconcile himself; he would just be glad he'd made it in time. And we would be together.

As the sun rose through the trees I grunted and sweated and watched for him. But there was no striding figure. No car.

When I went back up the steps May was waiting for me, just inside the front door; she'd seen me coming. My heart clenched but she said, "She's the same. Come inside and rest."

"We have to get Nick."

"I know. I'll go."

"Don't be ridiculous," I said. I waved out at the mountains of snow. "You can't go out in that."

"Neither can you," she said, and her voice quavered up, nearly out of control.

"May."

"What has *happened to him!*"

"He's stuck just like we are."

"He won't be able to stand it! He needs to get here in time! If he doesn't—he—"

It was as if the night had never happened. She had forgotten all our calm, all my excuses for him; her panic was fresh. I hugged her. I knew she was right; I had no words of comfort. Nick *would* fall apart. He *would* disintegrate. "May, you're so cold. It's so cold in here."

"I'm okay."

"Go shovel. Look, I'm sweating. It will warm you up. You can't just keep sitting. I'll stay with her. I should anyway. I need to."

May nodded and turned away, not looking at me.

She suited up and went outside and I went and sat on the mattress on the floor next to my mother. "Wood's getting low," I said. "I'll have to go get some more."

Silence, of course.

I didn't like the daylight. I wanted night to come back. It had felt holier. My mother's chest moved gently up and down. Every now and then the urge to speak came over me but I tamped it down: it was just fear. Ordinary fear of the extraordinary. If death could be called extraordinary—which, of course, it could not. There was nothing more mundane, more of the world, than leaving it.

As I sat there with my mother as she lingered, endlessly, on the threshold, I gradually began to realize her presence was changing, that what emanated from my mother and filled the room was an agitated impatience. This was why May was upset. She had felt it too. Gradually it overtook the holiness, the peace. It roiled it up. It became a wind, and then nearly a gale, roaring about my ears, urging me in some direction I could not identify. *I can't go with you. I don't know what you want.* I didn't say it aloud.

I was so encased in this silent struggle with the will of my mother that I didn't hear the noise outside at first; then I realized there had been shouting, May's shouting—and I stood up and went to the door, but before I reached it, it burst open. "The plow came," she said, her chest heaving.

"Good old Vince," I said.

"I tried to stop him—I yelled and screamed and waved my arms but he just kept going—what if he has a phone?" She shook her head to clear it. "God. I'm getting my keys. I'm going after him—"

"No. I'll go. If he got here, that means they're plowing everywhere. The roads will be clear enough. I'll go get Nicky."

"Maybe he's on his way right now."

"He can't get here in that crappy little car."

"I love that car," she said.

"I know. I know you do."

Her eyes were filling. "Charlie."

She wanted to save him but dreaded his grief—I saw it in her face. "I know," I said again—me who knew so little.

She went inward, inward, to Nicky. "Yes," she said. "Please. Please go get him."

I walked back into the living room and knelt down beside my mother. I touched her waxy forehead. I wanted to say *Wait for me, please don't leave yet,* but even motionless her strange agitated vitality was so strong that I didn't.

THE WORLD WAS WHITE and askew, trees and lines down, no cars anywhere, although there were orange cones around a telephone pole that had fallen half into the road. The glare was blinding; I put on my sunglasses. I stopped at the first convenience store I came to, to see if they had a working phone, but the place was closed and dark.

Only the main streets in town were plowed, just a first pass one car wide. When I got to the turn for Nicky's street I pulled my car as far to the side as I could in case the plows came by again and began to walk. By now it was almost nine. The world would begin to come alive. Sound, any sound, would be hard to take.

Sure enough, down the street two men were out shoveling. They gave me enthusiastic waves: we had all survived! "What a mess, huh?" one man called.

I had to clear my throat. "You're doing a yeoman job," I called back.

"Gotta be careful. This stuff is wicked heavy." He huffed a huge shovelful off the sidewalk and into his yard. "Heart-attack snow. Sleet on top. Started sleeting, at the end."

The other man was wearing a Russian-style fur cap and smoking a pipe. He removed the pipe and said, "Wife'ud be pissed if you keeled over."

I said, "You have power?"

"Not yet. I heard tomorrow."

"What a fucking mess," the pipe smoker said.

At Nick's I raised a fist to the door: nothing. I knew the bell didn't work. I almost knocked again but I didn't like the sound. I didn't want to draw attention. The guys down the street might come to help, ask what was what. I got out my keys and slipped the duplicate that Nick had given me into the lock, but then I realized the door wasn't locked.

Inside, it was cold and quiet. The place was not quite as messy as usual. I glanced in the open door of the bedroom: bed empty—not made, exactly, but the covers pulled up. What passed for made with Nicky. In the living room, there was a stack of papers and textbooks on the floor. The coffee table was clear. "Nick? Nicky?" I didn't call loudly; I didn't keep calling.

On the kitchen table, propped up against a dirty glass, was a manila envelope, addressed to me.

He was going to Congo. There were refugee camps, he had contacts. Anita had told him to go. *It is awful there Charlie its horrible and they need people. Not me I kno that but just peopl and you don't need me here and I kno that to. No one needs me here. This place was perfect when I got here your kind of place Charlie but I need distratcion that is bad but that is the way I am.*

I do not know from what I need to be distracted from. I do not think about it. Mom understands

I am sorry you will have to deal with all this shit Im leaving. Its better thogh. No one will want to see me or talk to me. There is a letter here for May

Im going to write it all down and this is the truth. You can do whatever you want with it. Everyone wanted so much from me and I was giving it to them I didn't sleep with Celia until after she and zack broke up that IS the TRUTH you should know that. She came over here all the time I didn't invite her she just showed up but then afterwards she was so sad and I couldnt stand it it seemed right jesus maybe it was. I thout he knew and I thout he would tell you and then he died I don't fucking know I don't Charlie. I loved her your going to ask what it was, well her feet, the way she walked so carefully, delicately like she doesn't want to leave footprints, I get that. I tried not too.

I loved May too more it was more real maybe. more adult I know that is the point charlie. I meant it please tell her I told you that. Maybe I could have stayed w/ her and I loved her and Charlie you know I don't say it if i don't mean it. This is not the place for me. I knew but i tried and you should have known but it was beautiful wasn't it charlie? In the snow. That night at Divya's after christmas with mom I will always remember it was perfect it was the peek the top of the mountain thank you charlie there are not many nights like that thats all i wanted. It was too much though too much and so i say thank you and i am sorry

I had never known before how he did it. How he pulled himself away, bit by bit, his beautiful face shining all the while, until before you knew it all you could see was his waving hand, the cloud of dust.

AFTER I PUT MY LETTER back in the manila envelope with May's, unopened, I became efficient.

I went through every room. I found bottles in the trash and in the closets. In the bathroom I found four empty prescription painkiller bottles with my mother's name on them. I put them in my pocket.

I called Salter's house and talked briefly to Bethie. Everything was fine, the generators were working in the gym, and they thought the power would be back within the hour. I told her my mother wasn't good and I wouldn't be in, nor would May. I let her assume Nick was with me. "I'll tell Adam," she said. "And there's nothing we can—"

"Nothing right now. Nothing at all."

I closed the door to Nick's apartment and locked it behind me.

I strode purposefully down the street, waving but not speaking to

Rosencrantz and Guildenstern. I got to my car and drove to the near-est open gas station, where I bought gas for my generator, two coffees, and two enormous cardboardish blueberry muffins. It was not until I was back on the road to the house that I let myself think that Anita could be dead by now. And that May was waiting not for me, but for Nick.

The road had been plowed again and was easily passable. My street had room for one car to go down it; Vince had done a decent job on my driveway. The sun by now was bright, almost celebratory.

May was at the door almost instantly when I walked through. "Charlie. She's still here." And I was surprised at the rush of relief. It frightened me, how glad I was. "But she's bad again. Where's Nick?"

"He's not here," I said. "I can't find him." The manila envelope was folded fat inside my coat.

She looked at me and I expected her eyes to be frantic and lost, little-girl eyes worrying over little-boy Nick. But they were resigned, unsurprised. "Did he tell you he was going anywhere?" I said.

"No," she said. "He didn't." The question seemed to mildly annoy her, a mere distraction. "Charlie, you have to talk to her."

I followed her back into the living room. The peacefulness was gone, and the look of gentle surprise; my mother was gray, her mouth roundly open. There was silence, and then finally a breath—or rather a rasping, barely human, the sound of a body reduced to failing machine, running on the engine of the reptile brain. I sat down next to her and smoothed her forehead. "Oh, Mama," I whispered.

"Do you think she's waiting for Nicky?"

"No," I said. "I don't think so."

May sat down on the floor, at my feet, looking up at my mother. "Then you have to tell her it's all right to go," she murmured. "Daddy did this. She's hanging on. She's hanging on for something."

"You're so stubborn," I whispered.

Another rasp, cheeks sunken in, her mouth a lipless gape.

"Mama," I said. "Please listen. I'm going to tell her. Listen, Mama, listen," crooning now, *It's all right. Hush little baby.* "I'm telling her everything."

Her lungs were dry as cliffs, her throat full of stones.

I turned to May. "Nicky is gone. He's going to Africa, probably. Anita told him to go."

Her mouth opened a little. And closed.

"I don't know much. I'll tell you everything I know. But there's something else. Please listen. I need to tell you about my father. Anita didn't tell you, because I wouldn't let her."

That gentle little furrow of her eyebrows. "He was a priest," I said. "Or, rather, a deacon. He was in St. Annes, Georgia, for a summer posting. It was good for him because his fiancée was in Savannah that summer. With her family. She was from Savannah. But he fell in love with my mother, and she got pregnant."

"Charlie."

I was in a trance. I was holding it away from myself. I was dismantling the house piece by piece. "But he went back to the fiancée anyway. He went back to Virginia. To seminary. Where his fiancée's father was a bishop. And then eventually he became a chaplain. At a school."

"Stop. Please stop." She was whispering.

My mother's terrible breaths. One. Then the next. "There was a man named Jimmie Garrett. He died in Vietnam. But he wasn't my father. My father didn't die in Vietnam. He didn't even go there. His name wasn't Jimmie Garrett. But Anita didn't tell me. She didn't tell me until it was too late. Until he was about to die. And until I had fallen in love with his daughter."

One more breath. "Don't tell it like a story," May whispered.

"I'm sorry."

"If it's not a story."

"It's not a story."

"Charlie. Charlie." I didn't reach for her. I couldn't. Instead I kept my hand on my mother's arm. Not moving or stroking. Just a connection. I felt her there. I felt her receding.

May could not get her breath. Sound wouldn't come. Then, finally, "I don't believe you," she said.

Silence. For a long time. And then we both realized: silence.

———

I FOLDED ANITA'S HANDS on her chest. I wanted ancient gestures. Where were pennies for her eyes? Who would pay the ferryman? May stood up, looking down at her, not at me, and then walked out of the room. I heard the back door open and close—she had gone out to the patio. I let her be.

The body of my mother didn't make sense: Was it presence and absence together? How was the absence so large? The body itself seemed to call for action. So I went down to the cellar with the gas, started the generator, and turned the water back on. I went and got more wood from the pile on the porch, brought it in, stacked it in the brass wood box. I found my charger and plugged in my phone; maybe I'd get a signal.

I stood next to my desk and made a list of people to call: the funeral home. Adam, Divya, various Satterthwaites. At the plugged-in phone, there was one bar, appearing and then disappearing. I called Nicky again, got patchy voice mail, didn't leave a message.

Then I remembered the breakfast I had bought what seemed like days ago, although it had been only a bit more than an hour. I got the bag of muffins and May's coffee from the car—I had drunk mine on the way—and, back inside, heated hers up in the now-functioning microwave. Then I got my coat and boots and went out the kitchen door.

She was sitting in the middle of the snow-covered patio, in one of the Adirondack chairs. The snow was a foot and a half deep, at least. Only the top of the chair and its arms showed. She was cradled in snow. Her red coat pooled around her like a train. It was early enough that the sun hadn't yet risen over the peak of the roof, but the shadows and light on the mountains in front of us were stark, and I had to shield my eyes against the glare.

It was ridiculous, comical, the way the chair was barely visible, the way she looked like she was floating in the white. Absurd.

I began to slog toward her, using the deep prints she had made. She didn't look at me when I came close. I set the coffee cup and the bag on the wide arm of the chair, at a level with the snow. Something about her stillness made me think I should stay, that she wanted me to stay, but the other chair was completely consumed, so I backed up and then just stood, the drifted snow past my knees. After another long minute she took the coffee and wrapped her gloved hands around it. She drank. She took the white bag onto her lap, peered into it, and brought out a piece of muffin, which she ate without comment; then she rolled the top of the bag closed again as though she'd just had a full meal.

I felt giddy. I realized a weight had been lifted. I thought about how this was Anita's gift to me. Somehow my horror and mortification had dissipated, for good, as I had spoken inside; the reality, out loud, somehow seemed smaller than my years of florid shame. I wanted to say these things to May, but I knew I was far, far ahead of her. The reality was still enormous. And there was the matter of Nick—all that she didn't even know yet. The envelope was still pressing against my chest. But suddenly I thought that maybe we could find him, bring him back, that now that the worst was over we could all be sensible, that he would be able to survive Anita's death as I was, already, splendidly—see, I was fine! And he would be too. It would be the three of us again. Somehow it was all right. I wanted them together. Yes, that was what I wanted! Now that the truth was out, how marvelous that there was this second act possible at all, that Nick and May could be together with my blessing, a real blessing. I had to figure out how to say all this to her. "May-May—"

She held up a hand, as though I had interrupted her listening to something far away. I waited. Her hand drifted back down and she said, "Did I tell you I went to Savannah this summer?"

"No, you didn't." The wind picked up and I hunched in my coat, my hands in my pockets.

She was speaking very slowly. "To see my mother. To check that box."

"And did you check it?"

She smiled at the mountains. "Oh, yes. I checked it."

"Well, that's good."

"Although I guess it was also checked for me."

I was eager as a puppy. I was practically bouncing up and down in the snow. I had plans, I had to tell her.

"Charlie." Her gaze hadn't moved from the view in front of us. She still hadn't looked at me. Her eyes were narrowed against the bands of blinding light. "I need to tell you about this lunch we had."

She was in shock, probably. I would let her natter on for a while. Where did we need to be? What was the rush? I needed to remember there was no rush. I hadn't called the funeral home. No one was coming, no one knew anything. We were in this suspended time. The two of us. It was a lot to absorb. Everything I'd told her. I'd known for years, she had known for an hour. When she gave me the chance, I would gently say that, and that we were in completely foreign terrain with no guide.

But for now I'd just listen. "It was in a ladies' tearoom—can you imagine such a thing?" she was saying. Looking straight ahead. "Did you know such things still exist?"

"Well, I'm not surprised."

"It was like a time warp, Charlie."

"I bet it was."

"You sit across from your mother and you behave. That's what you do."

"I expect so."

"You use all your good-girl training. Every bit."

"Every single bit."

She started a little and finally turned her head in my direction, although she didn't meet my eyes. I thought maybe I'd angered her. But I wasn't laughing at her—oh no! I was taking it all with utmost seriousness! Her face worried me. A strange softness to it. And also a slight, unnerving curl to her lip. The two things not matching at all.

"But you know about behaving," she said. "Oh, Charlie, you know all about it too. You know how it works."

"I suppose I do."

"No matter what your mother tells you."

"Right."

"Or doesn't."

"Yes."

"No matter what your mother says."

"May-May," I said. "What did your mother say to you?"

"She told me a story."

"Tell me, May."

She nodded. Said nothing.

"May."

She was still nodding. Absurdity had been confirmed. I went to her chair and knelt before her in the snow. She finally looked up and her eyes terrified me but that made no sense and I kept my voice calm. "Sweetheart, what did she say? Don't worry. It's only a story."

WALLPAPER WITH A BAMBOO DESIGN; chicken salad, on chinoiserie plates, iced tea in footed glasses: the decorum of ladies who are keepers of old codes. This was where Florence had taken May, a tearoom in Savannah: a good choice for a mother and daughter whose main intention is to behave. But the bamboo wallpaper, the blue-and-white china: some colonialist fantasy? A flimsy gazebo on a tropical river, fluttering white linen: helplessness? Is that what they were meant to invoke? But I don't know about such things.

May has gone to Savannah. She's checking the box. Savannah not the place where she grew up—it's her mother's home, her grandparents', yes, but she herself is a stranger in a strange land, made even stranger because her mother has transformed herself back into a native, and her friends, the old childhood friends who have welcomed her back, are surrounded by their southern children who are living lives like their parents, girls May's age who are married and now the mothers of children in smocked outfits and hair bows. And May strides in tall and olive skinned and speaking French and wishing she were in Paris or Massachusetts or anywhere else. And at the same time filled with that failure, the failure to marry, to have the blond children, to have lunch with her mother every week. But she's doing it today. Yes, today she is checking the box.

She's come from Dallas, where it's just as hot now, in June, but a dry heat, and all the blond ladies have a lacquered edge to them that isn't here in Savannah. She'll admit that. She will not admit, though, at least not to her mother, that Dallas feels like a long detour to her, or that she doesn't love her fiancé enough, that she has tried and failed and that he is not the answer to whatever her overarching question is.

She would rather take off the ring he gave her, it makes her feel cheap with falseness and subterfuge, but she doesn't want to discuss it with Florence so for now she leaves it there on her finger, glittering, Texas-sized. Her mother admires it every few minutes: yes, she does, and that doesn't help, no it does not. Her mother wants to plan a wedding, is talking about lovely venues in Savannah, about the club, this is why we're members, May, about the best months of the year, March being best, with the humidity low, the azaleas blooming—oh yes lovely, and the boys would be so glad to get out of New England, she can't believe they all stayed there, March had always been the worst, well that and April, oh and February too, she had barely been able to stand it but it hadn't bothered Preston, it had been so infuriating—her mother talks of her father lightly now, in this way, and as usual May can't decide whether she should be annoyed or furious or relieved.

Florence can't understand why they haven't set a date; probably this lunch has been designed to address the question. But what's on May's mind, along with her failing engagement, is her talk with Adam Salter just a few days ago, the call out of the blue, the remarkable idea that she could go back to Abbott—another thing she will not discuss with her mother. She has many things to keep to herself. Luckily she is a bafflement to her mother and always has been. Florence won't detect anything besides the usual discomfort. She'll criticize May for some minor aspect of manners or dress and May will let her, thinking, as always, of her father, to whom she was not a bafflement. As she grew up, his flaws had gradually uncovered themselves, and by the end he was autocratic and absurd—but when the three of them were together, May alone at the mercy of her parents, he had been ballast and safety.

Afterward, May is sure her mother brought her here because she'd known how hard it would be to make a scene. Florence must have known how in this time-warp of a place May would feel the weight of all her mother had ever wanted to be, all her mother had ever wanted *her* to be, how well behaved, how knowable; if she was going to have a daughter then it was going to be this kind; and Florence looked across the table at her, over their iced tea and their chicken salad amandine, and said, *There is something you are old enough to know, you are getting married and beginning a new life and I suppose one needs to know these things, it is part of being an adult, to be very clear on one's family. No, I have never believed in secrets.*

All right.

I was very unhappy, you have to understand, I was miserable up there. I had found myself about to not be young anymore, I was just—well I hope you never wake up and think, my God, how did this get to be my life?

Yes, that's exactly what I don't want.

He'd said he would get a church in the South, we'd have to move around but I was expecting that, my own father was a bishop and I knew how it worked. But then it was not at all what Preston promised, what I'd been led to expect. Your father was not what I'd been led to expect. I am not proud of it. Things happen. You fall into things—but it was a choice, I have to admit that. It is always a choice.

Mom. What are you saying. Mom.

Did you know his first wife was killed in a terrible wreck? So sad. They were barely married any time at all. A sweet girl. He was beside himself—the strong silent type, you know, but he was beside himself, and I remembered that. And he and I had always liked each other, we'd always had this little zing—that happens even when you're married, you should know that, you meet some-one and you know that, well, in another life—You can't be attracted to just one person. It doesn't work that way. I'll do you no favors by not admitting that.

And he was so different. An outdoorsman, you know, good with his hands—Preston could barely change a lightbulb. We knew it was a mistake, we felt awful. Your father and I were barely speaking anyway. It's a wonder no one ever knew. In that tiny town where everyone had their nose in everyone's business, oh, people think southerners are gossips, but a little academic town, you have no idea—

Please.

Preston is your father. In every sense that matters. He adored you from the moment you were born. He'd always wanted a girl. He's the only father that matters.

But—

Win never knew. He never did. I'm sure—it was timing, I won't get into that, God no. I never did show until the fifth month or so. I was terrified it would be different with you. Because it had been four years and the fourth baby and what if my body had been different? But you cooperated and he never knew.

I don't think he even suspected. And he met Divya and forgot all about me, it all worked out. He was so in love with her he never would have stopped to think. No, I'm sure he never did.

But Daddy said I looked like his mother. I've seen pictures! He said that I looked just like his mother!

I know, it's funny, so strange how things can work out that way. You do, a little. Your coloring. And she was tall. But Win was always tan. He said his grandmother was black Irish. Who knows.

Here's a napkin.

The powder room is that way, May-May, if you need it.

What you should remember is how much your father loved you. I've always felt bad about leaving you alone with him but also I knew you would have that time. Just the two of you. I suppose I thought it balanced things out.

You're an adult, and I thought you needed to know this. But it seems I should have kept my mouth shut. Stop that and drink some tea.

May-May.

No, thank you, we are just fine. Nothing right now. Oh, she's okay, aren't you? Thank you so much. No just the check. We are just fine. No, really. We are just fine.

Daddy was only seeing what he wanted to see, May says. In despair.

Sweetie. Sweetie, people do.

Twenty-five

The house was empty, for the first time since before Christmas.

I had longed for solitude, and now I had it.

The power was still out—they were saying a day or two more, out where I was. But the generator chugged, the phone was back, and I had made all my calls. Deferential men who moved with near silence had come with a gurney and a van from the funeral home, an ambulance but not quite, and had wheeled my mother away.

Divya didn't want to leave me alone. "I'm okay," I said.

"Come over for dinner."

"That's all right."

"I'll bring you something, then."

I knew I would never convince her. "Tomorrow, okay? I would love that tomorrow."

"Nicky's with you," she said, not a question.

"He's in and out."

"Is he all right?"

"I don't know."

I would deal with that tomorrow, too. The storm had given me cover.

"Charlie—"

"Tomorrow, Div. Please. I need to sleep." And that *was* the truth, and it would also be impossible.

May had the envelope. All the evidence. I had handed it to her, that morning, before she left. She had said she had to leave and I had said all right. She had said Charlie I can't stay and I said I know. She had said I just have to go I just have to leave and I could not read her face, not at all, and then she had embraced me. Or rather just stood in my arms. It was a purely formal gesture. I was sure she was, like me, at the end of astonishment. Everything was ended, everything thoroughly, thoroughly over.

And I had left her alone to deal with what was in the envelope. I had left her alone for more shocks—unchivalrous, if nothing else— this was just occurring to me—May sitting in the rooms I'd never seen, sitting on some sofa, at some table, the letters spread out in front of her, knowing she'd lost Nick, that she'd never had him, we'd all lost the Nick we'd imagined we had, the Nick we had created. How destroyed it all was.

I had been sitting for hours by now, in front of the fireplace, the ashes paled to gray. I'd drunk two whiskies for my supper. I had no idea what time it was. I was sitting where my mother had died. I let myself fall onto the sofa, my head where hers had been.

Ghoulish and strange but I felt covered, for just a moment or two, as if a blanket had drifted down over me. And then I was abruptly cold again. Perhaps the generator had stopped—but the lights were on, fool, fool.

I began to wish I had agreed to Divya's invitation after all. I wanted to walk into that front hall, see the colors, the stairs going up, remember Win's hands on every piece of that house—as he had touched mine, that very mantel, there—we had stripped it and sanded it down, he and I.

Then I'd have to come back home to my own empty house. But I would have to get used to that again. Abundance had been temporary.

I got up and went into the kitchen to look at the clock: midnight. And there were evening and morning, the first day. The wrong order, that was. But at any rate the first day nearly over, the first day of Anita's death—could you say that? The moment of her dying, of the storm, had seemed endless. But now we had moved along into the period of my mother's death. Now this was ordinary time.

I took my keys from the hook by the door.

———

SNOW COVERED THE LABYRINTH. In the path it was up to my knees. The boxwood was invisible. All white.

The sky was clouded over too; good. I put my hand out to guide me.

But even though it was night I could feel the temperature rising. Every now and then a thud as snow slid off a branch. Fog was gathering, low to the ground, as I moved close to the center, then back out, the maddening pattern, enforced patience. Win trimming the green. Oh the hours. Where had Zack pushed through? Over there? Maybe he'd thought, as he broke the green down to the root, *I am not playing this game anymore, and I am destroying the board.*

Such a long way.

I had never been good at prayer but I was good at thinking, it was in fact the only thing I was at all proficient in (*oh let me think these thoughts, let me; I will let myself; enough*), and I moved my feet and I thought of Anita. Of Nicky. Of May. Of Preston, Win, Zack. Hugh. I turned the pages.

I tried to crack myself wide to them. To spare myself nothing.

May's voice in the darkness, Nicky's baby fists on my knees, Hugh in his study, at his desk where a yellow pool of light shone down, my mother in a yellow dress, leaving, leaving, my mother in my arms, heavy and incomplete. When I got to Zack, I thought of Booker, digging, and had to stop.

I saw my students, hundreds of them now, there really had been hundreds. I saw them as rosy babies and as gray shriveled sexless crones, their lives and all the possibilities folding and blurring.

And the center. Here it was. Was it the still point of the turning world? No answer. *Neither flesh nor fleshless. And do not call it fixity.*

The weight of the clouds pressed on me and I sank to my knees, just gave down. As Anita would have said. The snow began to melt under my knees and soak through my pants. I thought of ascetics seeking such things out. Bloodied flagellants. Nuns binding thorns into the belts of their habits, monks in lice-ridden cilices. Oh, a little cold water was nothing. Bush league.

Whose woods these are I think I know. Let me not to the marriage of true minds. Love bade me welcome. Time present and time past are both perhaps present. And now good-morrow. There were secrets in the spaces and in the rhythms of the spaces and the vowels and the consonants. There had to be. I kept rocking along with the meter. With that music. *Ba dum ba dum ba dum ba dum.*

But to what purpose Disturbing the dust.

These are the feet. I'm marking the feet with the chalk.

I was sitting in the pew next to my mother. *In the beginning was the Word.* She said lay your head right here Charlie. *And the Word was God.*

Yes exactly.

Up at Divya's a light went on. A minute, two, three. The back door opening, closing. Then footsteps on the wooden stairs of the deck. "Charlie?" A sigh. "Charlie." That lilt. The warmth of another world. *Chaah-lee.* I wasn't sure if she could see me. But why would there be cause for alarm? With good old Charlie?

"Charlie, May called me. Come out of there. Charlie."

"Hello, Divya."

"Charlie." Her voice didn't change. "You mustn't feel so sorry for yourself."

"That is a fact," I said, more grateful than ever for the boxwood walls. A child in a fort.

Divya's outline at the bottom of the stairs was becoming clearer. Or rather her shapelessness. A puffy lump with a head. She'd have on her big down coat, her ridiculous wearable sleeping bag. And snow boots. May had called and she had come downstairs, to the coat on the hook, to the boots by the door.

May knew now that Nicky was gone. She knew we'd made Nicky because we wanted glimpses of the bright beyond. We had given him his own glamour. But the rest of us were getting older. And all we had was the warmth of one another's decrepit bodies. And time would not stop, even for Nicky, especially for Nicky—that was the horror and the beauty, we were in it, circle or line, we were in it, we were in it. Around and around, all of us.

"Charlie," Divya said. Was she whispering? Singing? "You must come out now."

May who had known where I would go.

The snow was water now. I was kneeling in water.

"This is the hard part," Divya said. The lights behind her, in the kitchen, were so warm. "You cannot stay. You must come back out."

I began to stand. Both legs asleep—not an ascetic, not close. I paused, one hand in the wet, ass in the air, a ridiculous tripod. Blood roared down to my feet. Electric shocks for my negligence. Oh how real the flesh. Then I stood, I was up, I could see.

"May is at your house," Divya said. "She is waiting for you. She said to tell you that. She said, 'Tell him. Tell him I'm here.'"

AND IN THE DARK, the warm dark, one more story.

When I was two weeks old, Anita received a small package. She removed the brown paper—a grocery sack, cut to fit, carefully taped. Inside was a picture book, the kind with the gold spine, from the dime store. Inside the book was the letter she'd written for Ann Fusco, unopened.

Holding the baby—holding me—Anita felt suddenly unsteady on her feet. She sat down in a kitchen chair and felt that both she and the chair were floating unmoored, out into a great void. Then there was a horizon, as when the Lord separated the heavens and the earth; and then on the horizon was a towering wave of tears. It came toward her, a tsunami of feeling, and passed over her while she somehow withstood it, ducking under it as she used to duck under the surf as a child, feeling the suck of tumult passing over, disappearing.

With one hand, she somehow slit the letter open, giving herself a paper cut. She spread the letter she had written out on the table, and then stuck her finger in her mouth before the blood smeared.

Dear Memaw and Granddaddy,
    If you are reading this, I am dead, and my baby is alive.

She didn't read any more. She simply read those lines over and over and held me, who was asleep on her shoulder, and the waves, calm now, lapped gently at her heels. She realized that all this time she had been making a decision. It had been the roiling in her heart, in the middle of the night when, exhausted, she had laid me down beside her in her own bed and instead of falling into oblivion had lain awake watching me and feeling in herself a great duality. She hadn't known she was making a decision but she had been and now it was done, and now she knew I was well and truly hers, and no one else's. And that she was not her mother. But mine.

She folded the letter back into the envelope and carried it to the range, where she kneeled down, awkwardly, keeping the bundle of me balanced on her shoulder, and opened the broiler at the bottom with her free hand and pushed the letter in. When smoke curled out from the edges of the closed drawer, she turned off the gas, and when the smoke died away and she opened the drawer, it was empty save for gray flecks of ash that disintegrated when she touched them. Then she stood up, with me, and began our new life.

Twenty-six

We cremated Anita's body and I scattered some ashes in the back of the house, beyond the patio—flinging them toward the mountains, pretending they were going far beyond where they landed, that they were winging away like birds. I told myself that this was the last vista she had seen on this earth and that she would understand if I wanted to look out and know she was there—although I thought also that she would not have cared at all where the last physical bits of her ended up. And it was true also that someday people would live in this house and look out its windows and have no idea of this particular aspect of their view. Perhaps sooner rather than later.

I took the rest to Atlanta, where I put them beside Hugh, in a small graveside service. There was a plot waiting, and there was no reason not to do what was expected. She wouldn't have cared either way, and for the rest of the family it was neat and tidy, and anyway burials are for the living. Although I did beg out of a bigger one by saying she wouldn't have wanted any fuss, which no one disputed.

I saved out a baggieful of ashes for Nick. If he showed up back in the States anytime soon, he could scatter his own pieces of her where he wanted, too.

Once I was back in Abbottsford I considered a spoonful or two on Preston's grave. (And thought that Anita would have rolled her eyes at this doling out of herself.) I even went there, bringing Nick's bag along, as a sort of test, and stood there a long time. I told myself I was deciding, but really the decision was already made, and I kept the bag in my pocket.

It was late March by now and we were in a glorious thaw. The sky was a brilliant blue, and the air was thick with snowmelt. On Preston's grave, shadowed by the headstone, a crystalline patch of snow remained, icy at the edges. I'd come here only a few times before, and this time was no different—the sense that I was trying to manufacture emotion and wisdom far different from whatever portion of those things I possessed. I tried, dutifully, to remember what he'd looked like, to summon his actual person, and for a moment he rose before me, standing in the snow, shadow-faced, the rest of him Disneyfied: robes and gray hair flowing, something almost obscenely fine about him. In a mythical way. An untouchable way.

I'd tell May about that vision, one of these days, but not yet. I turned away from Preston and went to look for her, and found her where I expected, at Win's grave, just over a little rise. His stone was one of those twofers, with a blank on the other side where Divya would go, her name and birth date already engraved, the hyphen ominous and a little absurd. May stood there, looking down at it, a hand shading her eyes. She was wearing her red coat with the proud black velvet epaulets and I thought she looked magnificent.

I went and stood next to her. We were silent a moment and then I said, of the stone, "Divya swears that isn't creepy."

"I know," May said, surprising me. "She calls it 'the other side of the bed.'"

"You're kidding," I said, and May just gave me a look. We stood awhile longer. The silence began to grow. Finally I said, "Do you think you'll tell her?"

"I don't know."

"You don't ever have to."

"I know." She sighed, tolerantly. "I suppose it would be interesting."

The gelid wind was picking up, and May brushed her hair out of her face. "I'm cold," I said.

"Me too."

Halfway back to my car she took my hand in her gloved one, briefly squeezed, let go.

Once we were in the car and I had cranked the engine May said, "Are you ready?"

I nodded, and headed slowly down the narrow road to the cemetery gate. As I drove, May twisted in her seat to face me. "I have the one class," I said. "And then my meeting. Then I'll go home."

I kept my eyes on the narrow road but in my peripheral vision I could see her face held out to me, still bright from the sodden wind. "Charlie."

"Yes."

"I could go with you. Wherever you go."

"Yes, you could."

We had said such things already; we would say them again. We took careful steps on a long and winding bridge, and did not look down.

I EXAMINED THE FACES of my seniors. "Don't stew too much. Try," I said. Most of them would be hearing from colleges over break. "Write your final papers instead. As a stress release." Eye rolling.

No one had sat in Zack and Celia's old seats.

"Please do not forget. Poets do not just see. They notice. They *look*. It's active. And writing poetry without *looking* is impossible. Decent poetry, anyway. And I would argue decent living is impossible without looking, too.

"Does anyone remember *Our Town*? From ninth grade?" Indulgent nods. "People, it's not a simple play. It's dark. The opposite of sentimental. Go reread it sometime. Anyway. Near the end. Emily says, 'Do any human beings ever realize life while they live it?—every, every minute?' And the Stage Manager says, 'The saints and the poets, maybe. They do some.'"

Dex's hand was up. I nodded at him and he started flipping through his *Four Quartets*. "Wait a second. Wait. Okay. Yeah." He started reading. "'Go, go, go, said the bird: human kind cannot bear very much reality.'"

"Exactly," I said. "Exactly. Today, Dex, you are on."

"Mr. G.," Minnie said. Her face deadly serious. "Will you be here when we get back?"

"Yes," I said. "I will be here when you get back."

Dex burst out, "They aren't making you leave, are they? Are they firing you?"

Immediate rumblings from the chorus. *Not his fault. He didn't know. I heard. I heard.* And one other undertone, seizing at fairy-tale logic: *They're only half brothers.*

I held up a hand. "No one is getting fired," I said. "One day at a time. Besides, you seem to forget *you* won't be here next year. You'll have flown the coop. You'll be long gone." They couldn't really believe it. For once, neither could I. I had been through this cycle seventeen times, but still my heart twisted, and a grief that was strangely close to euphoria hit me once again. "Go," I said. "Go. Have a wonderful break. When I see you next, it'll be spring."

THE ADMINISTRATION BUILDING WAS already silent as a tomb. But Salter was waiting in his office, as promised. "What are you doing over break?" he said.

"Headed back south. I'm cleaning out my mother's house."

"Mm." He made a regretful, clucking sound. "Never easy."

"No," I said. "But she wasn't a collector. Thank God. She traveled light. Materially speaking."

"Is Nick coming to help you?"

"I don't think so," I said. "He's in Darfur now. At a refugee camp."

"Holy cow."

"Congo didn't work out," I said. "Or something."

"You've talked to him?"

"Once."

Salter was shaking his head. Finally he said, "So much talent, Charlie. A born teacher. I don't know if I've ever seen so much potential. *Gone.*"

In the silence, I handed him my own letter.

Salter opened it and read it, unsurprised. He folded it up and put it back in the envelope. "Falling on your sword is very old-fashioned, Charlie."

"I suppose you're right about that."

"How about I keep this letter for a while, maybe over the break, and you think about it."

"Whatever you want," I said. He ran a hand, reflectively, over the stiff brush of his hair. I thought of him when Nick had disappeared and the truth had come out: his anger had been righteous and palpable, and laced with a sorrow purer than I would have expected from Adam. I'd been moved, and ashamed. "It will make things easier, Adam," I said. "I'm surprised the Paxtons didn't demand you throw me out."

Salter picked up his heavy gold-banded pen, flipped it slowly between his fingers. "They did, Charlie. And we told them no. That you bore no blame. And that you were too valuable to lose."

There was a long silence. "Well. Thank you."

"We said you were an institution. A young one, of course." We permitted ourselves to smile.

"Adam, that means a lot. It does. But." I cleared my throat. "I should have known. Maybe on one level I did."

"We talked about this, Charlie. Are you changing your story?"

"No. But I should have—"

"Brothers aren't supposed to suspect each other."

"I don't know if that's true."

"If it's not," Adam said, "then I don't want to live in that world." He shifted a little, awkwardly. "In the good old days, I would have offered you a drink now," he said. "I suppose they did some things right in the good old days."

"Some," I said.

We let the quiet stretch. And then, together, we stood, and buttoned our jackets. "I'll hang on to this," he said, patting his breast pocket, where he had stowed my letter. We shook hands. And that was that.

GOING HOME, I took the long way. Through Abbottsford, that is, around the square, up and down streets. I didn't go down Nicky's dead-end street, only to turn around again, but I did drive by the Bank-head house, yellow now, shutters mended, tricycle in the driveway—a house belonging to the present, which we were now in, rather than the past.

During my meeting with Salter, the clouds had rolled in; outside of town it was dreary March, the light flat, the patchy snow along the state road gravel gray. The convenience store, the snowmobile place, the gun shop, the organic coffee bar with its groovy lettering. *Charlie, you've gone native.* Spring soon. This *was* spring. I'd already seen cro-cuses in the snow. No use denying them.

I wanted more, though. The near future, that was all I asked— just a week or two, or three. The time when I will be driving home, just like now, and the light, changing so fast, already will be brighter, higher; when I will bump down the long driveway, through the gloom, burst through—there is the house on the hill; and park the car; and go up the steps, the good strong front steps, the solid wood of old trees.

And I walk in the door and through the hall, into the kitchen, and out the back; and leave the door open, the air is mild and dry; and then when I come to the middle of the patio, when I face west, when I am still and no longer feel my own body moving through the air, then I finally hear the birdcalls, gentle but incessant. There are hours left of the day. May is behind me, in my house, I hear her footsteps, she is coming. The early quince, down the hill, is pink orange. And beyond that, green; a breath; a haze on the mountains.

Acknowledgments

Deepest gratitude to Henry Dunow and Jenny Jackson for their enthusiasm, skill, patience, and faith.

Thanks also to Nita Pronovost for her wisdom, and to the teams at both Doubleday and Doubleday Canada, especially Michael Goldsmith, Lauren Hesse, Will Heyward, and Nora Reichard, for their unflagging and expert support.

This book would not have been finished, and certainly would not have been any good, without the insights and deep generosity of Jaime Clarke, Dana Gioia, Susannah Howe, Bill Pierce, Dawn Tripp, Liz Rourke, and Sam Howe Verhovek. Thaddeus Howe provided crucial information about lacrosse. Carter Howe provided comic relief. Atul Gawande and Liz Rourke checked my medical details, and were touchingly concerned about my fictional patient. The legendary Richard Baker, of Noble and Greenough School, allowed me to watch him work and gave me crucial insights into the art and craft of teaching.

I would be remiss if I didn't mention the extraordinary teachers who set me on my own path, in particular Kemie Nix, David Purdum, and the late Jane Lauderdale.

I borrowed the lovely phrase "the air of elsewhere" from

Russell Brand, writing about the late Amy Winehouse; and the notion of not seeing but looking from John Berger, via James Wood.

My brief quotations from the *Duino Elegies* are A. Poulin Jr.'s translation, which is my favorite.

My husband, Peter, is the foundation of it all.

This book is dedicated to my parents, Rupert and Virginia LeCraw, and my brother, Andrew—first, best, and most beloved teachers.

A Note About the Author

Holly LeCraw is the author of *The Swimming Pool*. Her work has appeared in *The Millions, Post Road,* and various anthologies, and has been nominated for a Pushcart Prize. A native of Atlanta, she now lives outside Boston with her family.

A Note About the Type

This book was set in a version of the well-known Monotype face Bembo. This letter was cut for the celebrated Venetian printer Aldus Manutius by Francesco Griffo, and was first used in Pietro Cardinal Bembo's *De Aetna* of 1495.

The companion italic is an adaptation of the chancery script type designed by the calligrapher and printer Lodovico degli Arrighi.